William Al-Sharif is a British philosopher, scientist, historian, and author of over 80 books and 400 essays. He and his family live in Scotland.

https://willalsharif.com

THE ANONYMOUS

WILLIAM AL-SHARIF

Chiteki Books

47 Fa side View

Tranent, EH33 2NS, Scotland, the UK

Copyright © William Al-Sharif 2024

William Al-Sharif asserts his right under the Copyright, Design and Patents Act 1988 to be identified as the author of this work.

ISBN 978-1-7394959-1-6

For Alicia and Mary, with much love

CHAPTER 1

On the evening of November 4, 1995, a twenty-five-year-old Israeli extremist concealed a semi-automatic pistol in his jacket pocket. A chilling air surrounded him as he pressed his lips against the pages of the Hebrew Tanakh. His mind spiraled into a twisted, bigoted conviction, envisioning himself on a sacrilegious quest to silence a prominent politician in the heart of Tel Aviv.

In the United States, Hannah Rogers, a university scholar and businesswoman, had celebrated her thirty-third birthday party in her six-bedroom house near Brookside Road in the coastal town of Darien, in the state of Connecticut. Like an elegant editorial supermodel, she possessed a glamorous allure-fair, svelte, and standing at an imposing six feet. Cloaked in sophistication, she graced social gatherings and official functions adorned with gold necklaces, stylish dresses, and the subtle elegance of Estée Lauder makeup. Yet, beneath the veneer of opulence, she was no frivolous spendthrift or wanton wanderer.

In the realm of creativity, her passions unfolded like a thrilling narrative during her idyllic getaways. From capturing the essence of green landscapes on canvas to immortalizing nature through her lens, she delved into house decoration, cultivated vibrant gardens, embarked on journeys to remote foreign lands, and immersed herself in indigenous communities and captivating cultures. These creative pursuits fueled her fertile ingenuity and curiosity, shaping a tale where the boundaries between luxury and enigma blurred into a suspenseful narrative of mystery and temptation.

Despite her grandeur and wealth, a concealed and impenetrable character lurked in her vibrant personality. While her dynamic social lifestyle, affluence, thriving career, and statuesque glamor painted a portrait of opulence, success, and pleasure, a deeper truth about the profound complexity of human existence had unfolded.

In the realm of her private life, she understood a profound, dire reality-that material fortune, though beguiling, could not serve as the ultimate wellspring of genuine fulfillment and happiness. Behind closed doors, away from the glittering facade, she bore a significant role-an independent, single parent for thirteen years. This silent narrative spoke volumes about resilience, sacrifice, and the intricate balance between the public persona and the personal struggle that defined her journey.

A shroud of mystery surrounded her distinctive choices,

a clandestine realm known only to her. Even her closest confidants-parents and friends alike- remained oblivious to the main reasons behind her steadfast and obstinate refusal to get engaged in a romantic entanglement, despite the temptation of winsome suitors. The prevailing assumption among those who had shared the tapestry of her life for years was that her heart remained devoted to the memory of her late husband.

Since her daughter's birth in February 1982, not a single soul-be it a man or a woman-had crossed the threshold of her lavish abode. The stoic solitude she embraced had hinted at an untold narrative, weaving a tale of unspoken grief, unwavering dedication to the past, and a resolute commitment to her own way of life. There was a spiritual ground for her sexual abstinence and moral decorum. When she was a schoolgirl at Choate Rosemary Hall in Wallingford, her sententious, Catholic upbringing had deterred her from having sex or any bodily pleasure with mature boys. She wished to kiss a puckish boy under a red maple in a remote forest, attend a profligate dance party with hedonistic girlfriends, and watch an erotic movie in her dull bedroom, whose shadowy walls were covered with Latin crosses, rosary beads, and somber prints of Jesus Christ, the Virgin Mary, and Roman Catholic shrines. When she celebrated her eighteenth birthday with her devout family and friends, she got engaged to Michael Rogers, a second cousin and a member of a reputable clan committed to education, social liberalism, democracy, industry, and philanthropy. A week after their ceremonial marriage on November 9, 1980, Michael became an executive director of his father's booming industrial companies and a financial analyst for

Citibank Overseas Investment Corporation. He cherished and adulated his reserved, inexperienced wife, and was ambitious and sedulous, but the inscrutable decree of nature had another scheme for him and Hannah. He died at twenty-five in a car crash on the Lowell Connector, a notorious highway in Massachusetts, before the birth of Sarah, who grew up without a doting father.

At the tender age of nineteen, Hannah ushered life into the world, welcoming a daughter into her arms. She also inherited Michael's estate and a sizable portion of his wealth, and refused to live an idle, prodigal life. With the munificent support of her parents and Michael's amiable family, she studied with diligence and got a top-grade doctorate degree in cultural anthropology from Yale University, where she became an acclaimed lecturer and an object of attention to educated professionals. This demanding career and her corporate business became not just a necessary means of financial fortification, but an explicit manifestation of a deeper mission. Amid the busyness of boardrooms and business dealings, she remained resolute in her commitment to embody elegance, benevolence, and ingenuity. These laudable virtues were the pillars upon which she constructed her professional identity.

The well-being of her daughter took center stage. The demands of her official work had not diminished her dedication to the role of a nurturing and attentive mother. Love and care became the currencies with which she enriched the life of her daughter, creating a caring bond and a harmonious balance between the demands of a thriving career and the responsibilities of parenthood.

In addition, her nonconformist friends were ardent

champions of liberal feminism and advocates for female emancipation, social justice, gender equality, human rights, and environmental causes. With them, she found a sympathetic community aligned with her values. These like-minded souls had boosted the camaraderie through their shared passion for positive activism. So, it became apparent that Hannah's personal inclinations had leaned away from intimate relationships with men.

An hour after the birthday celebration, Hannah sat alone in the living room, drinking hot coffee, and reading a *Good Housekeeping* magazine when her stylish, eloquent sister-in-law, Barbara Rogers, called her.

"Good evening, love."

"Hello, honey. How are you?"

"I am doing good. How was the birthday party?"

"Fantastic."

"I am sorry I couldn't come to the party. Two Canadian friends were here to refresh my wandering spirit with delightful reminiscences. What are you doing? How is Sarah?"

"We are fine and enjoying our happy life. Sarah is in her bedroom sleeping or reading a book. In the morning, we and Andrea and Julie went to Indian Well State Park. The birthday party was fabulous and bracing. Over thirty guests were in the house."

"Good. What are you doing tomorrow?"

"We have no specific plans."

"Come to lunch with me. I miss both of you."

"We miss you too. I was busy teaching and reviewing articles. OK, love, we will have lunch with you tomorrow. What will you cook for us?"

"Italian lasagna."

"We love it. Do you need anything?"

"No. There is enough food to feed a tribe. Your warm affection is what I want. Don't change your mind about coming."

"I promise to come. Thank you, gorgeous. You are the best shining star in my hectic life. OK, honey, we will come tomorrow. Good night. I love you."

"I love you too. Good night and sweet dreams."

With a grin, Hannah crossed her manicured fingers and rested her pointy chin on them for ten seconds before ascending the stairs to talk to Sarah.

Sarah has spindly legs, light brown hair, and hazel eyes. She was awake in her single bed studying a comic book when her mother came in to see her.

"Darling, we will go to New York tomorrow morning to see Barbara. She has invited us to lunch with her."

"Hooray! I love my aunt. She is funny, and I love her food and chocolate cakes."

"That's wonderful." A soft goodnight kiss touched Sarah's face.

Hannah closed Sarah's bedroom door and headed to her bedroom suite, where she removed her brown leather loafers, skinny jeans, and gray fleece sweater in front of a mirrored wardrobe and wore a short purple silk nightgown. After brushing her teeth in the attached bathroom, she went downstairs to wash the coffee cup and inspect the doors, the windows, and the lights. She got a small glass of water from the kitchen and tiptoed upstairs to the bedroom.

In the sleigh bed, she glimpsed, with reflective silence, at a gold-framed picture of her departed husband. There was a book beside her. She opened it but could not read more than a page. Her somnolent eyes closed after she sipped water.

At six o'clock in the morning, four federal agents were at the plush apartment of an influential investigative journalist named Ann Stone. Her condo is in Tribeca, Lower Manhattan. An agent rang the doorbell. Ann was asleep in a canopy bed. The doorbell buzzed again. After opening her eyes and leaving the bed, Ann put on a striped kimono robe, pulled a handgun from a drawer, and stood behind the main door. "Who is it?"

"The FBI. Please, open the door."

She hid the handgun in the back of her stretchy, cinched leggings and opened the door. "What's going on this time?"

An officer gazed at her. "Good morning. We want to inspect your apartment. We have a search warrant."

"At this time? Why?"

"For national security reasons."

"Hogwash. I am a journalist and a media personality. What are you looking for? Another conspiracy theory?"

"Please, let us do our job. We follow orders. We are not here to apprehend you. Have you received classified documents from a secret agent?"

"No. Do you think I am a spy?"

"Who is this guy?" The agent showed her a photo of her with a hooded, black-coated, gloved person cradling an orange envelope, and standing in a New York subway station.

Ann opened the drawer of a console table. "Here's the envelope."

The agent opened the envelope and found vintage copies of lesbian novels, such as *Her Private Hell, Lesbian*

Limbo, *Odd Girl Out*, and *A Labor of Love.*

She smirked. "They are marvelous stories. Your wife or girlfriend should read them to spice up her sex life."

With his face reddened, the amazed agent thought Ann was fond of lesbian pulp fiction. "Thanks. Excuse me. We need to search the apartment."

She pouted and opened her right hand. "Go ahead. Please, don't frighten my daughter."

"Where is her room?"

With a stolid gaze, she pointed at a closed door with a forefinger. "There."

"How old is she?"

"Twenty."

"What's her name?"

"Ayita."

"Ayita? What is this name?"

"It means the good and the wind."

"What does she do?"

"She is a model and a fashion photographer."

The agent stared at a wall picture of a young woman in a black triangle bikini. "Is this your daughter?"

"Yes."

The four agents searched Ann's cluttered office, living room, boudoir, kitchen, and bookshelves. One of them opened Ayita's room door and saw a pantless woman sleeping on her right side and piles of colored socks and underwear spread over the floor. He gawked at her seductive left leg and declined to inspect the room. Another agent entered a clean bedroom and found a business card on a desk. He came to Ann. "Where is Albert Russell?"

"Ask the angels. He left my apartment last night."

"Is he your boyfriend?"

"No. Albert is a British citizen. I interview him when he comes to New York."

"Why?"

"He is a distinguished philosopher."

He lifted his fingers under his chin. "Amazing! Do you interview British philosophers in your apartment?"

"He is a decent man. He is my daughter's dad."

When the FBI agents left the apartment without success, Ann rushed to a telephone and made a call. "The primates were here. Go to the second one. I love you." She went to her daughter's room. "Ayita, get up. Go to the NBC building. Your dad is there."

An hour later, Hannah woke up after hearing robins and tree swallows tweeting near the draped windows. Her half-sleepy eyes shifted to the right to see the silver alarm clock on an oak chiffonier. After getting up, she moved into the bathroom and had a quick shower. A white cotton bathrobe covered her body, and pink wool slippers encased her delicate feet. She descended the stairs to the windowed kitchen, where she and Sarah had a breakfast of tea, fried eggs, orange jelly, and smooth peanut butter with sliced, toasted bread. After that, she darted upstairs and wore a white blouse, a gold necklace, a gray suit, and a Cartier watch. The phone near the bed rang.

"Good morning."

"Oh, good morning, Deborah."

"Did you hear the awful news?"

"No. What's going on?"

"An ultranationalist Israeli has murdered the Prime Minister of Israel. This happened yesterday when we were in your house."

"Oh dear! That is heinous. Why did he kill him?"

"Reporters say the killer has killed him because he opposes the Oslo peace accord between the Israelis and the Palestinians."

"Is the killer a Jew?"

"Yes. His name is Yigal Amir."

"What will happen in Israel?"

"I foresee trouble there and here in America. This is the first incident in which a religious Jew murders an Israeli politician. Honey, I am so sorry to bother you at this early time."

"No problem at all."

"Your birthday party was marvelous, and I enjoyed it very much. I was so happy to see your parents and our friends."

"Thank you for coming over and for the lovely gift."

"Zita Marino's program will start after a minute."

"I will watch the news. See you soon. Goodbye."

"Have a good time. Bye."

Hannah rubbed the back of her neck and called her daughter, who sat in the living room. "Sarah, darling, stick around for ten or fifteen minutes. I need to look at the news."

A pivotal moment presented itself, offering Hannah a choice-to exit her home and dismiss the unsettling news about Israel's internal affairs. Why should she bother herself with the distressing intricacies of politics? The joy of the birthday party had lingered, and she had made a heartfelt promise to share lunch with Barbara in the bustling heart of New York.

However, in contrast to the prevailing apathy and egocentrism that gripped many individuals, Hannah stood as an exception. Her heart beat with genuine affection for her friends, a sentiment so profound that it needed no vocal articulation. Through the crucible of her experiences, marked by unwavering dedication, she had learned to hold dear those who cared for her and her daughter. So, in a quiet moment of reflection, she rested on her bed, held a remote control, and switched on the Sony TV to check the news.

"Back to our top story. We have been following the news from Israel. Dr. Albert Russell is with us to offer insights and answer questions on the current events taking place in Israel. Dr. Russell is a world-renowned British philosopher, an expert on the Middle East affairs, and a visiting professor at the British Research Institute for the Study of Philosophy and Religion in the Indian city of Hyderabad," said the sharp-witted, charming NBC news anchor Zita Marino.

Hannah bellowed in surprise and stretched her back and arms, with an electrifying look in her static eyes. An unexpected matter had cropped up when Zita Marino welcomed Dr. Albert Russell. She gazed at the TV screen and buried her lithe fingers in her straight hair. Tears rolled down the flushed face, her eyes bulging in wonder. "My God! Oh, my God! I don't believe my eyes." She picked up the remote control to turn up the TV volume.

"Dr. Russell, it is my pleasure to welcome you this morning. As an academic philosopher and professional intellectual, what do you say about the underlying causes or motives that contributed to the shocking assassination of Israel's Prime Minister Yitzhak Rabin?"

Dr. Russell, a personable figure in the prime of his mid-thirties, donned a distinguished navy-blue suit that accentuated his presence. With an air of contemplative assurance, he crossed one leg over the other, settling into the commanding space behind the circular news desk. His hands, entwined and bearing a delicate pallor, rested with confidence-a subtle embodiment of intellectual gravitas ready to unfold within the discourse about to happen. "The religious Zionist fundamentalists in Israel want to imperil the onerous peace negotiations between the Israeli government and the senior Fatah leaders of the Palestinian Liberation Organization. Their opposition to peace is due to psychological and cultural reasons."

Zita pushed a strand of hair behind her right ear. "What do you mean?"

"I mean, the stylized stories of the ignominious Nazi persecution of Jews have become ingrained in Jewish minds, cultural imagination, and poignant memories. Many Israeli settlers think an apocalyptic catastrophe will happen to them and their state if they allow pugnacious Palestinians to set up a hostile state in the West Bank and Gaza Strip. The recent suicide bombings in Jerusalem and Ramat Gan, by Islamist militants, have increased the cognitive sense of fear and menace."

Zita twirled her pen. "Israel calls herself a Jewish state. Does religion play a role here?"

"Yes. There are doctrinal and mythical incentives for repudiating the peace process. In the name of religion, the religious, Zionist chauvinists believe historical Palestine, from the Jordan River and the Arabah Valley to the Mediterranean Sea and Sinai, belongs only to the Jews. They do not want Israel to recognize the legitimate human rights of the native Christian and Muslim Palestinians because they opine God had chosen the people of Israel and given them Palestine, a hallowed land flowing with honey and milk, as the Old Testament says. In Jewish eschatology, a messiah from the Davidic line will come and build a temple in Jerusalem. Also, many Orthodox Jews think secularism is an evil ideology. Yigal Amir says he acted on the orders of God and according to Jewish law and believes that Yitzhak Rabin had betrayed the faith. The radical Islamists, on the other hand, enunciate that a peace deal between the Palestinians and the Israelis is a sacrilegious sin against God and the Quran, and that Muslims must fight the Jews and liberate the whole land of Palestine by military force."

Zita gazed at his serious face. "What is the solution?"

"There is no easy answer to a labyrinthine impasse because financial, media, and political powers want to hegemonize the Arabic-speaking Middle East, fearing the emergence of a dominant Arab-Muslim power. Arab dictators, Israeli warmongers, and British and U.S. policymakers want to keep the status quo to maintain their strategic interests. I seize this opportunity to appeal to the United Nations Organization, the European Union, the Arab League, and the U.S. government to make sure that dialogue between Israel and her neighbors and comprehensive peace, not military occupation and war, are the only means to deal with the intricate crises in the Middle East. We need to extirpate war, or war will annihilate us. Our world needs good knowledge and genuine compassion. Fear, ignorance, and the absence of love are the fundamental causes of human suffering. The wise win without a fight, and the unwise fight to win."

Zita Marino's political conversation with Albert Russell had left Hannah in a state of petrification. A weighty silence enveloped her as she sat with her left hand curved against her sealed lips, absorbing the articulate exchange of thoughts unfolding before her. The interview, a cascade of eloquence and complex ideas, held her captive. Her eyes became veiled with a tautness that hinted at the emotional storm within. As Dr. Russell delved into the intricacies of political discourse, a subtle transformation occurred-her steady gaze, once focused, became blurred and tearful. The soft palms of her hands touched her rosy face, with her legs crossed, and she breathed a silent prayer to assuage her abrupt disquietude. After turning off the square TV, she meditated with closed eyes and remained motionless for three minutes. She left the bedroom and bolted downstairs to the office room on the right side of the oak-carpeted stairs. The phone buzzed.

"Good morning, Hannah."

"Good morning, Nathan. What is the news?"

"We searched Ann Stone's apartment."

"The journalist?"

"Yes."

"Why?"

"We are looking for classified documents purloined from the CIA and the NSA."

"When did this happen?"

"A week ago."

"What are these documents?"

"They detail our intelligence operations."

"Who leaked the documents?"

"We suspect he is a double agent known to Aldrich Ames and other treacherous moles."

"What is the connection between Aldrich and Ann?"

"Ann's leftist newspapers and magazines publish

classified documents obtained by secret agents. Ann is the granddaughter of the radical journalist Peter Stone, who was born to rich Russian immigrants and who pledged to sabotage our intelligence work. One officer said Ann got an envelope from a shrouded man in the subway."

"Who is this man?"

"We do not know. He wears a ski mask, a hood, and shoddy clothes. Ann said he is a poor vagabond who gets her cheap lesbian stories."

"Ridiculous. Ann is the most famous journalist in New York. She earns over $450,000 a year. Does she need cheap stories from a vagrant? Did you find the documents in her apartment?"

"No. We think Ann passed the documents to her secret lover."

"Who is her secret lover?"

"An English guy. His name is Albert Russell."

Hannah put her left forefinger in her ear. "Albert Russell? Are you sure?"

"Yes. Do you know Albert?"

"He is an eminent philosopher and a grandson of Bertrand Russell, Britain's greatest philosopher in the twentieth century. Thousands of radical thinkers, feminists, rebels, and political activists quote Albert. I watched an NBC interview with him."

"We also saw the interview."

"Where are you now?"

"At 30 Rockefeller Plaza. We are waiting for Albert Russell to leave the building."

"Why? What do you want from him? He lives in India and has nothing to do with espionage."

"We want to ask him about his covert activities in the

country. He published leaked documents on Panama and the Gulf War. We think he collaborates with a double agent."

"I see. Keep me updated. Please, we do not need trouble with the British government and the SIS. I must go now. My girl is waiting for me. Talk to you later. Have a good day."

Hannah picked up a telephone directory lying on a mahogany desk. After sitting in a Boston rocker, she browsed through the phone book and paused on several pages that had arrested her bleary eyes. Her left index finger landed on a page. She held an ash gray digital phone and made a call.

"NBC. How can I help you?" a female secretary said.

"Good morning. I am Professor Hannah Rogers of Yale University. I have watched Ms. Zita Marino's interview with Dr. Albert Russell. How can I contact Ms. Marino or Dr. Russell?"

"Give me a minute, please." The young secretary dialed a number. "Hi, Martin. Professor Hannah Rogers, from Yale University, wants to contact Zita Marino."

"OK, Sandra. Please, put her on the line."

"Hello. Good morning, Professor. What can I do for you?"

"Thanks. I wish to get a quick appointment with Ms. Zita Marino and Dr. Russell."

"Dr. Albert Russell has left the building. You can meet Zita tomorrow."

"Can I meet her today?"

"Today is Sunday."

"This is urgent, please."

"OK. Let me see. Please, give me a few seconds." With

his protuberant eyes fixed on a computer screen, Martin, a stout, mustached man with curly hair, straightened himself up and readjusted his black-framed spectacles. "Zita. Zita. Zita. Zita. OK. You can see her today at one o'clock."

"This is great."

"Confirm your kind name, please."

"Hannah Rogers."

"Thank you for contacting us. Please, bring an official identity card for identification and security check."

"I will. Thank you very much. Bye."

A flicker of ecstatic excitement flew into her winning eyes. With a grin, she attached her left fingers to her roseate face and stared up at the ornamented white ceiling. Resting her tight buns on the angular corner of the desk, she sucked the middle knuckle of her right forefinger, contemplating her next move. Four minutes later, she tripped into the living room, where Sarah was ready to visit her favorite aunt.

Hannah drove her silver Ford car to New York City. Her left elbow leaned on the window edge, and her fingers danced with her shiny hair. Sarah sat reading a storybook.

An hour later, the car parked beside Barbara's six-floor building on Broome Street in Lower Manhattan. Hannah and Sarah stepped into an elevator. Sarah pushed the button for the fourth floor and rang the doorbell of Barbara's apartment. Barbara opened the door.

Like her sister-in-law, Barbara is a lissome, long-legged, ravishing woman, but with bobbed red hair and deep gray eyes. Clad in skinny taupe trousers, a fuchsia shirt, and high-heeled black shoes, her ruddy lips smiled. "Good morning, my lovely ladies. Come into the wonderland."

Hannah's lips touched Barbara's, and Barbara kissed Sarah's face. Hannah and Sarah sat beside each other on a claret couch in an extravagant living room and glimpsed at romantic oil paintings of shapely women.

"How are you doing, Barb?"

"I am doing well. Happy to see you. Let's go to the kitchen. My piquant lasagna and Italian cheese salad are waiting for our genial onslaught."

The three sat at a round table, chewing their food and gossiping about family matters. When Hannah finished her lunch, she beamed at Barbara and touched her hand. "Love, can you look after Sarah for two hours? I have work to do."

Barbara goggled at her in astonishment. "Work? What is this drastic work on Sunday? Is it a secret romance with a lover?"

Hannah hummed. "I don't have a liaison with a queer lover. I want to see a journalist."

"Love is gliding in the air. Is he sexy?"

"Are you hysterical this morning? She is a woman."

"Wonderful. Is your dancing heart turning toward the enchantment of a vibrant, feminine connection? Perhaps exploring the beautiful realm of sisterhood and embracing your femininity would be a splendid choice after all these years of solitude." She giggled. "Who is she?"

"She is Zita Marino, the famed NBC news anchor. The meeting is at one o'clock."

"Why do you want to see her today? What is this furtive meeting on Sunday?"

"My Jewish friend Deborah Goldenberg has told me about the Israeli guy who assassinated Israel's Prime Minister."

Barbara simmered with frustration and seethed with anger. "Who even cares anymore? I turned away from the news because men's nonsense has saturated it. Excuse my language, but the mad world of men, with its arrogance, contempt, and sheer stupidity, seems to be the root of all evil on this planet." Her right hand patted Hannah's left shoulder. "Love, get a respite, I implore you. Allow your body, mind, and soul a moment of solace, a reprieve from the ceaseless anxiety that grips them. Look at your fatigued eyes-they bear the weight of countless trials. Do not tread the path of the misguided bluestockings, who believe they grasp the world better than us. Cherish the elation that freedom brings and embrace the euphoria that dances in the air. Your well-being deserves this interlude. Grant yourself the gift of tranquility and meditation. Anyway, I wish you the best of luck. Do you want coffee?"

"No. Thanks, honey. The food is delicious. I need to go now."

Sarah hugged and kissed her mother. "Bye, mom."

"Bye, darling. Look after yourself."

Barbara kissed Hannah. "Sarah and I will have a lovely time full of frolicsome hilarity."

"Have a pleasant time. I love you."

Hannah hailed a yellow taxi, seeking refuge in the comfort of its back seat. As the vehicle glided through the city's busy streets, she reached into her stone leather purse, retrieving a diminutive mirror and a lipstick crafted from rich rosewood. With meticulous care, she painted her slender lips, a subtle ritual to prepare for whatever lay ahead. The taxi stopped on 6th Avenue between West 49th Street and West 50th Street. After closing the door of the cab, Hannah walked to the left, gazing at police officers, armed FBI agents, paramedics, silent onlookers, and reporters standing beside crime scene tapes. She shoved through the staring crowd. Her gaze fell upon a disturbing scene of chaos-three police cars lay toppled, a terrifying indication to the violent unrest that happened. Seeking clarity and answers, she approached a young man among the spectators. "What happened?" Her voice cut through the clamor of the surrounding confusion.

The young bystander turned to her, ready to share whatever fragment of information he had. "There was an intense fight between the police and female cyborg warriors. It was like a futuristic action movie."

That was a shock. "Female cyborg warriors? Are you sure?"

"Yeah. The women warriors wear steel cyber armor and speak strange words. Their arms fired arrows, knives, and laser beams."

"Why did they fight?"

"The warriors did not allow the FBI agents to arrest a white man wearing a blue suit."

"Who was the white man?"

"Some people say he is a famous philosopher."

She touched her face and paused for a moment. "Did the police arrest the warriors?"

"No. No one can arrest them or kill them. They are powerful machines. Two of them threw a car at the cops."

Confounded by what she heard and saw, Hannah entered the GE Building and found her way to the information counter.

"Hi. How can I serve you?" a receptionist said.

"Good afternoon. I am Dr. Hannah Rogers." She unzipped her purse and took out a business card. "Here is my university identity card. I am here to meet Ms. Zita Marino at one o'clock."

"Please, have a seat."

She sat in a brown chair, awaiting a response. Her right fingers kept playing with the watch.

"Hannah, get this elevator. Zita is on the ninth floor, in the fifth room on the left side of the corridor."

"Thanks." Hannah entered a stainless-steel elevator and pressed the ninth-floor button. She gazed at a large mirror and fiddled with the front side of her hair. The elevator door opened. She looked straight at a colorful poster of a movie called "Forrest Gump" before striding to the left.

She noticed Zita Marino's name on a door. "Here is Zita's office," she mumbled and tapped on the door.

"Yes, come in," Zita responded.

Zita has hazel eyes, high cheekbones, sharp lips, and red hair with golden blonde highlights. She was wearing a magenta skater skirt, a white shirt, and black spool heel shoes.

They shook hands and smiled. "Good afternoon. I am Hannah Rogers."

"Welcome. How are you doing? Thanks for coming. Please, sit here."

Hannah placed her purse beside her. "I am all right. Thank you."

"Tea or coffee?"

"I prefer coffee, please."

"With sugar and cream?"

"I would appreciate three drops of cream without sugar."

Zita stood next to a coffee maker and made two cups of coffee. She put a white cup on a square table beside Hannah and sat in her swivel chair with her alluring legs crossed. "What do you do?"

"I am a professor of cultural and women's studies at Yale University."

"Awesome! Are you a feminist?"

Hannah's eyes twinkled. "Without question."

"Great. Do you think the feminist movement has achieved its objectives?"

"It has achieved significant milestones, yet the ongoing struggle persists, concerning abortion, divorce, gender equality and identity, lesbianism, political participation, and beyond."

"Are you engaged in politics?"

"Yes. I am a liberal Democrat. After all, feminism is an aspect of politics concerned with women."

"Will our women have equal access to political power?"

Hannah twirled her right hand in a doubting gesture. "In an idealistic world, we can achieve political equality through collective unity, sustained pressure on misogynistic politicians, education, and challenging the influence of conservative clergy. The feminism I brace and engage in depends on resistance against political, legal, economic, and social discrimination directed at women. Together, we can strive for a fair world where individuals, regardless of gender, can flourish in a society built on equality and respect. My circle of close friends and I promote social anarchism, global egalitarianism, gender fairness, and the principles of free love."

"Free love?" Zita winked. "Amazing! Do you believe in religion?"

"I grew up as a devoted Catholic. My forebears came from Ireland, and my parents think Catholicism is God's true religion."

"I am a Catholic by birth and culture. My late parents worried about family customs and traditions rather than dogmas and doctrines. Do you lecture on non-American societies?"

"Yes. One main course I teach is on Mediterranean cultures."

"Interesting. I belong to a Sicilian family, and I am in perpetual love with that part of the world. Do you live in Connecticut?"

"Yes. I live in Darien in Connecticut, and my house is close to Brookside Road and the Goodwives River."

"I haven't been to your neighborhood, but I think it is a sedate place."

"Yes, it is peaceful and green where I live."

After this casual introduction, Zita wanted to know the purpose of Hannah's visit. "Well, today is Sunday, a day when people unwind in the comfort of their homes or bask in the sunshine, cherishing quiet moments with their family and friends. What is going on in your life that has you in such a rush? Why is the hurry on a day meant for relaxation?"

Hannah had a quick sip of her coffee. "Leisure time in my hectic life feels like a distant dream. Balancing the responsibilities of caring for my teenage daughter and working full-time Monday to Friday leaves me with minimal space for respite. Weekends and occasional vacations become the rare opportunities when I can step outside the boundaries of my daily routine."

"What can I say? The inescapable confluence of motherhood and employment outside the home presents formidable challenges for working women in contemporary times. Our society, often steeped in jingoism, overlooks the fundamental roles and responsibilities that diligent women and mothers undertake. Navigating this landscape becomes demanding in our capitalist era, challenging the assumption that our life is effortless.

As you see, the separation from my spouse and three children shows the sacrifices I make for the demands of this work. Even the sanctuary of a vacation break cannot afford our TV network a reprieve, underscoring our crucial duties in this fast-paced, interconnected world."

"Yeah, the predicament is intricate, and yet we must have the courage to reject the frenetic and disparaging stereotypes imposed on women. The call for justice and equal opportunities extends beyond gender boundaries to encompass all individuals. Our feminist struggle is an ongoing, uphill battle, gaining momentum as we strive for a more fair and inclusive society. However, that is not why I am here. Your exquisite interview with Professor Albert Russell was a rewarding experience. You asked him sensitive questions aimed at unraveling profound insights, and his responses were incisive and thought-provoking, promoting a stimulating and enriching conversation."

"Throughout my career, I have had the privilege of interviewing amazing thinkers, politicians, actors, singers, entertainers, and businesspersons. However, only a select few have left an indelible mark on my insatiable curiosity. Dr. Albert Russell stands as a phenomenal individual, akin to the wisdom embodied by figures like Confucius or the masters of Taoism.

My desire to delve deeper into his insights propels me to seek another interview, this time with a focus on revealing various aspects of his private life. He, as a polymath philosopher and exuberant globetrotter, manages a bustling schedule that involves lectures and writings on a myriad of subjects. The mystery of how he manages his immense commitments is a proof of his organizational prowess and intellectual depth."

Hannah blinked at her and beamed. "Passion is a driving force for innovation. I guess he has a sublime enthusiasm for knowledge and life."

"That's what I sensed when I interviewed him."

Hannah, at this moment, thought it was propitious for her to make a personal request. "Can I ask you a favor?"

"Yes, you can. What is it?"

"Can I get a visual copy of your interview?"

"May I ask why?"

"I am organizing an international symposium and writing a research paper on the minority cultures of West Asian nations. The adverse circumstances in the Arab Middle East have a crucial impact on the multiplex and dynamic traditions in that part of the world."

"I agree. The terrible crisis between Israel and the Arabs plagues the entire world. Nevertheless, you are a professor at Yale. Why don't you contact your school to get further data on the Middle East? Your university has world-class libraries and massive archives."

"You are right. It is reputable and dear to my heart. I wish to converse with Dr. Albert Russell and discuss his experience in Asian and Middle Eastern societies. Do you know where he is now?"

"No. We had no chance to talk about personal matters. He came to New York to deliver lectures at Columbia University."

"Is he at Columbia University?"

"I do not know. Call the university and try to find him."

"Thanks. Once again, can I get a copy of your excellent interview?"

"You can. Excuse me for a moment while I make a call."

Zita made a phone call. "Hi, Robert. Can you get me a videotape of my interview with Albert Russell?"

"Yes, I can. Give me five to ten minutes."

"Thanks."

Zita looked at her polished red fingernails. "Are you related to the Rogers family in Massachusetts?"

"Yes. I am a great-granddaughter of William Barton Rogers, the first president of the MIT."

"Wow! This is quite impressive. Your prestigious family had produced scientists, industrialists, thinkers, politicians, and philanthropists. What about your own family in Connecticut?"

"I have a daughter. My husband died in 1981."

"Sorry to hear that. Who was your husband?"

"My husband was Michael Rogers, the youngest child of the industrialist and financier Henry Rogers."

"How old is your daughter? What is her name?"

"My daughter Sarah is thirteen."

"Sarah is a cute name. Have you been abroad?"

"Yes. I visited Canada, Mexico, Brazil, Argentina, Hong Kong, England, Portugal, Spain, France, Italy, Greece, Turkey, Syria, Morocco, and Egypt. I wish to see other countries, such as India and China."

"It is a big world out there. Have you met Albert Russell in person? Our country is full of scholars of Middle Eastern studies. Last week, I interviewed Bernard Lewis, Edward Said, and Fouad Ajami."

"I know. There are scores of trained scholars in our

colleges. I met Albert once, but we had little time to discuss the Middle East and other postcolonial regions. Your excellent interview with him has let me admire his down-to-earth approach and empathy."

"I agree. I have found him humble, passionate, and even feminine."

"Feminine?"

"As you might have noticed from the interview, he is a soft-spoken, good-natured man. He was the first male academic to kiss my face before a TV interview."

Hannah smiled. "It is interesting to hear that. Well, no sensible, mature man can endure your Italian charm and beauty. Your astute intellect is unparalleled."

Zita grinned. "Thanks. I think his noble English aristocracy has affected his classic eloquence and gentle manner. One day, I read about his love for his grandfather Bertrand Russell and spirited campaign for gay rights in England. I had not seen him with a woman, even when I conferred with him in his London house before the Gulf War in 1990. Maybe he is a homosexual. Oops! Please, do not quote me. Anyway, I always prepare my questions in advance before interviewing him."

"I dare say ..."

Robert knocked on the door and handed Zita a videotape.

"Thank you. Hannah, here is the tape. It is free." She simpered. "Please, it is copyrighted. Here is my business card, which has my contact details."

Hannah opened her purse and drew out her Yale University card. "And this is my university card. Thank you so much. I appreciate your gracious kindness."

"You are welcome, darling. I hope to see you again

soon. Enjoy the rest of your day."

"Thanks. I am grateful to you. Bye for now."

After inserting the videotape in her purse, Hannah shook Zita's hand and left the skyscraper. She dawdled on a concrete sidewalk on the eastern side of Rockefeller Center, conjecturing how to face Dr. Albert Russell. "Taxi, taxi," she squealed and gestured. A yellow taxicab stopped. "Please, take me to the main gate of Columbia University."

The taxicab halted at the 116th Street gate. Hannah gave the South Asian driver money and exited the cab. She observed junior students loitering at the high black gate. "Excuse me. Excuse me. Where is the Visitors Center?"

"Ha! Hey, what's up, ma'am? Don't you see? Today is Sunday. The Visitors Center closes today. Come back tomorrow," a Caribbean student said with a diffident smile.

"Does anybody know Dr. Albert Russell?"

"What is his college?" another male student asked.

"He is a professor of Middle Eastern studies."

"Just a minute," another student requested before turning his face toward a brown-eyed, frizzy-haired student. "Leila, do you know Dr. Albert Russell?"

"Yes, I know him. He gave us lectures for a week. He left the campus in the morning."

"Where did he go?" Hannah asked with an anxious expression.

"He took off to JFK airport after a TV talk."

"Did he mention his trip?"

"He said he is flying back to India. He works with a British institute over there."

"Thank you very much." Hannah winced as if she had missed a romantic date with a sweetheart. She took a taxi to Times Square in Midtown Manhattan and ordered caffé macchiato and a lemon ricotta cheesecake in an Italian restaurant. While she was silent, meditating on her unquiet life and waiting for her coffee and cake, a smiling waiter gave her a small envelope. She opened the envelope and found a greeting card. "Hannah, go to India and see Albert. He needs a kind-hearted, fearless woman like you. The Anonymous." She turned the card over and saw a black-and-white picture of a female cyborg warrior with a silver capital letter A. With nervous eyes, she looked at the people in the restaurant and called for the waiter. "Who gave you the envelope?"

"A motorcyclist."

"Did you see his face?"

"No. He wears a silver mask and an oversized hood."

"Did he speak to you?"

"No. He pointed at you. He looks weird."

"How?"

"He moves like a futuristic cyborg."

"I see. Thank you."

The peculiar card and the chat with the waiter had perplexed Hannah's mind. How did the Anonymous, a mysterious group of warriors, knew her name and Albert's need for a valiant woman? Why did the Anonymous contact her? With a shaken face, she moved out of the restaurant and plodded along the edge of a sidewalk, glancing with sad eyes at stores and blinking commercial ads before catching a taxi to Barbara's building.

"Hello, charmer. Did Sarah behave?"

"What are you talking about? Sarah is my best niece. We are having amazing fun. We ate a delicious kuchen made by my own hands."

Sarah jumped up and hugged her mother. "Are we going home?"

"Yes, darling, we are going home."

"How was the meeting?"

"Good."

"Do you want a cup of tea and a cake?"

"Thanks, love. I have many things to do."

"All right. Next time, you spend more time with me."

"I will. I promise."

After a slow hour, Hannah and Sarah were in their home. Sarah threw off her black ankle boots and hopped upstairs to her bedroom. Hannah dropped her purse on a perpendicular table near the TV and hung her jacket on a standing coat rack near the stairs. She rinsed her face in the downstairs marble bath and prepared a cup of tea in the kitchen.

The doorbell rang. Hannah put the teacup on the kitchen table and opened the front door. A teenage blonde girl, wearing mint jeans and a red turtleneck sweater, was standing at the door. Hannah shook the girl's delicate hand. "Julie, how are you, darling?"

"I am good. Can Sarah come over to our house?"

"Yes, she can."

Hannah swung her face toward the wide stairs and called out. "Sarah. Sarah. Julie is here."

Sarah opened her bedroom door. "Yes, mom, what do you want?"

"Julie wants you to go to her house."

"That's cool." She leaped downstairs, scrambled into her boots, and rushed out with Julie to her neighboring home.

Hannah retired to the cozy living room after getting

her teacup from the kitchen. She opened her purse and inserted the videotape into a Panasonic video cassette recorder to see Zita's conversation with Dr. Russell. The phone rang.

"Hi, Hannah."

"Hi, Nathan. What's the news?"

"We are on high alert."

"Why? What's going on?"

"Nahatatama and his Anonymous fighters are here. They attacked nine FBI and police officers and damaged three cars at the NBC building."

She squinched her face up. "How?"

"The Anonymous commander, Homatakawa, hit three officers with a chain whip and kicked their faces. When the other officers used their guns, the Anonymous poltergeists overturned their cars and struck their heads, legs, and arms with nunchakus, spikes, knives, hatchets, arrows, and ninja stars. Homatakawa and the Anonymous fighters used traditional tools, but this time, three of their warriors fired laser beams to make it impossible for us to fight back. This is a perilous development."

"Oh dear! What did the NYPD do?"

"Nothing. Homatakawa and his Anonymous fighters are machines and can make themselves invisible. They are like ghosts."

"They were active in Latin America. How did they enter the country?"

"Nobody knows how they entered the country or where they stay. We do not even know who made them. It is difficult for us to fight cyborg assassins."

"What's the link between them and Albert Russell?"

"They protect him wherever he goes. We believe Albert

is the mastermind of the Anonymous."

She rubbed her left thigh. "How?"

"The Anonymous fighters protect him all the time and execute the people who try to kill him. Their elusive leader, Nahatatama Yamotika, had vowed to massacre millions of Americans and destroy our cities if we arrest or kill Albert."

"Oh, my God! Do they worship him? Are they a secret cult? Why do they protect Bertrand Russell's grandson? I thought Albert talks about love and peace."

"He is a manipulative phony. The Anonymous fighters started their executions of our officers after a special force unit had assassinated Peter Stone and his son Jamie. Albert became furious and said the CIA would pay a heavy price for its crime."

"Strange. Why did he say that? Why did the CIA kill Peter Stone and his son?"

"The Special Operations Group thought Peter and his son were an imminent threat to our national security."

"What's the connection between the Stone family and the Russell family?"

"Peter Stone was Bertrand Russell's closest American ally, and Albert is in love with Ann."

"Who are Nahatatama and Homatakawa?"

"Ann Stone's father created them in a secret lab outside the country. Nahatatama is the supreme leader, and Homatakawa is the commander of the Anonymous warriors who are also called the ARA or the Anonymous Robot Assassins. Homatakawa, or the Red Spike Thrower, is the robot assassin who uses ninja weapons and sprints like the Scarlet Speedster. His special bodyguards call him Mahpiya Luta or the Red Cloud. They mean he is like the legendary Oglala Lakota warrior who defeated the U.S. Army in the 1860s."

"You said Homatakawa is a robot assassin. Who made him? Is he a human being?"

"Nobody can answer these questions. He is like Arnold Schwarzenegger in *The Terminator*. I guess he is a human with cyborg limbs because he eats and drinks. He killed over thirty agents and officials in the last five years. If he gets the last leaked documents, all of us will be on his blacklist."

Hannah scratched her hair. "Oh dear! What do you know about Nahatatama?"

"The Anonymous call their leader Nahatatama. We do not know what the name means, and we know nothing about him."

"Where is Albert Russell?"

"Nobody knows. We searched the whole airport."

"Didn't he leave the country?"

"We don't know. Maybe he departed from another airport ... Excuse me for a moment." A female agent gave him a typed paper. "Here is an update. Albert left the country from Boston Logan International Airport."

"Who are his associates in New York?"

"He has many acquaintances, mostly academics and journalists. My hunch is that he passed the classified dossier to a leftist professor at Columbia University. Edward Said is his best buddy."

"Edward Said?" Her fingers passed through her hair. "Please, do not harass Edward. He is dying of cancer. We have enough trouble with the Left. Anyway, I will go to India and see Albert."

"Are you serious?"

"Yes. I will go there and spy on him."

"Be careful. The Anonymous might kill you."

"Don't worry. I know how to seduce a man. See you soon."

Inhaling and huffing with a deep sense of enervation, she reclined on an umber sofa facing the TV, swinging her legs forward and kneading the tense muscles of her neck. She watched a part of Zita's refined interview, and her shimmering eyes became tearful. At one point, she stood in silence, and her fingers swirled around the TV screen as if she wished to touch Albert Russell.

With eyes devoid of mirth, she sank into the couch with her gaze fixed on the unexpurgated interview unfolding on the screen. The weight of what she saw had hung in the air, casting a pall over her expression as she absorbed the unfiltered reality before her.

When the interview ended, she rose with her steps echoing the reluctant cadence of someone burdened by the unseen. In her hand, she clutched the card she received from the Anonymous person in the heart of Midtown Manhattan-a colored artifact imbued with significance. The walk from the living room to the office became a trudge, each step carrying the unseen weight of reflection.

Seated in an armless chair, she unfolded the card with anticipation and trepidation. Her eyes, now etched with worry, moved across the printed words as if she was trying to decode a message of consequences. The gravity of the information had settled upon her like a heavy shroud, and for a moment, the room seemed to shrink in the face of newfound reality.

As her attention shifted from the card to her hands, she couldn't help but marvel at the tangible proof of the twists and turns of life. She goggled the fingers that touched the pages of an unexpected story and the hands that held the weight of unseen revelations as if she saw her existence through a different lens.

In her customary moments of introspection, she contemplated the desolate and lovelorn aspects of her life, a silent observer behind the thick, paneled walls that enclosed her world. A disciplined existence as a single woman and a devoted mother had long been the armor that shielded her from the raw edges of anxiety and depression. In the depths of her being, an overwhelming sense of desperation for love had gripped her-a longing for love, a hug, a kiss, a bawdy touch. These desires, unabashed and fervent, had become a source of inner turmoil, fueling the flames of her angst.

As she confronted the paradox of her situation, questions lingered in the corridors of her thoughts. But why now? Why, with her striking beauty, prosperous fortune, and acute brainpower, did she yearn for affection? Why hadn't she harnessed these attributes to weave a tapestry of love that enhanced both heart and mind? Smart, handsome people exist, but her stubborn aversion to sexual liaisons with men or women was an obstacle to her felicity and peace of mind. Moreover, what is this unforeseen interest in a British philosopher who lives in India? She affirmed to Zita Marino that she had contacted him once. Where? When? How? Did she love him? Did she have an amour with him? Why did she get a special card from the Anonymous? Is she an underground member of this faceless, violent organization? With a fathomless feeling of bitterness, she thumped the chair with her right hand, regretting something she had done or said. She appeared befuddled, and a lugubrious shadow of bewilderment had hovered over her inclined, haggard head, akin to a black thundercloud casting a gloom over her entire being. Her baffled mind recalled disquieting bygone memories pertained to her private life. This quiescent solitude was not for long. Sarah came back and interrupted her solitary introspection.

"Mom, mom, what will we have for dinner tonight?" she asked with a stentorian voice before entering the office.

With a rapid movement, Hannah hid the Anonymous card in her white panties and opened a women's magazine, pretending to skim through it. "Yes, sweetheart. What do you want to eat?"

"Can you make fish?"

"Yes, let us have fish. We love fish."

After dinner, Hannah kissed her daughter and asked her to go upstairs to her bedroom. She set the Anonymous card ablaze in the sink, watching as the orange flames consumed the reminder of a new perilous venture. With the remnants reduced to ashes, she turned her attention to Zita's videotape, and moved up the stairs to her bathroom, where she brushed her teeth, moistened her face, and stared at an oval mirror-a moment of silent confirmation of her adorableness.

Lying in bed, her fatigued eyes looked up at a half-length portrait of her and Sarah. The back of her right hand rested on a white pillow, while her head lolled on the palm of her left hand. In this intimate space, her emotions were in tumult. Restless, her gaze fixated on the portrait, yet her mind seemed to wander somewhere beyond the walls of the room. Her thoughts drifted toward the vivid conversation between Zita Marino and Albert Russell. This contemplation, however, would appear abstruse to her family and friends, a realm of intellectual musings that might not align with the familiar landscape of everyday conversations. Why is a high middle-class white American Catholic woman interested in the vile murder of Israel's Prime Minister? She is not a Jew or a fervid Zionist Christian to fret about Israel's explosive politics in the Middle East, nor is she a British citizen to concern herself with Albert Russell's life and humanist philosophy. Besides, why did special agents pursue Albert Russell in New York? What did he do? Why did the Anonymous protect him? Why did FBI agents rummage around in Ann Stone's apartment? What is her relationship with Albert Russell? The main reason Nathan Goodman, an influential CIA director associated with the FBI, had contacted her, remained shrouded in mystery. Is she a secret agent? Perhaps Nathan reached out because of her expertise in a specific field, seeking practical advice or help on matters related to espionage and national security. It is not uncommon for intelligence agencies to consult individuals with diverse skills and knowledge of matters that go beyond the scope of their public persona.

As the gentle, misty night advanced, the overwhelming pressure of anxiety had intensified in the noiseless bedroom. Hannah needed to release the compressed, instinctive feeling of her sexual desire and emotional frustration. After taking off the white bra and squeezing the bell-shaped breasts with her palms, she wore red, sleeveless, short nightwear, and viewed Zita's debate with Albert. She muted the TV, ogled Albert, and caressed her body until she reached the climax of her pleasure. This quick onanism was like a sleeping pill. It revealed Hannah's sexual attraction to Albert Russell. Why? Did she meet him in a private place? Did she have an undisclosed affair with him? Does a past amour explain why she had never mentioned him to her family and friends?

Hannah slept, but Ann Stone was awake in her bedroom, waiting for a phone call. At one o'clock, the phone rang and interrupted her nervous rumination. "Hi, darling, I am at Heathrow Airport."

Albert's soothing voice had conciliated her. "Love, I have been thinking of you." She wiped a tear.

"I am fine, darling."

"When is your next flight?"

"After two hours. Did the apes hurt you?"

"No. They searched for classified documents."

"What are these documents?"

"I think they comprise the names and locations of the CIA officers who took part in state terrorism and money laundering transactions."

"Do you have these documents?"

"No. Please be prudent and keep your eyes open. The CIA and their collaborators in the FBI think I gave you the documents."

"They do not learn from their flagrant wickedness."

"What happened to you after the interview?"

"Two female warriors stepped forward to escort me once I left the NBC building. As we made our way to the plaza, three agents approached to arrest me or to engage in a conversation. But events took an unexpected turn. A lithe motorcyclist, having an aura of agility and power, entered the scene with a double chain whip in hand. With remarkable precision, the motorcyclist targeted the limbs of the approaching agents. The impact of the chain whip had incapacitated them, leaving them thwarted in their attempt to talk to me."

"What does the motorcyclist look like?"

"He was wearing a brown costume with a medieval cowl, a brown belt, leather boots, and long spiked gloves. His martial arts techniques are incredible."

"Was he sporting a mask?"

"Yes, he was wearing a silver mask. He threw a card with an image of a cyborg warrior on one side and a capital A on the other."

"Oh, gosh! That motorcyclist is the Anonymous military leader Homatakawa Tamojika, who pledged to eradicate the CIA. Do you recognize him?"

"No. I read about him for the first time in 1990. I guess whether, by any chance, he is a friend."

"How did he know the agents were waiting for you at the NBC building?"

"I do not know what to say. The street became a battleground as the cyborg warriors engaged in a fierce confrontation. They toppled police cars and punished policemen and FBI officers with sticks. They drove me to the airport and vanished without a trace. I felt delighted to see Ayita waiting for me, though she should have stayed in the apartment."

"These warriors are members of the Anonymous group. They call themselves *Nikakawi Wenawa* or Warriors without Names. I think they wanted to protect you."

"Why? If they are cyborgs, why do they protect a British man like me? How did machines become flexible, learn martial arts, and get superhuman power?"

"This matter is still a mystery. Maybe they protect you because you support the human rights of the oppressed peoples. Journalists call the Anonymous the Nameless Masked Warriors."

"Why do they call them that?"

"Because scientists of technology make them of bioelectronic and silicone material and because of their masked faces and extraordinary force and speed. They assassinated over thirty CIA officers in Latin America."

"Blimey! Why?"

"No one knows why they kill intelligence officers. They work for Nahatatama and Homatakawa."

"Who are they?"

"Nahatatama is the chairman of the Anonymous. Homatakawa is the military commander. No one has identified them, and nobody had met them. Because of their names, FBI investigators think they are lineal descendants of the Karankawa and Tonkawa tribes that lived in Oklahoma, Texas, and northern Mexico. Their voices are mechanical and robotic, and their swift assassinations are gruesome. They and the Anonymous warriors speak ancient and extinct languages."

"Why do they fight the intelligence agencies?"

"God knows."

"I forgot to mention that a kung fu guy came out of nowhere and hit two FBI agents with flying kicks when they tried to shoot Homatakawa."

"What was he wearing?"

"A black tai chi uniform, a blue eye mask, and a headband with a yin-yang print on it."

"That's Tilatowate Ma or the Black Flying Eagle. He is Homatakawa's new assistant. Reporters say he is one of the best martial artists in the world today. The FBI offered a three-million-dollar bounty for information leading to his arrest."

"We live in a crazy world. Anyway, I will call you after I arrive. Thanks for everything. I love you."

"I love you too."

In the morning, Hannah took Sarah to Hopkins School on Forest Road in New Haven and drove to her Yale college. In her book-jammed office, she made a call.

"Good morning, Shawn. How are you today?"

"Hi, Hannah. Good morning. I am doing well. How was your weekend?"

"Great. Parties and fun with friends. Could you get me the zip code and the phone number of the British Research Institute in Hyderabad, India?"

"Are you going to India?"

"I am thinking of going over there. India, as you know, is a huge multicultural country."

"Good. I will get the address and the phone number and call you back."

"Thank you."

A while later, Hannah's phone buzzed.

"Write the phone number and the address of the British Research Institute."

Hannah got a blue ballpoint pen. "I am ready."

"The phone number is 00 91 40 79472244. The address is 69 Chirag Ali Lane."

"How do you spell Chirag?"

"C, h, i, r, a, g."

"Thanks a lot for your help. See you at lunch."

By midnight, she went downstairs and made a phone call from her home office.

"The British Research Institute," an Indian woman spoke.

"Good morning. I am Dr. Hannah Rogers, an American professor at Yale University in the United States of America. Can I see Dr. Albert Russell on Monday, December 18?"

"Hang on a minute, please."

The woman dialed two numbers. "Dr. Albert, an American scholar wants to see you on 18 December."

"The 18th of December?"

"Yes."

"Let me look at my diary." Dr. Russell opened a leather notebook. "Yes, that's fine. I am free before the lunch break."

"Hello. You can see Dr. Albert on 18 December between ten and twelve."

"That's wonderful. I will visit your institute on December 18. Thank you very much. Bye."

Hannah smiled and switched on the TV. A news anchor said the Anonymous had released a dubbed video statement, asking the intelligence agencies to stay away from Britain's philosopher Albert Russell or they would face severe consequences. Hannah sat on a couch, and a masked, hooded person appeared on the TV. "To the CIA and FBI. The Anonymous are here. We do not intend to kill or hurt you. But you made us furious because you tried to arrest Professor Albert Russell in New York. We want peace. In the meantime, we will destroy your cities and towns and crush you and declare war if you try to seize or hurt anyone of us or Albert Russell. Goodbye."

Hannah switched off the TV and went to her bed. In the morning, she dropped Sarah off at her private school and headed to a travel agency on Chapel Street. After entering the agency's office, she greeted a brunette receptionist wearing red-framed glasses.

"Hello, gorgeous." She kissed the receptionist.

"Good morning, Hannah. So glad to see you. How are you? How is the prettiest girl?"

"We are all right. Sarah is at school. How are doing, Martina?"

"I still breathe through my tiny nose and toil like a pouncing pronghorn."

"Well, surprise, surprise! I want to go to India. Can I get a flight to Hyderabad on December 14?"

"India? Wow!" She stared at her computer screen. "Sorry. Direct flights to Hyderabad do not exist. A flight to New Delhi is available on December 13, and multiple flights from New Delhi to Hyderabad city operate daily."

"Great. Can you get me a flight from New Delhi to Hyderabad on December 16?"

"How many people are going?"

"Just me and Sarah."

Three minutes later, Martina smiled. "Your flight will be on Wednesday, December 13, at nine a.m. from JFK International Airport. The Indian flight from New Delhi to Hyderabad will be on Saturday, December 16, at 9:30 a.m. Is this all right?"

"Yes. Wonderful."

"When do you prefer to come back?"

"Before January 10."

"Is Sunday, the 7th of January, OK?"

"Perfect."

"For your eyes, the tickets cost $1085."

After fetching a checkbook from her buff clutched

purse, Hannah signed a check and received the air tickets.

At home, she was jubilant and eager to talk to her daughter about the Christmas and winter holidays that were approaching. Sarah was watching the animated film *The Lion King* when her mother came into her bedroom. "Sarah, do you wish to go to India? Do you like to spend the winter vacation there?"

"India? Fantastic. I do not know. I mean, as you wish, mom."

Hannah sat on the edge of the bed. "Love, I want to tell you a secret. My maternal grandfather, Joseph O'Neill, was a Jesuit missionary in India in the 1930s. He told me fabulous stories about it when I was seven or eight. So, since my childhood, I had always dreamed of flying to India to explore its gods and temples and pass through its spectacular mountains, monuments, scary jungles, and wildlife reserves. I love its rich and spicy cuisine. My old dream is turning into a reality. We should not hole up here in our outlying home. Let us flee to India before our relatives ask us to take them to our ranch in Vermont."

"That's cool, mommy."

Hannah stood, patting her girl's shoulder, and smiled. "Great, sweetheart. It will be a wonderful adventure. Do you remember *The Jungle Book* movie? It is all about India. We will eat Indian curries, coconuts, mangos, and guavas. We will take photos of the Taj Mahal, forests, elephants, tigers, monkeys, dancing cobra snakes …"

Chapter 2

After enduring twenty hours of tiresome travel, Hannah and Sarah arrived at Indira Gandhi International Airport in New Delhi. In the crowded, malodorous airport, they looked at swarthy Indians decked out in salwar kameezes and gaudy sarees. A mustached immigration officer stamped their dark blue passports, and they met a scrawny Indian woman wearing a periwinkle saree and carrying a rectangular piece of white cardboard with Hannah's full name on it. Two dusky, gaunt Indian men wanted to hold their wheeled suitcases, but the Indian woman frowned and admonished them to stay away. A whitish taxi took them to the Ambassador Hotel near Sujan Singh Park.

In the evening, they ventured out for a brisk walk near the bustling Khan Market. The clamorous tumult of the packed streets had amazed them, and everything seemed exotic and irregular. The hazardous roads were muddy, obstreperous, and overcrowded. Mucky people cooked, and others ate food on the grubby sidewalks. The toxic air, heavy with caliginous and choking smog, had created a stifling and disconcerting atmosphere. Frenetic pedestrians navigated the swarming streets with a sense of urgency, crossing whenever a narrow gap appeared between the chaotic flow of small and large vehicles. The thoroughfares were a tumultuous mix of cars, buses, scooters, bicycles, and rickshaws, each moving in directions that seemed more like a dance of disorder than a structured flow. A scene of lethargy and chaos unfolded as drooling, slothful cows reclined on the sides of the roadways, showing indifference to the surrounding frenzy. Meanwhile, berserk monkeys showed unrestrained exuberance, leaping from brick facades to layered trees in a display of wild agility. Witnessing a family of five people on a single motorbike left Hannah and Sarah in a state of profound disbelief. To describe their reaction as a culture shock would be an understatement. The sight defied their accustomed norms and expectations so much that the term "culture shock" seemed insufficient to capture the magnitude of the experience.

On Friday morning, they boarded a hotel tourist bus and visited the colossal Red Fort and Taj Mahal in Agra, over 130 miles south of New Delhi. The architectural ornaments, the decorated minarets, the iconic Mughal structures, and the extensive gardens were entrancing. Hannah and Sarah snapped memorable photographs. Joyous Indians gazed at the beauty of their faces and beamed. Hannah suggested they should cover their heads with the colorful silk scarves they bought from a bazaar a day earlier.

On the next day, they got a flight to Hyderabad, the

capital of Andhra Pradesh, after Hannah had told Sarah about a Muslim kingdom that was there until 1948, a year after the triumphant independence of India. They stayed at Taj Residency Hotel, in an urban, commercial area called Banjara Hills. They admired the capacious hotel and its glossy marble floors, swimming pool, non-spicy buffet food, and live music.

On Sunday morning, they toured historical buildings, such as Golkonda Fort, Salar Jung Museum, and Taj Falaknuma Palace, and trekked through Nehru Zoological Park (Hyderabad Zoo), near a vast reservoir called Mir Alam Tank. In the evening, they dined in the hotel restaurant and greeted an old American woman sitting next to an Indian scholar who worked with the American Studies Research Centre in Osmania University for twenty years. After introducing herself and her daughter as cultural tourists, Hannah asked the scholar about the city of Hyderabad and the British Research Institute, which multinational students, academics, diplomats, volunteers, and travelers liked to visit. He penned the address of the British Institute on a small piece of paper and passed it to Hannah.

Hannah and Sarah visited the British Research Institute on Monday morning. The Institute was on Chirag Ali Lane, a congested, sordid, vociferous, narrow road in the midst of the metropolis. Sarah felt nauseous when she saw mooing cows and scruffy men urinating on the damaged sidewalk of the street. She and her mother had wondered to sight an educational institute in an unsanitary environment.

The British Institute was on the second floor of a vast chartreuse building. After opening a steel gate, Hannah and Sarah walked upstairs, entered the Institute, and seated themselves in a square waiting room. An Indian assistant, called Sandeep, offered them plain biscuits with spiced tea mixed with milk. No other person had spoken to them, and the members of the staff were in their closed offices. They got up and moved into the imposing library. An Indian woman in a garish red saree was sitting at a large counter and typing library cards.

"Good morning," Hannah greeted.

The Indian woman stood with a broad smile. "Good morning. I am Maghi, the librarian."

"Hello, Maghi. I have an appointment with a British scholar called Albert Russell. I also hope to read texts on Islam in India."

"Please, come with me."

Hannah and Sarah walked behind Maghi in the library and advanced toward a white man poring over an old, shabby book, and sitting at an oak escritoire.

"Dr. Albert, this lady has mentioned you, and she wants to learn about Islam in India."

A collection of sundry books created towering piles, engulfing the oaken top of Albert's antique escritoire. Chromatic bookmarks, ballpoint pens, text markers, and lined papers adorned an illustrated script, creating an organized chaos that spoke to a mind immersed in academic pursuits.

Amid this literary haven, Albert emerged, clad in a red-blue checked shirt paired with navy jeans. As he angled his face toward Hannah and Sarah, rising with a grace reminiscent of a fashion model, the long hall seemed to transform into a curated space, reflecting intellectual depth and sartorial elegance.

His physical presence echoed the traits of a highborn gentleman-standing at a healthy six feet, he exuded good looks and robust vitality. The short, light brown hair and the bright, clean-shaven countenance underscored a polished appearance, leaving an impression of a man who embraced the world of knowledge and carried himself with the demeanor befitting a highbred person of refined upbringing.

Albert beamed and shook the hands of Hannah and Sarah. "Good morning. Welcome. My name is Albert. What can I do for you?"

There was an odd silence as Hannah and Albert gazed at each other. With dazzled eyes, Albert swallowed his saliva and wished to utter mordant words, but Hannah halted him with politeness and alacrity. "Thank you very much, Dr. Albert Russell. I am Hannah Rogers. I am privileged and honored to meet Bertrand Russell's most preeminent grandson in this remarkable city." Hannah put her right hand on Sarah's left shoulder. "This is my daughter Sarah. Honorable sir, I seek your advice as to how I can get enlightening works on Islam and Muslims in Andhra Pradesh and other regions of India. I will very much appreciate your invaluable and wise insights."

Hannah's terse, amiable statement was a coded message to Albert because Sarah was standing beside her. Albert grinned and looked at Sarah. "Do you wish to join us?" Before she could say a word, her mother touched her shoulder. "Honey, you stay here." Albert glanced at her. "Come with me."

"I'll wait here," Sarah said when her mother and Albert were about to leave her in the library. Albert turned his twinkling face toward her. "Please, feel free in the library.

You may find comfort in this upholstered armchair." With a gesture of his right hand, he directed her attention to the expansive magazine racks. "You are welcome to pursue and check out any magazines or journals that catch your interest over there."

"Thank you."

Hannah and Albert walked to an office outside the library. Sarah wandered around in the reading hall for a short while, picked up a *National Geographic* magazine, and rested in a vintage wooden armchair. Indians and non-Indians surrounded her, praising her appeal, and asking personal and ordinary questions. Her lips muttered imprecise words, such as "fine" and "OK," to quell their impertinent curiosity.

Albert closed his office door and sat in an accent chair. His office was air-conditioned and crammed with metal bookshelves filled with nonfiction books. On the top shelves, volumes of ancient encyclopedias stood beside each other like engraved headstones. Hannah rested on a fawn sofa.

A peculiar tranquility settled over the scene. Albert brought his hands to his flat abdomen, staring at Hannah with questioning eyes. In that moment, an unvoiced anticipation prevailed, as if he awaited a cogent explanation for her unexpected visit at this time of the year. A heavy silence hung in the air, pregnant with an unspoken expectation of clarity.

Hannah, in response, sucked in her flushed lips, betraying a mixture of emotions. Her face became florid, revealing tension or embarrassment. "Good morning, dear Albert. How are you doing these days? How is your exciting life in India?"

Albert's left fingers brushed the bottom rear of his skull. "Good morning. What a fantastic revelation! Is this a seraphic and miraculous amazement before Christmas?" He quirked his mouth.

"Yes, it is a miracle and my utmost pleasure to meet you in an unfamiliar place. You look well and charismatic as always. Do you remember me?"

Albert's left fingers traced his temple. "It is an intriguing question! Do I remember you? What do you think?" He rubbed his Nordic nose and gazed at her. "Yes, I remember you. You are the enigmatic, flippant woman who exploited me for her sexual gratification and dumped me for no plausible reason when I was a student in Hong Kong."

"What is this sexual gratification? With all due respect, I think you were a remarkable member of this sexual gratification, as you call it. I had never exploited and humiliated you. What should I say now? It had been a long time since my departure from Hong Kong. It is impossible for me to stop thinking of you and your amazing love. God is my witness. I," she paused and grabbed her hair, "I loved you," she responded with an apologetic glance.

Unconvinced by her plain assertion, he glowered at her glinting eyes, as if he wanted to squawk. "Did you love me? Love is an attachment of caring and fond hearts. With no remorse, you disappeared and abandoned me in 1981, and now it is December 1995. You had been away for fourteen years. What do you call this occult absence in America? Do you call it love?"

"I am sorry. I swear by God, I did not mean it."

"Didn't you mean it? Did anyone force you to forsake

me and vanish without warning? I thought you had an affable mind. Where was your feminine heart? Where was your natural compassion? You did not even drop a note or send me a letter. You faded away for over fourteen years. I do not imply you must have continued your relationship with me, but at least you should have contacted me."

"It was not easy as you might have thought."

"Not easy? What do you mean by that? Why didn't you contact me?"

"I understand your profound agony, and you have the full right to be resentful and angry with me. What do you want me to say now?" She nodded her head forward. "I was married to an American businessman when I had the love affair with you in Hong Kong."

Albert seemed uninterested in her anomalous confession, though he wanted to hear the conclusion of her anecdote. He turned his face toward his desk, and his left middle and index fingers moved two books and printed papers. "Were you married? As far as I recall, you were eighteen years old. Did you get married when you were a minor? This is fascinating! So, you admit it was a casual liaison?"

"For emotional reasons, I had not intended to love you in the beginning. It started as an inadvertent affair, but then it became a blaring flame, an emotional storm, a burning love. Unlike you, I lived and grew up in a strict Catholic household. Catholicism was everything. My parents did not allow me to go out with boys or have a boyfriend. Without my consent, they arranged a marriage for me with my cousin right away after celebrating my eighteenth birthday. I got married and had no experience in life or sex. But after I met you, I wanted a new venture in my life. My body needed to explore its desires and sexuality with you. My spirit wanted to be free with you. I got a glimpse of the beauty of your tender heart and the brilliance of your mind. Oh, Albert, my husband Michael Rogers was in Hong Kong when I had that unforgettable and venturous amour with you. He died in a grisly car accident a few days after we left Hong Kong. His sudden and horrible death at an early age had devastated me. I became pregnant and depressed. Yet, I could not give up thinking of you. I wished to leave America and be with you, but I was pregnant, and my family was with me all the time. I had to stay in America to give birth and sort out Michael's will. So, three or four months after Sarah's birth, I flew to Hong Kong to see you, but you were not there, and nobody in your university and club knew your whereabouts and contact details."

Albert raised his hazel eyebrows and stared at her. "Why did you have an affair with me if you were married? Was your husband wealthy?"

"Yes, he was a tycoon. But, you know, women have emotions and sentiments. They indulge in love affairs when their apathetic men treat them as solid chunks of furniture and deprive them of meaningful attachment and communication. Michael was a notable millionaire, and he made me rich. But money and fame do not heal women's crippled hearts."

"Did you go to Hong Kong to see me?"

"Yes, and baby Sarah was with me."

"Why did you want to see me?"

"I wanted." She faltered and gasped. "I wanted to say you are an exceptional person."

Albert's right fingers banged on the corner of his

wooden desk. "Yes, I am a special person from an American point of view." He gave her a sardonic gaze. "Why are you here? Nice-looking, educated men would love to be with you. Why me? I am not an American. Do you want to revive that painful torment in my heart? Do you intend to discard me again?"

"What do you say? I am not your formal spouse to walk out on you. Why do you think I want to leave you again? Do you infer you are not in a relationship?"

"This is a private matter."

"A private matter? Is this how you talk to me, to your foremost lover? You told me I was your first girlfriend in Hong Kong. You lost your virginity because of me. Have you forgotten our love and what we shared?"

"Did I lose my chastity because of you? Suppose I have a partner. What would you do?"

"I know you are unmarried. I know many things about you. Your grandfather Bertrand Russell was a famous thinker, and you are a renowned philosopher, even when you hibernate like a polar bear in this distant institute."

"What do you expect me to say after these prolonged years of bitter chagrin? If you sought to reconnect with me, why didn't you contact my family? You know I belong to a well-known English family."

"Actually, I flew to England in 1983 and talked to your parents. I met your blonde sister, Dora, who said you did not have a postal address because you continued to travel all over the world. She further said you called your family from post offices. So, how did you want me to find your home? I gave your family my address and phone number in America."

A smile came to his face after feeling reassured and

revivified. "I see. Dora mentioned she met an American woman, but no member of my family had informed me about your phone number. What did you tell my family?"

"I told them I was your close friend in Hong Kong. As you know, your father is an Anglican priest, and your mother is a pious Christian. Fear made me disorientated and unable to disclose my affair with you." She opened her moccasin purse and pulled out a wrapped gift. "Take this."

"What is it?"

"This is your astounding interview with Zita Marino in New York. I watched it ten times. You are a genius like your grandfather."

"Thank you. How did you get it?"

"I met Zita in her office and got the tape from her."

"Where do you live?"

"I live in an affluent small town called Darien in the State of Connecticut."

"What do you do?"

"I am a professor of cultural and women's studies at Yale University."

"Brilliant. When did you meet Zita?"

"After your interview. I even visited Columbia University and asked about you, but you were in the air. To grasp the entire truth, I have come to India to meet up with you, wonderful man." She wiped away a few tears. "Yes, despite all these painful years of our separation, you are so dear to me. Ah!" She paused and wept. "I have been a single woman for fourteen years. Yes, fourteen years without love and sexual affection. Do you know why? God, God knows why I want to meet up with you."

This unfeigned ardor had kindled Albert's forgiving

heart with flaming love. He could not believe a cultured, rich, beautiful woman had been single for fourteen years because of her love for him. Hannah shielded her face with her hands and sobbed like a distraught widow. Albert stood beside her, placing his right hand on her left shoulder. "Hannah! Please. Oh, my God. Please, do not cry here." He handed her a white tissue paper and a glass of water.

"Hannah, this is not a proper place for us to discuss emotional matters. I am busy in the afternoon, but, with full sincerity, I hope to spend time with you tomorrow. Let us move to the library."

She wiped away her pearly tears and drank water. "Please, do not tell Sarah about our past. I told her nothing about you. Promise me not to tell her about my affair with you."

He caressed her shoulder. "I promise you that and understand your legitimate concern. I appreciate your friendly visit, and I am gratified to see you again."

They went to the library shelves in an enormous, tenebrous hall. Sarah, concerned about her mother, ambled to the bookshelves to see her. As she walked between the tall and wide bookshelves, she heard mumbling and saw her mother carrying two books and talking, in a cheerful tone, to Albert, who rested his left elbow on a bookshelf.

Hannah noticed her daughter. "Oh, darling, you are here. I am sorry. We have been talking about exciting things. Let us go to the reading hall."

The three moved to the well-lighted reading hall. "You may sit here. Sorry, Hannah, the library does not allow the visitors to borrow books." Albert looked at Sarah. "Do you need a drink?"

"No. Thanks."

Over an hour later, Hannah and Sarah met Albert in his secluded office. "Thank you very much for welcoming us here."

"My pleasure. I hope the books were helpful to you."

"Yes, they were good and informative." A smile glimmered across her face. "When do you finish your work?"

"At five o'clock."

"Thanks once more. I promise to see you tomorrow."

"Sure. Thank you. I am pleased to meet both of you." Albert shook their hands. "Bye. Take care." They waved and left the Institute.

On their way back to the hotel, Hannah touched Sarah's hand. "Albert is from England. He is a nice guy and a clever philosopher. His grandfather was famous all over the world. We should see him again." Sarah made no comment.

In the late evening, Hannah and Albert spent more than an hour in their bedrooms, pondering upon their unexpected encounter and conversation. Hannah was uncertain about Albert's initial reaction to her sudden visit, though she felt satisfied when he expressed his delight at the prospect of rekindling their friendship. Likewise, her uncharacteristic, audacious appearance had left Albert astonished. The boldness of her action had prompted him to pose a simple yet profound question to himself: "Why does Hannah want to reconnect with me after many years of separation?" The query echoed through his deep thoughts, adding an element of introspection to the unfolding reunion. So, he called Ann

Stone. "Hannah Rogers is in the city. Do you know why she is here?"

"She is attractive and rich. Trust her and be kind. What did she say?"

"She said she loves me. What do you think?"

"Do you love her?"

"I am not sure. It is too early to tell."

"Be yourself. Love Hannah and do not forget me."

At three o'clock in the morning, Albert woke up after hearing an automated voice in his head. "Love and trust Hannah. She is one of us. You need her, and she needs you." He stared at the lines of his sweaty palms and thought he had an unusual dream.

On Tuesday morning, Hannah and Sarah went to the British Institute. Albert was in the library hall, drinking black tea and reading an Indian English newspaper.

"Good morning."

Albert put the newspaper on a round table and stood to receive them. "Good morning, Hannah. Good morning, Sarah. How are you this morning?"

"We are all right. Thanks. Are you busy?"

"I have a lecture on the history of Indian philosophy after two hours. Please, have a seat."

Seated in a trance, Sarah puzzled over her mother's fanciful idea of a holiday abroad. The vivid imagery painted by her mother's descriptions came to life in her mind-Indian tigers, majestic elephants, and untrodden jungles had formed a mosaic of exotic landscapes, each detail etched with the attraction of adventure.

Her thoughts stayed on her mother's illustrious portrayal of the Himalaya Mountains in Northern India and Nepal. The amazing grandeur of these towering peaks, described with a richness of detail, had unfolded in her mind's eye. Leering at her mother, she wished to say, "Mom, I feel sluggish today. What would we get from seeing a philosopher who prattles on about books and ideas? What are we doing in this uninteresting institute? Why are we here? What are we aspiring for in this grimy city? Let us go to a warm place. Or let us go back to America. Look at these dirty and cracked walls. Disgusting lizards and spiders are creeping on the webbed ceiling. The stinging, buzzing mosquitoes are sucking my blood …" But what could a thirteen-year-old girl do? She felt she had no choice but to be a dutiful daughter.

To be fair, her classy mother, her best friend in the universe, was beatific and perky. She had a vivid talk with Albert about their professional interests and social activities. His unpretentious modesty and extensive expertise had impressed and captivated her. He, one should say, had asked Sarah six times if she needed something to drink.

Hannah turned her beaming face to Sarah and sensed her discontent. As a wealthy, vivacious girl, she favored a stimulating environment. "Sarah, let us return to the hotel." Sarah felt happy, but her mother touched Albert's hand. "Do you like to have dinner with us?"

"That will be great. I look forward to having dinner with you and Sarah. Where do you like to go?"

"Taj Residency Hotel has a pleasant restaurant that offers a wide variety of cuisine. We will meet up there at six."

"See you then."

At ten to six, Albert and a copper-haired, gray-eyed, sylphlike girl entered the bright hotel premier restaurant. Albert was in a white shirt, dark blue pants, and a navy jacket shining with gold buttons. The girl was wearing an orange shirt, blue jeans, and pink sandals.

"Good evening. This is my daughter Olivia."

Without hesitation, Hannah stood radiant in natural beauty, shook Albert's hand with a rare elation, and kissed Olivia's gleaming forehead. "Good evening. Hello, Olivia. Thanks a lot for coming."

Olivia rested between her father and Sarah. Hannah sat to the left of Albert and could not take her inquisitive eyes off his attractive daughter. "Great to see you, father." She tapped his hand. "Olivia is gorgeous. How old is she?"

"She is eleven."

"Where is her mom?"

"Her mother died in an airplane crash in Japan."

Hannah's left hand gripped her chin. "Oh, my God. I am so sorry to hear that. When did that happen?"

"The tragic accident occurred in August 1985."

"Is Olivia's mom buried in Japan?"

"The Japanese authorities told us the explosion of the plane had incinerated her body to ashes. We found her valise and cuff bracelet. The plane crash killed another U.S. citizen and a British national."

"What was her name?"

"Eva Kelly."

"Kelly is an Irish surname. Was she Irish?"

"She was an Irish American from Brooklyn."

"When did you get married?"

"In 1983."

"Where does Olivia live?"

"She is always with me. She goes where I go."

"Is she in school?"

"Yes. She goes to an international school in the city."

Meanwhile, Olivia glanced at Sarah with a childish smile. "How did you find India?"

"Primitive and dirty."

"How is the food?"

"I don't like spicy food. It irritates my stomach, though I like Indian fruits and juices."

The four guzzled, bantered, conferred, and listened to live music. At first, Sarah, reserved and jittery, thought Albert would come to the restaurant and inundate them with insipid lectures on religion, philosophy, politics, and science. That was her inceptive impression of him. But, to her astonishment, he was lovable and jaunty that evening. With great zeal, he expressed his fervent passion for life and peace and supportive affection for the good people of the world. He laughed, joked, and showed Hannah and Sarah his shrewd sense of English satire and playfulness. It seemed that he sought an untethered time away from his monotonous academic habitat. Yet, as a cultivated scholar of letters, he awed Hannah and Sarah with his encyclopedic knowledge of literature, history, and science. Besides, Sarah felt happy to talk to an English-speaking girl. She and Olivia chatted about their countries, schools, friends, and hobbies.

Feeling the pleasure of seeing her old beau, Hannah was ebullient and rapturous. She was wearing a short, ecru, floral skirt and a sleeveless white camisole top, displaying her enticing cleavage and back. She touched Albert's hands and knees several times after she rested beside him on a separate couch.

The pleasant time moves fast like a flying arrow. Albert checked his watch. "Wow! I do not believe it. It is midnight."

"Thank you for this lovely night. We have learned new things and enjoyed your wonderful company."

Albert stood and kissed Hannah's grinning face and Sarah's forehead. Hannah kissed Olivia's cheek, and Sarah shook her hand. "Good night." Albert waved his right hand.

Hannah waved back. "Good night and God bless you."

Sarah grumbled. "Mom, could you carry me up to the room? I am too tired to walk."

"Come on, you are not a baby."

Albert turned his face back to them. "Hannah, if you do not mind, I will help you."

"Thanks, Albert. You have had a long day. She is just lazy."

Albert smiled. "Please, Sarah, give me your magical hand."

Sarah, with a tired body and listless eyes, put her right hand in Albert's until they were in an elevator. Albert embraced her upper back when the elevator door opened and walked until she settled down in her bed. "Good night, Sarah."

"Thanks, Albert. You are an honorable gentleman and a wonderful nobleman," Hannah complimented.

"No problem. Good night."

Albert and Olivia left the hotel, and Hannah sat on the right edge of Sarah's bed. "Albert is a sweet dude."

"Do you love him, mom? We met him yesterday. He held your hand most of the time, and you touched him on the knee."

"You are perceptive, my little girl. Sleep now. I love you."

On Wednesday morning, Hannah and Sarah took a

taxi to see Albert and Olivia near the General Post Office building in a rowdy area called Abids, three hundred yards away from the British Institute.

"Good morning," Hannah said.

"Good morning. It is a fine, rainless day. Have you ever ridden an auto rickshaw?" Albert asked.

"No."

"Let us get one. We will go to a place called Charminar in the old city."

They rode an uproarious rickshaw with a bulb horn and three wheels. Sarah and Olivia squeezed themselves between Hannah and Albert. The oily-haired ebony driver steered the ear-splitting rickshaw at full speed. Hannah grasped a metal edge. "Oh, my God! Oh, my God!" Albert appealed to the driver to slow down.

They arrived at Charminar, a historical monument erected in 1591. Albert looked up. "Charminar means four minarets." They visited Laad Bazaar and Mecca Masjid (Mosque) at Charminar Road after Albert had asked Hannah and Sarah to take off their flat, strappy sandals and veil their heads. In the evening, Albert invited Hannah and Sarah to a multi-cuisine restaurant, called Rich and Famous, at Nampally Station Road in the city center. Sarah sat next to Olivia, and Albert rested beside Hannah. Albert looked at the bemused faces of Hannah and Sarah when they found it difficult to choose a meal. He smiled and expounded Hindi words such as *pulao, biryani, korma, dal, Mughlai, jhal faraizi, gosht, keema,* tandoori, naan, and chapatti.

After dinner, Hannah rejoiced like a whirling dervish. She patted Albert's left fist. "Where do you want to spend your Christmas vacation?"

"We have no ideas."

"We are thinking of going to Goa."

"Goa is a paradisal state. It has a long, idyllic beach."

"Do you wish to come with us?"

"We will not say nay. Thank you."

On Saturday morning, December 23, they flew to the village of Dabolim in Goa. Albert proposed they should hire a car and stay in south Goa and explained the salubrious and mental benefits of having a sanitary environment "away from the smoky, hippie tourists."

"Anything you say. Anywhere is fine with us if it is clean and safe."

In the evening, Nathan Goodman was in the CIA's New York office in the World Trade Center when a woman spy called him. "Hannah and Albert are in Goa."

Albert, Hannah, and their daughters stayed in a two-room cottage on Varca Beach, where they loved the stunning seaside, the food, and the stupefying sunset. Albert wore long-sleeve shirts and said, "I dislike the sun." He had declined to swim, though he immersed his feet in the tepid seawater. Sarah thought he was too bashful to shed his shirt and uncover his body in the presence of women and unfamiliar strangers because of his scholarly reputation and polished upbringing.

A week later, Sarah and Olivia wore mini shorts and sat beside each other on the beach. Their bare feet were in the warm sand. Albert came out of his room in beige shorts and a blue, long-sleeved shirt. He squatted beside Olivia.

"How are you, girls? What are you reading?"

"I am reading a story about a family adventure in Egypt," Olivia responded.

Before Sarah could utter a word, her elated mother

caught Albert's hand and pulled him against her. "Get up. Come on. Let us walk." She was wearing a mustard sarong skirt, which Albert gave her on the Christmas day, and a white tank top. They held each other's hand and strolled barefoot on the delicate beach. Hannah leaned on a curved coconut palm tree, hugged Albert, and brushed his lips. Albert inserted his right knee between her thighs, placing his left arm around her exposed shoulders and letting his lips touch hers. They mumbled words into each other's ear and cackled. No one else heard what he or she had said.

For the first time, Sarah became interested in her mother's sexual dalliance. She stopped behind a tree and sneaked a peek at Albert and her mother when they fondled and kissed under a circular thatch umbrella. She exhibited singular fascination and wonder at their overt amorousness. "Olivia, look. My mom and your dad love each other. Weird. My mom had always refused to love a man."

"They are adults. They can do what they like."

All stayed out, under the starlit sky, until midnight and celebrated the New Year. After singing "Happy New Year" in a gruff voice, Albert hugged them and kissed their faces. He held the girls' hands. "Come to my spooky room." Olivia and Sarah got tin ankle bracelets, and Hannah received a gold pendant. "The finest gift is in the hearts of the people we love." He whooped again, "Happy New Year."

Hannah hugged him and sucked his mouth in front of the girls. "Honey, you are very kind. Thank you so much." Intoxicated with sexual craving, she willed to proclaim her love for him. She fetched two glasses of red wine from the kitchen.

Sarah held Olivia's hand. "We want to go to bed."

Hannah kissed her. "OK, honey. Good night."

Albert smiled. "Good night, princesses."

Sarah and Olivia shambled to a room and slept beside each other like sisters.

Hannah was sleeping unclothed and without a sound when Albert woke up beside her. The girls awoke and moved out of the cottage after washing their faces. Albert rested on the right end of the cabin, dangling his muscly legs back and forth, and reading an illustrated booklet on Goa. Sarah and Olivia sat beside him.

"Hi, dad." Olivia kissed.

"Good morning," Sarah greeted.

"Good morning. Did you sleep well?"

Sarah stretched her arms above her head. "Yes, we slept well."

"Do you want a cup of tea?"

"Yes. Stay here. We will make tea," Sarah replied.

When Sarah and Olivia were in the kitchen waiting for the water in an aluminum kettle to boil, the former noticed that Albert's bedroom door was half-open. She purported to draw a hand towel from the bathroom, peeped into Albert's bedroom, and saw her mother braless and sleeping on her left side. Licking her lips with the tip of her rosy tongue, she wished to know why her mother had made love to Albert. That was natural, for she knew her mother had refused to love men. Her instant curiosity was instinctive and uncomplicated. As an educated, grown-up teenager, she was well-informed about women's sexual behavior and desires. At once, she asked herself, "Why did not my mom have sex in America? Why does she love a British philosopher in India? Was she his friend? Does she hide something from me?" Anyhow, she felt glad that her mother had found a companion to love.

Sarah and Olivia made three cups of tea and rested again beside Albert. They had a little chat about their schools, friends, and general pursuits. Later, Hannah came out wearing chino shorts and a black bra. With her wet hands on Albert's shoulders, he tilted his face up. She crouched toward his face and smacked his lips. She yawned. "Good morning, folks. Did you have breakfast?"

"No. We have been waiting for your majesty."

In the late afternoon, Albert covered his left ear with a hand after hearing a mechanical voice in his head. "Be careful. The enemies are behind you." Ten seconds later, he, Hannah, and their daughters halted their slow steps on the coast when a deafening explosion occurred behind them. They turned their faces toward a roaring fire and a cluster of people in a circle.

"Hannah, please, stay with the girls. I'll come back soon." After running for a half minute, Albert saw a car on fire and found startled people surrounding a dead white man with a handgun in his hand. "What happened?"

"Three strange women threw petrol bombs on that van and killed a man with tonfas. One of them hit this man's neck with her fingers," an Indian man said.

Albert stared at the lifeless man's neck and saw five blood spots. He remembered the finger punching in the Shaolin Temple and thought a kung fu martial artist had killed the white men. "What do the female attackers look like?"

"They wear armor and silver masks. Their hair is long and dark. I did not understand their language. They look like the cyborg warriors," another Indian said.

"Where did they go?"

"They said something and disappeared like ghosts."

Albert eyed the dead man, recalled Homatakawa and the Anonymous warriors who thrashed federal agents at the NBC building in New York, and became convinced that they murdered the two white men in Goa. "Why was this man carrying a gun?"

A woman covered her belly. "I saw him following you and your family. Do you know him?"

That was a surprising statement. "No." Albert came back, and Hannah hugged him. "What happened?"

"There was a fight. Let us go back to the cottage."

Despite that incident, the next few days were full of delectation and happiness. Albert loved to carry the girls on his robust shoulders, and they were like a privileged, happy family. On Friday, January 5, they flew back to Hyderabad and stayed in Albert's three-bedroom apartment. On Sunday morning, it was hard for them to say goodbye. Hannah gave Albert her home address and phone number and begged him to communicate with her. "Don't forget to write." At Hyderabad airport, Albert hugged and kissed her and Sarah with intense affection. "It has been our best holiday for ages. We are grateful for your revitalizing visit. We expect to see you again soon."

Chapter 3

Hannah met Nathan Goodman in a bar-restaurant at the bottom of Greenwich Avenue, Greenwich. "I searched Albert's apartment and office in Hyderabad. He has none of the official documents."

"Any news about Nahatatama, Homatakawa, and the Anonymous?"

"Albert has no contact with them. He had never mentioned them."

"But they killed two fellows in Goa."

"Why were they there? Who sent them to Goa? Killing Albert is not a solution. The Anonymous guys shield him all the time and everywhere."

"Why do they protect him?"

"I don't know. We are tracking the wrong man."

"How? The Anonymous organization protects him for a reason."

"Maybe because he loves Ann Stone. I assure you both have nothing to do with the Anonymous. Ann is in her New York office most of the time, and Albert is pacifist and busy with his academic work. He weeps when he hugs his daughter and when he calls his family in England. It is impossible for him to be associated with the Anonymous because he hates war and violence. I think Nahatatama wants to see a war between the leftist revolutionaries and us. As you told me, the Anonymous vowed to blow up our cities and slaughter the Americans in Latin America if we kill Albert."

"What do you suggest?"

"Let me contact Albert again, and then, if necessary, we will change our strategy. We need to act on serious matters and postpone our program to assassinate him."

"How does he feel about you?"

"He trusts me. I told you I know how to seduce a man."

"Good. Keep me posted."

Meanwhile, Hannah wrote exquisite letters to Albert, and he sent droves of messages and books to her. Sarah kept photos in her bedroom and made funny cards for Olivia. She once drew tigers standing near lofty woods and scribbled, "Olivia in the jungle."

One day, Hannah and Sarah rested beside each other on a couch in the family room and watched the animated film *Beauty and the Beast* when their phone buzzed. Sarah stood. "I will get the phone."

"Hello, Sarah. How are you, darling?"

"I'm all right. Thank you."

"How is your lovely mom?"

"She is well."

"How is the school?"

"It is in order, and I am doing well. My exams are next week."

Hannah stood. "Who is that?"

"This is Albert. Albert, here is my mom."

"Thanks, sweetie."

Sarah gave her mother the phone. "Hello, Albert. This is a pleasant surprise."

"How are you getting along, sweetheart?"

"I am well. How is your life? What are you doing?"

Albert asked Hannah about her summer vacation and invited her and Sarah to visit him in Hong Kong.

"Hong Kong once again? I do not believe that. Do you visualize a wild fantasy there? My sinful body is craving for effleurage and a sexual escapade." She laughed. "We were in India four months ago. Let me speak to Sarah."

Hannah turned her face to Sarah. "Albert and Olivia want us to spend the summer vacation with them in Hong Kong. What do you think?"

"I would love to go to Hong Kong. We have never been there. Yes, I would love to go there."

"Well, Albert, Sarah is eager to go to Hong Kong." She then mentioned personal and general matters and said loving things to Albert. "Goodbye, Albert. I love you too."

"Hooray, Hooray, it's a holi-holiday. What a world of fun for everyone, holi-holiday." Hannah sang with joy, stretching her arms forward, and hopping up with a jolly grin. She sat and put her left arm around Sarah's shoulders. "Honey, finish your exams, and we will fly to Hong Kong to have fun with Albert and Olivia. Are you happy now?"

"Yeah, I am so happy to see you joyful. It will be so cool to see Olivia and Albert once again. I love them."

Hannah and Sarah flew to Hong Kong. Albert and Olivia waited for them at Hong Kong International Airport. Albert saluted and bowed to Hannah and Sarah as traditional Chinese do. "Hi, darlings. Welcome to Hong Kong." He kissed them. Hannah kissed Olivia, and Sarah shook her hand.

They got a taxicab to Kowloon, where Albert rented a two-bedroom flat on the eleventh floor of a building near Sheraton Hong Kong Hotel.

In the apartment, Albert kissed Hannah's pink lips, dragging her body closer to his, and running his fingers on her back. "I missed you." He glanced at Sarah with joy. "This was my flat when I was an undergraduate at the University of Hong Kong."

Sarah peered through the window of the living room. "It is high up here. The cars look like ants."

"My empty stomach is roiling and hungry." Albert rubbed his abdomen. "Shall we go somewhere to eat?"

"Sure," Hannah replied.

Albert held Hannah's left hand and spoke of a luxury hotel restaurant on Salisbury Road near the spectacular coast. They entered the restaurant and got a table beside a vast window overlooking the dazzling beach. Albert sat beside Hannah. He and Olivia ordered chicken corn soup and Chinese noodles. Hannah and Sarah asked for beef brisket with egg-fried rice.

Hannah saw a white, overweight man wearing a boater

hat, and consuming a glass of beer. "Excuse me. I need the restroom." She left her seat, and the man followed her. Hannah stood beside the main door of the restroom. The man came to her. "Hi, Hannah. What are you doing in Hong Kong?"

"Hi, Matthew. I am on a special mission. Why are you here?"

"I am keeping an eye on the English imposter."

"He is mine now. I am here because of him. Where do you stay?"

He handed a card to her. "Here is my phone number."

"Nice to see you. I must go. See you soon." Hannah entered the restroom and washed her hands.

After dinner, Albert, Hannah, and their daughters strolled near the sea before going back to the apartment. "This is your bedroom," Albert told Sarah. "Put on your pajamas. I will go to the kitchen to make green tea."

Hannah, Sarah, and Olivia changed their clothing, and Albert brought square slices of fruitcake and green tea in Chinese bowls. He sat beside Hannah on a scarlet sofa and massaged her left hand. "I am happy to be with you." Hannah stared at him and smiled. He gave her a gentle kiss on her lips. Sarah and Olivia were tired and sleepy.

"Mom, I want to sleep."

"OK, love. Give me a kiss and a nice kiss for Albert."

"Good night, dad. Good night, Hannah." Olivia kissed and yawned.

Sarah and Olivia woke up at eight and saw Albert meditating like a Buddhist monk, with his half-closed eyes on the floor, and wearing blue Chinese pajamas with an embroidered ivory dragon on the left side of the jacket and Chinese button knots. Sarah told him she loved his silk pajamas. Later, Hannah got out of Albert's room, wearing an amber towel, and kissed them before going to the bathroom.

After breakfast, they wandered through a traditional market on Shanghai Street and noted people pottering around in Chinese garb. When they were in front of a Chinese clothes store, Albert held Sarah's left hand. "Come in with me. These are Chinese pajamas. Select the one you like."

"She has loads of chic pajamas," Hannah said.

"Does she have a Chinese one?"

"No."

"Then let her get Chinese pajamas. I think you should also get one."

"OK. I will get one, but I will pay for it."

"I will pay for Sarah's."

Sarah chose wisteria pajamas, and Albert gave her a pink umbrella with a red Chinese dragon image printed on it. "This parasol is to protect you from the sun."

Albert was right. The weather was scorching that day. They ate vanilla ice cream and strolled along the beach sidewalk. In the evening, they walked north to a movie theater on Nathan Road and watched *The Pelican Brief*, a political thriller starring Julia Roberts and Denzel Washington. Hannah and Albert enjoyed the riveting movie, while Sarah and Olivia had found it hard to follow.

On the next day, they went to the Space Museum on Salisbury Road, where they spent two hours learning about the universe. After having lunch at an adjacent restaurant, they boarded a green ferry to Lantau Island, the largest island in Hong Kong. Sarah and Olivia saw Chinese girls holding cosmetic mirrors, facial brushes, mascaras, eyeliners, powders, cream palettes, and lipsticks. Sarah smiled and glanced at her mother, who used crimson lip rouge.

On Lantau Island, they rode a mini cable car to look over the verdant hills and other small islands. They also dropped by a theme park on the island. After coming back to Kowloon, they had a peaceful night in the apartment, except when Albert acted as a panther and asked Olivia to sit on his dorsum.

They spent most of the fourth day at Ocean Park in Hong Kong Island. Next day, Albert wore a bright shirt, a checked jacket, a gray tie, and dark blue pants. He told Hannah he had to deliver a lecture on ancient Chinese philosophy in a Hong Kong college.

"How do I look?"

Hannah touched the knot of his striped tie and let her smooth left forefinger rub his nose. "You are gorgeous." A soft smack on his pinkish lips was divine.

An hour later, Hannah, Sarah, and Olivia went out for a walk on Canton Road. After buying soft drinks, they sat on a bench in Kowloon Park and praised the variety of plants. "God damn you," Hannah yelled.

"What's wrong, mom?"

"That Chinese man on the bike has taken my bag."

"Are our passports and money in the bag?"

"No. Let us go back to the apartment."

They raced south on Nathan Road. Homatakawa came on a motorcycle and put Hannah's bag on the brick edge of the sidewalk. Hannah embraced Sarah and Olivia and gazed with terror at Homatakawa's silver face mask. "Please, don't kill us." Homatakawa waved and fled from their sight.

Hannah took her bag with a tight grip and sped back to the apartment. In Albert's bedroom, she opened the bag and found a pistol, a silencer, and a white card. "Welcome to Hong Kong, our valuable friend. Prepare yourself for a new mission. You will receive further instructions soon. We are a regiment. We do not acquit. We do not neglect. We do not rest. We are the Anonymous." Hannah looked at the back of the card and saw the Anonymous iconic image of a cyborg warrior and a silver capital letter A. She burned it in the bathroom and panicked.

In the evening of that day, Olivia told her father about the incident and the masked motorcyclist who brought back Hannah's bag. After dinner, Hannah and Albert became inseparable and sensual. They kissed, caressed, jested, and flirted as if they were on a honeymoon trip. Hannah leaned back on a sofa, put her half-naked legs on Albert's thighs, and lured him to massage her velvety feet.

"The Chinese mugger had frightened me."

"I am with you. We live in a safe area, and crimes are rare in Kowloon. Did you see the motorcyclist's face?"

"No. He wore a renaissance hood and a metallic mask."

"A metallic mask?"

"Yes, an eerie metallic mask. He looked athletic and rangy."

"I guess he is a martial arts friend who wanted to keep you safe. Do not worry. I will ask Chinese friends to safeguard you and Sarah."

"One of these days." She held his hands. "You haven't told me about your private and emotional life after the death of Olivia's mom. We are alone now. Do you like to tell me about your intimate affairs with other women? I love to hear your romantic stories."

Albert moved his right hand on her bare thighs. "Are you a spy for the underworld? I thought women don't like men to mention their ex-lovers." He tickled her nose. "Do you want to dissect my amateurish love secrets?"

"I do. Say anything you want. I am not prudish."

"A year after the death of Olivia's mom, I befriended a Chinese woman in Singapore. Her name is Li Chen. Our brief friendship was artless and fluky because of our conflicting views on life and morality. I stood as a fervent advocate of liberal humanism, while she, hailing from a conservative, deprived town in mainland China, embodied an introverted and squeamish demeanor. Despite the contrasts in our backgrounds, we both yearned for a carefree companionship to chat and revel in the simple glee of life. Then came the moment that shattered the fragile friendship we had crafted. One day, she said she would not abandon her familial ties and commit to a life away from Singapore. So, with heavy hearts, we agreed to part ways, and our carefree journey closed with an unavoidable farewell.

My second love relationship was with a permissive, tall brunette woman from Oakland in Northern California. Her name is Rachel Miller."

"Awesome. Is she a U.S. citizen? What was the story with her?"

"Rachel is a U.S. citizen. She has a shiny, bonny face, hazel eyes, and long, sheeny hair."

"I feel jealous now."

"She loves music, dancing, parties, hiking, reading, and writing."

"When did you meet her?"

"I met her seven years ago at a book fair in London.

She introduced herself as an independent publisher of
literature and agreed to publish one of my literary articles
in a book. We loved and cared for each other for fifteen
weeks. We thought we would spend our life making love,
traveling, reading, photographing natural wonders, and
authoring didactic books for adults and children. But I
became despondent and suspicious after I discovered she
was married with two little children in the U.S. Having an
occasional affair with a married friend is not an ethical
problem for me, but I wished Rachel was honest. At the
same time, I was on the verge of despair because of my
overt conversion from traditional aristocracy and Anglican
conservatism to pacifism and humanism."

"What do you mean by conversion?"

"My conversion was an intellectual rejection of our
cocksure Anglicanism and vain traditions. I despised the
hypocrisy of our hollow religiosity. Think of the insolent
idea that the British monarch holds the title 'Defender of
the Faith and Supreme Governor of the Church.' Our
patrician sanctimony has been aberrant and fallacious. For
ages, the British government's pride of superiority, ferity,
and war has been nefarious and inimical to civil rights and
world peace. Politicians in Westminster still think Britain
is the British Empire that rules the seas. I condemned the
misogynist, homophobic, psychological, and sexual abuse
of women. My dissent included a frank criticism of the
hubristic intellectuals who blustered about their monotone
ideas and censured the dissenting voices. Their modish
suits and false politeness cannot cover up their support for
hegemony and power. For the sake of fame and glory,
many of them supported Britain's miscreant wars and the
Conservative Prime Minister Margaret Thatcher and her

xenophobic, sexist, and sycophantic Tories. So, I stood by the gay people when the psychotic bigots conflated homosexuality with AIDS and moral turpitude. Creativity, freedom, and peace have become my passion."

"Do you consider yourself an Anglican?"

"No. My religion is the religion of love. It has no temples and creeds. Religions may talk about love, but true love has no religion. I was not afraid to advocate free love and sexual freedom. So, I proclaimed my opposition to religions, wars, and archaic convictions. This bold and public declaration, which resembled my grandfather's *Why I am not a Christian*, had annoyed official and ordinary people. Yes, the best way to understand the world is to rebel against its deplorable conditions and have the courage to change. Only the fools who do not change their opinion."

At this moment, Hannah wanted to know if he had any connection with the Anonymous. "Why are you so popular in Latin America?"

"Because I pillory the U.S. foreign policy. While the Leftists and the socialist radicals perceived me as one of their iconic heroes, the harsh reality unveiled a different narrative. I existed in solitude as an outcast for a prolonged stretch of five years. The weight of isolation bore down on me, creating an emotional abyss that transcended the mythic cult of the hero they had constructed around me. Behind closed doors, the perception of heroism crumbled, revealing the raw and unfiltered reality of a soul grappling with introspection and the heavy burden of societal exile. My English family and friends had abandoned me. So, I resolved to live and work in Asia."

Hannah pressed Albert's hand against her breasts and kissed it. "Oh, love, that was too difficult to endure."

"It was like running into a blustery hurricane. Yes, it was debilitating for me to undergo such an abrupt personal transformation. But true satisfaction is doing what people think you should not do. I determined to do what I always wanted to do no matter what people think."

"What about the Californian woman?"

"I loved Rachel. She was amiable, pretty, intelligent, and visionary. Yet, a pervasive sense of disillusionment and weariness had engulfed both of us. I felt dispirited when she refused to share her life with me and revealed her engagement in sexual activities with her oppressive husband. When I wanted to help her, she said she would not divorce her husband because of her fear for the safety of her little kids. Not to mention her anger whenever I dared to inveigh against her country's foreign policy. Our equanimity shattered into a myriad of fractural emotions, and we found ourselves locked in a relentless cycle of torment-a surrealistic blend of love and pique."

"Cycle of torment?"

"I imply that there was a sense of ambivalence and skepticism about each other's intentions. I have a British-American daughter, and she was with her two kids and husband in one house."

"Two kids?"

"Yes. A boy and a girl. They and their father live with her in one house."

"Do you have any contact with her?"

"No. Rachel does not know I am here. What matters is that a luscious American woman has seduced me and healed my shattered heart. I am so lucky to be with her now. She is my adorable sweetheart."

Albert wept with grateful emotions and kissed Hannah's hand. She cradled his head and placed it on her comforting chest, sensing his heartwarming and sensitive personality. His innocent tears had increased her love for his heart, though she wondered why he did not reveal his immense love for Ann Stone and Ayita.

Upon opening her bedroom door, Sarah gazed into Albert's tear-filled eyes, and a sense of mild melancholy had overcome her. She placed her book on a table near the sofa and stood next to her mother. "Mom, why is Albert crying?"

"Nothing serious. Albert misses his English family."

"But we are his family now, aren't we?"

"Yes, darling, we are one family."

Olivia came out of her bedroom, glancing at them. Albert grinned and stretched his arms forward. "Olivia and Sarah, come here and sit on my knees." After sitting on his thighs and leaning their backs on his chest, he hugged them and kissed their heads. "I love you, beautiful girls." Two drops of warm tears rolled down Hannah's face when she embraced them all.

The next day, Hannah wore gym leggings and running shoes. "Albert, I am going out for a run."

She jogged on the beach sidewalk and entered a phone booth. "Hello, Matthew. This is Hannah."

"Hi. When are you coming to see me?"

"Where do you live?"

"156 Waterloo Road, Kowloon Tong."

She wrote his address on a small piece of paper. "I will see you tomorrow at 2 p.m. Is this okay?"

"Yes. What about your girl?"

"She will stay with Albert."

"Okay. See you tomorrow."

On the following day, Albert went to his bedroom to catnap, and Hannah wore dark, casual clothes. "Sarah, darling, I am going out to get a few things. I won't be out for too long."

Hannah walked for ten minutes and got a taxi. Homatakawa followed her on a motorcycle. Later, Hannah shook Matthew's hand, and a toned man came out of the kitchen. "This is Anthony Taylor."

Matthew puffed a Corona cigar. "What are you doing with Albert Russell, who passes himself off as a serious philosopher? His anarchic and Marxist terrorists killed many of our people. He is a dangerous gangster."

"I disagree. We are wasting our time with him. He told me the other night about his lovers and wept like a bambino. I am afraid Nahatatama and his warriors are preparing for a war with us. They want to distract us by focusing on Albert, who does not know how to use a knife and a screwdriver."

"So, why are you here?"

"To retrieve classified documents."

"Did you recover any document?"

"No. There are no books or files in Albert's apartment. Does he have another place in the city?"

"We don't think so."

"Have you tried to contact him?"

"This is impossible. Albert is the Mafia godfather in Hong Kong. Secret Chinese bodyguards protect him all the time. Most of the storekeepers in his building are his hired guns. Last month, they killed one of our men and a South Korean friend. Did you suspect anything?"

"No. Albert teaches philosophy and religion."

"Does he call anybody?"

"He calls his English family."

"Any word about his connection to the Anonymous?"

"No. Albert had never talked about the Anonymous. Be careful. Homatakawa is in the town."

"Have you seen him?"

"Yes. He threatened to kill my daughter and me if I betray Albert."

"Who is this masked guy? His arms and legs are like steel. He is like Steve Austin in *The Six Million Dollar Man*. Once he overturned and pushed my truck off a cliff in Mexico. What do you think we should do to Albert? I wish to kill him."

"Albert is nobody. Leave him to me. We cannot kill him in Hong Kong. His Chinese allies would slay the Americans here and blow up our consulate."

"I know. Do you want to eat or drink?"

"No. Thanks. I must go back to my girl."

"How is she?"

"She is fine."

"Does she know about your work with us?"

"No. She is still a kid."

"Okay. Let us see you after two or three days."

Hannah left the house, and Matthew gazed at Anthony. "What do you think?"

"Do you trust her?"

"She has been with us for over ten years. She gave us information on drug cartels and Muslim terrorists."

"But she claimed Homatakawa has threatened her. In what manner? Did he communicate with her? He does not speak English, and his videos are subtitled."

"I don't know."

"We need to keep an eye on her. She might be a double agent."

"How?"

"She went to Latin America, where Nahatatama and his terrorists killed our colleagues. She could be the insider who transferred the classified documents to Albert."

"I am not sure. Hannah met Albert a few months ago, and Albert published classified documents in 1990. I think someone else gave him the documents. At that time, Hannah was in Latin America to spy on the guerrilla movements. She said Albert doesn't have the documents."

"Does she know who killed her husband?"

"No. She has never mentioned him."

Three days later, Hannah visited Matthew's house and sat on a chair.

Matthew rested his feet on a coffee table. "Do you love Albert?"

"What is this question?"

He gave her an envelope. "Open it."

Hannah opened the envelope and felt offended when she saw romantic photos of her with Albert. "What is this? Have you been spying on me?"

"Why do you kiss Albert like that?"

"Excuse me! I want him to trust me."

"And what?"

"How would I know his undercover work with the radical Leftists and the Anonymous before I create a trust relationship?"

"Is that true? Are you a double agent?"

"How dare you speak to me like that? The Agency knows everything about my work. I am not staying here."

Matthew pulled a handgun on her. "You are not going anywhere? You said Homatakawa had threatened you. How? Does he speak English?"

"No. He gave me a piece of paper."

"Do you work for the Anonymous?"

"What happened to you? Don't you trust me?"

"Who gave Albert the classified documents?"

"I met Albert for the first time last December, and he published the classified document six years ago. So, someone else gave him the documents. I searched his apartments here and in India. He doesn't have classified documents."

"Tell me the truth if you want to see your daughter again."

"What? Damn you. Leave my daughter alone. Do you threaten me? The Agency knows I am here."

With a derisive smile, Matthew stood with his back to a window. A seven-inch steel kunai moved through the window and into Matthew's neck. Matthew fell on his face and died at once. Hannah looked at the kunai and noticed the engraved signs of the Anonymous mask. She drew her gun and aimed it at Anthony Taylor, who was lying on a bed. "Who is the head of the clandestine unit?"

"What do you want? Ask the CIA."

"To hell with the CIA. Who is your boss? Who asked you to spy on Albert Russell?"

"Ryan Mitchell."

"Where is he?"

"He works for the Consulate."

"Where is the camera?"

He opened a drawer beside the bed. "Here is it."

"Hell is your place, moron." Gunshots shattered the

silence as she fired two bullets, extinguishing his life. She moved to collect the damning evidence-the camera and the envelope filled with photos of her. Panic surged within her as she made her way to the kitchen, fueled by the urgency to erase any trace of her involvement.

In the steel sink, the incriminating photos met their fiery demise. She watched as the flames consumed the images, leaving behind ashes. The sound of running water masked the ominous crackle as she washed away the remnants of her dark secret, desperate to cleanse any lingering evidence.

With fear pulsating through her veins, she left the house, her fingers trembling with the weight of her actions. As she stepped out of the steel gate and into the street, a terrifying sight awaited her-a masked person, enigmatic and foreboding, perched on a motorcycle. "Hannah, come. I am Homatakawa." Hannah heard a robot voice, and Homatakawa took her back to Albert's building without saying a word.

In the apartment, Albert noticed specks of blood on Hannah's top dress. "Are you okay?"

"Yes, I am fine. My nose hit an umbrella when I was taking photos."

"Be careful. Some Chinese guys use the umbrella as a weapon."

Two days later, Hannah kissed Albert's face. "I want to go out to buy tampons." She left the apartment and got a ferryboat to Hong Kong Island. A taxi took her from Wan Chai Pier to Des Voeux Road West. She put on a sun hat and prowled for ten minutes until she reached a building at number nine. She entered an elevator and pressed the fourteenth button. When the elevator door opened, she stepped out and knocked on a door. The door opened with a security chain attached to it.

"What can I do for you?" a handsome man in his mid-forties asked.

"Ryan, I am Professor Hannah Rogers from the Intelligence Agency. Here is my ID."

Ryan looked at the ID and gave it back to her. "See me at the Consulate."

"Please, it is about Matthew and Anthony. I know the guys who killed them."

Ryan unhooked the door chain. "Wow. Please, come in."

Hannah locked the door and stared him in the face. "Who killed Michael Rogers and Peter Stone?"

"Who are they? Ask the FBI. I am a diplomat."

"Why did you want to kill Albert Russell? Why are you spying on him?"

"I don't understand."

"I work for the CIA and know who you are?"

"You are talking to the wrong guy."

Hannah picked up her gun. "Sit down, jackass. Who killed Michael and Peter?"

"Cool down, lady. I do not know their real names. The guy who killed Michael is called the Black Wolf, and the guy who killed Peter Stone is called the Angry Jaguar. They directed the CIA's covert assassination operations."

"And you are called the dumbass. Go to hell." After shooting him in the face, she wore rubber gloves and placed an Anonymous card and a note atop his lifeless chest.

Two days later, Albert and Hannah walked at a slow pace in Kowloon and noted a front-page headline that said, "THE ANONYMOUS STRIKES BACK." Albert held the newspaper with both hands and read in a feeble voice, "The Anonymous group has declared responsibility for the murder of three CIA agents in Hong Kong ... The Anonymous left a note beside the dead body of the U.S. diplomat Ryan Mitchell. The note said, 'We say to the CIA operatives around the world: We know who you are and what you do. If you do not stop your dirty work, we will get you out of your holes, and we will kill you. We are a regiment. We do not acquit. We do not neglect. We do not rest. We are the Anonymous.' Are we seeing an anti-American revolution in Hong Kong?"

Hannah hugged Albert and acted as if she was horror-stricken. "I am terrified. Why do the Anonymous guys kill Americans? Who are they?"

"The Anonymous is a group of mercenary wights. Do not be afraid. Hong Kong is my backyard."

Chapter 4

After returning to the U.S., Hannah asked Sarah not to talk about her romantic liaison with Albert Russell. She justified her demand by saying they are notable academics, and there is no formal commitment and cohabitation between them. Sarah put photos of Albert and Olivia on the door and the walls of her bedroom and kept their gifts in a wall wardrobe and in a wooden box with a lock. When school classmates asked her about Albert, she said he was their gregarious escort in Hong Kong.

Albert and Olivia invited Hannah and Sarah to spend the Christmas vacation in England and Jordan. Hannah and Sarah flew to Heathrow Airport in London. Albert put his gloved hands on Hannah's face and kissed her and hugged Sarah and kissed her. Olivia got hugs and kisses too.

In his Victorian apartment on King's Road in West

London, Albert cooked herbed penne pasta with creamy mushroom chicken and grated Parmesan cheese. They spent a quiet night talking about the delightful things that make life congenial and worth living.

In the morning, Sarah was reading a *TV Times* magazine in the living room when she heard a rustling at the main door. She went to the entryway and realized a mail carrier had inserted letters and leaflets through the bronze mail slot. After picking up the post from the floor, she met Albert who was sitting beside Hannah and drinking tea in the kitchen. "Here are letters for you."

"Thank you."

Albert scrutinized the junk mail and the envelopes as forensic detectives do. "Here is a letter from Sweden."

He opened a white envelope with a propeller letter opener and read a printed letter. "Brilliant news. Uppsala University has offered me a two-year grant for my research work in Bangalore in South India. It will pay for my travel, food, and accommodation expenses. The research will start in August."

Hannah cheered and kissed his rosy face and rubescent lips. "Congratulations. This is great."

Albert called his Welsh brunette mother Lady Janet Russell. "Good morning, mum. How are you, darling?"

"Good morning, son. I am fine. How are you today? How is Olivia?"

"We are doing well. Mum, a Swedish university has offered me a two-year scholarship for my research work in South India. The research will start in August."

"This is brilliant, my son. I am chuffed for you. Come for dinner tonight."

"We will come. An American friend and her daughter

are with us."

"They can come too. No problem."

"Thanks, mum. We will see you in the evening."

In the evening, Albert, Hannah, and their daughters warmed themselves with winter coats and left the apartment to meet Albert's Anglican parents, Janet and John, who lived in Kingston upon Thames.

Janet and her gray-bearded husband, John Russell, opened the main brown door of their cottage-like house after they saw a black taxi carrying Albert and Olivia and their friends.

"Good evening, dad. Good evening, mum." Albert kissed them.

Olivia loped and hugged her joyful grandfather and grandmother. "Hello, granddad. Hello, grandma."

"This is Dr. Hannah Rogers. She is a professor at Yale University. This is her daughter Sarah."

John smiled. "Welcome to England. It is cold today."

After they came in, Albert and Olivia met Dora Russell and her sixteen-year-old daughter, Ruth. Dora welcomed them with tender kisses and shook the hands of Hannah and Sarah.

They assembled around a hardwood dining table and enjoyed eating grilled beefsteaks, roasted potatoes, boiled carrots and peas, and apple pies. Hannah briefed them about her academic career, and Sarah presented a keen description of her school. Albert told his parents and sister he and Hannah and their daughters would spend the Christmas vacation in Jordan.

When Albert, Hannah, and their daughters left John's home, Dora glanced at her parents. "I have been thinking of Hannah. Do you remember her? She is the American woman who came here thirteen years ago and asked about my brother. Albert hadn't mentioned her."

Janet took a sip from her cup of tea. "You know your bookish brother. He knows many scholars from all over the world."

On Friday morning, December 20, Albert, Hannah, Sarah, and Olivia flew to the capital of Jordan, Amman, where they stayed in a four-star hotel in an uptown area called Jabal Amman. Albert did not want the girls to remain alone in a separate room because of his practical concern for their personal safety. He asked them not to tell the hotel workers that Hannah is his girlfriend and fleshed out that Jordan is an Arab-Muslim country and most of the local citizens would not tolerate his free, unconditional relationship with Hannah because their interpretation of Islamic laws is rigid and literalistic.

In the morning, they had a tasty Arabic breakfast in the hotel restaurant. They ate hummus, fava beans, falafel, baba ghanoush, tabbouleh, labneh, and green olives, and drank mint tea. After that, they took a yellow taxi and visited the Roman amphitheater in the city center. They strolled in al-Balad (city center) and dropped into traditional stores. Albert bought Olivia and Sarah Arabian cocktail dresses, embroidered and handmade with cotton silk fabric, and got Hannah a silk shawl. She wanted to kiss his lips, but he moved his head to the left and hugged her. "Don't kiss me here. I will get extra kisses from you when we go back to the hotel." Their slow walking had ended at a restaurant near the old Bukhari Souk. They ate roast chicken with salad and cucumber pickles and quaffed fruit cocktail juice.

In the evening, Nathan Goodman received a call from

the mysterious woman who monitored Hannah's movements. "Hannah and Albert are in Jordan."

On Sunday, December 22, they hired a South Korean car and traveled down to the Dead Sea. Hannah was the driver, and Albert's job was to decipher a roadmap and guide her. Hannah parked the car three yards away from the Sea. Though it was December, they dipped their feet in the seawater. "You will not get drowned here. The seawater is salty and rich in minerals," Albert explained. "Olivia, Sarah, put on your swimming costumes."

There were no changing rooms at the stony shore. Sarah and Olivia got into the car, changed their clothes beside each other in the back seat, and smiled when they saw their naked bodies. After wearing their swimming outfits, Albert asked them to lie back in the water.

Sarah raised her legs. "The water is awesome. I am floating like a canoe."

Twenty minutes later, the girls left the seawater, and Hannah covered them with orange towels. They walked on the rugged beach. Albert held Hannah's hand and pointed toward the other side of the Dead Sea.

"Hannah, that's Palestine."

"Do you mean Israel?"

"Palestine or Philistine is the historical name in Syriac, Aramaic, Latin, and Greek languages before the birth of Jesus. There is no archeological evidence about the so-called Jewish Kingdom of Israel, or even about the mythical figures David and Solomon."

"So, that's the West Bank?"

"Yes."

"Is it possible for us to visit Palestine?"

"Yes, but the security situation is terrible. Under the

guise of faith, the Zionist state occupies Palestine by military force, and there have been atrocious suicide bombings by delirious Palestinians. So, where will we go, my darling? What we do not need is a bitter dose of pestilent politics. Let us have lunch."

They strolled to a small eatery and ate lamb kebabs with tomato salad, yogurt, and handmade bread. After lunch, they visited King Hussein's Bridge, which connects Palestine with Jordan, and saw Israeli soldiers carrying automatic shotguns on the other side of the Bridge. With discerning eyes, they inspected an ancient site called *al-Maghtas* where John the Baptist lived and baptized his followers, including Jesus.

When Albert touched a natural spring at the baptism site, a tiny voice in his head whispered. "Be careful. Watch your back." A dark Land Rover stopped, and a gangling man stepped out of the car. "Well, well, Albert Russell. What a surprise!" He pointed a gun at Albert's back.

Hannah screamed at the girls. "Go to the car and put your head down."

When the girls entered the car and lowered their heads, Albert spoke to Hannah, "Go to the car and leave me alone." The gunman turned his face back when two Anonymous female fighters smashed his car windows with sledgehammers. Albert kicked the gun out of the man's hand and punched the side of his left knee. The man groaned and genuflected. Hannah kicked his head and sat on his back. "Albert, go to the car now."

"I can't leave you with this thug."

"I said go to the car. Please. I know this guy."

Albert sat in the car with uneasy feelings.

Hannah slapped the man's head. "What the hell are

you doing here? Get up. Who are you? I am supposed to kill Albert."

"I am Logan Moore."

"Let me help you." The man got up and limped. "Who told you about Albert and me?"

"Nathan Goodman."

"Do you work for him?"

"Yes. He asked me to kill Albert if he refused to talk about the leaked documents and the Anonymous." After saying these words, a broadhead arrow pierced through his neck and killed him. Hannah's scream pierced the air as she writhed in distress. In a state of shock, she turned her gaze behind her, only to be met with the terrifying sight of Homatakawa, who gestured while brandishing a hunting crossbow, casting a shadow of dumb horror that left Hannah transfixed in a moment of inward fear.

Her white teeth chattered, creating a staccato rhythm, as she returned to the car with folded arms. Quavering and stammering, she fumbled for the right words. Albert hugged her. "What happened? I heard you screaming."

She trembled. "I ... I saw Homatakawa, whom I met in Hong Kong. He is creepy. He looks like a medieval Viking warrior."

"How? Did you see his face?"

"No. He wears a mask and fur and animal skins."

"What about the other man? You said you know him."

"He needed money."

"What happened to him?"

"He can't walk. You broke his leg."

"How did he know my name?"

"He saw you in the hotel. Let us go back to Amman."

The next day, they toured the ancient city of Jerash and

its vast Roman amphitheater. A brown Jordanian boy apprised them of the bygone history of the place, and they admired his exceptional brilliance. Albert spoke to him in classical Arabic and gave him five Jordanian dinars. After having falafel hummus sandwiches and orange juice at an adjacent restaurant, they dropped by the high town of Ajloun and its outstanding castle.

On Tuesday, December 24, they were in the south, where they discovered the ancient town of Madaba. At Mount Nebo, they entered a primitive church with no roof, windows, or electricity. Builders made its benches of enormous limestone. Albert pointed out that biblical scholars think people had buried Moses there.

Later, they visited another old church in Madaba and prized its artistic mosaic floor. After that, they drove south to the rocky city of Karak, where it was tedious for Hannah to drive on its narrow, jammed roads. They inspected the ruined castle, which the Crusaders built in the twelfth century, and ate grilled chicken and kebabs. Their trip ended up in Petra, and they stayed overnight in a hotel.

On Christmas Day, Albert walked to the reception counter, picked up a copy of *The Jordan Times*, and read about the death of an American citizen on the east bank of the Jordan River. The paper said local people found a drowned American man in the baptism pool and the Anonymous claimed responsibility for his death because he was a CIA spy. Irked by the crime, Albert thought Hannah had caused his death. Hannah came to him. "Are you ready to go?"

"Yeah ... Yes."

"Are you OK? You look pasty."

Albert had declined to discuss the death of the American citizen. "I think I didn't have enough sleep."

"We will sleep early today."

On lean horses, they ventured forth to survey the primeval, Nabatean, ruddy monuments. As they marveled at the colossal landscape, a question lingered in their minds-how could the aboriginal people carve such mighty mountains and rocks and construct prodigious buildings and theaters? After taking memorable photos, Albert told them that an *Indiana Jones* movie was shot there.

When Sarah and Olivia sat on a rock, Albert took Hannah aside and caressed her hand. "Darling, what's going on?"

"What do you mean?"

"The Anonymous murdered two Americans in Goa when you were there. They slew three Americans in Hong Kong when you were there. Two days ago, they executed an American when you were with him. Who killed these men?"

"You have just said the Anonymous had killed them."

"Why did the Anonymous warriors kill them when you were with me?"

"I am a university professor, not a killer." She paused and placed her palms on his face, and her eyes became tearful. "It is because of you. The Anonymous warriors do not execute CIA and FBI agents because of me, but because of you. I read what newspapers and magazines say about you. Many contemptible guys want to see you dead. I do not know why, but it seems you had done serious things. Do you hide something from me?"

"No. I wish to know Nahatatama, Homatakawa, and the Anonymous to know why they protect me."

"I think the U.S. government had done something horrible to them and their families. But why do the Anonymous warriors follow us? How do they know where we go?"

"I don't have the answer."

From Petra, they moved south to Wadi Rum. After taking photos, they gathered around a flaming brazier in a tent, sipped tea, and greeted tattooed Bedouin women in long embroidered costumes, and unshaven, wrinkled men wearing red-black headscarves.

They later turned up in the tourist town of Aqaba and had an Arabian Christmas supper. They enjoyed the delicious food and the serene beach. On Boxing Day, they toured the town center and could not swim in the Gulf of Aqaba because the seawater was chilly.

On Friday, December 27, they stopped at the neglected city of Ma'an before driving north to Amman.

Hannah proposed they should make a quick trip to Palestine to catch sight of the consecrated birthplace of Jesus Christ. Albert was averse to travel because of his intelligible consternation about their security. After some time, Hannah persuaded him to go to Palestine.

Early on Sunday morning, December 29, they traveled to Palestine by a blue tourist bus. A sense of shock had enveloped Sarah and Olivia after they crossed the Allenby Bridge. The landscape transformed as armed soldiers clad in green uniforms appeared everywhere. Bearded citizens wearing Jewish kippahs carried machine guns.

Hannah patted Albert's arm. "Look at these armed people. What is this state? Is this a free country for the victims of Nazism?"

"Many things have changed in the world except the

harm that people do to each other. Our cocky politicians do not care about democracy and human rights in the Middle East. Their demonic allies are venal Zionist warmongers and Arab despots. Other superstitious halfwits think this small territory is Jehovah's Promised Land of honey and milk for His chosen children. The idea that there is a Holy Land is so foolish that only the cocksure sticklers regard it as true. Of course, this is America's foremost ally for love and peace!"

Hannah stared at Israeli soldiers trailing around military checkpoints and holding machine guns. "How do the indigenous Palestinians manage their daily lives in this militarized country and with these Israelis?"

"Do they have another choice?"

"I feel pity for them. Blessed are the meek. Blessed are the peacemakers, as Jesus says."

In Jerusalem, they strolled to the Dome of the Rock and the Wailing Wall, inspected the Via Dolorosa, and saluted Palestinian shopkeepers selling rugs, rosaries, crosses, and other religious ornaments.

After having lunch at a restaurant, they agreed to visit Bethlehem. They got a Mercedes taxicab owned by an obese Palestinian. Hannah, Sarah, and Olivia sat in the back seat. Albert saw Orthodox Jewish boys holding pebbles and chipped stones and trotting toward the taxi.

"Put your head down. Olivia, Sarah, kneel on the car floor and put your head down," Albert yelled, placing his left hand on Hannah's head, and forcing her to lower her body. A flying stone smashed the rear window, and the shattered glass fell on their bent backs. Hannah screamed. "Oh, my God! Oh, my God!" The girls cried like babies.

Albert lowered the car window and shouted at the

delinquent youngsters. "*Shalom.* Please, behave for Yahweh's sake!" They looked at him and halted their juvenile offense. One of them apologized in English. "Sorry. We didn't know you were Jews."

"Thank you." Albert turned his face toward the back seat. "Olivia, Sarah, don't worry, my love. You are safe now. Hannah, are you all right?"

"Yes, I am fine. That's frightening and vile."

The Palestinian driver steered south while his nose bled after a stone had hit it. Later, they arrived in Bethlehem. Albert insisted on taking the driver to a local pharmacy and paying for his treatment. He gave him fifty dollars to fix the taxi's rear window.

In Bethlehem, they entered the Church of the Nativity and touched the Silver Star beneath the small altar, which symbolizes the birthplace of Jesus.

Their last historical city was Hebron, where they explored the Abraham Mosque. Albert told them the biblical story of Abraham and his patriarchal family. An hour later, a taxi drove them to an Arab restaurant in the commercial area of Bab al-Zawiya, where they consumed shawarma sandwiches and mint tea. After dinner, they came back to Jerusalem by another taxi and had a peaceful night in the Ritz Hotel.

In the morning, a tourist bus took them back to Amman, where they got a room in the Marriott hotel, in a locale called Shmeisani.

On Tuesday morning, December 31, Albert delivered a public lecture on Arab philosophy at the University of Amman. In the evening, he and Hannah and their daughters celebrated the New Year in the hotel and recalled the New Year's Eve in Goa.

They spent the next two days sauntering around Shmeisani and its adjacent neighborhood, Jabal al-Hussein, before they flew back to London. In London, they visited places of interest, such as the British Museum, the British Library, the Natural History Museum, Tower Bridge, Hyde Park, Trafalgar Square, and the Neasden Temple.

This time, Hannah's heart was in profound love for Albert. Their hands intertwined, a constant conviction that transcended the mere physical touch. She cast away the constraints of conventional morality, and her academic eminence held no relevance. It was as though she desired to proclaim her deep affection for him to the entire city, a sentiment that exceeded social conventions and academic hierarchies. She caressed and kissed him in taxis, in frosty parks, in restaurants, in bookshops, in museums, at royal palaces, on bridges, and at the Thames River. In the snug apartment, she embraced a hedonistic, licentious, and sensuous demeanor, a celebration of pleasure that persisted even in the constant company of Sarah and Olivia. She showered with Albert, sat on his thighs, and kissed him like a ravenous person who had found a slice of meat. She bared her seductive legs, enticing belly, and alluring breasts. It was hard to explain how she felt about Sarah and Olivia. She wished to be alone with Albert in his apartment and take her clothes off in the living room or in the kitchen. But Sarah and Olivia were big girls then, and their bodily hormones were raging and out of the whack. To Sarah, Albert was the first man to kiss and fondle her mother's curvaceous body in front of her. She suppressed her sexual fantasies and attraction to him because of her age, and because of her mother's abounding affection for him. To Olivia, Hannah was coquettish, and her body was provocative and stunning. She felt Hannah's voluptuous pleasure and elfish beauty had stimulated her physical attraction to women.

Albert's attitude toward Sarah had become ideal. He looked upon her as his charming, privileged princess. Darling, honey, sweetheart, and sweetie had become her favorite names. She felt happy when he tended to her, even when her flirtatious mother sat on his thighs and kissed his face. Holding his hand when they ambled into the city was extra excitement. He entertained her, cracked jokes with her, and always gazed at her sparkly eyes to see if she wanted to get something for herself. Before leaving Britain, he bought her swanky clothes and voguish accessories.

Chapter 5

Hannah controlled her fury and indignation at the CIA's attempts to kill Albert and met her CIA director Nathan Goodman in a Port Chester restaurant. When Nathan mentioned Logan Moore's death in Jordan, she informed him that insiders had revealed to the Anonymous the names of the agents who conspired to murder Albert Russell. With a deliberate manipulation of facts, Hannah managed not to show the identity of the insiders or how she knew about them. In the summer, she and Sarah flew to Hong Kong to meet up with Albert and Olivia. This time, they stayed in a three-bedroom apartment in an upscale area called Mid-Levels. The weather during that season was sweltering and humid.

Upon meeting her lover, Hannah's sexuality knew no bounds. The yearning for him was so intense that she found herself unable to contain her desires, succumbing to eroticism in the confines of the living room. After taking off her half-cup balconette bra, she wore a sleeveless, short swing dress and told Albert about her endless love for him.

The next morning, they took a boat across to Macau Ferry Terminal. After their arrival, a shuttle bus drove them to Hotel Royal on Estrada da Vitoria. They relaxed in the hotel for an hour and walked to Macau's ancient center, where they sensed the Portuguese influence on the design and color of buildings and streets. They visited Kun Iam Temple and the statue of Bodhisattva Avalokitesvara, located south of Avenue Dr. Sun Yat-Sen. After that, they had food in a traditional restaurant before going back to the hotel. Hannah and Albert slept in a full-size bed, and Sarah and Olivia were in twin beds. They wrapped themselves with wool blankets because the temperature of the room was arctic. Thanks to the air conditioners!

Next day, they wandered around for three hours and had a Portuguese lunch in a restaurant. Sarah suspected the food she had was Portuguese. Albert clarified that the Portuguese cuisine in that part of the world includes Macau and Chinese flavors. In the evening, a ferry took them back to Hong Kong.

On a Friday afternoon, they boarded two trains to the Chinese city of Guangzhou. A taxi drove them from the train station to a four-star hotel in Tianhe district. The petite receptionist did not know more than four or five words in English. Two Chinese Malaysians helped them with the translation. They got a room on the fourth floor. An hour later, they moved downstairs to have dinner. Albert went to the straight-haired receptionist and pointed his fingers toward his gaping mouth. The receptionist realized they needed food to eat. She extended her right arm to the left direction. After sitting at a table, Albert, Hannah, Sarah, and Olivia looked at the menus and understood nothing because they were in Mandarin. The best language for them was to use their hands and fingers. A waiter came to them, and they let her understand they wanted to eat fish. Twenty minutes later, the waiter brought four plates of white rice and fish on the top, four tureens of green vegetables in a light soy sauce, and a big bowl of white dumplings made of cornstarch. There were porcelain chopsticks on the table. Hannah and Albert told the waiter they wanted forks or tablespoons. The waiter fetched four teaspoons. The white rice was tasteless, and the bland fish were poached in unflavored water. However, they smiled and swallowed the food. At least they liked the Chinese green tea after the meal.

The following day dawned with a sense of adventure as they set out to ramble around the CITIC Plaza. The nearby streets, under the blistering sun, were teeming with an excess of humanity, and the air was thick with noisome smog from the pervasive carbon pollution. Massive buses rumbled by, and people navigated the bustling scene on tricycles with trolleys.

Despite the humming, chaotic surroundings, an unexpected contrast was noticeable. The Chinese people they met there had exuded an unusual calmness and friendliness. Amid the crowded chaos, there were no screams or quarrels. It was as though a peculiar serenity prevailed, a stark departure from the typical tumult one might expect in such overpopulated streets.

When they drifted around a shopping mall, Albert noticed a special eating place. "That restaurant is for

Muslims because its front sign says it serves *halal* food and makes lamb kebabs and skewered chicken. Let us go there."

As they entered the fanned restaurant, a lean Chinese man with a long gray beard greeted them with a cordial smile.

Albert nodded, and his left hand enclosed his right clenched fist. "*Assalamalikum* [Peace be with you]."

"*Waalikumassalam* [And peace be with you]. How are you?"

"*Alhamdulillah* [Praise to God]. We are well. Where are you from?"

"I am from Xinjiang."

"How are you here?"

"My father came to this city when I was a kid. I worked for ten years in Saudi Arabia and learned Arabic and English."

"That's great. Are there many Muslims in the city?"

"There are about ten thousand Muslims here. Most Chinese Muslims live in the northwest."

"Do you have a menu?"

"We make barbecued chicken and kebabs."

"We want a small chicken, four kebabs, and fresh orange juice."

"Please, sit here."

They spent forty-five minutes eating the flavored food and drinking the juice. The Chinese man thanked them and gave Albert a warm squeeze.

They left the restaurant and got fruits from a farmers' market and proceeded back to the hotel to unwind. To their luck, there were two Hong Kong television channels in English. They slept early that night.

On Sunday morning, they planned to return to Hong Kong. After breakfast, they came across an attractive Chinese woman, wearing a tight white shirt and dark blue pants, and standing beside the hotel receptionist. Olivia gazed at her seductive bosom, eyes, and lips, and felt drawn to her. She placed her mouth on Sarah's ear. "Wow! She is a nymph. I wish to suck her lips and lick her body."

"What? Behave. Are you mad?"

"Hi. Good morning to everyone. My name is Shuang Chen."

"Good morning, Shuang," Hannah and Albert said.

"What do you want to do today?"

"We want to go back to Hong Kong. Albert has work to do," Hannah responded.

"Oh no! That will make me feel down. I came over here because the receptionist told me that English-speaking people are here. I had hoped to spend the day with you."

"Alas, we have to go back to Hong Kong. We hope to meet you again," Albert said.

"Are you going to the train station?"

"Yes, we are."

"Please, wait here. I will ask a cab driver to get you to the train station."

Ten minutes later, Shuang and a chubby taxi driver came in. "This taxi driver will take you to the train station. He will guide you to the right counter. Please, do not pay him over thirty-five renminbi yuan. This is the deal."

Hannah patted her shoulder. "Thank you very much. It is so wonderful to meet you."

Olivia bit her tiny lips and thought of Shuang until her arrival at the crowded train station. The merry taxi driver took Albert, Hannah, and the girls to the right platform, and they thanked him for his service. People stared at them when they were on the train and smiled when Sarah and Olivia took photos.

The next day, Hannah and the girls went to Victoria Peak, the highest point on Hong Kong Island. When the girls took photos, a hooded person gave Hannah a small, folded piece of paper and disappeared. Hannah unfolded the note. "Ask Nathan Goodman to come to Hong Kong and kill him. We are here. Love. The Anonymous."

In response, Hannah entered a phone box and called Nathan Goodman. "Hi, Nathan. Come to Hong Kong. I got the leaked documents."

"Great. I will come soon. I will call you tomorrow at 6 pm. What is the phone number?"

"It is 25410360."

Next day, Hannah waited at the phone box. Nathan called. "Meet me on Thursday at 7 pm in front of Man Mo Temple."

On Thursday evening, Hannah stopped at the locked gate of Man Mo Temple, bearing a brown satchel. A bald man came to her. "Hi, Hannah. I work for Nathan. Can we cross the road?"

"Ok."

They crossed Hollywood Road and stood under a tree. "Where is Nathan? Who are you?"

"I am Colin Wilson. Nathan apologizes for not coming to see you. He is not well today."

"Where is he?"

"In a house in the Central area."

"I need to see him."

"Can I get the file?"

"No."

"Why not?"

"I don't know you."

"Nathan asked me to see you. So, please, give me the file. We don't need trouble."

"We? Who are we? I will give the file to Nathan. Take me to his place."

Colin gripped her brown bag. "Give me the bag. What happened to you?"

"Leave me alone."

"You asked for it, bitch." The tension increased as he slapped her face, sending her crashing to the ground. In a sinister twist, he reached for a concealed gun, reflecting the malevolence of his intent.

As the ominous scenario unfolded, a sudden turn of fate intervened. Two throwing spikes found their mark, piercing his neck with fatal precision. A chilling silence reigned, broken by the thud of his collapse. His face hit the tree trunk, and his body crumpled to the ground.

With her right hand on her forehead, Hannah looked up at the road and saw Homatakawa pointing at the seat of the motorcycle. She remembered the motorcyclist who handed over her bag and executed two CIA agents in the previous year. With trembling limbs, she scampered and sat behind Homatakawa, who was wearing a black jacket, gauntlets, and leather boots. Homatakawa opened a tail box and gave her a helmet. Hannah covered her skull and rested her head on Homatakawa's back. "Thank you. Thank you so much."

Two men in a Toyota car followed Homatakawa, who

moved south to Caine Road, entered Old Bailey Street, and drove through Chancery Lane and down the cement stairs that lead to Arbuthnot Road. The driver of the chasing car swore. "Shit! There are stairs here."

After speeding on Arbuthnot Road and Caine Road, Homatakawa stopped the motorbike at the blue gate (No. 16) of Victoria Prison and sat on a concrete step on the right side of Chancery Lane.

Because of the narrowness of Chancery Lane, there was no chance for the driver of the chasing car but to reverse. When the car reached the entrance of the Lane, Homatakawa threw two daggers that killed the driver along with his companion. Homatakawa searched the motorist's pockets and found identity cards. Hannah got these cards after she noticed a black leather mask attached to Homatakawa's silicone face.

"Who are you? How are you so strong?"

Homatakawa made a silent sign. A few minutes later, the motorcycle halted on Bonham Road. Homatakawa placed a reassuring pat on Hannah's hand and gave her a card that said, "Be strong and don't be afraid. We will punish your enemies. The blind will see, and the deaf will hear. Keep up the excellent work. We love you. We are the Anonymous."

"Be careful, my dear. I will watch you. Goodbye," Homatakawa spoke like a robot.

"I wish to know you. Thank you so much. You are a wonderful person."

Homatakawa held and rubbed Hannah's hand. "I love you." Homatakawa gave her a flying kiss and disappeared.

In the apartment, Albert looked at her cheek. "Why are you late? What happened to your face?"

"A jerk asked me to go out with him to a nightclub. When I refused, he became angry and slapped my face."

"Oh dear! Please, do not go out without me. Look after yourself."

Hannah and Sarah spent three weeks in Hong Kong. Albert worked in the mornings, and they roamed around the city in the evenings. They watched movies, played games, quipped, read, and conversed. They were a happy family and had no arguments or irksome disagreements.

On Tuesday, July 1, they traveled from Hong Kong to "the land of the free," Thailand. They stayed in Sheraton Grande Sukhumvit, a newly built hotel in Bangkok. The weather was sizzling and muggy, and the streets were teeming and raucous.

On Thursday morning, a tourist bus took them to the ravishing city of Pattaya on the east coast of the Gulf of Thailand. From Pattaya, they sailed to a dazzling island called Ko Lan (Koh Larn), where they had succulent grilled fish. Tattooed men ate raw fish. Sarah and Olivia found that nauseating.

After lunch, Hannah, Sarah, and Olivia took off their T-shirts, loose shorts, and sandals, and sat on portable chairs looking at the enthralling horizon and seawater. In silence, Olivia surveyed women wearing string bikinis and experienced abnormal physical sensations.

Hannah took off her black, oval sunglasses and turned her tanned face toward Albert. "Albert, look around you. Haven't you noticed you are the only guy here who is wearing formal shoes, cotton socks, pants, and a long-sleeve shirt?"

"What is the problem with that?"

She chortled in response. "It is a sunny and torrid day.

Don't you feel feverish and roasted in these freaking clothes?"

"You know I dislike the sunlight and the heat. I am fearful of skin cancer."

"What about this?" She left her chair and sat on his thighs, putting her hands on his chest, and kissing him.

"You will break the chair."

She hid her fingers in her permed hair and cackled. "I am wearing a bikini and on the top of you, and you are worried about a two-dollar chair? Man! Are you an iron man? Men!"

"Darling, I love your hugs and kisses, but the chair isn't ours."

"Okay! Get up." She heaved him and walked with him for a spell. When Albert rested his back on the soft beach sand, Hannah unbuttoned his shirt and rocked her revealing body on him. Sarah, at fifteen, could not resist the erotic temptation. She twisted her face to the left and ogled her mother and Albert when they kissed and caressed. She had lecherous feelings and wondered when she would have a sweetheart to kiss and fondle on a tropical, sandy seaside.

The next day, they visited Safari World in the northeast of Bangkok. With other tourists, they watched dancing alligators and elephants and a Thai magician performing incredible magic. The short magician asked an American tourist to stand beside him. He put a bucket in front of the tourist and said, "Do not urinate in public places." After saying that, the audience saw water coming out of the tourist's shorts. Where did the water come from? The magician asked the tourist to raise an arm and used the other arm as a pump. The astonished crowd saw water coming out of the tourist's armpit.

In the evening, Albert went out to dine with Thai scholars. Hannah and the girls walked along Asok Montri Road to do shopping. Sarah and Olivia got ice cream from a shop and walked six yards behind Hannah. Without a hint of warning, Olivia wriggled, the ice cream slipping from her grasp as she let out a piercing wail. "Hannah, Hannah." Hannah, caught off guard, turned her face back only to be confronted by a ghastly sight-a Thai man holding a knife to Olivia's delicate neck, dragging her toward a waiting car.

"Calm down, Olivia." Hannah picked up her pochette. "Please, take my wallet and all my money." A second later, she noticed Homatakawa driving toward her on the sidewalk. "Olivia, down," she screeched. Olivia lowered her body, and Homatakawa inserted a sai dagger into the abductor's larynx. A female Anonymous warrior appeared and threw the Thai man on a car. Homatakawa held Olivia with one hand and put her on the motorcycle. "Oli, sit." Homatakawa looked at Hannah. "Hannah, go, go. Go away."

After taking Olivia to the hotel, Homatakawa gave her a trinket box and put a forefinger on the neck. "Your neck, your neck, your neck." Homatakawa patted Olivia's chest. "I love you."

Olivia dashed up to her room and sat on her father's bed. Ten minutes later, Hannah and Sarah came in and rested beside her to comfort her. Albert also came back. Olivia jumped on him. "Dad, dad, I am scared."

Albert kissed her. "What happened, sweetheart?"

"A wanker put a knife on my neck and tried to abduct me, but Homatakawa killed him and gave me this box."

"Oh, sweetheart!" He wept and hugged her. "I love you, sweetie. What is in the box?"

She opened the box and saw a gold heart necklace and a girly watch. "I think Homatakawa wants me to wear them all the time to protect me. He put his finger on my neck and said words three times."

Albert examined the necklace. "This side of the heart says Olivia, and the other side says Albert. How does Homatakawa know our names?"

"I don't know. He also knows Hannah's name. He rubbed my hand. I think he knows us."

"How is his accent?"

"He speaks like a robot."

"What do you mean?"

"His voice is robotic and throaty. When I looked into his eyes and hugged him, I sensed he is like a cyborg."

"Strange."

"He moves like a robot, and his arms are strong as steel. I guess he is a computerized machine."

"Come, let me bathe you." After bathing her, Albert dressed her in a clean outfit and asked her to sleep with him in his bed.

Hannah brushed her hair. "Who is Homatakawa? I saw him in Jordan and Hong Kong."

"How would I know? Maybe he is a Chinese friend."

"How does he know we are here?"

"I do not know. Only my family knows we are here."

In the morning, they traveled to Kuala Lumpur and toured pleasant places for four days. After that, they stayed in Singapore for two days before heading to Colombo in Sri Lanka, where they got two attached bedrooms in the Galle Face Hotel, a few steps from the breathtaking beach and the endless blue ocean.

One day, they scuttled to the sizzling beach. Albert, for the first time, removed his long-sleeved shirt and white undershirt and became topless. Sarah stared at his upper body and licked her brittle lips. "Wow! What is this, Albert?"

"What's up, darling?"

She wished to tickle his rocky belly and muscular shoulders and chest. Her fingers wanted to run down and up his naked back, and her carnal body experienced concupiscent pleasure and attraction. This was the first time she had desired to touch Albert's uncovered body.

"This is awesome. I am surprised. How did you get this powerful body? Did you go to a gym?"

"No. I practice kung fu."

"Kung fu?"

"Yes. I traveled to Hong Kong when I was sixteen years old to study philosophy and learn kung fu and tai chi. I loved the Shaolin monks and Bruce Lee and wanted to be proficient and powerful like them. Do you know now why I leave our accommodation early in the morning or before I go to bed? I go out to practice kung fu when few people are around."

With her lips drawn together, Sarah absorbed her spittle and gazed at her half-naked mother. "Mom, why didn't you tell me about Albert's athletic body?"

"His body is mine. Do you have any objection?"

Sarah became jealous and sensitive, suspecting her mother's quirky relationship with Albert. But what could a girl make out with a mature, intelligent man? How would she wheedle a gifted philosopher? "Please, can you show me kung fu movements?"

Albert kicked like a shot, jumped high, and punched the air like a gust. "Let us swim."

Sarah felt this would be a rare opportunity to satisfy her aphrodisiac reverie. "Wait, Albert. Wait. I want to take photos." She brought a Canon camera and got flattering photographs of his beautiful body.

Albert did not demur or reprove her action, though he sensed her concealed intention. It was natural for her to think her mother was lucky to be with a sagacious man with such a seductive body. She lusted after Albert and could not resist peeking at his appealing physique when they swam. Yet, she was wary not to raise suspicion about her lustful desires. "Do you like to teach me kung fu when you are free?"

Albert splashed water on her face. "This will cost you thirty bucks per hour."

On that sweltering day, bathed in the heat of the sun, they experienced a delight beyond words. They swam around a protruding rock and lobbed green coconuts over their wet heads. Albert asked Sarah and Olivia to stand on his broad shoulders and leap into the lukewarm water. He then dived, pressing his head between Hannah's thighs, and held her on his firm shoulders for a while before plunging together into the water.

Albert taught Sarah kung fu every morning and evening and informed her about the main kung fu stances. "This is a horse stance. This is a cat stance, and this is a rooster stance." Sarah marveled at the brisk movements and the kung fu styles that were inspired by animal moves. Albert was careful not to put much pressure on her supple body, though she developed an infatuation for him when he touched her feet, knees, waist, arms, hands, shoulders, and neck. One day, she lost her balance and plummeted on his body like a falling tree. With a flirty smile, she was so gratified that she ignored her mother's presence and emotional sentiments when she shared guiltless merriment and kittenishness with him. As a caring mother for sixteen years, Hannah discerned she had no alternative but to smile and encourage her daughter to do her best.

A week later, Albert was at a Jesuit research institute for an interview with a local newspaper. Hannah, Sarah, and Olivia had a long walk around the city center. When Olivia entered a restaurant's restroom, Hannah said to Sarah, "I want to suggest something. Albert is a great guy, and both of us love him. I wish he would live with us in America. It is not good we see him every six months for a few weeks. What do you think?"

She felt exhilarated. "I would love that, mom. I love him. He would teach me kung fu and help do my homework if he lives with us. We had not had a man in our house since I was born. I also love Olivia."

"Excellent. Would you like to tell Albert that?"

"Yes, mom."

Albert came back to the hotel where he, Hannah, and the girls had chicken and cashew curry. After stuffing his belly, he moved to his white bedroom to change his clothes. Hannah, Sarah, and Olivia followed him and rested on his bed.

"What's up, ladies? Can I have some privacy? Or do you want to see my underwear? I have nothing to hide."

"Sarah wants to tell you something."

He kissed Sarah's head. "Yes, darling, what do you want to say?"

Sarah sat beside him, and he placed his arm around her

shoulders. "We want you and Olivia to live with us in our home in Darien."

Olivia clapped in joy as her pleased father stood and lifted Sarah with his arms around her chest. "This means you need to arrange two extra beds for us."

"There are six furnished bedrooms in our house; so, you won't sleep in a mummy sleeping bag."

Albert turned his beaming face toward Hannah and kissed her. "So, what is the story, sweetheart?"

"There is no story. We want you and Olivia to live with us."

"Thank you, love. Both of you are very kind."

Hannah's smile, a radiant reflection of happiness and elation, had painted her face with a glow that bespoke of fleeting bliss. Yet, a subtle shift occurred, as Albert uttered the words, "Just give me two years." A hushed silence enveloped the scene, and the playfulness that danced in Hannah's eyes had faltered for an instant, and her jubilant expression crumbled into a demoralized expression. The nuances of her downturned lips and the faint creases that etched her forehead had betrayed the vulnerability beneath the facade of merriment.

She put a hand on her face and could not believe what she had heard. She became outraged and baffled. "Two Years? Why do you need two years?"

"Darling, I ought to go to India."

She grabbed and compressed a white pillow. "No. You don't have to go to India."

He glanced at her flaring eyes. "Please, calm down, love. What happened to your adept memory? You know I must work in India for two years. Don't you recall the official letter I received from a Swedish university when we were in England?"

Bowing her head in an acknowledgement of the burden she carried, she contracted her brow, the furrowed lines revealing the internal struggle playing out within. Resting her hands on her tempting thighs, a subtle tension emanated from her figure. The surrounding air seemed to thicken as the tempest of emotion within intensified, and an aura enveloped her being.

In the depth of her silence, there lay an untold story-a harrowing ordeal etched into the recesses of her awareness. The knowledge of a clandestine world, marked by the cold-blooded murder of CIA operatives in Hong Kong, remained shrouded in the secrecy she bore. "But I say you can change your mind and come with us to America."

"Uppsala University has already sent me money, and my Indian colleagues are waiting for me."

"You can say you changed your mind."

He took a deep breath into his gut. "Change my mind? I am not a little boy. And say what? Do you want me to say to my relatives and friends I have changed my mind because I need to live with an American woman?"

"What is this nonsense?" She hurled a white cotton cushion at him. "And what do you mean by an American woman? I am your girlfriend, for God's sake."

"I have never said you are my girlfriend."

Albert's impertinent, unequivocal statement had cut through the air like a lightning bolt, a shocking confession that landed with a force that shattered all expectations. In response, she stroked his shoulder and became furious. "Am I not your girlfriend? Who am I? A prostitute? One of your secret mistresses?"

"You are a dear friend and an admirable lover. But how

many people know about our liaison? What happened to you today? We were epicurean and overjoyed. Did you forget my two-year contract? Why didn't you ask me to decline the Swedish offer when we were in England?"

"What is this ridiculous and pointless jargon? I was unsure of our relationship, but now we are a family."

"I am glad we are a lovely family. Even so, I promised my Swedish and Indian friends to work in India. Cannot you be patient and benignant for a couple of years?"

Hannah was aware of Albert's defiant mind and recalcitrant spirit. "I beg you to come with us. Come with us if you love me. I need to feel I have a true partner. I want to feel I have a family. Asia is not our continent. India is not our country. Both of us are academic scholars. We cannot continue to be secret lovers, and we cannot continue to travel. India is far away from America. I will give Uppsala University money. It seems you do not appreciate why I want both of you to live with us."

"Darling, I do not doubt my love for you or your love for me. I understand why you need us to live with you. It is hard for you to be without a spouse in America. I know that. I know Sarah loves us. You can live with us in India for two years."

"India? Where? In a dirty and putrid hotel? With cows and monkeys and with those obnoxious morons who piddle and spit on the scuzzy streets? We have a big and elegant home in Darien. Sarah cannot leave her school and friends. Look at yourself, man. You live like a roving vacationer. Despite your international fame, you do not own a house or even a car. You spent twenty years of your life traveling around the world. For what purpose was that? For freedom and academic prestige?"

"My way of life is a vocation, not a career. My life is not a job. Nature created me not to be like you."

"Please, this is not only about us, but Olivia needs to live an ordinary life in a comfortable home. I cried the whole night after that Thai guy wanted to kill her. I will send her to the best private school. Don't you recognize I have emotions and sexual desires? What about our sex life? Don't you have feelings and desires? Do you want us to have sex every five or six months? Cannot you sense the aching pain in my heart? You are obsessed with books, peregrinations, and martial arts. Do you want us to live in hotels and keep flying?"

"You sound like my waspish grandmother. If you disfavor the life in India, move to England and be with my family until I finish my work in India. You know I am a staunch man of principles. I repeat, I promised my Swedish and Indian friends to work in India for two years. For Heaven's sake! I will be with you for the rest of my life after I complete my work in India."

"How can you convince me? You might change your mind and say you want to work in Antarctica."

"Yes, I want to play chess and dominoes with the emperor penguins in Antarctica. Please, listen. I need time to organize my stuff. We need to think about Olivia's school. Olivia will start her school day after ten days. We should say goodbye to our English family before moving to America. I require four or five months to collect and send my books and files to your house. Last, I need to apply for a job in your country."

"Books and files? I haven't seen your books and files. We are in this hotel, and you talk about your imaginary books. You do not need to work in America. I am rich, and you know that. There is enough money for us.”

“How much money you make is not my concern. I care for the people who are compassionate, positive, and respectful. The monotonous work-and-spend-till-the-grave lifestyle causes anxiety and unhappiness. I can earn scads of money if I choose to be a rapacious media expert or a political advisor. Our temporal life is greater than money and sex. Where are your imaginative and visionary dreams in life? I do not dwell in a hermitage. I let you see wonderful places.”

“Here we go again with your repetitious parlance. Why are men insensitive and phlegmatic? You concern yourselves with your damned work and pastime.”

“I am not men. I am a person, and my name is Albert Russell. Don’t I care about you and Sarah? Am I heartless and iniquitous? I phoned you every night when you were in America. I paid for your air tickets and for your deluxe accommodations.”

“Is it about spending and payments? You have always refused to take money from me.”

In a moment of candid sincerity, he addressed her with a measured tone. “I recognize your emotional and psychological aspirations, but you told me you would never get married again and have kids.” These words had revealed the unspoken tensions that had woven their way into their relationship. The revelation of her aversion to marriage and the prospect of having children had echoed as a fundamental contradiction to his understanding of their amorous connection. Yet, seeking to reconcile the incongruities, he posited a hypothesis. “I thought you did not want your friends to expose our free love relationship because you are a university professor.” The mention of a "free love relationship" hinted at a desire for privacy, driven by the constraints of societal norms that encroach upon the personal lives of individuals, especially those in academia. "I thought you and Sarah would be glad to travel and see new fascinating countries. Olivia and I will get a permanent house, but not now. I will never break my contractual promise to my Swedish and Indian friends. What happened to you?"

Hannah bit a lip and moved her hands between her thighs. "What do you mean by that? Why do not you want to sacrifice your job for our love?"

"I can ask the same question. Please, focus and open your ears. I am not a schizophrenic man. I can speak Shakespearean English. What should I say to persuade you? All I say is I must work for two academic years in India. Is this a big deal?"

"I demand a straight answer right now. Are you coming with us to America?"

"Is this a challenge? My answer is no. We are not going with you, and we will not live with an ungrateful, mercurial, capricious woman who intends to break my heart and our family for a trifling reason. I did not travel to America to philander with you, but you came to India on your own free will and beseeched me to be your lover. Did you forget that fact? Did you forget my love for you? Did you forget my hugs and kisses? Did you …?"

Albert rasped, a raw edge to his voice revealing the turmoil within. Closing his eyes for a poignant moment, he grappled with emotions that seemed too heavy to bear. So, with a decisive force, he stomped out of the hotel. "Dad." Olivia followed and hugged him. "She is a witch."

"Darling, do not hassle yourself with this trivial matter."

Hannah's unprovoked argument had also infuriated Sarah. She glared at her mother's flaming eyes for a second and wished to utter unpleasant words to her.

"Sarah ..."

"Leave me alone."

Sarah rushed out of the hotel and ran to Albert until she clutched his left hand. "I hate my mom when she is obstinate and stupid."

"Please, Sarah, don't scorn your beloved mother. She is my friend, and I love her. She is concerned for all of us."

"She keeps my dad's photos everywhere in our house. A photo of him is near her bed, and she kisses it every day. No photo of you is in our family room. My mom didn't tell our family and friends about her love for you."

"That's fine. I dislike bickering."

They kneeled on the beach sand and stared at the fascinating horizon. Sarah sat beside Albert, clinging to his left arm and sticking her head on his shoulder. She became resentful of her tetchy mother and afraid of losing Albert and Olivia. She supposed her mother should have said they would wait for Albert. Should they abandon their best friends because of a two-year job?

She rubbed her right face on Albert's left biceps and wept. "I love you, Albert. I would never imagine a life without you and Olivia. My friends have fathers. I wish to have a dad. I want to be with you." This was the first time she uttered the words "I love you, Albert."

Albert circled his left arm around her and kissed her head. "I love you too. Thank you, sweetie. Olivia and I will not desert you, regardless of what your mom might do. I know your mom well. She does not have the grit to leave me. Well, come with me if you want ice cream."

They got up and walked two hundred yards until they arrived at a convenience store. Albert got three ice cream cones. "Let us go back to the hotel to cheer up Hannah."

They came in with a calm spirit. Hannah sat by an open window, contemplating with a wistful face. Albert stretched his arms toward her. "Hannah, come here. Come and give me a big hug."

She embraced him and put her head on his shoulder. He placed his hands on her hair and kissed her head. "I want you to know that I love you. Do not lose hope. Miracles are in hidden places. A mild argument may refresh our memory of love. True love is like a cliff in a raging sea. Maybe it is right for us to be platonic friends. You are a good friend, and a wonderful friendship with you is a pleasure." He pointed a finger at Sarah. "This gorgeous young lady deserves our love and care. Please, let her stay in contact with us."

She gazed at his sparkling eyes. "You are beautiful. I have never loved a man like you. Sorry. I cannot be patient anymore. I have lived alone for many years. We cannot fly every five or six months and live in hotels. I cannot resign and quit my job, house, and friends. My house is in my heart. Sarah will call you because you are her favorite man, and she loves you. I need a break to think of our friendship. It is not possible for me to give up our home and my university. I must be there. There is excruciating anguish in my heart because of you and circumstances thrust upon me. Someday you will thank me for the many things I have done for you. I have been looking for an important thing, but I could not find it. I trust I would someday have enough courage to talk about it." She kissed his face. "I want to sleep with Sarah tonight."

Olivia slept with her father that night. The next day, they visited a Buddhist college. Hannah and Sarah went out to an airline office and asked a female secretary to confirm their flight to America. When Albert and Olivia came back to the hotel, Hannah told them she and Sarah would leave Sri Lanka after three days.

Sarah spent the last three days speaking to Olivia and Albert with a substantial deal of emotions. She hugged them and wished to be with them all the time. But what could a teenager do? The sad moment came when she articulated a word of farewell and embraced them for a long time at the airport.

Albert touched his chin. "I love both of you. You are my other family."

"We love you too. We will miss you. Sarah and I will wait for you. I mean it with lots of love. Best wishes for your work in India." Hannah wiped tears. "God knows why I love you. I will never forget you. Please, stay connected with us. You both have a special place in our hearts. Sarah loves both of you very much."

With a crushed heart, Albert kissed and hugged them. "Look after your mom."

"I will. But she should care for me too."

Albert put his right hand on Hannah's left cheek and gave her a tender kiss near her lips. "Be well and take care. Please, contact me if there is something I can do for you. Goodbye, love."

Sarah sat in an airplane seat, putting her right hand on her face, and leaning her head on a window. That was the longest and saddest flight of her life.

Chapter 6

Hannah bought Sarah an IBM personal computer and floppy disks to save her typed work. "This is to keep you connected to Albert and Olivia. I will show you how to use the Internet."

The computer in her bedroom was the best gift Sarah had received. She told Albert about it and emailed him every night before retreating to her bed. Her emails ended with the two words "always love." Albert was quick to respond, and she enjoyed reading his eloquent, wise words. This undisclosed correspondence was a form of chaste intimacy and transcendent togetherness. No one else, not even Hannah and Olivia, was supposed to see their private messages. Sarah felt Albert was her dearest friend, personal counselor, and faithful mentor. Without reservation, she told him about her emotions, dreams, clothes, family, school, classmates, parties, and even about her menstruation and biological growth.

In secret, Hannah found herself glum and wrathful because she had separated from Albert and because CIA operatives had sought to assassinate her. She probed the identity of the American secret agents, whom she and Homatakawa had slain in Hong Kong, and realized that Nathan Goodman was their supervisor. On a Friday, Julie asked Sarah to spend a night in her home. Hannah seized this opportunity to travel to a town called Gilford in New Hampshire. After parking her car on the northeastern side of Edgewater Drive, she wore velvet lining gloves and broke into a mansion at Lake Winnipesaukee. Nathan and his Hispanic wife were sitting on a couch and consuming liquor. Nathan tried to move, but Hannah pointed a silenced gun at him. "Don't move. Put your hands on the table."

"Who are you?" Nathan's wife asked.

"Shut your hole."

"Hannah, for God's sake, hold on for a minute. My wife has nothing to do with our work."

"Really? I know her terrorist acts against Cuba."

"Cuba? What is this bosh? Are you a Communist? Cuba is our enemy."

"Why did you want to kill me in Hong Kong?"

"I would never do that. You are a dear friend."

"Who is spying on me?"

"Nobody spies on you."

"Who told you about my travels? Tell me the truth if you wish to live."

"OK. Please put the gun down. Your best friend Linda keeps us posted on your moves."

"Linda?"

"Yes. Linda works for us. We asked her to keep an eye on you."

"Why?"

"We think you are a double agent."

"A double agent? For whom? Russia? China?"

"Who leaked the CIA documents to Albert Russell?"

"Albert published the documents in 1990, and I met him in 1995. So, how do you think I gave him the documents? You know we are still looking for classified documents, and somebody leaked a file on my work for you. Don't you remember?"

"Who are the Anonymous?"

"I don't know."

"How don't you know? The Anonymous killed over twenty CIA officers after you met them."

"This is not my problem. Is Linda a CIA agent?"

"Yes."

"Who killed my husband? Who killed Peter Stone?"

"I do not know their real names. They are called the Black Wolf and the Angry Jaguar."

"Isn't it ironic that your family name is Goodman, and you are an evil man? I lied. You won't live." She fired four shots and killed Nathan and his wife. Then she placed a card on Nathan's head. The card said, "We know who you are and what you do. We will get you out of your dark holes and we will kill you. We are the Anonymous."

A bulky, bearded man came into the house and kicked Hannah's lower back. "Drop your gun."

"OK." With frightened eyes, she placed her gun on a coffee table.

"Who are you?"

"I work for Nathan."

"Are you an agent?" The man saw the Anonymous silver card on Nathan's head. "Do you work with the Anonymous? Are you Homatakawa?"

"No. I am Homatakawa." Homatakawa moved into the room and flung a hatchet at the man's forehead. The man's eyes widened in shock as the hatchet embedded in his forehead. A visceral scream escaped his lips. His body convulsed, and in his agony, he tumbled forward, crashing onto the coffee table. He lay sprawled on shattered glass and debris, with blood oozing from the wound. As he yowled in agony, Homatakawa pulled a steel spike from a sleeve and sunk it deep into his neck. Hannah bent over and vomited after she saw the repulsive slaughter. Homatakawa gave her a small bottle of water and patted her shoulder. "Drink. Go, go. Have a safe trip." A burning chimney was four yards away from the dead bodies. Homatakawa torched the house and fled the scene.

A week later, CIA officers met Hannah and asked her about the leaked documents she mentioned to Nathan Goodman. "I gave the documents to Kevin Wilson in Hong Kong."

"Why in Hong Kong?" a CIA officer asked.

"Nathan Goodman asked Kevin to get the documents from me when I was there."

"Where are these documents?" another officer asked.

"I do not know. Someone killed Kevin Wilson after I gave him the documents."

"Who killed him?"

"A member of the Anonymous."

"Who killed Nathan Goodman and his wife?"

"I do not know. I think the Anonymous have insiders who spy on our communications."

Meanwhile, Hannah started a liaison with her best friend, Linda Jones, to explore her engagement with the CIA. Linda was a white lesbian scholar in New York City. She and Hannah had agreed to keep their affair a secret.

Albert worked two academic years in India before settling in Edinburgh, the capital city of Scotland. When he told Sarah about Edinburgh city, she entered the library room in her house, viewed a large world map hung on a wall, and felt bubbly and optimistic. "Good. Only the ocean separates the east coast from Scotland," she whispered to herself.

When she finished the first half of her last year at the school, her mother asked her to ring Albert and seek his advice on college education.

Sarah called Albert. "Hello, Albert. This is Sarah."

"Hi, Sarah. How are you, darling?"

"I am fine. How are you doing? How is Olivia?"

"We are doing well in Edinburgh. It is wintry here. How is your mom?"

"She is good. Albert, I want your advice."

"Of course. What advice do you want?"

"This is my final year in the school. Which American college should I join? What should I study?"

"Have you considered Yale University? It is in your state, and your mom is associated with it."

"I want to move out of my mom's house and rely on myself."

"Your education should depend on your spontaneous creativity and on what you like to study. You should come to Scotland. Olivia and I miss you."

"Is that OK?"

"Come on, darling. Yes, that is okay. Come over here,

and we will talk further about your learning."

"Thanks so much. Where would I stay? I do not want your family and buddies to ask you unnecessary questions about me."

"No problem at all. You can stay with Olivia in our apartment."

Sarah had become enthusiastic to go to Scotland and meet Olivia and Albert. Hannah was delighted too. "Go and see Olivia and Albert. Albert will give you good advice. Tell him I still love him. Remember, he is a busy scholar. You understand what I mean."

Two days later, Sarah informed Albert that her aunt Barbara would travel with her.

"I will get a room for her in a nice hotel."

In March 2000, Sarah and Barbara flew from New York to Edinburgh. Olivia and Albert were waiting for them at the airport. Words cannot describe how Sarah felt when she spotted them. She hugged them for two minutes and let them give her kisses on her face.

"Welcome to Scotland," Olivia said.

"It is so great to see both of you again. Could you imagine to what extent I have missed you?" she said, with tearful eyes. "Oops! This is my aunt, Barbara Rogers." Barbara was wearing a cream suit and a black blouse. Her lips were red. Albert shook her hand and kissed her face.

"Welcome to Scotland, the fertile land of invention, tranquility, and whiskey." Albert beamed. "It is my pleasure to meet the celebrated novelist."

"Thank you. Sarah told me wonderful things about both of you. Please, I am not a media celebrity; I am just an author."

Albert kissed Sarah's forehead. "Look at your height.

You are a tall woman now, though I do not allow you to be taller than me. I love your long hair."

They took a black taxi to Edinburgh city center. Sarah sat beside Olivia and held her left hand while Olivia put her right arm on her shoulders. Albert relaxed beside Barbara on the opposite seats. He and Olivia asked Sarah quick, usual questions such as, "How are you doing?" "How is your health?" "How is your mother?" "How is your school?" Sarah kept saying "fine." She did not want to gibber. All she yearned for was to attach herself to Olivia and Albert and get hugs and kisses. Albert told Barbara about the places they had seen while on their way.

Barbara got a high-ceilinged room in the Balmoral Hotel, a stone's throw away from Princes Street in the city's heart center, which encompasses commercial stores, historical monuments, and splendid gardens. In the evening, Albert, Barbara, Sarah, and Olivia dined at an Indian restaurant on Antigua Street and had pleasant conversations.

The next day, Albert took Barbara and Sarah to an enormous bookstore called Waterstone's on Princes Street. He bought books by Bertrand Russell, Noam Chomsky, and Edward W. Said and gave them to Sarah. "Read books that challenge your views, broaden your thinking, and foster a sense of connection with others. Let nobody kill your dreams. Great inventions sprout from dreams. Craft a proactive life plan and resist the temptation to relinquish your autonomy to the thoughts of others. Become the sole architect of your own circumstances." He also advised her to join Columbia University in New York and said his cherished comrade and mentor Prof. Said works there. He added it would be convenient for him to travel and see her in Manhattan.

After that, they visited Edinburgh Castle on the Royal Mile and the National Museum of Scotland on Chambers Street. They spent the next five days wandering around in Edinburgh and the Lothians.

This trip to Scotland had revealed Albert's nonpareil adulation, affection, generosity, and polymathic intellect. He informed his guests about his sociopolitical work for justice, peace, the LGBT, and women's human rights, and spoke of his passionate admiration of the feminists who struggled against inequality and men's macho, sexist hegemony. He was glad to hear about Barbara's best-selling novels and passion for writing. She gave him her address and telephone number. Of course, there was a rapturous, esoteric closeness between him and Sarah. Sarah's beneficent warmth had endeared her to Albert, who did not forget to show her his tremendous love and adoration. While in Scotland, she expressed her genuine emotions and opinions. Barbara's libertarian personality was helpful when Sarah expressed her happiness to be with Albert and Olivia without the overshadowing presence of her mother. In Asia, she presupposed they cared for her because Albert was in love with her mother. But in Scotland, she was with them without her mother's scrutiny. She hugged them, confided intimate matters to them, and got their entire attention and love.

Chapter 7

Sarah told her mother about her desire to join Columbia University and said Barbara would care for her when she lives in Manhattan, and Albert would travel to New York to give lectures and meet up with her. Later, Columbia University had accepted her formal application to the Department of Arts and Humanities, and her mother bought her a two-bedroom apartment in the Flatiron District in Manhattan. There was a sensible reason for this purchase, though the accommodation was far away from the university campus. As a protective, prosperous mother, Hannah did not want her daughter to settle with frivolous students and learn harmful habits. One day, she visited

Sarah and said it would be convenient for Albert to stay with her when he comes to New York. Sarah enjoyed her new freedom, luxury, and space.

At a gradual pace, Albert's private emails became more romantic and less intellectual. He used the words "lots of hugs and kisses" at the end of his messages. This non-sexual friendship was not enough. He and Sarah felt they needed physical intimacy and more than a platonic rapport on the Internet. So, when Sarah completed her first semester exams in December, she conveyed to Albert her intense longing to meet him and delve into confidential matters. Albert refrained from probing into these matters, despite harboring a sense of influence over the world in his imagination.

Sarah traveled alone to Edinburgh in December 2000. Albert and Olivia welcomed her at the airport and exchanged warm hugs, kisses, and smiles. They spent the second day roaming the downtown area and the European Christmas Market, on East Princes Street Gardens, and chatting about families, studies, and general topics.

In the morning, Olivia left the apartment to see Scottish classmates, and Albert and Sarah traveled by train to a country town called Pitlochry. River Tummel runs through the township and its lush hillsides. Albert and Sarah walked on a pedestrian teetering bridge stretching over the river and moved upward to the visitor center, where they had a snack, coffee, and Scottish shortbread. With hands nestled in their warm pockets, they ascended to a gigantic hydroelectric dam, immersing themselves in the sophisticated process of generating electricity through the synergy of gushing water and power turbines. Following this enlightening experience, they strolled along the serene river behind the dam. During their slow wanderings, a charming discovery awaited them-an antique wooden bench surrounded by pine woods. Taking a respite, they reveled in the enchanting allure of the river and the woodland that enveloped it.

It was now the time for them to consider their intense affection and love. "So, Sarah, how is your emotional life? Do you have a handsome boyfriend in New York?"

It turned out for a moment that Albert was unaware of Sarah's deliberate intentions and desires. She poked his right shoulder with her left fingers and placed her hand on his knee. "Do you pretend to forget why I am here? No, I don't have a boyfriend in New York."

"Do you fancy a Scottish ginger-haired boy wearing a tartan kilt and plaid socks?"

"I heard the Scots do not put on underpants when they wear the kilt. Is this true?"

"It depends on the weather, the winds, and biological things."

"I want to discuss a personal matter. Please, I want nobody else to know about it."

"Yes, what is it?"

"I will be nineteen in February and am struggling hard to figure out my sexuality. I do not know who I am and what I want. This matter is coming up in my crazy head, bringing me down into a sort of despondency."

"Do you have a physical, biological problem?"

"No. As you see, I have a perfect and healthy body. I think I have an emotional and psychological problem."

"In what sense?"

"I mean my sexual orientation."

"Are you a lesbian?"

"I am not sure. I am disoriented and indecisive about my lesbianism. A part of me is homosexual, and the other part is heterosexual. I love nubile women, maybe because I dislike the penis and do not want a man to stare at my vagina. I buy women's magazines and love to look at beautiful women's figures. You know, no man had ever lived in our home since I was born in 1982. My mom's friends are progressive feminist women, and some of them are lesbians. One of these lesbians is my mom's best friend. My aunt Barbara writes romantic and erotic books though she has never mentioned she loved a man. By the way, my aunt told me she had a crush on you. Don't tell her that."

"Well, she is attractive, intelligent, and a brilliant author. Tell me, are you still a virgin?"

"Yes. I did not have sex with anybody. Sometimes I use sex toys like dildos and vibrators. I don't know how women live with men and copulate with them."

"Do you mean you are ambivalent about your sexual desires?"

"It is not only about sex. I love my gender though I feel I want to be with a caring and smart man to express my true feelings and thoughts. Excitement and sexual desires make me confused. What do you think of homosexuality?"

"I am heterosexual. I do not think I can outlive without a woman. Our sexual life should be natural and based on mutual freedom. What do you want to know about homosexuality?"

"What do you say about the gay people?"

"I have no problem with them. I supported the gay people when the bigoted idiots and their misleading propaganda fused homosexuality with immorality and

AIDS. Dogmatic simpletons believe that natural disasters, such as hurricanes and earthquakes, and epidemic diseases, happen because of homosexuality. The gay people are human beings, and I stand up for their legitimate human rights, even though I question the unscientific theories of homosexuality. Love should inspire our life."

"It is great to know that."

"The world needs true love guided by an excellent knowledge of ourselves and the world. We do not need hatred and wars in the name of patriotism or religion. I oppose the homophobes who mistreat the gay people and call them awful names. Governments have no right to interfere in people's private lives and sexual orientations."

"I saw nude men in movies and magazines. I have never seen a naked man in my real life. My pedantic Catholic mom is uninformed about my sexual needs and fantasies. I do not know how to tell her or my friends about my disguised love for a special man. Who knows? You are this special man. I love you. I really do. Have I offended you?"

Albert held her hand and kissed it. "No, my love, you haven't offended me at all, and I am proud of you." He put his right arm on her shoulders. "Darling, I think you are bisexual because you experience emotional and physical attractions to women and men for their sexual appeal. I know you and Olivia had showered together. I have been polyamorous even after I married Olivia's mom, who was bisexual. Honey, be whatever you want to be. Love is not a sin. Do not be afraid of speaking up your mind and heart, and do not stop doing what you want because of someone else. I will support your right to be who you want to be. Do not pester yourself with people's spite. I will be on your side. Happiness depends on the power of will, desire, and knowledge. I am happy and perky because I have chosen my way of life. Do whatever you like provided you do not do illicit harm to other people."

Sarah felt reassured and vitalized to perceive Albert's positive support and understanding. His affection had filled her throbbing heart with profound gratitude for him. At that moment, she thought of her mother, who sat on Albert's knees and kissed his face and lips. And moved by her recondite desires, she rested on his thighs and placed her hands behind his neck. Albert's hands moved under her dress and touched her slim waist. She gazed at him and put her nose on his and had a fervid desire to kiss his beaming face, but crystal tears slipped from her gleaming eyes, and her heart danced with joy for being with the only man she loves. Her head bobbed to his right chest after she embraced him. Albert put his right hand on her head while his left hand moved up and down her spine.

After touching the sides of his face, she looked at him again, and the flames of love were blazing and roaring in her trembling heart. "Ah, Albert, oh, my love, I wish you fathom the depth of my heart." She paused and wept. "I have been dreaming of you since we were in Sri Lanka. My eyes looked at your photos every night. I loved you when you taught me kung fu and touched my hands and feet. I became mad after I saw your naked body on the beach. To be honest, I did not regret what my mom had done to you because I foresaw your love for me and my love for you. My lips kiss your glamorous photos, and my love for you is so powerful that I cannot stop thinking of you. I want to be with you all the time. My happiness is bound to integrate with you. My body and soul crave you as my heart craves blood. I dream of you every day and every night. My passion cannot get enough of you. I have never loved a man. I am too mystified to know what to do about my twitchy sexuality and my love for you. Ah, Albert, I wish you would be mine. Am I ridiculous to say such a thing?"

Albert kissed her hands. "You know, love, my mom told me once that God wanted to make me a woman, but He changed His mind at the last minute. I lived my childhood with my mother and sister Dora. My school friends were girls. I love women for who they are, and I had wished to be a woman. If I were a woman, I would have been a lesbian. I do not feel relaxed with men, especially the arrogant ones. I had always declined to go out with men to pubs and cinemas. My philosophical mind cannot comprehend why I keep myself away from men and loathe the hogwash about masculinity. The notion that nature creates men to be practical, rough, and tough is foolish. I flout the stupid conviction that men should not show forth their deepest emotions and talk about their private feelings. The men who did not know love were the main causes of human misery. But what can we do? God created us in this way to be who we are and say what we feel."

"You are a woman in a wonderful man's body with a white heart. I am not a vivid writer and may not pick out the right words, but be sure you have a special place in my heart."

"Thank you, sweetheart. Be certain that my love for you is indestructible."

Sarah wept again. Albert looked at her red face and let his index finger wipe her diamond tears and rub her ideal nose. She touched his cold face and kissed his lips for twenty seconds. This was her first sensual kiss on Albert's lips. She had never kissed a man's lips before.

When Albert grinned, she placed her right hand on his left cheek. "Why are you smiling at me, Dr. Russell?" Her left fingers petted his lips. "What is your problem, man? Is it illegal for an American girl to kiss an English man in Scotland?"

Albert beamed and blinked. "No, it is not illegal for an American mistress to kiss me in Scotland." His tender cuddling and benign cheerfulness had persuaded her to encircle her arms around his scarfed neck and share another kiss on his lips.

"What is going on, Ms. Sarah Rogers?"

"What do you mean?"

"Why did you kiss my lips?"

"It is cold, and I am keeping your lips warm." She tee-heed and kissed him. "I am not in bed making love to you. I can kiss you, however, whenever, and wherever I want. When I say, look at me Dr., when I say I love you, I mean I have the full authority to kiss you. I am the boss now. The end."

Albert sensed Sarah's amateurish and honest love for him. He put his forefinger on the side of her nose and remained silent. Her smile waned, and she thought he was unwilling to squabble with an inexperienced student.

"Let us walk."

They held each other's hands and walked around the dammed river until it snowed. "Scotland is an astounding country of racing clouds and seasons."

They sheltered themselves under a bushy tree. Albert unbuttoned and erected the collar of his overcoat and covered Sarah's body after she crossed her arms and shivered. His chest squashed her tender breasts, and she sensed the warmth of his body. Her eyes gazed at his radiant face with her hands on his lower back, and she kissed his lips for a long while. Albert smiled and pointed out that her snuggle under the dripping tree was "very romantic."

When the snow stopped falling, Albert kissed her lips and held her hand. "Senorita, let us go to a restaurant to celebrate our love and have a Scottish toast for our sublime friendship." Their faces dimpled into smiles when they went to a restaurant on the main A924 road and had two pints of beer and a warm toast.

They sauntered to the small train station in the town and bought second-hand books from a tiny bookshop. With their hands together, they waited for the train. Sarah, with immense excitement, looked at his glinting eyes. The blue train arrived, and they sat beside each other as if they were going on a fairytale honeymoon. With their eyes looking through the train window, they talked a little about themselves.

Two hours later, they departed Edinburgh Waverly Station and strolled up to the three-bedroom apartment on Spottiswoode Street near the turfy Meadows. Thirty minutes later, they were in the heated kitchen.

Sarah took off her coat. "Do you like a cup of tea?"

"Yes, please."

After putting on a silver teakettle, she hugged Albert and reposed her head upon his chest. "Do you love me?"

"Yes, darling, I love you. I have been thinking of your

sweet kisses and warm hugs in Pitlochry. We know what we want from each other. But, please, be patient for a short while. I am concerned about your family's reaction and the repercussions of our romance."

"Our love is about us."

"I know. Your mom was my intimate lover for a couple of years. In a cheerful sense, you have surprised me in Pitlochry. I thought our love at this time was mystical and platonic, because I wish you focus on your studies and succeed. We will be together after you finish your exams in May."

"The simple fact is that my witless mom was not your wife. She ditched you in Sri Lanka after you had done many good things for her. If she wanted to repair a relationship with you, she would have come with me to Scotland. I don't have a moral problem with a love relationship with you."

"Our ineffable love is not an ethical predicament, but you need to have emotional confidence and strength before you show off your bisexuality. I guess we should have an agreement on how we want our love to be."

"I am not an experienced pioneer in love. Yes, I have lesbian desires and fantasies, but I am not a lesbian in the strict sense of the word because I want to be with you. I think I talked about lesbianism because I was afraid of rejection." Her right fingers brushed the flesh of his left jaw. "You are a famous philosopher, and I am a first-year college student. Pretty and educated women would love to be with you. It is difficult for me to ask you to be my boyfriend, though you are the only man I love. The other issue is that I am afraid of my mom. She will kill me if I have sex with you."

Albert laid his hands on her shoulders. "I love you too. Fear nothing and no one. I will be with you. We will discuss our courtship later. Give me a hug."

After hugging him, she felt her amorous propinquity and thought of the days when she wanted to caress his muscular body in Sri Lanka. "Can I kiss you?"

"Yes, you can."

She circled her arms around his neck and kissed his lips with great lust. When her vaginal hormones were about to bawl and explode, she raced into a white bathroom, stripped off her clothes, and massaged her body under the hot shower. Though exuberant, she wondered what Albert was doing and pondering when she pampered her lecherous body. After the shower, she put on a turquoise towel around her body and left the bathroom barefoot.

At that moment, Olivia came into the apartment and yelled with joy, "Hello, everyone!" However, her cerise face scowled when she saw Sarah wrapped in a small towel, exposing her bare shoulders and legs. She thought she had made love to her father and goggled at her, without greetings, without a smile. "Where is my dad? Where is he?"

Sarah felt Olivia's glum ire. "He is in the kitchen."

"Dad, dad." She entered the kitchen and saw her composed father sitting at a round wooden table, reading an *Economist* magazine, and drinking a cup of tea. "Dad, dad."

"Yes, darling."

With a tremulous body, she sat on her father's thighs and kissed his lips, as if she wanted to say to him, "You belong to me. No one in the entire world would dare to take you away from me. I am the only woman who loves you." However, she became uncertain after seeing him in his blue tonic suit, navy striped necktie, and oxblood brogues, though her natural incertitude roamed in her watchful head. Her arms surrounded the nape of his collared neck, and she muttered words in her private mind. "Am I a dolt? My dad is wearing shoes and a suit. Did he make love to Sarah? Did he put on his shoes and suit after making love to her? Let me wait and see what he would do and say?"

Olivia idolized her father and could not take the risk of asking him a brazen question such as, "Did you make love to Sarah?" He is her best and only custodian who cared for her all her life. He had told her about his secret emotions and love relationships. Besides, he is an intrepid thinker who is not afraid of speaking up his critical mind. If he had a sexual liaison with Sarah, why would he shroud his love for her?

"Dad, how was your day?"

"It was fine, love. Sarah liked Pitlochry and its high dam and river, and we had a smashing time there. I got books for you. Did you have dinner?"

"No. I didn't eat."

"Let us make dinner."

Albert got three beef steaks, oyster mushrooms, cherry tomatoes, and sour cream from the refrigerator. Olivia placed three ivory plates and silver forks and knives on the table. Sarah came in wearing baby pink culottes and a lilac T-shirt. Albert asked her to open a bottle of red wine.

They sat around the table eating and drinking. Olivia, filled with tension, directed her eyes on her plate and wondered when her father would divulge his amour with Sarah. Instead, he talked about food, the weather, music, and TV programs.

After dinner, Albert suggested they should move to the drawing room and watch the TV. To his delight, there was a *Father Ted* episode on Channel 4. "I love *Father Ted*; it is hilarious."

Olivia put her stockinged feet up on a couch and huddled next to her father, while Sarah leaned on a vinaceous chaise. Albert glanced at Sarah and thought he should not discriminate between her and his daughter. "Sarah, darling, sit beside me. I want both of you to keep me warm."

Sarah left her chaise and sat next to him. He put his left arm around her shoulders and kissed her head.

Though the *Father Ted* episode was humorous, Olivia and Sarah did not laugh as if they were in a funeral home. Olivia cuddled her father's right arm, and her demon had speculated about his clandestine intimacy with Sarah, who, with a degree of wariness, was fearful of Olivia's testy response.

Albert stood. "My brilliant darlings, I have work to do in my office. Good night."

Olivia kissed and hugged her father. "Good night, dad. I love you."

"I love you too, sweetheart."

Sarah stood and hugged Albert, who gave her a soft kiss on her lips.

"Good night. Thanks for the wonderful picnic."

"Thanks also to you. You are always welcome. Good night. Take care, darling."

Feeling of something pressing on their chests, Olivia and Sarah dragged themselves to their bedroom like mute mummies. Olivia switched into a fresh set of attire, donning a white floral chemise. She selected a colorful book from a wall shelf and retired on her pink bed to unwind. Without a word, Sarah sat on her bed, resting her head on her bent knees. A strange silence prevailed in the dim room for ten minutes.

Olivia exposed her naked legs and white thong and waited for Sarah to explain more things or anything, but she did not. She, it should be said, had always loved Sarah and looked upon her as one of her best friends. Both traveled, lived, and slept side by side when they were in Asia and Britain. They also sent confidential emails to each other for over two years.

Olivia gazed at Sarah and broke the eerie placidity. "Sarah, what's up with you? You have been silent this evening. Do you want to tell me something?"

"Tell you what?"

"Anything."

Sarah rubbed her shins. "I don't know."

"Are you downhearted? Did my dad agitate you?"

"No. I am thinking of a few personal things."

"Is this a riddle or what? What are these personal things? What happened to you? Am I a stranger now? Do you hide something from me?"

"No. You know everything."

"Do I know everything? Why don't you tell me? Am I not your best friend?"

"Yeah, you are my best friend."

"Are you afraid of something?"

"I guess so."

"Come and sit beside me."

She left her bed and sat next to Olivia before covering her legs.

Olivia's left fingers touched Sarah's wispy hair. "Come on, honey. You told me many things about your personal life. What's going on?"

"Do you promise not to get angry at me?"

"Do you think I am a monster? I pledge not to make your eyes blue."

Sarah licked the back of her left hand. "Where should I start? I came to Scotland because I love your dad."

"This is not a secret. I know you love my dad, but love has infinite meanings."

"I have sexual feelings for your dad. I cannot stop thinking of him."

"Sexual feelings? Are you indiscreet? Are you under the false impression that my dad would have a sexual relationship with his ex-girlfriend's daughter? My dad is a world-renowned professor and philosopher. Do you imagine he would have sex with a first-year university student? Where is your reasoning mind?"

"You don't know how he feels about me. Your dad loves me, and I love him. I can't control my heart."

"Can you be honest with me? What did you do with my dad?"

"We went to Pitlochry."

"What else did you do?"

"I do not know how that happened."

"What happened?"

"I kissed your dad, and he kissed me."

"Did my father kiss your lips?"

"Yes. I hugged him and kissed his lips. He even said my kisses were very romantic. If that was wrong, he wouldn't have allowed me to kiss him."

Olivia let Sarah's left hand touch her right thigh and

laughed. "Don't you know my dad? He can challenge any philosopher in a debate and kill five people with a kung fu strike, but women are his weakest links because of his womanly pneuma. His feminine heart sees beauty in every woman he loves. He hugs and kisses his women friends even at his university. If a woman friend takes off her clothes and asks him to give her a hug, he won't refuse."

"I don't think your dad kisses the lips of his friends."

"I hug my dad and kiss his lips, but this does not mean we have a sexual relationship."

"You are his daughter, and he looked after you since you were born. I kissed your dad's lips as my mom kissed him. I do not think it is against the British law that an American college student falls in love with your dad."

Olivia stroked Sarah's left hand. "Honey, I am not talking about legal rules and regulations in Britain. In simple words, how do you expect my dad to make love to his ex-girlfriend's eighteen-year-old daughter?"

"Your dad says he loves me."

"Was he serious? What else happened?"

"I told your dad I am a different woman?"

Olivia howled like a wolf. "You are amazing. You always make me laugh. How are you a different woman? Are you an invisible ghost or a zombie from another planet? Ha! What do you mean?"

"I told him I have lesbian feelings."

"Lesbian feelings? You say you love my dad. Do you think my dad is a lesbian too?"

"Your dad says I am bisexual. He said he wished God had created him as a woman. Your dad has a lesbian atman."

"Atman? Are you a Hindu? Well, I am a lesbian."

"Are you a gay girl? I thought you were kidding when you talked about your attraction to women."

"My homosexuality is not a joke. I am a proud lesbian, though I am not in a relationship. Do you want to have sex with my dad?"

Sarah blushed at the strange question. "Excuse me! What do you suppose me to say? Yes, I adore your dad. I love him, and this is my problem."

"Can you explain?"

"I don't know how to tell him about my desire to be his girlfriend."

"Tell me the truth. Did you make love to my dad after you came back from Pitlochry?"

Sarah paused for a while, and her face turned pink. "What did you say? No. No. I kissed him in the kitchen, and he did not stop me. Why do you think I made love to your dad?"

"I saw you wearing a small towel around your waist. Did you want to seduce my dad and make love to him?"

"No. Your dad is not a little boy."

"Are you sure?"

"Yes."

Sarah's affirmation had diminished Olivia's vain suspicion. "How did you kiss my dad? Look at me." Olivia put Sarah's left hand between her bare thighs and kissed her lips with a great passion. "Did you kiss my dad like that?"

"Why did you kiss me?"

"Shut up! I love you. Don't you know that yet? Can't you read between the lines? You saw my naked body. We showered and masturbated together."

"So?"

"Don't you crazy, bragging Americans understand our English finesse? So, I love you." She kissed her once again.

"Olivia, you are sixteen. Please, your dad and I love each other."

"Love each other? Read my lips, baby. Your romantic feelings are unreal and irrational. Not that I blame you. You did not have an experience with a man in your house. Besides, why didn't my dad ask you to sleep with him tonight in his bedroom? He said nothing about your assumed love for him. My dad is a sweet and humble chap, but you must know one important thing about him. To many people, my dad is the Che Guevara of the intellectual world, though he does not like war and violence. The anti-capitalist leftist revolutionaries say my dad is their hero because he says nasty things about America's wars. The corrupt governments hate him because he fights for justice and freedom. And like my great-grandfather Bertrand Russell, my father says critical things about religion, politics, morality, and sex. An assassination organization -it is called the Anonymous- protects my dad wherever he goes. The Anonymous killed CIA agents because they tried to hurt my dad. Honey, you are too young and delicate to face the dreadful wrath of governments, intelligence agencies, the corrupt media, and religious institutions."

Olivia's argument seemed convincing. "I guess I am a dunce. Why would a renowned philosopher like your dad have a relationship with an eighteen-year-old girl?"

"Now you talk sense. Forget all that. What about a sexy massage?"

"What do you want to do?"

"Be quiet." After undressing Sarah's T-shirt, she licked

her shoulders, breasts, thighs, and back. She took off her nightdress after moving behind her and made love to her.

"You see, you won't become pregnant if you make love to a woman."

"Unless by chance you were an extraterrestrial alien from Mars."

Sarah felt excited after making love to Olivia and getting the first experience of lesbian love away from her homeland. Yet, she was speculative about her sensual romance with Albert.

"Can I say something about your dad?"

"Of course you can. What do you want to say?"

"Your dad's romance has amazed me today. He is an eminent professor and twenty-two years older than I am. Why did he allow me to caress him and kiss his lips?"

"He loves you, but not as much as he loved your ravishing mom. He has been single for three years. You are gorgeous, and you remind him of your sexy mom. Men kiss their partners and dream of other women they like. I once asked my dad to get a girlfriend after we moved to Scotland, but he told me that my mother and your mother were his greatest lovers. He said, 'My love life with your mother was like a dream, and Hannah had dashed the hopes for new love and shattered my fragile heart. I cannot have a spouse when there is no harmony between my mind and heart. I have a feeling that someday I would marry a unique woman.' Yes, your wacko mom had ravaged him. That is why he is without a partner."

"What amazes me is that my mom had rejected rich and educated Americans, but without hesitation, she loved your dad when we were in India. I even recall the day when she asked the librarian of the British Institute about your dad. How did she know him?"

"They are academics, and my dad travels around the world. Maybe they met at a conference."

"Why did my mom love your dad? I feel they are hiding a big secret."

"That is quirky. My dad told me about his lovers. He had never mentioned your mom before we met you in India. By the way, I have an American half-sister in New York. Her name is Ayita."

"Wow. Your dad has never spoken of her. What does she do?"

"She is a glamor model. She appears in Victoria's Secret catalogs and *Vogue* magazine. My father adores her mom. Her name is Ann Stone. She was his first girlfriend, and I think she is his secret mistress. My dad has never been monogamous."

"What do you mean?"

"Ann came three or four times to Scotland and slept with my dad in his bedroom. My dad stays with her when he visits New York."

"Why didn't they get married?"

"No one knows. Relatives say my dad's family and Ann's family were against their marriage for religious reasons. My dad belongs to an Anglican family and Ann belongs to a Russian Orthodox family. Ann phones my dad before he sleeps, and he says he loves her."

"Interesting."

"Ann and my sister visited us when we were in Asia and Latin America. I guess my dad will never marry a woman if she asks him not to see Ann and my sister. As they say, love is blind." Olivia put her left arm on Sarah's chest. "Sweetie, I have known you for four or five years. I love you. Do you wish to be my girlfriend?"

"Do you want me to be a lesbian forever?"

"As a matter of fact, yes, I do. And who knows? Maybe your sweet lover will someday become your father-in-law."

"But I live in America."

"I am an American citizen. I will join your university soon."

"What about your dad?"

"You are my girlfriend now. Do not think for a moment that my dad would be your boyfriend. I will talk to him tomorrow. Do not brood over this matter. My dad is a liberal humanist."

"Can I tell him? I still feel attracted to him."

"You can talk to him, but I will finish you if you take off your clothes and make love to him. He is my only man, and I deify him."

"Let us make love once again and sleep. Can I sleep with you?"

"Yes, you can, but do not snore."

The following morning, Olivia left the apartment to see a Scottish friend and do shopping. Sarah woke up naked at nine o'clock and showered and had breakfast before she entered Albert's office. Albert was wearing a tartan robe and sitting on a couch reading a Scottish newspaper.

"Good morning."

"Good morning, darling. How are you?"

"I am fine. Can I talk to you?"

"Yes. Any time."

She looked at his impressive library. "You have an amazing library."

"Thank you. Knowledge makes me sense the arcane

essence of our existence. The Earth is like a grain of sand, and human history is a page and a footnote in the gigantic book of the universe. The vanity of our life is like a tome, and the wise read the good pages."

"Wisdom in the morning. I am here to apologize for what happened yesterday."

"Why do you want to apologize?"

"I don't know. I wish I could express my true self. You were my mom's only lover after the death of my dad. You are a preeminent philosopher and a grandson of a famous man, and I am an average college girl. I must respect you. You are not a young boy."

"What do you want to do?"

"I have no intimation of what I should do with you. I know I love you with extreme intensity."

"Make hope your confidential ally. You may not see it, but it will not fail you. So, what do you want me to do for you?"

"I want your love to live and make myself happy. Is it possible we become devoted and unconditional friends? We can hug, kiss, and do other things. What do you think?"

"Do other things? There are noble things, and there are ignoble things. Can you be more specific?" He blew a kiss to her and clapped. "You should be a philosopher of love. What do you think?" He smiled. "Sweetheart, I need your love, and you need mine. Please, forget the idea that I am a recognized scholar, and you are an undergraduate student. We are equal humans. I was silent last night because I wanted to think of our exceptional love. Likewise, I thought of your mother."

"My mom jilted you without penitence. I believe my

love for you is real. Do you think you and my mom will be together again? She dumped you. She did not come to Scotland to see you. Did you forget that? I am young. I did not have sex with a guy, and I am in love with you. You are the first and only man I love. I do not need money, cars, or a big house. I want your hugs, kisses, and love. We can keep our intimacy a secret between you and me. We do not need to tell people about our love."

"Darling, we can have an intimate relationship, but you need to have the courage in your heart to talk to your mother. Your mother, though she adores you, will never forgive you or give you permission to have a love relationship with me. I was her confidential lover for two years." Albert stared at her face. "Are you ready to lose your mother and crush her frangible heart forever? Your mother ought to know what we do. Think of what she did for you. She looked after you all these long years on her own and bought you a luxury flat in New York. She pays for your college and travel expenses. I do not want her to chastise you, eject you out of her apartment, and stop funding your necessary studies. I need to safeguard you and arrange something for you in case she disowns you. Also, I cannot have a secret relationship with you because I am a notable public intellectual and activist. I must tell my family and friends about you. We are human beings trapped in conditions, desires, and passions."

"I want to be with you even if my mom ends her relationship with me. I am not a little girl anymore. I love to hug and kiss you. Is there a middle way?"

"Do you mean the Buddha's middle way?" He giggled. "Darling, you can hold my hand and kiss me whenever and wherever you want, but you need to be sincere with your feelings. Reconcile your heart with your mind to achieve happiness."

At this moment, she wanted to know why he allowed her to kiss him. "Can I ask you a private question?"

"Be careful. The ancient walls of Scotland have long ears."

"Why didn't you stop me from kissing you?"

"Genuine relationship is like a romantic story. It starts with an attraction and ends with love. I love you. Your warm tears in Pitlochry had permeated my broken heart. I detected the depth of your pure love. I loved your smooth kisses. True love is the one that makes us free. I want us to be free with each other. Only with you I can be free. Come and sit on my knees. I hope I have good news for you."

Sarah sat on his thighs, and he twiddled with her long hair.

"Darling, you are talented, kind, and well-informed. I love to touch you and kiss your lips because I love you, and to let you know why love makes rational thinkers like me irrational. My love for you is inexplicable. I did not think of having a relationship with you before your current visit, though your lucid, warm emails were full of intimate feelings. When you kissed me yesterday and told me about your love, I could not resist the innocent lure. You kissed me when I needed an affectionate woman to heal my broken heart and make me celebrate the fullest excitement of life. You are the one who has healed my split heart and made me cheerful. My love, do you like to be my fiancée?"

Sarah gasped, cried, and screeched like a gurgling rivulet. The word "fiancée" is more impressive and precise than the generalized word "girlfriend." "My, my God!" That was a stupendous revelation. She had not expected an official relationship with Albert before her graduation from the university. "Do I like?" She pressed his face against her chest and cried again. "I would love to be your fiancée. My love for you is timeless, like the air we breathe. You have made my dreams come true."

They kissed and fondled each other until they heard Olivia's voice. Albert stood upright like a pillar when Olivia came into his office. "Good morning." Olivia kissed her father.

"Olivia, sit beside our sweetheart, Sarah. I want to tell you an important matter." Olivia sat beside Sarah and thought her father was about to say positive words about her lesbian intimacy with Sarah. "Darling, I am conscious of your desires and feelings and of the special passion between you and Sarah. I told you about my innermost emotions and informed you about the women I loved and the women I did not love. Both of us exalt and love Sarah. Sarah and I have decided to get engaged."

Olivia sprang upward like a tabby, hugged her father, and sniveled. "What should I say? This is a delightful surprise. Congratulations, dad. Sarah adores you. She will be a great fiancée." Olivia hugged and kissed Sarah. "I love you, honey. Be benign to my dad. He is the only man I love."

After a jovial exchange of hugs, kisses, and romantic badinage, Sarah suggested she should join the University of Edinburgh, but Albert disagreed. "You should stay at Columbia University. Your thriving future will be in America, not in Scotland. Olivia will join your university soon, and I will get a house in New York and be with both of you. Let us wear warm clothes and go out to celebrate our wonderful love."

In the evening, Sarah entered Albert's bedroom and was reluctant to ask him about his affair with Ann Stone. She feared losing him by bringing up such an issue. Albert kissed her painted lips, and his hands landed on her shoulders. "As you have proposed, the engagement will be in the church on Saturday morning. I also respect your decision not to invite people from your country."

"Thank you, love. I need to buy a chiffon dress and party shoes for the engagement. I have something else to add. It would be unfair if I sleep with you tonight and leave Olivia alone in her room. I do not want her to think I want to take you away from her. So, please, let me sleep with her tonight."

"Be free here. Kindness brings about the beauty of our hearts."

After kissing Albert in a lustful way, Sarah moved to Olivia's bedroom. Olivia was standing like a lonesome maid beside a framed mirror and brushing her sopping hair. Sarah hugged her back, and her lips moistened her sleek neck. "I will forever love you. Please, pardon me. Your dad surprised me today. What could I do? Can any woman of sound mind resist your dad's incredible heart and charm? You are my first love. I will always love you and be with you. I will always care for you."

Olivia turned her face and kissed her lips. "All I want is to see you happy with my dad. You will be an excellent stepmother."

"Thanks, honey. We will have sex after I jot down a few words from my heart about us. Take off your clothes and keep the bed warm for me."

"Do you want me to betray my dad?"

"This is love, not a betrayal."

Sarah sat at an oak desk and opened her diary. She wrote,

"I have kissed Olivia's beautiful lips with a great passion. The new ecstasy of love is intoxicating and overpowering.

Tonight, I am the happiest woman in the world. I will be Albert's fiancée. Our betrothal ceremony will be on Saturday. I have told Albert about my unfathomable love for him. This, I am sure, is the beginning of my eternal relationship with him. We fondled, kissed, and carried each other's hand. Our most profound love is not as erotic as it seems. It is a mystical affinity between two spirits, two souls, two minds, two bodies. We have never argued, disputed, or disagreed. Both of us love the way we are together. We are free. No conditions. No pretense. No formality. We say the things we like to tell. We do the right things we want to do. Darling, honey, love, sweetie, and sweetheart are our new tags.

I do not dissemble my affection for Olivia. I have told her about my unshakeable love for her, about my body, about my true feelings, about my close friends, about my dreams. I love to hug and kiss her and hold her pretty hands. She is thoughtful, gentle, and supportive. She had never rebuked me and had never been angry with me. Her face is always shining. Her bright lips are smiling.

A sense of profanity and contrition was overwhelming. I don't know why. I do not mean the Catholic dogma of sin, which I scorn. There is no regret for my intense love for Albert. I am happy because I love him. He is a wise man and has natural qualities and hopes that I should recognize. What would a young student do with a gifted scholar who was my mother's only boyfriend after the death of my father? Yes, I love him, and nobody in the world can stop my titanic love for him. He is an eminent savant, and I am an ordinary college girl. I must respect him. His charming daughter is my adorable sweetheart. What can I do for both of them? Can I be their shared inamorata? Ah! My love for Albert has set my soul on a raging blast. I want to kiss his lips day and night. I wish to go to his bedroom now and make love to him.

Am I off my head? I love Olivia, and I am in love with her father. She wanted me to be her girlfriend, but her dad asked me to be his betrothed. I love her, and I am in love with her dad. He is the only man we love.

My marriage to an international philosopher will be a big news story all over the world. I must be unswerving. It will not be easy for me to tell my mom about my marriage to her greatest lover. What should I do? My love or my mom? Love will always win. I love Albert. I love him. I love him."

Chapter 8

A week post her engagement, Sarah ventured back to New York, exuding a vibrant aura of resilience and optimism. Reveling in the privilege of being the beloved partner and cherished fiancée of a distinguished scholar, her erstwhile desire to love an American individual had dwindled and withered away.

Contemplating Albert's academic renown, she reflected on the way she should present herself to the public and the media once she entered into matrimony with him. The impending union with a distinguished philosopher had prompted her to consider the narratives she would share with her family and friends. This concern became a catalyst for her meticulous attention to her appearance, encompassing aspects such as beauty regimen, dietary choices, cosmetics, trendy hairstyles, and wardrobe selections. She changed her coiffure and subscribed to women's magazines, such as *Cosmopolitan, Curve, Shape, Vogue, Glamour, Marie Claire*, and *Girlfriends*. Yet, she could not dare tell her mother about her betrothal, lascivious behavior, and sexual relationship with Albert and Olivia, or about her entrenched aversion to Catholic moral philosophy. She worried about her family's stern response, financial security, and university expenses.

In February, Albert surprised her with a pleasant phone call. "What will you be doing in the next week?"

"I have no plans. As usual, I will attend classes, type an essay, buy food, clean the apartment, and wash my clothes."

"I will be in New York in the next week. I will give lectures on Tuesday, Wednesday, and Thursday."

"Love, that's great. I will attend your lectures. Where will the lectures take place?"

"In your university."

"That's awesome."

"Should we visit your mom? We need to tell her about our betrothal."

Sarah twirled a lock of hair around her left fingers. "Forget this matter now. I do not need a war with my mom. She is bloody obdurate, and will not, under any circumstances, allow me to hook up with you. I don't want her to spoil our love."

"As you wish. Whatever happens, you have my total backing. But, love, we need your mom to be with us when we get married. I think I should talk to her."

Her right foot kicked a baseboard. "We will discuss this galling matter after you come to New York."

Albert arrived at JFK International Airport. A female immigration officer looked into his eyes. "What is the purpose of your visit?" Albert picked up an official letter from his jacket pocket and showed it to her. "Columbia University has invited me to deliver lectures and attend a conference." The officer made a call, and two security agents came. "May we have a word with you?"

"Sure."

The agents motioned for Albert to follow them down a dim corridor that seemed to stretch into the shadows. As they traversed the narrow passageway, a chilling silence prevailed, interrupted only by the echo of their footsteps. But without warning, a long-haired female cyborg warrior materialized behind them, her metallic presence causing fear.

In a swift and calculated motion, she hurled the agents forward with a supernatural force, as though they were mere pawns in a malevolent game. The unsuspecting agents crashed into a row of seats with a disturbing thud, their bodies contorting in unnatural angles. The cyborg's cold, unfeeling eyes surveyed the aftermath of her display of strength.

Before the agents could understand the gravity of the situation, four security officers came with their weapons drawn and aimed at the unidentified cyborg. "Stay where you are." The cyborg stared at them. "You coward pigs." The tension in the air was palpable, and the corridor became a battleground between humans and the enigmatic, cybernetic foe. The lights flickered overhead, casting eerie shadows on the unfolding confrontation. As the standoff reached a critical juncture, the corridor pulsated with the unspoken threat of impending violence.

The relentless stare of the cyborg froze the security officers in their place. With an ominous hum, her outstretched arms unleashed fiery red laser beams that seared the air and punctured the floor, leaving smoking craters. Panic seized the hearts of the officers as they retreated, seeking refuge behind a nearby wall.

As the officers cowered in fear, two female Anonymous warriors appeared, with their arms extending with lethal intent. In a synchronizing dance of destruction, the warriors fired lasers, cutting through walls and shops with lethal precision.

The airport descended into chaos. The terrified screams of workers and travelers echoed through the halls as they sought shelter. Panic-stricken individuals sprinted toward secure locations with the atmosphere fraught with an unrelenting sense of danger. The Anonymous warriors, undeterred by the chaos they had unleashed, continued their assault, turning the bustling hub of travel into a battleground.

The three Anonymous figures surrounded Albert to protect him. "Hurry. Let us go." They transferred him to an arrival hall where Sarah was waiting. Another female Anonymous warrior surfaced and gave Albert his passport and luggage. With a troubled look, Albert hugged Sarah, and the Anonymous warriors covered their heads with alpaca ponchos and disappeared.

Sarah gaped. "Who were they? What happened? Do you know them?"

"No. They fought the security officers who wanted to interrogate me. I do not know why the Anonymous fighters protect me. Let us leave the airport."

They got a taxi to the Flatiron apartment, where they kissed, fondled, and said affectionate words. Albert could not take off his clothes and make love because he thought of the Anonymous warriors who frightened people and caused damage to the airport. He expected the FBI to arrest and interrogate him. In the evening, they took a drink of red wine and watched an entertaining film called *American Beauty*. They sat beside each other on a couch and put their stockinged feet on a wooden coffee table. Holding each other's hand, they viewed the movie with lazy eyes and mentioned the pleasurable things they had done together in Scotland.

Albert retired to his bedroom to sleep. Sarah could not sleep in her bed. Her mind thought of Albert, of his kisses, of his hugs, of his beautiful love. She tiptoed to his bedroom. The bedroom door was a little open. Albert was wearing brushed cotton check pajamas and sleeping on his right side. Sarah, wearing a white strap camisole, slid under the thick cover, and lay behind him, molding her body to his. Her breasts touched his back, and her thighs joined his. She put her left arm around his waist and let her hand and fingers rub his belly. His right hand pressed her hand. She kissed the back of his neck and fingered her body.

At nine o'clock in the morning, Sarah took Albert to Columbia University and guided him to his lecture auditorium. She entered the hall and occupied a seat in the middle section. Four scholars encircled Albert. When he stood at the podium, Sarah beamed and wished to declare that this outstanding philosopher is her adored fiancé. Albert glanced around for a moment and started his lecture with a gleeful grin. "Good morning, ladies and gentlemen. How are you this morning? I hope all of you are happy and well." The keen audience felt he wanted to assert his easy affability and truthful care for human relations. To their astonishment, they noticed that his intelligent lecture was extemporary. The massive trove of information had accumulated in his encyclopedic mind. He peered at his Omega watch five times, and after the fecund lecture, delighted scholars and students shook his hand and asked him quick questions. Sarah had the chance to talk to him. "I will meet you at the main door of this building at 12:30. We will go out for lunch."

At 12:30, they held each other's hand and walked into a Greek restaurant on West 113th Street. After lunch, Sarah told Albert she would attend a lecture and they should meet each other at four. Albert seized this time to see Ann Stone and Ayita. He met them at a café near *The New York Times* headquarters on West 43rd Street. Ann touched his hand. "You are right about Michael Rogers."

After four, Albert and Sarah walked into a food store. Albert fetched a bag of noodles from a shelf. "Do you like Chinese chicken noodles?"

"Yes, I love Chinese noodles. Do you remember the aromatic Chinese meals in Asia?"

"Yes, I do."

They got Chinese egg noodles, boneless chicken thighs, red bell peppers, green chilies, scallions, light soy sauce, corn flour, rice vinegar, and a white wine bottle.

An hour later, they unpacked the food in the kitchen. Albert kissed Sarah. "How is your kung fu?"

"It is not good, I guess. I became shiftless after I joined the university?"

"Do you like to do kung fu?"

"Yes, but not much."

They took off their linen sweaters and shoes and warmed up in the living room. Albert taught Sarah how to avoid a punch in the face and hit an opponent's upper neck with the knuckles of her hand. He also showed her how to squat and strike an attacker's sensitive genitals. She loved it when he touched her hands, knees, and feet. With delight, she felt it was pleasant to blend kung fu training with sensual acts.

Albert entered the bathroom to shower, and Sarah chopped the chicken thighs, the bell peppers, and the scallions into small pieces. Albert came in wearing Scottish woolen pajamas.

"Have a shower. I will cook. Thanks for cutting up the chicken and the vegetables."

She walked into the bathroom and had a shower. After drying herself, she wore a gray T-shirt with an I-am-with-her front print. The chicken noodles were on two white plates on the dining table. A white wine bottle, two lead crystal glasses, and a purple scented candle were also on the table.

"Thanks, honey. This looks like a five-star restaurant. Thanks for cooking."

"It's my pleasure. Cheers!"

While they were eating the noodles, Albert touched her hand. "How, when, and where do you want us to live together?"

"I don't know. I am still a student. We will discuss this topic later. I am not in a hurry. I am happy with the things we do. You are with me."

After dinner, they sat on their favorite couch and watched a romantic comedy movie called *Notting Hill*, starring Hugh Grant and Julia Roberts. Sarah put her bare feet up on the couch and leaned her head on his right chest. He kissed the top of her head and put his right arm around her. She had an indescribable feeling of euphoria. Other types of ecstatic excitement prevailed and enticed her to remember Albert's superb love for her in Scotland. She recalled his travels, and the sad day in Sri Lanka when her mother argued with him, and when she told him about her desire to be with him. Her mind reminisced about the pleasant trips to Scotland and prompted her to think of her mother, who said that "Albert is a busy scholar." She thought of her resistless sexuality and student life in New York. Her mouth uttered no words on these undying things, and fanciful dreams had trifled with her libidinous desires.

Taking her time, she stretched her half-naked thighs on Albert's legs and persuaded his hands to massage them. Her hand ran under his pajama jacket and on his warm stomach muscles and chest. She asked him to kiss her and close his eyes. A moment later, she sprinted to her bed and buried her hand under her black lace thong. She quivered, squawked, and thanked Heaven for the joy of love. After exchanging goodnight hugs and kisses with Albert, she slept alone in her bedroom that night.

On Wednesday morning, they moved into a university lecture hall. Sarah sat close to the lecturer's platform, aiming to look with glee at Albert's face, and hear his euphonious voice and classical English accent. Albert gazed around for a little while. "Good morning, ladies and gentlemen. How are you on this gelid day? I hope you all are happy and well."

After the lecture, scholars invited Albert to lunch with them. Sarah saw him walking and talking with Professor Edward W. Said and other notable scholars. With an egotistical pride, she susurrated, "How many people know this distinguished scholar is my fiancé and bosom lover? Albert's family and I are the only people who know that." She had an absurd sense of pride and contentment.

She met Albert at three o'clock. They sauntered in the Upper West Side and walked to Central Park where they spent time at the Jacqueline Kennedy Onassis Reservoir (the Central Park Reservoir). After getting a yellow cab to Times Square, they had an Italian dinner at Carmine's. From there, they got a taxi to the apartment.

"That's a lovely day. Thank you."

She gave him a quick kiss on his lips and a hug. "I am grateful to you for being with me. You have refreshed my love life. You could have spent your day with academics, but you preferred to be with me in my apartment. This means a lot."

He hugged her. "But no one is like my special true love. I thirst for a cup of tea. What do you like to drink?"

"I will get a glass of vintage port."

He held his cup of tea, and she got her wine glass.

"What about some music?"

"What do you like? I have Madonna, Bob Dylan, Paula Abdul, Whitney Houston, Johnny Cash, Merle Haggard, Martina McBride, Elvis Presley, Michael Jackson, Tina Turner, Celine Dion, Kenny G. ..."

"Kenny G.?" he interposed. "Do you remember his music when we were in Hong Kong?"

"Yes, I do." She smiled. "You are awesome. How many serious philosophers care about Kenny G.?"

"I like his gentle personality. His calming music helps me think of reality. Country and rock music let me escape from the stressful problems of life."

The CD player played Kenny G.'s jazzy music, and

Sarah sat beside Albert, sipping her port wine. When Kenny G. played "The Moment," he put her glass on the coffee table and induced her to dance with him. He placed his right hand on her left waist, and his left hand held her right hand. She put her left hand on his right shoulder. The soothing music, the enamored dancing, and his sensual touch had enraptured her voluptuous body and electrified her heart. She could not explain to herself how she felt about him.

She carried his hand after they danced and sat close to him on the couch. When Kenny G. played "Forever in Love," they held hands and spun like ballet dancers. Sarah leaned her head on his chest and looked up at his tearful eyes. "Don't cry, love." She touched his eyelid.

"The tears of love are beautiful when a caring hand touches them."

"What is going on in your head? Why are you crying?"

"I have remembered our happy days and mirthful life in Asia and Britain. I still recall that sunny day when you straddled on my shoulders in Goa. Do you remember the clay and mud masks on our faces when we were in Sri Lanka? Our love is incongruous and inexplicable. It is like God's plan, as people say. Your mother and I split up, and here I am dancing with you and in love with you." He kissed her. "Oh, love, I know you as I know Olivia. A mysterious magnet draws me closer and closer to you. My heart has partnered with the whole of you. What would we say when we meet your mother?"

"I know how you feel. Please, do not peeve yourself with my mom's manic hysteria. I'm your love and fiancée."

He put his hands on her face and kissed her sharp lips.

"Love teaches us a vocabulary that no language can describe. You are charming and clever."

"Once you asked me to ignore what people would think of me. I love you, and my love differs from the artificial love we see in most Hollywood movies. I will tell the world I love you. My crazy mom knows I adore you. I understand you were her secret lover for two years, and you care a lot about your academic work. I want to share my passions and sexual needs with you. You are exceptional, and I will always love you." She gave him a swift kiss on his lips and took him to her bedroom. "This is my private, sexy room."

With a broad smile and astounded eyes, Albert gazed at the colorful posters of Linda Evangelista, Cindy Crawford, Farrah Fawcett, Claudia Schiffer, Michelle Pfeiffer, Amber Valletta, Brooke Shields, Madonna, Sharon Stone, Carolyn Murphy, and Elle Macpherson.

"Do you like my bedroom?"

"It is warm and romantic. Why don't I see posters of men?"

"Who cares about men? Women are sexier than men. Don't you think so?" She smiled and held a framed photo of him. "But secretly, I have a love affair with this handsome man. He is the only man I love. Tell nobody about him." They giggled.

Albert sat on her bed, and she picked up two slip-in maroon albums of their photos when they were in Asia and Britain. "I took this photo in Hong Kong. My mom took this photo in India. I took this one in Sri Lanka ..."

"Great. These were wonderful days and memories. Darling, I have an important conference tomorrow at nine o'clock. We need to wake up early in the morning. Thank you for this special day. Good night. I love you."

"I love you too. Good night. Dream of me."

He slumbered in his room, and she looked around at the walls of her room and thought of the sweet words they said to each other. She was confident of her love for him, yet she reminded herself of the fact he was her mother's greatest lover. It was difficult for her to know what to do about her forceful love for him. She wanted him to be with her all the time, but what about his work and prolific writing? What about Olivia and her lesbian love? What about her dearest aunt, Barbara? What would happen when Olivia settles in New York? Would she make love to her? Or would they put an end to their secret affair? She could not think further and put her head on a soft silk pillow and slept, hoping the other day would be better than today.

The next day, she woke up and spent ten minutes in bed reflecting on a sweet dream she had. Her spirit was jaunty, and she planned to do exciting things with Albert that day. She exited her bedroom and found Albert sitting at the dining table, wearing his dark blue suit, and drinking tea.

She approached him and gave him a kiss on his lips after she pulled her hair back and tucked it behind her small ears. "Good morning, honey."

After taking a shower, she wore a short satin robe and seated herself across from Albert. "What are you going to do today?"

"I have an academic conference at nine o'clock. I will be free after 12:30. Can we invite your aunt Barbara to dine with us? I do not want her to think I am ignoring her."

"No problem. I will call her later this morning. We will go out to the town after your conference. I need to buy a few things. It is cold and snowy. We need to take an umbrella."

They went to the university, and Sarah found a seat in the nook of the symposium hall. She thought she should not distract Albert's attention and hinder his enjoyment of his scholarly work, which he loves with great affection.

Around 10:30, she left the hall to call her aunt and attend a lecture. At 12:45, she met Albert and told him her aunt would come over to dine with them at six o'clock.

They exited the university campus. Ice and snow blanketed the slithery sidewalks. Albert held a mauve umbrella with one hand, and Sarah grabbed his arm until they reached a Spanish Latin American restaurant on Amsterdam Avenue. After lunch, they plodded on until they arrived at Victoria's Secret, a woman's top-end underwear and beauty store. Sarah held his hand and pulled him into the store. He peeked at provocative underwear styles, and his face became rosy.

"What are we doing here?"

"I want to buy underwear and lingerie. For your information, women wear bralettes, bikinis, thongs, corselets, shorts, and briefs. Should I teach you that, Dr. Philosopher? Didn't your dazzling, sexy eyes see my red underwear? Don't you want to know what I wear?"

"I am at your service, my queen."

"Olivia told me you buy sexy underwear and swimsuits for her. So, stop pretending to be Mr. Innocent."

He kept his sight down. Sarah assumed he did not want close acquaintances to see him traipsing around in a women's underwear store. Her liberated love for him had stimulated her to brush aside his academic preeminence and seduce him. "What about this balcony bra? ... Do you want me to wear these see-through string panties? ... Do you like these black gauzy panties? ... What about this sexy bikini?"

She yanked him to a changing room and let him see her naked breasts before she tried on a bra.

"Touch the bra. Do you think it is soft?"

He simpered and showed her kung fu strikes. She smiled and held a pair of transparent panties. "Which one do you like?"

"I like the plum one."

"You have a good taste of women's underwear." She took off her boots and pants and gave him a fervent kiss. "Let us be adventurous and make love here."

"Not in the store."

"Why not? Are you shy?"

"This is an inappropriate place for sex."

"OK, honey. I just want to be close to you."

They got a cab to their apartment. After removing their trendy clothes, they had a cup of tea with cakes. Sarah recommended they should go out for a brisk walk in Madison Square Park, despite the icy pathways and the freezing weather. Albert agreed.

They went out for a ramble and said pleasant words to each other. They found their way to a secluded seat under an elm tree. Sarah sat on his knees and kissed him for five minutes. After shivering in the cold, they left the park and entered a food store after they had decided to make butter chicken curry that evening.

In the apartment, Albert wore a white shirt and navy

jeans, and Sarah put on a taupe satin negligee covering half of her thighs. They cooked a meal, and the doorbell clanged.

"I will get it."

"Hello, my charming lady. How are you doing, love?" Barbara kissed Sarah.

"Good evening, aunt. Perfect. You have come at the right time."

Barbara was wearing wild rose lipstick, a brown jacket made of jacquard wool, tawny trousers, an ivory shade silk blouse, and high-heeled chestnut brown shoes.

Albert came out of the kitchen, wearing a pink bib apron. "Good evening."

Barbara kissed his face. "Good evening, Albert. I am so delighted to see you in New York. It is a lovely apron. Are you the chef here?"

"Sarah and I cooked the dinner."

The three sat at the dining table and ate the chicken curry.

Barbara wiped her lips. "Yummy yum! The dinner was delicious. It was not picante as I thought."

"Thank you," Albert responded.

"Sarah told me you are leaving the country on Sunday."

"Yes. I do not want to disturb Sarah's studies."

"Can you come to my place tomorrow at 2:00 pm? I would be thankful if you could look at my new novel."

"With my pleasure. We will see you tomorrow."

Later, Barbara told them she had to leave to meet a friend and discuss work with her. "Thank you for dinner. The vino was superb. See you tomorrow."

Sarah sat beside Albert and watched a crime film called

L. A. Confidential. Exhaustion weighed on her weary eyes as the final credits rolled on the movie. After a lingering kiss, she retreated to her dark bedroom, collapsing on the bed in a dramatic sprawl, her head tossing in a restless manner. Despite weariness, her eyes refused to succumb to sleep, holding an unyielding vigil over the storm of thoughts that swirled within her troubled mind.

A myriad of unsettling thoughts agitated her as she lay there alone. The complexity of her relationship with Albert loomed over her like a tempest, casting shadows of doubt and uncertainty. Not to mention the impending storm of her mother's inevitable retribution that thundered in her head. After some time, she walked out of her bedroom and wobbled on Albert's thighs.

"I could not sleep. Can you sleep with me tonight? I promise to be good to you."

After flicking off the TV, Albert put his arms around her thighs and carried her to the bedroom. He took off his shirt and rested on the bed, and she put her jaded head on his bare chest. His right fingers sank into her hair. Five minutes later, she was in another world.

At the stroke of eight, she woke up to find her fiancé still sleeping and breathing beside her. As the morning light caressed his exposed body, her gaze lingered, probing the contours of his face, arms, and chest. She pondered the abnormal suppression of his carnal desires. They could have made love in her elegant bedroom after his arrival in New York. They could have spent time together in the bath. She should have asked him to massage her nubile body with sweet almond oil. She did not think for a minute he did not want to make love to her and assumed his quotidian kung fu training and bookish addiction had impelled him to control his sensual desires and mettle. Though the evocative ghost of her mother had haunted her mind, she thought of keeping their unsurpassed love as a secret liaison. Why should other people know about their great love? Their love is their business alone.

But the racking dilemma is that she had made love to his captivating daughter and was too scared to tell him about their lesbian lovemaking. Besides, Albert was her mother's first lover after Michael's death. Her mother once said he caressed her body every night when she slept with him. Even so, his affection for Sarah seemed amatory, sensual, spiritual, and emphatic. He called her darling, honey, love, sweetie, and sweetheart. His hands had never dissuaded her from hugging him, kissing his rosy lips, and touching his private body parts, and he had never stopped her from saying erotic things to him.

In Scotland, she and Albert had consented to sex before marriage and to enjoy the guiltless pleasure of intimacy. For a swift moment, she thought her mother was the reason that precluded him from making love to her in the apartment. Hannah is beautiful, wealthy, and a successful scholar and businesswoman. Albert had preoccupied himself with her unpredictable reprisal.

Sarah walked into the kitchen and made two cups of tea. She brought the teacups to her bedroom and put them on a side table. Filled with excitement, her eyes looked at Albert, and her lips wished to suck his colorless lips and pink nipples, but he was sleeping without a sound. She rested her head on his chest, feeling gleeful to be with him. As she wished to dream of their love, Albert's right hand titillated her back, and she sensed his fingers on the back of her neck before they rubbed her head.

"Good morning, love."

"Good morning, sweetheart. What's the time now?"

"It's 8:30."

She did not want to speak or debate. This was her opportunity to make love to the man she loves. She flexed her body, pressing her breasts against his chest, and licking his face. "Thanks, honey, for sleeping with me."

With a blushed face, he kissed her twice and persuaded her to sit on his rocky abdomen. His hands massaged her bare legs and moved up to her hips and waist. The tender tips of his fingers stroked her armpits and tickled her. She laughed and pushed his arms down. Her body fell on his chest, and her mouth sucked his lips. He held her hands and let his lips and tongue fondle with her fingers. Her breasts rested on his chest again, and he put his arms around her. His fingers played with the end of her hair and touched her neck and chest cleavage after she stretched her body up. At that salacious moment, she desired to be naked in bed the entire day. He gripped her hands and induced her to rest beside him. When he sat on his bended knees and sought to brush her lips, she turned her face to the door, palpitated with anxious fear, and shrieked like a banshee. "Mom, get out. What are doing here? Get out."

He put his right hand on her face and stared at her wary eyes. "Darling, look at me. Look at me. Your mom is not here. You seem chary. What can I do for you?"

With a disoriented murmur, she rubbed her filmy eyes, a sudden jolt disrupting the tranquility of the moment. "Oh, my God. Sorry. Sorry. I imagined my mom standing in the doorway and watching us."

Albert sensed her realistic fright and inexperience,

though he had never tried to instruct her in sexual matters. He wanted her to gain a gradual understanding of human sexuality. She became edgy and susceptible to her mother's disownment and recrimination. In that moment of awareness, she recognized she was not only with a loveable, sensitive, warm fiancé but also with an erudite, meticulous philosopher who evaluates and rationalizes everything he conceives and perceives, including his romantic infatuation and sexual life.

"I am sorry," she reiterated. "I am so happy to be in love with you. Your presence here is the most important thing that happened to me. I am the luckiest woman in the world."

Albert gave her a quick kiss on her lips. "Thank you, darling. Stay right here. I need to go to the other room."

Feeling frustrated, she clutched her rumpled hair. Was she with an extraterrestrial superman made of steel? Her body wished he continued his wanton foreplay. She did not want him to discuss anything but their erotic love. Why didn't he ask her to remove her negligee and thong?

Unaware of Albert's purpose, she thought he wanted to go to the other room because she reminded him of her mother and his love for her. "Honey, forget my mom's rage. I am also nervous about her retaliation."

Poor Sarah! Did she mention her mother once again? Her mother was not in the apartment to scold her and evict Albert. She should converse about her mother after she displays her prurient love for him.

"Love, I am here with you. Why did you mention your mother?"

"What's wrong? Why don't you want to make love to me?"

"Darling, I haven't talked about your mother. I did not say I do not want to make love to you. You turned your face away from me, shuddered, screamed, and said you imagined your mother standing in the doorway. I felt something has sidetracked you."

"Can we stop talking? Let us make love. It will not take over five minutes."

Albert touched her chin. "Love, as I have said, I stopped touching your body because you twisted your face away from me and spoke of your mom. Patience is the path to happiness and wisdom. Be patient for a minute. I want to go to the other room."

Perplexed and afraid, she grappled with the challenge of articulating her emotions with poise. "Trust me. An inexplicable awe tugs me close to you. I cannot fathom it. You are a woman in a man's body. Your heart is a woman's heart. You have a woman's love. Your touch is a woman's touch. You talk about your deep emotions as women do. You kiss and caress as lesbians do. I love you and love to touch you. I feel excited when you touch me."

Albert sat on the edge of the bed and smiled again. "Darling, why are you telling me all these things? You are my fiancée and love. Be patient for a minute."

"To hell with patience." It seemed she inherited some of her mother's melodramatic genes. "Why don't you want to make love to me? I am your sweetheart. We made love in Scotland. Don't you remember that? Why are you unwilling to make love? Why, honey? Do you love another woman? Tell me why? Are you afraid of my mom's fury? Are you concerned about your job and reputation?"

He laughed. "Darling, I still do not understand your

dispute. You are my precious fiancée. I apologize if I have hurt your feelings. I am fallible. Please, I love you in the fullest sense of the word."

"But why did you say you want to go to the other room? Where is your love for me?"

He shook his head. "My little angel, come with me to the other room."

They went into the other bedroom. Albert opened a tote leather bag and picked up a burgundy box. "Open the box."

She opened the box with shaking hands and peered at a glistening diamond ring and an expensive necklace. "What is this?"

"They are for you, my dear love. Today is your birthday. Did you forget that? Sweetheart, do you like to marry me?"

That was like receiving a Nobel prize in love. She stuck her right hand in her mouth, crying like a hungry baby. Her body crouched beside the bed. She could not believe what Albert had told her. "I don't believe this. Oh, my God!"

He laid his right hand on the back of her neck. "What do you say, love?"

She wiped her streaming tears. "Oh, my gosh! I am a stupid idiot. I thought you wanted to come here because you did not want to make love to me. Honey, I am sorry. The ring and the necklace are fantastic. Yes, love, I want to marry you and put the world on fire."

"Put them on."

"I will." She wiped her nose with the back of her left hand and placed the ring on her finger and the necklace around her neck and secured the clasp. After getting up on her feet, she looked at a mirror, kissed Albert, and asked him to turn around. With her hands on his naked chest, she stood behind him and kissed the back of his neck and firm shoulders. Her dress dropped to the floor, and she pressed and rubbed her breasts on his back and rested her left cheek on the top of his shoulder. He did not move.

"Please, honey, I want to come. Don't look." She rested her left hand on his neck, and her right hand rubbed her wet pudendum. "Yes, yes," she yelled and fell on the bed.

A linen comforter covered her naked body. "The orgasm was terrific and super-fast."

Albert grabbed the comforter off the bed and stared at her body. Her waggish smile and provocative allure had captivated him. He slithered like a serpent and made love to her. With a hearty laugh, he threw two soft pillows at her. "How can I live without you?"

She stayed in bed, caressing her body when he went to the bathroom. Later, he came in wearing a white boxer brief, and she watched him wearing his clothes. He wore navy jeans, a baby-blue shirt, a ginger sweater, a checked brown coat, cocoa-brown shoes, and a gray fedora. Sarah went to the bathroom and had a shower. After the shower, she asked him to come to her bedroom. He sat on the edge of the springy bed, ogling her. She looked at him with a charming expression on her face. After getting dressed, she sat on his knees, resting her arms on his shoulders, and kissing him.

"Do you think my wacky mom will kill me?"

"I think she will murder me first."

"I don't faze about what she would do and say about us. You are my heavenly lover. My happiness craves for you. Someday I will let the world know you are my dearest man. I love you, honey. Are you ready? We will eat outside."

They went out to Brooklyn and had breakfast in the River Café. Sarah sensed Albert's immense love when they talked about their marriage and strolled hand in hand to Brooklyn Bridge Park before taking a cab to Barbara's building.

Sarah rang the doorbell of Barbara's apartment. The door opened. "Why is it dark here?"

"Surprise! Happy Birthday." Barbara and her four women guests cheered and sang the Happy Birthday song.

After the birthday party, Albert and Sarah returned to the apartment. The phone buzzed.

"Happy Birthday, sweetheart."

"Thanks, mom."

"I called you ten times. Where have you been?"

"Out with friends and Barbara."

"I got gifts for you. Come tomorrow."

"I will come with a foreign friend to catch up over lunch. Is that okay?"

"No problem, love."

"I will talk to you tomorrow. Bye. I love you."

Sarah smiled with an impish grin. "My mom will have a heart attack when she sees you in her home. Please, do not tell her about our engagement. I do not need trouble now."

The next day morning, Albert reaffirmed his love for her. "We have agreed to get married. No one will break us apart. I promise. You have my full love and support. Let us see the big chief."

"I thought of what I said to you yesterday. Can you tell

my mom about our engagement and marriage? I am too terrified to talk to her. She might kill me.”

“Don’t live in fear. I am with you.”

Albert sat in the car. “Darling, can you stop at a flower shop? I want to get your mother a bouquet.”

“Sure.”

While passing through Stamford, Sarah stopped the car in front of a flower shop on Bedford Street. Albert walked into the shop and bought a posy of red and white roses.

“They are lovely.”

“This red rose is for you.”

They entered Darien. When they were a hundred yards away from Hannah’s house, Sarah stopped the car.

“That’s my mom’s house over there. I will go first to see her. Do not let her see you. You knock on the door after I get in.”

Albert left Sarah, who parked the car beside the house garage. Her mother opened the main door and stood on the top of the front steps.

“Hi, mom. I am here.” She waved.

“Hello, gorgeous. How are you, love? I miss you so much.” Hannah kissed her and gave her a warm hug. “Come in, sweetheart.”

When Hannah closed the door, the bell rang.

“Oops!” Hannah opened the door. “Yes.”

Albert tipped his hat and bowed. “Good morning, madam.”

With a stoic gaze, Hannah vibrated and put her shaky hands on her dazed face. “Oh, my God! Oh, my God! Albert. Albert.” She stretched her arms toward him, kissed his face, and gave him a tight hug.

“Oh, darling, come in. Come in. It is so good to see

you again. Look at you, man. Nothing has changed, just a few white hairs here." She glared at her daughter. "Did you say he is a foreign friend? I will spank your stinky butt after a while. Why didn't you tell me Albert is here?"

Sarah laughed. "He is here now."

Albert gave Hannah the roses, and she held his left hand. "Please, sit. I am so happy to see you. Do you like tea or coffee?"

"I like tea, please."

Sarah saw her mother's tearful eyes after they entered the kitchen. "Mom, are you well?"

"Yes, I am well. Oh, my God. I cannot believe Albert is in my house. When did he come to America?"

"A few days ago."

"Where did he stay?"

"He stayed with me."

"Good girl. Did he say anything about me?"

"He is eager to speak to you."

"I still love him. I cannot forget him. Don't tell him that." After saying these words, she saw a gold necklace hung around Sarah's covered neck. "This is a beautiful necklace."

"Albert gave it to me." Sarah's left hand touched the necklace. Her mother held her hand when she noticed the diamond ring on her finger. "When did you get this ring?"

"Albert bought it for me for my birthday."

"He adores you, doesn't he?"

"I think so."

After they prepared the tea, Sarah sat beside Albert, and Hannah rested on another couch.

"How are you, Albert? What about Olivia? How is your family?"

"We are well. Olivia is in her final year in the school."

Hannah's eyes became teary. "It is so wonderful to see you here in my house. Why did you come to America?"

"I came to see you. Didn't you miss me?" He smiled. "I came to deliver lectures at Columbia University."

"That's good. How did this girl treat you?"

"She has starved me."

"She is a naughty girl."

"Stop it, both of you. We have had the best food in the town."

"Sarah is very benevolent and caring. We have had an interesting time together."

"Good, good. There is a chicken in the oven. We will have chicken for lunch."

"That's brilliant. So, how are you? How are you doing?"

"I am fine. This is my hometown, and this is our home. I still work with Yale University."

Sarah held Albert's hand. "Come on. Let me show you the house ... This is the kitchen ... Here is a bathroom ... This is the office, and this is our library ... This is the swimming pool ... A gym room ... Let us go upstairs ... This is my mom's bedroom ... This is my bedroom, and these are photos of you ... Two bedrooms are here ... This is another bathroom ... Do you like to make love to me here?" She laughed.

"No, I am not dying to make love to you. We made love last night. Behave. We are in your mother's house."

They descended the stairs. "You have a beautiful house. I like the contemporary homes in America. The new houses in Scotland have small rooms and low roofs. I love big rooms with high ceilings."

"The houses in this area are large. My husband bought this house two months before we got married. I love it and love its scenic location, though it is far away from the university. A stream is in front of the house, and a park is in the backyard."

Albert touched a framed picture on the stone chimney-shelf. "Is this Michael?"

"Yes."

"He was a handsome man. Sarah inherited the shape of his lips and chin."

"He is in heaven. Shall we have lunch?"

"Let me give you a hand."

Sarah smiled. "I am your honored guest. Both of you must serve me."

Hannah looked at Albert's face. "What happened to the girl?"

"I have no idea. We will find out a final solution for her after lunch."

Hannah and Albert entered the kitchen and hugged each other for ten seconds. Hannah put a hand on his face and kissed his lips. "I love you. Thanks for coming."

"I love you too. I am happy to reconnect with you. Is there anything you want to tell me?"

"Be yourself and enjoy your wonderful life. I will go abroad for a one-year sabbatical leave. I hope to see you after I come back."

Albert brought a tray of roast chicken and baked vegetables, and Hannah fetched China plates, silver forks, stainless steel table knives, a bottle of Grgich Hills red wine, and three glasses.

Sarah sat next to Albert, and her right hand touched his left thigh under the table. Hannah sat on the opposite side. They ate and discussed food choices, the weather, Connecticut, New York, and Scotland.

Hannah placed her knife and fork on her plate. "What should we do on this wintry day?"

"You can show me your county and its surrounding areas and beaches."

"That's fine. We will take Sarah's car. How was her driving?"

"She is an excellent driver when she drives 120 miles per hour."

"Thanks for the compliment! Get out and sit in the car before I kick something."

Albert laced up his shoes a little tighter. "I am ready to go."

"Mom, wait for a while. I want to introduce Albert to Julie. Albert, Julie is my best friend. She was my schoolmate for twelve years." She and Albert held each other's hand and walked to Julie's house, a detached mansion surrounded by swamp oak trees.

Sarah knocked on the door. "Open the door, sassy girl."

Julie opened the door and clinched Sarah. "Oh, my gosh! Hello, sexy devil! I missed you very much. Come in and give me a big kiss."

Sarah kissed Julie's lips. "This is Albert Russell."

"Is he ...?"

"Yes, he is," she interrupted.

"Hi, Albert. How are you? Please, come in. This is my mom, Andrea."

"Hi," Albert said.

Andrea shook Albert's hand and kissed Sarah's face. "Please, have a seat. Do you want tea or coffee?"

"Nothing. Thanks. My mom and we are going out. We have popped in to say hello and introduce you to Albert, or I should say, Professor Albert Russell. He is our sweetheart and something else."

"Are you on holiday?"

"I came to deliver lectures at Columbia University and see Sarah and her mother."

"Sarah mentioned you live in Scotland. It is one of the fascinating places we wish to see."

"You are welcome to visit. Give me a shout."

"Thank you."

"We have to go. Julie, I will call you on Monday."

Albert and Sarah left Julie's house and came back home. Three minutes later, Albert sat in the back seat behind Sarah and requested Hannah to sit in the passenger seat beside her daughter. Sarah looked in the car mirror to see Albert and winked.

They went to nearby coastal towns before Sarah parked the car in downtown New Haven. They walked around the city and ended up in a restaurant where they had a nutritious dinner.

Hannah's eyes were weepy most of the day. "Mom, are you well?"

"Yes. I am so happy to see both of you."

They returned home. "Mom, we must go now. Albert's flight is in the morning."

Hannah kissed and thanked them for visiting her.

Sarah drove the car with an unsettling feeling of what might happen because Albert did not tell Hannah about the engagement. "You asked my mom random questions, which reminded her of my dad. Why didn't you tell her about our relationship?"

"It is a long story. I need to protect you."

"Protect me? From what?"

"From your mom."

"Why? My mom loves me so much. She told me in the kitchen she still loves you. What's going on?"

"Yes, your adorable mom loves me, but she feels guilty of duplicity in her private life."

"What are you talking about?"

"She contrived a plan to reconnect with me and get me involved in things related to you."

"Is this a puzzle? I do not understand. She saw the diamond ring on my finger."

"What did you say?"

"I said you gave it to me on my birthday. My mom sensed I am in love with you."

"Darling, I want to close my drained eyes and take a nap. Many things are jerking up and down in my heart." Albert closed his eyes and thought of Ann Stone, who said to him, "You are right about Michael Rogers."

In the Manhattan apartment, Sarah wore an ivory camisole and brushed her hair before standing before Albert, who was in an introspective mood. "Are you OK, love? Did my mom say something to you?"

"Wait here for a moment." He went to her bedroom and fetched a framed picture of Michael Rogers. "Come here, darling." She sat beside him on a couch, and he put his right arm on her shoulders. "Do you recall when my dad came to Scotland and asked you about your father and family?"

"Yes, I do."

"Please, I beg you to be calm and brave."

"Why?"

"Because Michael Rogers was not your father."

She put her hands on her face when she heard Albert's disturbing affirmation. "What's this you say?"

"I have been thinking of your relationship with Michael, your alleged father, since our engagement. Michael's photos in your mom's house have confirmed what I doubted for some time."

"Alleged father? What do you mean?"

Albert held Michael's framed photo. "Look at this photo. You do not look like him."

"Yes, I do not look like him. I am a woman."

"Michael had blue eyes and blonde hair, and your mom has blue eyes and golden hair. You have hazel eyes and light brown hair. Why didn't your mom make a comment when I said you inherited the shape of Michael's lips and chin?"

"I am not an expert in genetics. Barbara's eyes are not blue."

"When did Michael die?"

"He died in 1981."

"In which month?"

"I don't know."

"Switch on the computer and type Michael's name."

Sarah sat at a desk after turning on a computer and typed "Michael Rogers."

Albert stood behind her chair, bowing his head near her right ear, and staring at the computer monitor. "Type his name and the name of his father."

Sarah typed "Michael Henry Rogers."

"Scroll down ... Check out this one."

She clicked the mouse button and put her left forefinger on the computer screen. "*The Boston Globe* newspaper says my dad died in a car crash on Thursday, April 9, 1981.”

“If he died on April 9, how were you born on February 23?”

“I don’t understand.”

Albert got a blue ballpoint pen and a white paper and did mathematical calculations. “There were 320 days between Michael’s tragic death and your birthday. If Michael impregnated your mom on the day of his death, your birthday would not have been on February 23. I do not think your mom was pregnant for 320 days.”

“Oh, my God. What are you saying?”

“I say normal pregnancy lasts about 280 to 300 days, not 320 days. I am sure now that Michael was not your biological father.”

Sarah gazed at Albert’s musing face with a puzzled expression. “Unbelievable! This is a serious matter. We can’t accuse my mom of lying without evidence.”

“Your mom has a kind, simple heart, but she is hiding a significant secret to protect herself and you. Do you remember when she said in Sri Lanka that someday I would thank her for doing many things for me and she wishes to have the courage to talk about an important matter? Did she have an affair after Michael’s death?”

“I don’t think so. Barbara and Michael’s family love my mom very much.”

“Maybe your mom had adopted you.”

“I suspect that. Barbara and my four grandparents were with my mom when she gave birth to me in a New Haven hospital. My birth certificate says she is my mom and Michael is my dad. My mom loves me very much. Why would she lie about my real dad?”

"This is weird. Either your mom had, say, a one-night stand, or someone forced her to have sex with him."

"Oh dear. What should I do?"

"Don't tell anyone, including Barbara and your mom, about this matter. My best friend and your teacher, Edward Said, is suffering from terminal leukemia. His wife, Mariam, is a wonderful woman. They know you are my fiancée. I will give you their phone numbers and address. They have a son and a daughter. Contact them if you need emotional support." Albert opened his black wallet and gave Sarah a card. "Please, talk to Ann Stone if you want to know specific information about the Rogers family. Ann is my top confidante and the head of the investigative unit of *The New York Times*. Please, be cautious and do your undercover investigation. I will do my research and keep you updated."

Later, they listened to soft music and fondled each other. Albert realized Sarah would feel apprehensive and lonely after his departure to Scotland. He advised her to go to college, mingle with good friends, and get involved in justice and peace activities. "Darling, the happy life is to love yourself and live for others." He paused for ten seconds. "Do you like to invite me for a drink in a quiet bar in the town?"

"Of course, love. I will put on my boots and coat."

They went out to a restaurant bar on West 35th Street in Midtown Manhattan and talked about their emotions, marriage, Hannah, Olivia, and Barbara, and had a drink of vodka cocktails. A barmaid stared at a TV screen and saw images of Albert when he was at the airport. A news anchor said that the airport security cameras could not display the Anonymous warriors who protected Albert and caused damage to the airport. The barmaid went to a bartender. "Look at the TV." She pointed at Albert. "That's the guy who works for Anonymous. We should call the cops."

"Wait here." The bartender entered a back room and held a phone. A female Anonymous warrior, wearing a silver metallic dress, appeared and smashed the phone with her fist. The bartender quavered. "I am sorry. Please, do not hurt me." The warrior grabbed his shoulder and stared at his eyes. "Don't call the cops and do not cry, little man." She disappeared.

Upon returning to the warm apartment, a surge of restlessness and agitation gripped Sarah, rendering her jittery and tetchy. Stripping the layers that shielded her vulnerability, she implored Albert to sleep with her in her bedroom. He eased into a semblance of relaxation, while her eyes darted toward him several times, as if seeking reassurance of his presence.

As the weight of the night pressed upon her, she couldn't help but steal a kiss in the quietude of his slumber. Memories of their intimate love flooded her mind, juxtaposed against the looming specters of academic responsibilities and impending graduation. The urgency to refocus on her studies bore down on her, demanding answers to the hows and whens.

Yet, in the night's stillness, a far more profound turmoil had stirred within her. Thoughts of Michael Rogers not being her biological father had clawed at the edges of her consciousness, a traumatic revelation she must grapple with. The deception woven by her mother over the years had unfurled like a dark tapestry, leaving her entangled in a web of questions without simple answers.

How would a young woman like her forget or endure such a seismic truth? The echoes of betrayal had reverberated through her thoughts, casting shadows over her identity and familial ties. Why doesn't love come with easy happiness? Despite this anguish, she believed Albert was the only man she loved. She continued to think of him. Imagine a physician says you have only seven hours to live. You count the minutes and the seconds. "Ah! Albert will leave me after six hours ... Ah! Albert will leave me after five hours."

In the morning, they had a hurried breakfast. Sarah hugged him and cried on his shoulder before they left the apartment. With tears, her gnawing heart entreated and whimpered. "My love, please, do not leave me. Please, do not forget the woman who loves you. You are the only man I love. Do not desert me and break my heart. My love, let me go with you. I have found love in you and with you. Is our life about work and money? How can you leave me? How can you turn your back on your love? What kind of heart do you have? Nobody will love me after you go away. Who will kiss me after you leave? Who will hold my hands as you do? I will miss your smiling lips, your glowing face, your love ..."

They arrived at JFK International Airport, and their eyes were red and tearful. Sarah hugged Albert and kissed his lips for two minutes. They cried, and when Albert went through the security checkpoint, she followed him and yelped. "Albert, I love you. Come back, love. Come back." Albert turned his face and wiped his tears. She jumped over a stanchion and ran toward him, but two security guards stopped her.

When Albert gave his British passport to a female

immigration officer, a secret agent asked her to let him go. Albert felt relieved because he did not want the Anonymous warriors to start a fight and harm innocent people.

With a ruptured heart and wretched eyes, Sarah returned to the apartment and had no desire to eat or read or do anything. She did not even call her mother to talk about Albert's departure. After wearing a cap sleeve tunic, she got a glass of rose wine and listened to love songs by Chely Wright, Deana Carter, Martina McBride, LeAnn Rimes, Tracy Chapman, Melissa Etheridge, Trisha Yearwood, and Shania Twain. She remembered her hugs, kisses, and love, and slept in her bedroom. That was the longest and saddest day of her life.

In Scotland, Olivia and her grandparents were blissful to see Albert, who told them about his cosmic love for Sarah and exquisite lectures at Columbia University. In the evening, John and Janet told Albert and Olivia about their desire to go back to England on the following day.

Albert phoned Olivia's school in the morning and said his daughter would not go to her class on that day. He asked Olivia to stay at home to say goodbye to her grandparents. "Olivia, darling, I want you to stay with me today. I need to talk to you about a crucial matter."

"What about the school?"

"I have phoned the school and said you wouldn't attend your classes because I am not well."

"Why? What is going on? You look exhausted and abstracted. Did somebody hurt your feelings?"

"No. I will tell you the matter after we say goodbye to your grandparents."

After breakfast, Albert and Olivia hugged and kissed

Janet and John Russell and wished them a safe journey to England.

"Olivia, come with me." Albert held her hand and took her to his office. She sat on his thighs after he rested on a brown couch. "I want to tell you a secret. Michael Rogers was not Sarah's biological father. I told Sarah that fact. She is distressed and enraged."

"How did you know that? Why didn't the lewd bawd tell Sarah about her real dad?"

"It is a lengthy tale. God knows how I feel about Sarah. Please, darling, Sarah loves you and needs you. Call her."

Olivia cried and kissed her father. "I love you and know how you feel about all of us. I lived all my life with you. No one knows you as I do."

In her wallpapered bedroom, Olivia gazed at a mounted picture of Sarah and became despondent. An hour later, she called Sarah. "How is the raffish trollop? I heard your louche dad was a migrant from Mars. I love you, stinky face." They cried.

"I love you too, honey. Yes, my invisible dad was a shameless lecher from Mars. Please, love, take care of your dad. He is a genius with a big heart. Why didn't anybody tell me about my biological dad? Thanks to your dad, who discovered the truth."

"Don't worry about my dad. Both of us need him. Poor you and dad. Thank God you did not get a heart attack when my dad told you about Michael. Anyway, we will come to America after I finish my exams and kick your fetid arse."

"Yeah, I need a big kick in the ass. I want to tell you a secret. I wept when I made love to your dad. It was like losing my virginity and total privacy. I did not allow him to look at my vagina. I describe your dad as a male lesbian.”

“Ha! So, you have two lesbian lovers? Did you cheat on your first lesbian girlfriend?” Olivia chortled.

“I don’t know. I love you and can’t wait to see you again.”

“So, there will be no more sex between us?”

“I wish to make love to you right now. We can use dildos and vibrators.”

“Did you tell my dad about our sexual shenanigans?”

“No. Thank heaven.”

“Keep it a secret between us.”

“I will. Did your dad tell you about our marriage?”

“No. Congratulations, honey. When and where are you getting married?”

“We will get married in England after I finish the exams.”

“Great. I will be so happy to be your stepdaughter. I must see my dad. His voice is mute. I love you.”

“I love you too. Give your dad lots of hugs and kisses from me. Bye, honey.”

A quarter of an hour later, the phone rang in Sarah’s apartment. “Good morning, darling.”

“Oh, love, I am so glad to hear your voice. Last night was the longest night of my entire life.” She paused and wept.

“I love you. Let your lonely nights produce your most glorious thoughts.”

“Sorry, love, I don’t want to upset you. You know my heart.”

Albert talked to Sarah about his immense love for her and requested her to go to college on that day. She went to her university classroom and had no desire to read a book or talk to a friend. She was so flustered and incensed that she could not understand what her lecturers said. Her physical body was at Columbia University, but her soul and mind were with Albert and Olivia in Scotland.

In the evening, Sarah called her best friend Julie. "Good evening, Julie."

"Hello, babe. What a lovely little surprise! Where are you calling from?"

"I am in my apartment. Could I ask you a favor?"

"Yes. What can I do for you?"

"Could you tell your dad I want a DNA test?"

"What? Why do you want a DNA check?" She reacted with a surprised look. "Honey, what happened? Tell me, did somebody commit a crime?"

"No. There is no crime. The DNA test has something to do with my mom."

"With due respect, your mom is an eccentric weirdo. My dad's head office is on State Street in New Haven."

"Can I see him in New York? I don't want my mom or her friends to see me driving in Connecticut."

"I will call you back after ten or fifteen minutes."

Ten minutes later, the phone rang. "I have talked to my dad about the DNA test. He will come to your apartment on Saturday at eleven o'clock."

"Does he know where I live?"

"Yes, he does."

"Thank you, honey. Please, tell nobody about the DNA thing. You are the best of all. My life without you would be like a blazing inferno. I will see you soon and have a special chat with you."

On Saturday morning, Sarah met Julie's father, Dr. John Palmer, a giant bearded man with gray, short hair.

"Hello, Sarah."

"Hi, John. Please, have a seat."

"How are you doing in New York? How is your mom?"

"My mom and I are fine. I am doing well in college."

"What can I do for you?"

"I hope you can examine my DNA. I want to be certain Michael Rogers was, or was not, my biological father. Please, do not tell my mom or any member of my family about this matter."

Dr. Palmer rubbed his beard. "This is strange. Your family and friends know Michael was your father."

"But he died on April 9, and I was born on February 23. Why didn't anybody think of this matter?"

"I see. I forgot the name of the investigative journalist-I think his name was Peter Stone-who said Michael's death was not an accident. This influential journalist argued that Michael had arranged to expose official money laundering through bank accounts. After that, some shooters killed Peter, and the FBI did not investigate his allegations."

"Unbelievable. Did my mom have an affair after Michael's death?"

"I am not sure. Andrea was with her most of the time. Your mom lived on her own all her life after Michael's death."

"Strange. How could she become pregnant? Please, do not tell my mom about the DNA test."

"I understand." Dr. Palmer opened a dark bag and got a cotton stick and put it on the backside of Sarah's gum for fifteen seconds. He took a sample of her blood from her index finger. "That's it." Dr. Palmer picked up an official paper. "You need to sign this paper to allow us to examine Michael's DNA. We will exhume his body if necessary. We need your approval."

"No problem." Sarah got a pen and signed the paper.

"I will contact you after I get the result of the tests."

A fortnight later, Dr. Palmer called Sarah. "I am in New York. Can I see you this evening?"

"Yes, you can."

"I will see you around five o'clock."

At ten to five, Dr. Palmer rang the doorbell of Sarah's apartment. Sarah kissed his face. "Please, come in."

Dr. Palmer sat on a sofa in the living room and gave Sarah a flavescent envelope. "Here is the report of the DNA tests."

Sarah opened the envelope and read this statement,

Dear Ms. Sarah Rogers,

The DNA analysis has proved that Mr. Michael Rogers was not your biological father. Please, contact me if you have any concerns.

Sincerely yours,

Dr. John Palmer.

In an emotional embrace, Sarah clung to Dr. Palmer, seeking solace in the refuge of his chest. Unrestrained tears flowed down with a torrent of emotions. Dr. Palmer, with a compassionate touch, gave her white tissue papers to staunch the cascade of sorrow. Her anguished moans resonated in the room, making her unable to find the strength to stand, as the weight of her emotions left her vulnerable and unsteady.

"Who is my dad?"

"I don't know. We do not recall your mom had a partner after Michael's death. I think she had a secret affair."

"How would I know my real dad?"

"Does your mom have a secret relationship with a man?"

"No. My mom's best friends are women."

"We need to know Michael's close friends. I guess one of them had a brief affair with your mom."

"Why didn't my mom tell me about my real dad?"

"Michael was a wealthy man, and your mom was a young girl when he died. So, I think your mom was too fearful to speak the truth and make serious troubles with Michael's influential family or with her Catholic parents. She lived on the inherited wealth before she got a job at Yale."

"What should I do?"

"Get me photos of Michael's friends. Be vigilant and don't let anybody see what you do."

Dr. Palmer left the apartment, and Sarah called Albert. "You are right. Michael was not my dad. I have no dad. What more can I do? I love you. You are the most wonderful lover in the world. I want to be with you forever. Please, do not leave me. I need your hugs and your love. My existence is incomplete without you. You are my love and soul."

"Sweetheart, I am the happiest man because of your love. I am so fortunate to have you in my life. I love you and will always love you. No one in this insane world will take you away from me. Words cannot describe how I feel now. Thanks to God for you. Thanks to God, who has given me the sweetest woman I adore. You mean so much to me. Be patient for a short while. Focus on your studies and let us get married after you complete the exams."

"Yes, let us get married in May. I can't wait to be your wife."

Five minutes later, Sarah called Barbara. "Aunt, can I see you tomorrow in the afternoon? I want to tell you a private matter."

"You can. We will have dinner together."

The next day, Sarah visited Barbara. "It is so lovely to see you."

"Thank you."

With eager eyes, Sarah looked at the new surrealistic oil paintings on the walls. "They are magnificent and romantic."

"I love the paintings that help me contemplate, envision people, and think of fresh stories. Do you like tea or coffee?"

"I need a glass of wine. Crazy things are raging in my groggy head."

"We will drink wine." They went to the kitchen.

"Red or white?"

"Red, please."

Barbara opened a wooden cupboard and drew a bottle of Californian red wine from an oak rack. Sarah lifted her glass. "Cheers."

"Cheers."

Sarah cried after she took a sip of wine.

"Oh, darling, what's wrong?"

Sarah placed her glass on a table and picked up Dr. Palmer's letter from her satchel purse. "Read this."

Barbara put her glass on the table and unfolded the

letter. "Jesus Christ! Oh, my God! Wasn't my brother your biological father? Is this a joke? How did this happen?"

"Your brother died on April 9, and I was born on February 23. I guess my mom had an affair after the death of your brother. I had no idea about all that."

"Oh, my God! Your mom had always been single. All her close friends have been women. What should I say about this dissipated woman? I don't believe she had deceived us all these years. I have been her best freaking friend since I introduced her to my brother. And you Sarah ..." She cried, and Sarah squeezed her and wept as well.

"I must call your depraved mom and berate her. This is a scandal."

"Please, aunt, do not speak to her."

"Why? I am not afraid of her."

"Just ignore her. Albert and I will get married after I finish the exams. I want you to be with me."

"Are you getting married? You are still a student."

"Albert adores me, and his love is the main thing."

"He is a great man, and you need to be strong. Does he know Michael was not a father?"

"Yes. He who told me about my mom's deceit."

"Oh, dear! Let us have something to eat before we burst out with all sorts of nonsense and kill somebody. I have cooked macaroni."

During the dinner, Sarah asked Barbara not to tell Hannah about her engagement and future marriage.

The next morning, Sarah pulled out Ann Stone's business card from her purse and remembered Dr. John Palmer, who said the investigative journalist Peter Stone believed criminals had killed Michael Rogers. She also recalled Olivia, who said Ann is her half-sister's mother and Albert's occasional secret lover. She made a phone call.

"Hi, Ann. I am Sarah Rogers."

"Hello, Sarah. How are you doing?"

"I am all right. Can I see you in person?"

"Yes, of course."

"When?"

"Can you see me today at 5 pm?"

"Yes, I can. Where can I see you?"

"At 131 Duane Street. I am on the third floor."

At five, Sarah was in Ann's apartment. She sat in a room surrounded by wood bookcases and ogled Ann's beautiful face and hair.

Ann, a woman aged forty-two with a Russian heritage, has striking blue eyes and golden blonde hair cascading down to her shoulders. Her attire consisted of a batwing top with white-gray stripes paired with a dark broomstick skirt. "Nice to see you. How are you doing?"

"I am doing well."

"Best wishes on your engagement. Albert told me the pleasant news."

"Thank you."

"When are you going to get married?"

"After the exams in May."

"Great. Shall we go to the dining table?"

After sitting at a walnut table, Ann held her wooden chopsticks. "Albert told me you like Southeast Asian food. So, I cooked egg-fried rice and chicken curry."

"That's fantastic. How do you know Albert?"

"Nobody knows Albert as I do. I first saw him in

England when he was one year old. My dad and granddad were close friends of Albert's grandfather Bertrand Russell and his family. I saw Albert for the second time in 1967 when my dad and granddad met Bertrand Russell and released a statement against the war on Vietnam. I then met Albert in Wales in February 1970 when Bertrand Russell died. Albert was nine or ten years old. We became friends and loved each other. Six years later, I gave birth to our daughter Ayita. Albert always stayed with Ayita and me in this apartment when he came to New York."

"Did you meet Bertrand Russell?"

"Yes, I met him three or four times when he was in his nineties. As I have said, he was one of my dad's best friends."

"Did your dad love Albert?"

"Oh yes, very much. My father called Albert every week. They worked together on many projects and opposed the U.S. military intervention in Central and South America."

"What did your dad do?"

"He was a scientist and inventor of robotics."

"What do you know about my family?"

"The CIA killed my eighty-one-year-old grandfather and grandmother in 1989, a day after they met your mom. The CIA thought my granddad knew something about Michael Rogers. A year later, the CIA murdered my dad and mom. That's why Albert cares much about me."

"Sorry to know that. That is horrible. Did the cops catch the killer?"

"They were six or seven killers. The mysterious assassin Homatakawa Tamojika executed five of them when they were outside the U.S. and said he assassinated them because they killed my parents and grandparents."

"Who is Homatakawa? How did he know who killed your parents and grandparents?"

"No one knows him. Maybe a CIA insider had told him about the hitmen's operations."

"The CIA?"

"Yes. Homatakawa said the hitmen who murdered my parents and grandparents were CIA operatives."

"Why did my mom meet your granddad?"

"She wanted to know the truth about the death of her husband. My grandad said officials had killed Michael and told your mom he gave somebody important documents related to Michael's death."

"Was Albert involved in this matter?"

"Not really. My grandfather trusted Albert and admired his intellectual integrity and struggle against injustice."

"What about my mom?"

"As I have said, the CIA murdered my grandfather after he met your mom. I thought your mom had taken part in his murder. Therefore, I investigated your mom and the Rogers family."

"What did you find out?"

Ann's right hand rubbed Sarah's left arm. "Can you keep a secret?"

"Yes, I can."

"Your mother is an undercover agent. She works for the CIA and other intelligence agencies."

Sarah gazed at Ann's face with burning eyes. "Oh, my God!"

"Please, do not misunderstand me. Your mother is a good woman. She joined the CIA to know the truth and protect Albert."

"Protect Albert? Why?"

"Because CIA agents pursue him."

"Why? What did he do?"

"He did nothing. CIA operatives thought Albert got secret documents from my grandpa. Homatakawa and the Anonymous killed many of these operatives."

"Oh, my God! But my mom loves Albert very much."

"That's another story. In 1995, federal agents searched my apartment and looked for classified files. Your mom knew about this matter and visited India. She went there to know the truth and protect Albert."

"Was my mom his secret bodyguard? I don't think my mom had spied on Albert. She adores him. They had sex everywhere."

"I recognize that, but we dwell in a complex world where interests collide. I need a favor from you."

"What is it?"

"Your mom will leave the country after a month. She hides stacks of classified documents in the basement of her house. I need some important documents. You will stumble on staggering information."

A red-haired, green-eyed, athletic woman in her mid-twenties entered the apartment and kissed Ann's lips. Sarah looked at the feather tattoo on her left wrist.

"Ayita, this is Sarah, your dad's fiancée."

"Hi," Ayita said and shook Sarah's hand with a vague smile. "Mom, what did you cook tonight?"

"Egg-fried rice and chicken curry."

After proceeding to the kitchen, Ayita filled a wood bowl with food and retrieved two melamine chopsticks. In silence, she made her way to her bedroom, offering no words to Sarah.

Ann and Sarah continued their informal discussions about families and politics. Later, Ann took Sarah to a bedroom after she asked her to stay with her that night.

"This is Albert's favorite bed."

Sarah touched an old wooden dummy. "What is this machine?"

"This is a *muk yan jong* or a wooden dummy. Albert used it for his kung fu training."

"Were you Albert's girlfriend?"

Ann smiled. "Albert had never had a girlfriend. He is like the goldfinch that sings on many trees."

"But he is your daughter's dad, and he had lovers. My mom was one of them."

"That's true, but he had never called his women lovers girlfriends. For philosophical reasons, he thinks the word girlfriend is derogatory to women. Please, Albert doesn't sleep around, though he loves his women friends. Do not cage him if you want to have a good relationship with him. He adores you and will never thwart you from doing what you want. That's enough for today. Good night."

A month later, Hannah started her one-year sabbatical and traveled overseas to do research work on the native peoples of New Zealand, Australia, Papua New Guinea, and the Solomon Islands. Sarah seized her mother's absence to search through their house in Darien. She remembered Ann's private conversation and how her mother had never allowed her to go down to the basement. After opening and closing every drawer in the house, Sarah could not find the key to the basement door. Therefore, she asked a locksmith to come to the house and unlock the door.

After getting a new key, Sarah switched on a light and descended the narrow stairs to the large basement, which appeared like a research library. There were eight high steel shelves, loaded with books, magazines, newspapers, archive boxes, and lever arch files, and six silver file cabinets attached to two walls. Sarah walked around, pulled out a top drawer, and found colored, labeled folders arranged in alphabetical order. She opened files and inspected clips of official letters, newspapers, journals, and miscellaneous reports about banks, politicians, businesspersons, journalists, and corporate firms. Later, she unlocked a bottom drawer and discovered a folder that contained unposed photos of Albert Russell, when he was in his twenties and thirties, and snippets of his statements, interviews, and short essays published in newspapers and magazines. Another drawer had albums containing intimate pictures of her mother and her best friend Linda Jones, an outspoken lesbian scholar of psychology at New York University. These pictures proved Hannah and Linda were more than best friends. Another file cabinet preserved photographs of Michael Rogers and his relatives and friends. Filled with suspense and an awakened curiosity, Sarah spent over three hours trawling through her mother's classified files.

Chapter 9

After an exhaustive, painstaking scrutiny of classified documents extracted from the basement of Hannah's house, Albert and Sarah concluded that Hannah and Linda Jones were lesbian lovers. Hannah had been involved in undercover operations for the CIA and had sex with a man after the death of Michael Rogers. Frightened, addled, and aggravated, Sarah thought her mother was the major CIA operative who spied on Albert and supervised espionage operations against him when he was in Latin America, Asia, and Europe. She requested Albert to marry her soon to feel secure.

On Friday, May 25, 2001, Sarah, Barbara, Ann, Ayita, Julie, and Andrea arrived in London. Albert and Olivia transported them to the May Fair Hotel on Stratton Street. After dinner, Albert told them Dora and Olivia would guide and take them on an excursion to the capital.

He kissed Sarah. "Did you tell your mom about our wedding?"

"No."

"Why?"

"Barbara and I despise her. Why does she work for the CIA and the FBI? She betrayed everybody. She tricked me and lied about my dad."

"That is all right. I will see my adorable bride on Sunday."

On Sunday morning, a beautician, a hairdresser, and a fashion designer came to the hotel and made Sarah look like a flawless white angel. At eleven o'clock, Dora took the American guests to her father's Anglican church in Kingston upon Thames. Dressed in a navy blue suit, Albert stood on the top step of the church. He radiated with great geniality when he saw Sarah in a strapless wedding dress, exposing her pretty neck and shoulders. He kissed her hand, and both entered the nineteenth-century church. Albert sang in a muffled voice. "Here comes the bride dressed all in light. Radiant and lovely she shines in his sight."

Sarah smiled. "Be quiet."

Albert, Janet, Sarah, Olivia, Dora, and the American friends rested on the front pew. Over 120 British men, women, and children were in the church. Father John Russell welcomed them and asked Albert to stand at the pulpit and give a speech. After greeting his relatives and friends, Albert talked about Sarah's last visit to Scotland and her immense love for him. "I was a hermit in the earthly city of Edinburgh, but Sarah has opened the gates of heaven for me." He was heedful not to bring up his love relationship with Hannah.

With immense pride, Father John Russell conducted the wedding ceremony. "I now pronounce you husband and wife, in the name of the Father, and of the Son, and of the Holy Spirit. Amen." Albert and Sarah kissed each other and grinned.

After the ceremony, Albert, Sarah, and their guests returned to the May Fair Hotel and had a memorable wedding party.

The clock struck two in the eerie stillness of the night when Albert woke up and heard a cacophony of thuds and clunks emanating from the room above his bedroom. Alarmed, he stole a glance at his slumbering, half-naked wife before darting toward the closed window. Tension tightened his nerves as he yanked aside the curtain, revealing the moonlit scene outside.

As the curtain fluttered, a horrifying crash shattered the silence, echoing through the serenity of the night. Albert's senses heightened, capturing an unmistakable sound of glass shattering, accompanied by a subdued hubbub of screaming and shouting. His heart raced as he strained to discern the source of the commotion.

In the dim street below, the shadows played host to an unexpected spectacle. Two people, cloaked in dark suits, tumbled through the air, plummeting from a shattered window above. The sight unfolded in a twisted battle of chaos, culminating in a bone-chilling impact as the two people landed on Stratton Street with an unsettling thud. Albert clenched his fists, ready to confront the enigma that had breached the tranquility of his sleep.

"Albert, why are standing at the window?"

"There was a loud noise. Two men fell on the street."

"Come to bed. We need to rest before the flight."

Albert moved to the bed and hugged his bride. A minute later, they heard sirens of ambulances and police cars coming closer to the hotel. Sarah pushed back her hair from her face. "What's going on?"

"Maybe some men had a fight."

On Monday, Albert, Sarah, Olivia, Dora, Barbara, Andrea, and Julie flew to Paris for what Albert called "a collateral honeymoon." A day later, Albert got an English newspaper and read about the Anonymous assassin who murdered a British secret agent and a U.S. spy in the May Fair Hotel. The paper did not reveal the identity of the killer, but it published a dim photo of a slim masked person. Albert stared at the picture and realized that the masked person was Tilatowate who protected Homatakawa in New York in 1995.

Two weeks later, Albert and Sarah flew to Miami and stayed in a hotel for a week doing what lovers do. They spent the next few weeks making love, exercising their fit bodies, shopping, and buying furniture for their new house in the village of Larchmont, in Westchester County, New York. In August, Olivia moved to the United States and lived with her father and stepmother in their home.

On the Sunday evening of September 9, 2001, Zita Marino interviewed Albert to get his views on the assassination of the Afghan military leader Ahmad Shah Massoud. After elucidating the military and political situation in Afghanistan, Albert made a startling statement that created a furor in the country. "Muslim terrorist attacks on the United States are imminent. The attacks will take place within seventy-two hours."

"Oh, my God! What are your sources?"

"Former students inform me about the Islamist groups

in Pakistan and Afghanistan."

"Where will the attacks take place?"

"The attacks will hit financial, political, and military centers. The radical terrorists want to bomb the World Trade Center in Manhattan, the White House, the State Department, the Pentagon, and the CIA headquarters. I informed the FBI about the matter. Senior CIA officials recognize this grievous issue, though nobody knows when the strikes will take place. I hope the authorities will take immediate steps to ward off the attacks."

After the interview, Albert visited Ann and asked her to publish classified documents on Muslim terrorism and the CIA's military plans in the Middle East. "Who gave you the documents?"

"The Che Guevara guy."

The next day, Albert, Sarah, and Olivia moved to a hotel in Philadelphia, and *The New York Times* published the classified documents, which exposed the U.S. army's plans to occupy and change the regimes in Afghanistan and Iraq and to threaten the geopolitical interests of Russia and Iran. Conservative media accused Albert of being "a fabricator of conspiracy theories."

Albert became a Distinguished Professor of religion and philosophy at Columbia University, the most controversial British philosopher in the United States, and an eloquent public speaker after the terrorist attacks on September 11, 2001. The secret lovers, Sarah and Olivia, continued their affair and enjoyed going together to the university. Leftist thinkers, activists, and journalists manipulated Albert's political prognostication and said the U.S. government, the Saudi government, and the CIA knew about the terrorist strikes in advance. Outraged CIA operatives charged Albert of being "a professor of terror." They watched his moves to figure out how he obtained classified documents from the CIA and the Pentagon headquarters.

On Saturday, October 13, Albert and Sarah visited Ann to dine with her. After dinner, Sarah entered a restroom, and Ann and Albert lay on a sofa in the living room. Albert glanced at an opposite mirror and jumped over Ann to shield her. A silent bullet pierced through a window and broke an Oriental vase. Ann yelled. "There is a gun under the couch."

"I don't need it."

Sarah opened the restroom door and saw Albert covering Ann with his body. "Albert, what's going on?"

"Stay in the bathroom. There is a sniper."

Albert crawled to the main door. With a quick, silent flick, he extinguished the lights, plunging the room into a shroud of shadows. Heart pounding, he raced to the rooftop, driven by an imperative urgency that gripped his alert senses.

As he swung open the door to the roof, the scene that unfolded before him was from the pages of a heart-stopping thriller. Tilatowate, obscured in the inky blackness, hurled lethal steel spikes with perfect precision toward an adjacent building. The spikes sliced through the air with a sinister intent, finding their mark on the neck of an unsuspecting gunman positioned on the opposite rooftop.

The night air crackled with tension as Tilatowate orchestrated a macabre dance of justice. In a swift and calculated move, Tilatowate followed the projectile assault by delivering a powerful flying kick to the chest of the incacitated gunman. The unfortunate assailant tumbled like a marionette with severed strings, crashing on the unforgiving surface of a parked car below.

As Tilatowate vanished into the shadows, Albert scampered downstairs and entered Ann's apartment. "Come here. It is over." He hugged Ann's back and kissed her neck. They looked at the street below and saw a dead man on a car with a rifle next to him.

Albert said rested his chin on Ann's shoulder. "Do not worry. I am with you."

"Who killed him?"

"Tilatowate. Sarah, come out now."

Sarah peeked at Albert when he hugged and kissed Ann. "What happened?"

"A sniper wanted to kill Ann and me."

"Why?"

"We don't know."

"Why don't you tell me the truth?"

"Which truth?"

"We got married five months ago. What's going on between you and Ann? You hugged and kissed her, and you are holding her hand. Why do you do such things in front of me? Is Ann your mistress?"

"Darling, sit here. We will tell you the truth. Ann ..."

Ann shut Albert's mouth with her hand. "Let me tell her the truth. Sarah, I told you Albert was my first and only boyfriend. You know he is my daughter's dad. The bad guys murdered my parents and grandparents. So, I lost my family. I have no sisters. I have no aunts and uncles. A psychopath wanted to kill me tonight. Albert hugged me to calm me down, not to have sex with me. Albert is the only man who cares for me." She sobbed out.

Sarah embraced her. "Oh, my God. I love you. I did not mean to hurt your feelings."

"I love you too. I hope you realize why I need Albert."

"Please, call us whenever you need us."

Albert gave her a kiss. "Thank you, darling. I stayed here when I visited New York to look after our daughter. As you have seen, hitmen want Ann dead because of her relationship with Jamie and Peter Stone."

"I am sorry." Sarah hugged Ann again. "It is so great to be with you. I love you."

"I love you too. Please hide your affair with Olivia. Keep it a secret."

Ann's unambiguous statement caused Sarah to blush and stammer. "What, how, how do you know? Did Olivia talk to you?"

"I am the best investigative journalist. Did you forget?"

"Tell me the truth. Who told you about me and Olivia?"

"One day, Albert saw you and Olivia make love in his Scottish apartment. On another occasion, he came back to his Larchmont home to get his wallet and heard laughter in the upstairs bathroom. He peeped through the keyhole and saw you and Olivia do lesbian things. You know what I mean."

Sarah nodded and felt ashamed of being unfaithful. "Albert, I am sorry. I cannot control my lesbian desire. I love Olivia. Please, forgive me."

"No problem. Do what you like with Olivia. Just keep the liaison a secret."

The following day, Ann received this text: "I Hope you and Albert are doing well. I killed the sniper. Bye for now. Tilatowate." In the evening, Albert visited her. "Why didn't you want me to tell Sarah the truth?"

"Are you insane? Did you want her to know I am your sister? Did you want to tell her your mom had an affair with our dad? She is too shallow to hold a secret and understand. What would happen if Ayita and Olivia knew I am your sister? You must keep in mind what the CIA criminals would do to you if they discovered you are my dad's son. Our war with the CIA is not over. You are the last man from the Stroganov family. Do we need a new bloody war with the Russian Mafia? We don't want the Anonymous to start another war front with the Russians. I love you, Albert. You are my everything." She put her right hand on his face and kissed him. Albert took her into his arms and kissed her.

When they fondled on a couch, Ayita came into the apartment and smiled when she saw them. "Mom, what are you doing? My dad is married now."

"So? You know I love your dad."

"I love him too." Ayita tickled her father and kissed him. "Dad, please, stay with us tonight. I miss you so much. My mom told me what happened yesterday."

"I wish to meet Tilatowate and thank him for saving our life. I still do not know why he and others protect us from the wicked men."

Hannah returned to Darien in May 2002. She drove to Flatiron District to see her daughter. After entering Sarah's apartment, she got a weird, vexatious feeling. The quiet, vacant apartment seemed like a ghost's sanctum. The closets and the bookshelves were empty. Feeling flustered and perturbed, she called Barbara's apartment, but Barbara was in Toronto promoting her new book. She called Julie, Sarah's best friend, but there was no answer.

She phoned Julie's mother, Andrea.

"Hi, Andrea. This is Hannah. I am back."

"Hello, honey. How are you? How was your work in Oceania?"

"I had a wonderful time there. It is a different world over there. I got gifts for you and Julie."

"Thanks."

"I am in New York. Where is Sarah?"

"She is in the last house on Pryer Lane in Larchmont Westchester County."

"What is the house number?"

"Two or three. It is a bright mansion overlooking the water."

Hannah paused for a moment. "Thanks, love. I must go. See you soon."

Forty minutes later, Hannah moved her car in low gear on Pryer Lane and scanned the sides of the narrow road. After a while, she stopped the car in front of a house when she saw her daughter cleaning and tidying up items on a windowsill.

"What is she doing here?" Tears filled her eyes before she left the car and knocked on the house door.

Sarah opened the door. "Hi, mom. When did you come back? Come in."

"Two days ago. I called you many times. Why is your apartment deserted? What are you doing here?"

"I am Albert's wife."

Hannah's blood boiled in her veins, and she became furious and aghast. "What? Albert's wife? When did you get married?"

"Last year."

"Last year? Are you an idiot? Why do you humiliate

me? Did you forget who I am? I am your mom, for God's sake. Don't you know what this means? I am your only parent and guardian. Why didn't you tell me about your marriage?"

"Because I know who you are. You are a big liar."

"Shut your mouth." She slapped Sarah's face and wrenched her ponytailed hair. "I have never ever lied to you. Why did you delude me? What have I done to you? You are an ignorant fool. You do not know the cruel world outside your home. Shame on you. Shame on you."

"You are hurting me. Stay away from me." After pushing her to the floor, Hannah kicked her backside and placed a knee on her waist. "You lied to me." She grabbed Sarah's left hand. "You said Albert gave you this ring on your birthday. Why didn't you tell me about the engagement and the marriage proposal? Why?"

"Do you beat me because I married Albert? Why didn't you tell me about your work for the CIA? I am your girl. Shame on me? Why did you spy on Albert? Why do you hate me? Who am I, mom? Who is my biological dad? Why didn't you tell me the truth?"

"What is this babble?"

"I looked at the official documents in the basement of our house. The FBI says Michael was not my dad."

"The FBI?"

"Yes, the FBI."

Hannah stood and rubbed her hands. "I have never said Michael was your biological dad."

"Why do you work for the CIA? How did you get old photos of Albert? Why did you spy on him? What were you looking for? Why didn't you tell me about Linda Jones and your affair with her? Could you imagine how I felt when I realized you work for the CIA? Do you have any idea how I slept when the FBI told me Michael was not my dad? I cried for so many nights. Thank God for Albert, who looked after me and made me happy."

After listening to her daughter's evocative common sense, Hannah soothed herself. "Sweetheart, I am sorry for hitting you. I love you. You are my only child. God knows how I nurtured you on my own. You went to the best schools. I showed many countries around the world and bought you expensive clothes, a good car, and an apartment in Manhattan. I pay for your education."

"Thanks for everything. This is my life now. I know who you are. Who is my dad? Who is my dad, mom?"

"You will know your dad after you divorce Albert."

"Are you mad? I will never divorce Albert. I love him so much."

"You can't be Albert's wife?"

"Why?"

"Because Albert is ..." Before she could complete her sentence, Albert entered the house with a smile. "What a pleasant surprise! My mother-in-law is in the house."

"Mother-in-law, stupid moron?" Her fists pounded his chest. "What did you do to my daughter, you son of a ...? This is ridiculous. Are you out of your mind? I was your girlfriend. You are older than I am. Am I now your mother-in-law? Why do you want to inflict pain on me?"

"Because you made a huge mistake. You should have trusted me when I was your lover. Try to be a good mother-in-law."

"You must divorce my daughter."

Sarah scowled. "You are a madwoman."

"Am I a madwoman?" Hannah tried to smack her, but

Sarah attacked her on the arm. "Come on. Hit me if you can. I will break your arm if you touch me."

"Pity on you. You are so stupid. Did Albert teach you martial arts to punch your mom?"

"I do not allow you to assault and yell at my wife."

"Shut up. Sarah is my daughter. Piss off. I ask you to annul your marriage to her."

"We don't live in the medieval ages. You are acting like a fascist dictator. Why are you here?"

"To tell my daughter the truth."

"You are a bestial liar. Albert, tell her the truth."

"Sarah is my love. I will never leave her."

"You cannot be Sarah's husband."

"Why? Did I violate any law?"

"Because you can't."

"Why? What are afraid of?"

Hannah sat in an armchair, broke down in tears, and covered her face with her hands. Her face turned reddish and wet. Her fingers rubbed the back of her neck. "Because, because you are my love. I have been a single woman all these long years because I love you. Yes, I love you, moron. I wept when you visited me last year. I thought you wanted me to be your partner once again, but you married my daughter without my consent. Are you a philosopher or a jerk? How dare you marry my daughter without my assent? I implore you to leave Sarah. Where is your rational judgment? Do you know any wise philosopher who married his girlfriend's daughter? She is too callow to be your wife. She is a student for God's sake."

"What is wrong with you?"

"Are you afraid of the truth?"

"Which truth? Why don't you tell Sarah about her real father?"

"Are you blind? Look at the color of her eyes and hair and look at the color of your eyes and hair. You are her dad."

"This cannot be possible."

"Why not? I was pregnant for ten months. I had sex with you and Michael. Did you forget our sex in Hong Kong?"

"You betrayed your family."

"Shut your mouth. I investigated your love affairs with other women. Did you tell Sarah about your long affairs with journalists? You had sex with other women when I was your girlfriend. So, stop your bullshit. You became a father when you were fifteen. Yes, you had sex with Ann Stone when you were fourteen. You continued to have sex with her even after your family did not allow you to marry her. Did you tell Sarah about your first daughter, Ayita? Did you tell her Ayita is a Victoria's Secret and *Vogue* model? Tell Sarah about your long liaison with Ann Stone and the other women."

"Ann Stone? You are paranoid and hypocritical," Sarah interrupted.

"Shut up, gink. Yes, Ann Stone. Albert sleeps with her. He slept with her in Scotland. So, keep your foul mouth locked. I am talking about your stupid and perverted marriage to my daughter."

Sarah elbowed Albert's chest and seized his right hand. "This woman is a dunce."

Hannah stood and caressed Albert's shoulders. "Tell Sarah how I was your first girlfriend in Hong Kong. Did you forget that?" She stared at her daughter. "I am your mom who has always loved you. God knows how I lived and worked after Michael's death. The CIA murdered Michael. I joined the CIA to bring his killers to justice. Do you think this was easy? God knows how I cared for you and guarded you. Why did you discomfit me? I sent you to Scotland twice to tell Albert about my love for him, but you seduced him and became his wife. Why didn't you tell Albert about my love for him? Why don't you appreciate what I have done for you?"

Albert felt embarrassed and guilty for not telling Hannah about his marriage to her daughter. His left fingers struck the armrest of a couch. "Please, tell us the truth."

Sarah glared at her mother. "You said you were Albert's first girlfriend in Hong Kong. We met him in India when I was thirteen. Do you remember that?"

"I had an affair with Albert when he was a junior."

Sarah pressed Albert's hand and frowned at his crestfallen face. "Did you have sex with my mom before I met you in India? Why didn't you tell me that? Why?"

"Your mother ..."

"Albert promised not to tell you about the affair when I was in his office in Hyderabad. He is a principled man. He will never break a promise."

"I do not understand your gibbering."

"Here is the truth. Michael Rogers was my best cousin. He was a smart and prosperous businessman. I loved him and thought his charm, integrity, and wealth would make me happy. I married him when I was eighteen. After we got married, I realized he adored his work more than anything else, though he worshipped me. Twenty years ago, we flew to Hong Kong because he had business over there. He spent his time with workaholic and thriftless entrepreneurs. I became friendless, though he gave me lots of cash to spend on whatever I needed. One day, I entered a McDonald's restaurant. After I got my meal, I looked around and could not get a vacant table. A young guy looked at me. 'You can sit at my table. Here is a seat for you.' I sat and thanked this young guy. He said, 'No problem. You are welcome. My name is Albert.'

I said, I am Hannah. I am an American. You do not look like the Chinese.

I smiled when Albert said, 'Do I have lidless eyes?'

I said I like your suit. What is it?

Albert said, 'This is a kung fu suit. I practice kung fu at a club here. You can come if you want.'

I said, can I see what you do?

He said, 'Yes, you can. You can learn tai chi if you are not interested in fighting.'

That is interesting, I said. Where is the club? How can I get there?

Albert said, 'I will take you there. It is not far away from here. I am going to the club tomorrow morning at ten o'clock. I will meet you at this restaurant. What do you think?'

That is wonderful. Where are you from? I said.

He replied, 'I am from England.'

I said, England? What do you do here?

He said, 'I am a student in the department of philosophy. What about you?'

I said I am a tourist.

The next day Albert and I visited the kung fu club, and I liked to learn tai chi. I told Michael I had found something that would keep me occupied. He did not mind.

Albert charmed me with his hospitality, intelligence, and goodness. One day, we went up to his apartment to shower and eat. We made love on that day, and I made love to him every day for three weeks.

I told Albert I had to leave Hong Kong and promised to see him again. I intended to divorce Michael and live with Albert in Hong Kong. But Michael died in a horrendous car accident, and I got pregnant.

After your birth, I said nothing about your dad. You have light brown hair and hazel eyes. I have bluish eyes and fair hair, and Michael had blue eyes and blonde hair. When people asked me about the color of your eyes, I said my Irish grandmother had hazel eyes.

I was eighteen when I became pregnant. And because I grew up in a strict Catholic family, I could not go to a clinic to abort or tell our families and friends about my love affair with Albert. It was impossible for me to say you were a love child. I inherited Michael's house and wealth, and my vocation was to care for you and meet Albert. I could not find Albert anywhere. He left Hong Kong, and there was no Internet in these days to search for him. I visited libraries and collected his articles, interviews, and photos which you saw in the basement. To my luck, Albert had a TV interview in New York in 1995, and I got his address in India. That is why I traveled to India. I went there to see Albert."

"Why didn't you tell me about Albert?"

"I was not sure about Albert's response, or about his love for you. You were young. But now I am certain he loves you, and you love him. I could not tell our family you were not Michael's biological daughter. I sent you to the best schools. You are now a student at a reputable university. I bought you an apartment in New York because of my good relationship with Michael's family."

"Who is my dad?"

"I think Albert is your dad."

"You think? Don't you know the man who made love to you?"

"Listen. We will do a DNA test and know your dad after you divorce Albert. Do you want me to go out of the house and say you are an illegitimate child?"

The words "illegitimate child" had infuriated Albert. "Do you underrate my intelligence? You cannot fool me anymore. I am not Sarah's dad. So, stop fabricating stories. I will never divorce Sarah. Do you understand?"

"I have told you the truth. Do you want to live the rest of your life in sin?"

"I do not believe in your Catholic sins. You swindled your husband and his reputable family. Michael was infertile. You wanted to inherit his wealth. A man had sex with you, and you became a mother to defraud everyone under the guise that Sarah is Michael's daughter. You falsified an official birth certificate, though Sarah was not Michael's daughter. You could go to prison for forgery. The FBI and your relatives know Sarah is not Michael's daughter. You have no right to tell me about groveling sins. You duped your daughter and me. Michael's family distrusts you."

"I swear, I have told you the truth."

Sarah frowned. "Am I Albert's daughter? You are a despicable idiot. What about Albert, the man you allege to love? What about his colleagues and family? What about me? What about my ... my ...?" She discontinued and cried. "What about Olivia? What would Albert say to his daughters and family? The world knows I am Albert's wife. Did I marry and have sex with my dad, you cheap hooker? Do you want Albert to divorce me because I am his daughter, as you say? Do you want Albert to leave me because he made love to a married harlot in Hong Kong? What would you say to my grandparents? What about my aunt Barbara, who loves me and always cares for us? Why do you want to ruin my heart and love? You are a selfish whore. You are a dipshit. You are a filthy goon. You are a depraved sociopath."

"Darling ..."

"Get lost, psycho. Leave me alone. I hate you. Get out of my house. Get out." Sarah ran upstairs to the bedroom and draped her quivering body across the bed, weeping with bitter umbrage. Doleful thoughts had roamed in her explosive head. She could not believe her mother, her best friend in the world, had hoodwinked her. She could not imagine her mother had lied about Michael for many years. Her doubtful demon whispered ribald things. Yes, her mother had always loved her and done wonderful things for her since she was born. The unthinkable became an unfortunate reality. Imagine a mother asks her married daughter to divorce her husband because she might be his illegitimate daughter. This excruciating nightmare would haunt her emotional life forever. How would she forget what her mother had said?

Hannah left the house and rested in her car, whining like a wounded soldier on a battlefield. Albert followed her and sat beside her. "Are you happy now?"

"Please, get out of my car."

"Your daughter is with me now. I will not leave you this time before you tell me the whole truth."

She rested her hands on the steering wheel. "Moron. When will you ever appreciate how much I love you?"

"I know you love me, but I wish you realize you have lost a glorious daughter and a great family. You should have congratulated Sarah for becoming a wife, and we would have discussed our problems without saying nasty things. You have devastated kind hearts because of your doltish, treacherous prevarication. We must keep certain secrets at the bottom of the sea, and we must reveal matters for the truth. People hold back secrets from their friends when they do not trust each other. Trust is the bedrock of love. You did not trust me, even when I kissed your ass."

"Believe me, I am honest with you."

"Why didn't you tell me in India or in Hong Kong that you think Sarah is my daughter? I married your daughter because I love you. Yes, I want the three of us to be together. I could have married a European woman and stayed away from you and your mad country. I hoped to reconnect with you because I love you. I wanted to invite you to Scotland to spend time with me, but people told me about your intimate liaison with Linda Jones. Why didn't you tell Sarah about Linda?"

"Were you spying on me?"

"You spied on me, and I spied on you."

"I traveled to Scotland to surprise you, but I saw you with Ann Stone. You held her hand and kissed her lips. That is why I did not propose a relationship when you visited me last year. I was with Linda for a purpose."

"Are you bisexual? Was it a coincidence that Linda traveled with you to Australia?"

"You don't understand. I killed Linda."

Shocked and horrified, Albert gazed at her unmoved, callous face and stretched his back and shoulders. "Oh, my God! Why?"

"She was a CIA bitch. She informed the CIA about my travels to see you."

"How did you kill her?"

"I dropped her off a cliff in Papua New Guinea. She directed CIA agents to kill you in Hong Kong, but Homatakawa and I killed them."

"You and Homatakawa?"

"Yes. I work for the Anonymous. Homatakawa gave me a gun in Hong Kong to protect you."

He wiped the corner of his mouth. "I see. I found a gun in the toilet tank. Please, tell me everything you know about the Anonymous."

"It started when Peter Stone exposed the CIA's crimes in Vietnam and Latin America. The CIA was unhappy with what he did and said. Then came my husband, who was a righteous man. Two months before his death, Michael gave Peter bank records on the CIA's covert companies, defrauded money, and arms trade deals with South American dictators. When the CIA and its mafia could not get the bank records, they killed Michael. Michael told me he prepared a list of CIA names before his death. Anyway, Peter Stone invited me to his house in 1985 and told me CIA operatives and politicians were behind Michael's death. He asked me to join the CIA to get classified documents on its money laundering through American banks. I was the CIA insider who gave Peter CIA documents. CIA hitmen killed him in 1989 and thought he gave you the CIA documents. His son Jamie created Nahatatama, Homatakawa, and the Anonymous to avenge the death of his parents and protect you. The CIA assassinated him after he refused to disclose the identity of Nahatatama and Homatakawa."

Albert wept, and Hannah caressed his left thigh. "Sorry. I know you love Jamie's daughter. She is a wonderful woman and a great investigative journalist. Many agents and civil servants wish to gag her, but the Anonymous warriors protect her."

"How do you work for Homatakawa? Who is he?"

"He is like a machine, and no one knows his origin. My mission is to leak classified documents and inform the Anonymous organization about the CIA's conspiracies. Hatakachita—we call him the Messenger- tells Homatakawa and other leading members of the Anonymous about the agents who plan to hurt you."

"Are you the Che Guevara guy who gives me classified documents?"

"No. The Che Guevara guy is not associated with the Anonymous. He was a guerrilla revolutionary in Central America. He killed many American agents and spies."

"Who is Hatakachita?"

"He is the only person who can talk to Homatakawa. I think he is the mastermind of the Anonymous."

"Who is the leader of the Anonymous?"

"He is Nahatatama or the Blue Chief."

"Who murdered the American in Jordan?"

"Homatakawa killed him with an arrow. I killed his CIA director Nathan Goodman because he plotted to kill you and me. Homatakawa burned his house."

"What else?"

"Homatakawa and the Anonymous assassins are bionic machines. Their mission is to safeguard you and kill the people who try to harm you."

"Why do they look after me?"

"Nobody knows why. Maybe they protect you because you love Ann."

"Why do CIA agents want to kill me?"

"Because they think you have official documents that contain their names and addresses."

"What about Sarah?"

"I avoided men because I love you. Believe me, I sent Sarah to Scotland to tell you I love you, but she tempted and deceived you."

Albert's hand touched hers. "I love you too, but I cannot divorce Sarah and break her heart. The world knows she is my wife. Sarah will commit suicide if I divorce her and marry you. It is too late for us to discuss a new love relationship, though we can see each other when we are free. What about your work for the CIA? I abhor the CIA and its unethical work. You said you joined the CIA to uncover the people who killed Michael. You also said you wanted to leave Michael because he cared more about his business than his love for you. Do you see a contradiction in your statements?"

"There is no contradiction. Michael was my closest cousin, and he adored me. I realized later he was busy because he wanted to expose the CIA and the corrupt companies and politicians. Besides, a good man does not mean a perfect husband. I was immature when I had sex with you in Hong Kong."

"Who killed Michael?"

"I don't know. I will resign from the CIA after I catch his killers."

"Please, be careful. The FBI agent Robert Hanssen is in

jail because he spied for Russia."

"I am careful. Did you get a list of CIA names from Peter Stone?"

"No."

"Peter told me somebody has a list of the CIA agents who killed Michael."

"I didn't get a list from him."

"Please help me find this list. You can ask Ann to help you find it. I hope you understand I wanted you to live with me in Darien to make it easy for the Anonymous and me to protect you. The Anonymous asked me to go to India to love and protect you. The CIA tried twenty or thirty times to assassinate you after you published classified documents before the Gulf War in 1990. The CIA thinks you have evidence related to its agents and Michael's death. Who was the guy who gave you the documents which you published?"

"He was the Che Guevara guy. He wears a helmet and a mask."

"Can you describe his helmet and mask?"

"He wears a Che Guevara helmet, a Che Guevara mask, and a Che Guevara beret. I tried to catch him in London, but he kicked me."

Hannah paused for a while. "He is the mysterious assassin who shot down CIA planes in Latin America in the 1980s. When was the last time you saw him?"

"Last September."

"But why you?"

"What do you mean?"

"I mean, why did this professional assassin give you the classified documents? Why didn't he give the documents to journalists?"

"I do not know."

Hannah put her right hand on Albert's left knee. "Do you appreciate how I and others had protected you?"

"Thank you, my dearest friend." Albert kissed her.

"Please, help me find the devils who killed Michael. I will do my best to protect you. Be careful. You cannot fight George W. Bush, the CIA, and the Pentagon by writing books. Do you understand?"

"What about Sarah? She needs you."

Hannah pshawed. "It is hard for me to forgive her. I sent her to Scotland to tell you about my love for you, but she lied and married you."

"The past does not exist. Sarah is my wife now. She wants to know her father. Who is her father? Don't you remember the man who made love to you?"

"I don't remember. I swear. Please, I thought you were Sarah's father. Are you sure you are not her dad?"

"Yes. I had a DNA test. I am not Sarah's father."

"Please, I didn't become pregnant to inherit Michael's wealth. Michael hid his will from me. Many male friends visited me after his death, and I do not recall I had sex with a guy. Maybe someone had drugged me and made love to me. Anyway, this matter is between Sarah and me. Do not tell her about my work for the Anonymous. I hope you understand."

Albert touched her face and kissed her lips. "I love you. Thank you for saving my life."

"I love you too."

"Go home and have some rest. You are a good friend, and I love you. I will see you soon." They kissed again.

After closing the car door, Albert picked up a photo album from an antique oak coffer in his office and moved upstairs to his bedroom. He sat on the bed and massaged Sarah's back and legs. "Sweetheart, give me a hug."

She hugged him and put her groggy head on his chest. "I will never ever allow the strumpet to break our love."

"Our life is like a moving story. The way to happiness and wisdom is to know how to remain calm. I have a splintered heart because of my love for you and Olivia. Please, darling, love your mom. She is an exceptional woman. We make mistakes and need to fill our hearts with love and forgiveness."

"Are you my dad?"

"I am Santa Claus. No, I am not your dad."

"Tell me the full story without frills. No more secrets between us."

"Rest your head on the pillow. My story with you began after I traveled to New York City in 1982. I told Ann about your mom's relationship with me in Hong Kong. She said the Rogers family is rich and influential. We found your mom's house and snooped on her. We saw her holding a baby girl. Ann joked and said the baby girl might be my daughter. In 1984, I and Olivia's mom came to New York. Ann gave me a photo of you when you were two years old and said, 'I think she is your girl. She looks like you.' I thought you were my daughter when a private investigator told me Michael was infertile. Look at these photos."

Albert opened the photo album. "Look here. This was you when you were two. That was you when you joined the elementary school. That's you when you were ten …"

Albert put a white pillow under his head. "When your mom visited me in India, she said she became pregnant after she left Hong Kong. She insisted she was single for fourteen years because of her love for me. I assumed she reconnected with me because of you, and not only because of her love for me."

"Can you explain?"

"I had a love relationship with your mom because I wanted to be close to you. Your mom was too timid to divulge the relationship between you and me. It was probable she became pregnant after we had sex in Hong Kong in 1981. I also had an inkling of your mom's tacit intention. If she was poor and a lower-middle-class worker, I would have understood her purpose, but your mom is glamorous and rich. I doubted she was single for fourteen years because of her love for me. I could have asked her about your real dad. I could have given up my job in Asia and lived with you in Darien, but I played the patient game?"

"What is the patient game?"

"I wanted your mom to speak the truth about herself and you, but, as you know, she lost her composure when we were in Sri Lanka."

"What about Michael?"

"Michael was impotent. He visited a private clinic to treat his impotence before he died in a car accident. The other issue had to do with money and Michael's will."

"What was his will?"

"Michael told his lawyer Laura Hoffman if he passed away before having a child, your mom would get $100,000, and his family would provide her with a two-bedroom house for five years. But if he died when your mom is pregnant or after having a baby, your mom would get the estate and a third of his wealth."

"What about me?"

"Three weeks after Michael's tragic funeral, Laura Hoffman visited your mother and informed her about Michael's conditional will. So, your mom responded by saying she was pregnant to inherit the house and Michael's money. Your mother had sex with a man and became pregnant."

"Who is this man?"

"He is a mystery. Your mom told me she doesn't recall the man who made her pregnant."

"Do you believe her trash?"

"That's what she said."

"How do you know I am not your daughter?"

Albert caressed her back. "Do you remember the colored lollipops in Scotland?"

"Which lollipops?"

"I gave you lollipops when you and Barbara were in Scotland to get bits of your saliva. I also took samples of your menstrual blood. It was Olivia who collected your menstrual napkins."

"Disgusting. Medical detectives, huh?"

"Yes, we were like the FBI forensic investigators. I asked a Scottish medical lab to check my and your DNA. I became glad when the DNA tests affirmed I am not your biological dad. After that, my emails to you became more romantic and less philosophical and intellectual. Besides, a friend informed me about your mom's relationship with Linda Jones."

"Is my mom a lesbian?"

"Not really. Linda was an appealing, liberal, lesbian scholar. She was your mom's best friend for fifteen years."

"Why do you say she was?"

"Linda died a few months ago."

"How? She was still young."

"She fell off a cliff in Papua New Guinea."

"Was Michael a CIA officer?"

"No. Michael was a man of dignity and virtue. He wanted to unmask the CIA's money laundering and arms deals through bank accounts. Peter Stone thought secret agents had killed him. So, some guys murdered Peter in 1989, and we do not have his evidence."

"Enough politics. Kiss me. Make love to me. Caress me and lick my body. Ah! I was happy before I saw the witch. The hateful beldam says you must divorce me. Do you believe her nonsense? My mom is a retarded ignoramus. She is a rotten hag. Nobody would take you away from me."

"No one would separate us. But, please, be kind to your mother and my mother-in-law." He declined to reveal Hannah's dangerous work for the Anonymous.

"I do not want to see the wretched mother again. She is vicious."

"Sweetie, do what you wish. Again, please, do not say rude things about your mom. I love her, and she has done many good things for you and me. Let us eat."

Overwhelmed by emotions after dinner, Sarah lay in bed, tossing and turning, unable to find comfort in sleep. Her turmoil was palpable, a storm raging within. Casting her gaze upon Albert, she felt the weight of his unparalleled love, triggering a flood of memories. The echoes of her joy and glee reverberated in her mind, contrasted by the haunting revelation from her mother's tale. How would she leave Albert? How would she give up making love to him? She could not believe her mother's narrative.

"I cannot sleep."

Albert put a book on a side table. "Darling, come here."

She cowered beside him and placed her head on his chest without saying a fulsome word. She needed a cuddle, a kiss. "Please, switch off the light. I want to sleep."

"No problem. Close your eyes and try to sleep." He switched off the light, and she slept beside him after giving him a deep kiss on his lips.

In the breezy morning, Sarah covered her sleeveless, lavender-rose sleepwear with a white bathrobe after she woke up at eight. After washing her pastel face and brushing her unkempt hair, she moved downstairs to eat and make coffee. When she approached the side edge of the kitchen wall, she saw her husband stretching a leg on the backside of a chair.

Albert rested his hands on his stretched leg and sensed Sarah's presence. "Good morning."

She hugged his back. "Good morning, love. Do you still have the desire to do kung fu after listening to my mom's satanic story?"

"The past is history. Kung fu keeps me sober."

"How do you feel this morning?"

"I feel refreshed and young."

"Do you believe my mom's diabolical anecdote?"

"Sweetheart, I am with you. I will never make a public statement and say Michael Rogers was not your dad. I love you and do not care about our society's moral quackery."

She gave him a warm kiss and rested her face on his left shoulder. As his muscular arms encircled her back, she felt contented and safe. "You have an amazing heart of gold?"

"Love must be the essence of our existence. You are my

intimate soul. I will sacrifice everything for you."

"You are an angel sent down from heaven. Who wants to see tears in the morning? Let us drink coffee. What do you like to have for breakfast?"

"Two boiled eggs with salad."

She touched his left hand and gazed at his face. "You are amazing. Do you know why I love you?" She shed tears.

"Yes, I do. I love you and love our soulmate, Olivia. I have not stopped thinking about her."

They relaxed for two hours before they left the house for a jaunty walk in a nearby green park. Vexed and perplexed, she kissed him several times and expressed her boundless affection for him. She suspected her mother was conspiring to take him away from her.

They returned to their home. "Yes, Sarah. What do you want to do?"

She rested on his thighs, placing her left arm around his shoulders, and letting her right fingers touch his hair, forehead, eyebrows, eyes, nose, lips, and chin. She kissed his left ear and licked his earlobe, and her lips mopped his smooth face. Her eyes became tearful. "What can I do? Am I manic and foolish? My love for you is in my blood and flesh like a chemical bond."

Albert placed his hands on her face. "Thank you, darling. Let us be patient."

"Patient? How could I be patient with you? My love for you is about my soul. My debased mom cooked up that damned story because I love you. I will never trust her again. She did not tell you she was married when she made love to you in Hong Kong. And after leaving Hong Kong, she did not care about you and did not give you her address and phone number. She left you for fourteen years. We were with you in India, Hong Kong, England, and Jordan, and she said nothing about the relationship between you and me. We traveled to Macau, China, Thailand, Malaysia, Singapore, and Sri Lanka, and her slimy mouth uttered nothing about my dad or about her work for the CIA. Remember how she left you in agony in Sri Lanka. I have given up faith in this crone."

Albert remained mute because he didn't want to upset his wife and unveil Hannah's dangerous work for the Anonymous. After supper, Sarah thought no more of her mother's disquieting account. Feeling aroused, she fondled Albert to sate her emotional and sexual desires. She put on a red thong and a golden straw satin blouse. After sitting on Albert's knees, she kissed his face. "How is my man?" Her fingers opened his mouth, and her bare feet touched his legs. "Hold me on your back." Her arms encircled his collar, and her breasts leaned on his back. His arms gripped her naked thighs. When he dropped her on the bed, she clutched his shirt collar, forcing him to swing at her, and kissed his lips. He turned his back to take off his clothes. She spanked his buttocks. "Look." He stuck his tongue out when she rolled up her blouse and showed him her braless bosoms.

She giggled. "Come and make love to me. The bed is hot as an oven. I will massage you with my tongue."

After making love, she lay on her back. "I am scared."

"Don't fear the things that do not exist. Wonder should be one of our highest dreams. Be what you are, and I will be with you. Yes, curious things might happen, but one thing will never change. My love for you will never recede."

"I wish we go to a remote and uninhabited island in the Pacific Ocean. My survival depends on our love. Our love makes me see my real world. Do I sound like a ninny?"

"You are smart and have a light heart. Love expands and sprouts forth in various directions as trees bloom."

"What should we say to Olivia?"

"We should tell her the truth, but without saying offensive things about your mom."

"I wish many fathers were like you. You and Olivia are like best friends."

"Yes, I adore her. There are no secrets and gender barriers between us."

Sarah's demon reminded her of the possibility that she might be Albert's biological daughter. "Suppose I am your daughter; would you leave me?"

"I haven't thought of this hypothetical matter."

"I won't leave you, even if you are my father. I watched a program on sexual behavior. What is this daughter-father business? Daughters should love their fathers, and fathers should love their daughters without a sense of shame. I do not mean daughter-father incest. I mean our human love. There is social and religious hypocrisy about love. The conservatives say it is a sin for a daughter to love her dad and kiss him, but it is not a felony to make wars and murder thousands of unarmed civilians. The world needs love. I hate war."

"Yes, the world needs love, not war. The father-daughter liaison is a complicated issue. If we suppose Adam and Eve were the first human beings, their sons and daughters made love to each other for survival. Imagine in our days a father makes love to his daughter, and she becomes pregnant. Her baby would be his child and his grandchild. There is an ethical and legal problem here. Religions forbid incest, and countries proscribe marriage between father and daughter."

"I don't endorse sexual intercourse between fathers and daughters. What I say is that girls should talk to their dads about their biology and about their sexual desires. They should talk about emotional dreams and fantasies and about the size of their breasts and underwear. Why can't a girl say she is in love with her dad? If I had a wonderful dad, I would caress and kiss him and have fun with him. I feel happy when Olivia brushes your hair, shaves your face, massages your back and feet, or when she sits on your shoulders and asks you to take her upstairs to her bedroom. You buy underwear for her. Most fathers do not buy underwear for their daughters. People make false boundaries between dads and daughters, and many of them are depressed and frustrated because they repress their true feelings. Daughters should tell their dads about their puberty and physical changes. Many crazy girls do not know how to talk to their dads about private matters. I don't think affection and love between dads and daughters would make them perverted."

"Excellent, love. I have no problem with what you say. Fathers must be responsible, caring parents. They should care for their daughters and see what they love and need. Daughters should speak to their fathers about their personal lives, emotions, and sexual desires. Fathers should listen to their daughters. The problem in our society is the absurd superstition that a girl's private things are only her mom's affair. Conceited men claim to be pragmatic and refuse to talk about their emotions under the pretext that they are powerful and practical. However, we need to be clear about one thing. I mean, God or Mother Nature didn't make us of solid rocks. We cannot eradicate our sexual desires. Natural human desires should be free and normal."

"Enough lectures. I love you. Let us sleep now."

Chapter 10

In the heart of Washington Square Park, Albert delivered a speech that echoed with the weight of truth. Before a congregation of political activists, he exposed the sinister machinations of the Republican President George W. Bush and his hawkish followers. His words cut through the air like a clarion call, revealing insidious schemes that trampled on the sacred grounds of constitutional freedom of speech. The ominous beat of war drums reverberated in his condemnation as a stark reminder of a perilous path laid out by those in power. Albert laid bare the ruthless tampering with fundamental human rights-a dark canvas painted with twisted strokes that blurred the boundaries of privacy, oppressed women, and marginalized minority groups. The atmosphere crackled with the intensity of his fearless message, each word a rallying cry against the encroaching shadows of oppression.

Encouraged by her outspoken father, Olivia became an active member of a student group called "Liberal Students for Human Rights," and opposed the U.S. foreign policy, religious fundamentalism, and the wars in Afghanistan and Iraq.

A valorous, anarchist student called Mary Lee Hanks headed the human rights group. She has gray eyes and mocha hair. Olivia saw her at an antiwar protest, berating the President, Dick Cheney, Donald Rumsfeld, Colin Powell, Condoleezza Rice, hidebound politicians, and eminent Christian fundamentalists. She pondered over Mary's striking courage.

One day, Olivia was making antiwar and human rights banners in a college hall when Mary addressed her. "Hi, there. How are you today?"

"I am fine. Thank you."

"I am Mary Hanks. I study political science."

"I am Olivia. I am a humanities student."

"Do you know Professor Edward Said? He is my hero."

"Yes. I have his work in our house. He is my dad's best friend."

"Who is your dad?"

"Albert Russell."

"Wow! Is Professor Russell your dad? He is another hero of mine. You are a lucky girl."

"Luck is not a choice."

"Sorry, I must go now. I hope to see you again and talk about your fascinating dad."

"Thanks, Mary."

Four days later, while Olivia was nibbling her lunch in Ferris Booth Commons, Mary came to her table. "Hello, Olivia. How are you doing?"

"I am doing well. Thank you."

"Can I join you?"

"You can. Please, have a seat."

"I saw you the other day with a stunning girl. I think her name is Sarah Rogers. Is she your buddy?"

Olivia smiled. "She is my stepmother."

"She is young."

"Love knows no age."

"Is she a student?"

"Yes. Sarah is in my department."

"Do you have a boyfriend?"

"This is unimaginable."

"Why?"

"I do not dream of psychotic boys. What about you? Do you have a beau?"

"No. I am a lesbian."

"Interesting. I am an out lesbian too. Do you have a girlfriend?"

"No. I am single."

"I am single too."

"Can we go out for dinner?"

"Yes. What about this Friday night?"

"That's fine. Where do you stay?"

"I live with my dad in Larchmont."

"Where is your mom?"

"My mom died when I was one year old."

"Sorry to hear that."

Olivia and Mary sensed their ingenuous, intimate closeness and continued their conversation about their households, ambitions, and studies. On Friday night, they got a taxi to a French seafood restaurant in Midtown Manhattan and discussed their emotions, desires, and expectations. Mary's political activism, tenderness, and solicitude for women and the destitute had impressed Olivia.

They left the restaurant, smiling and holding each other's hand with comfort. Olivia invited Mary to her house. "Here is our home. I hope you would like it."

Mary glanced around at the contemporary lounge. "It is elegant and full of books. I like the faint colors of the walls."

"Do you want wine?"

"Yes, thank you. The house is quiet. Where are your dad and stepmom?"

"In Florida."

Olivia got a rose wine bottle and two glasses and sat beside Mary. After chatting for ten minutes and taking tots of wine, she touched Mary's hand and scrutinized her face and thin pink lips. Her rouged mouth brushed her lower lip, and she wanted to know what Mary would say and do. When Mary kissed her back and sucked her tongue, Olivia moved her into her bedroom and stripped off her clothes. She licked her body and peeled off her clothes. They caressed and made love for an hour. Mary, the disobedient activist who challenged and cursed politicians, entrepreneurs, and televangelists, was a bashful angel in bed. Olivia enjoyed her gentle fondling, smooth hands, beaming grin, and seductive body.

They spent two days in the house, bathing and massaging each other. They made love on couches, on carpets, in the kitchen, and in the bathrooms. Their undisturbed intimacy had made it possible for them to grasp the subtle meaning of women's love of women. Without interference from anybody, they debated how, why, and when women fall in love with other women.

Later, Albert and Sarah arrived at LaGuardia Airport in Queens, New York. When Olivia saw them, she hastened toward them. "Dad, dad, Sarah, Sarah ..." She hugged and kissed them for a minute.

"Oh, love, oh, sweetheart, I missed you. This is my girlfriend, Mary Hanks."

Albert and Sarah kissed Mary's face and moved to the house in Larchmont. Olivia rested between her father and stepmother and gripped their hands. When Albert and Sarah went up to their bedroom, Mary whispered. "I have never seen a daughter who loves her dad as you do. You kissed and hugged him many times as if he was your boyfriend."

"My dad is the only man I and Sarah love. He has a delicate and feminine heart."

The next day, they visited Barbara to dine with her. After dinner, Barbara stood in silence when Olivia kissed Mary's lips in the kitchen. Albert took Barbara to a room after he noticed her tears and change of face.

"Their kiss has moved me and filled me with love and passion. I am happy that Olivia is a homosexual."

"We should respect her free love and choice."

"I am surprised."

"You are a feminist author. You write romance novels and believe in women's sexual freedom. Your novel, *Shadows of Love*, is about two female fashion designers who love each other. Olivia loves women as other women desire men."

"Olivia is free to do what she likes. I see a Canadian woman friend in Toronto. She is an author of lesbian fiction. I will introduce you to her. Please, keep this matter a secret. Did you read that racy novel? Is there a book you have not read?"

On that day, Mary felt happy when Albert and Sarah persuaded her to live with Olivia in their house. This made it easy for her to enjoy herself and express her lesbian sexuality without prejudice. Sarah and Olivia had agreed to put an end to their affair to respect Mary's feelings and commitment.

Albert's scathing criticism of U.S. foreign policies had irritated the politicians, military personnel, and intelligence officers, who reviewed the CIA and FBI reports on the Anonymous organization and wondered why it guards him all the time. The government and the FBI had refused to harm or arrest Albert because the Constitution protects the freedom of speech and Britain supports the U.S. wars. However, four CIA officers met in an apartment in Lower Manhattan and schemed to silence Albert and Homatakawa. An officer suggested they should hire a gunman to murder Albert, but his colleagues argued that Nahatatama, Homatakawa, and the Anonymous warriors would kill tens of thousands of Americans and make the conflict against the U.S. look like a World War Three. Another agent proposed they should kidnap Olivia or Sarah to compel Albert to hand over classified official documents. In the end, they agreed to trap and kill Homatakawa with a rocket launcher. A week later, two agents abducted Olivia when she strolled on Third Avenue and forced her to remain in a blue Ford van. Two hours later, Albert's cell phone beeped. "Dad, dad," Olivia screamed.

"What is wrong, darling?"

"Hello, Dr. Russell."

"Who are you?"

"That's not important. Bring the CIA's documents, and we will give you back your daughter."

"Where do you want me to meet you?"

"Come alone to the Rocky Point Pine Barrens State Forest. We will wait for you at Rocky Point Yaphank Road."

"OK. Please, do not hurt my daughter. I will give you what you want."

Albert entered his home office and inserted a file in a messenger bag. Sarah saw him. "Where are you going?"

"I need to see Olivia."

"Where is she?"

"I don't know. Please, lock the doors and don't open them to anyone." He kissed her.

When Albert was on Rocky Point Yaphank Road, he gazed at four police cars, a SWAT van, and two ambulance vehicles blocking the road. He left his car and walked to a police car. "What is going on, officer?"

"There is a crime scene here. Please, go back to your car."

Albert saw a puddle of blood, four lifeless bodies, and a burning vehicle. He rested in his car and became distraught with grief. Five minutes later, his cell phone rang. "Yes."

"Did you find Olivia?" Sarah inquired.

"No."

"Where are you?"

"In Rocky Point."

"What are you doing there?"

"I came to see Olivia here."

"What happened to her? Did somebody abduct her?"

"This is a possibility. I will talk to you later."

Ten minutes later, Albert's phone buzzed. "Yes."

"Dad, I am OK."

"Darling, where are you?"

"In Brooklyn."

"What happened?"

"I am with Homatakawa, who saved me in Thailand. See you at home."

Albert returned home and embraced his daughter. "What happened, love?"

"Two armed guys abducted me when I was on Third Avenue and threw me into a van. Their driver drove to Rocky Point. When the three guys stood on a sidewalk, two masked girls, with long, dark hair, walked toward us. A guy in another car prepared a rocket launcher to kill the girls, but Homatakawa turned up from nowhere, slaughtered the guy with a knife, and blew up his car with the rocket launcher. After that, Homatakawa and his girls killed the other three guys with chopsticks."

"Chopsticks?"

"Yes, metal chopsticks. Homatakawa is so powerful that he held two abductors and knocked their heads on the windshield. He is a humanoid cyborg."

"How?"

"He speaks a strange language as a robot, and his arms are like iron rods."

Sarah sat next to Albert. "Who is Homatakawa?"

"I guess he is one of my Shaolin friends."

"How did he know Olivia was in Rocky Point?"

"I don't know."

Olivia drank water. "Homatakawa touched this necklace. I think he wants me to keep it on."

Albert examined the gold necklace. "Maybe there is an electronic chip inside it. Keep it on."

"Homatakawa knows me."

"How?"

"He hugged me and clutched my hand for a minute."

"I see. Anyway, you are now sound and safe."

The next day, the media said the Anonymous killed four men in Rocky Point because they abducted Albert Russell's daughter. The FBI issued a five million dollars reward for any information leading to the arrest of the leader of the Anonymous organization. In the late evening, Zita Marino interviewed Albert.

"Can you tell us what happened?"

"I was in my house when I got a phone call from my daughter. She screamed, and a man took her cell phone and said I should bring classified documents if I wanted to see my daughter again."

"What are these documents?"

"They are CIA classified files."

"Do you have these files?"

"I do not have classified files. The police or the FBI can go through my house and university office. As a British citizen, I do not need U.S. classified documents. I am not a party politician or a secret agent."

"Why does the CIA think you have secret documents?"

"Ask the CIA. I regret to say that the Anonymous had executed the CIA operatives who intimidated me in the last fourteen years. There is a surreptitious war game between the CIA and the Anonymous, and I am stuck in the middle. I appeal to the CIA to stop threatening me. I am a university professor and a pacifist man of love and peace."

On Thursday, September 25, 2003, Albert, Sarah, Olivia, and Mary were having dinner in the Larchmont house when Albert's phone buzzed.

"Yes ... Oh no! When did that happen? ... God bless his soul ... I have lost a remarkable friend and mentor ... My deepest condolences to you all ... You are in our thoughts and prayers. I am here for you if you need anything ... I will see you soon. Take care of yourself. I love you all."

With his back to a wall, Albert thrust his hands into his pockets and looked sorrowful.

Sarah stood beside him. "What's wrong?"

"Edward Said has died in Long Island Hospital."

She clung to him and cried on his shoulder. "I am at a loss for words. He was a fantastic teacher."

On Monday, September 29, Albert and Sarah went to Manhattan to condole the Said family. Albert gave a brief speech and pointed out that Edward had always said to him, "When I see you, I recall your grandfather Bertrand Russell, one of my intellectual heroes."

In the second week of January 2004, Ann, Albert, Ayita, Sarah, and Olivia traveled to England to attend the funeral of Father John Russell, who died of lung cancer. Olivia saw Ann holding Albert's hand and leaning her head on his shoulder when they stood at the grave. She took her father aside. "Dad, the media is following us. You will be an Earl. I know you love Ann. You are married now. Sarah might feel envious, and the media might wonder why you hug and kiss Ann."

Albert hugged her and remembered that day when Ann asked him not to tell anyone about her real relationship with him. He didn't want Olivia to think her grandmother was an indecent woman or to know Father John Russell was not her grandfather. Olivia loved John and Janet, and they adored her. "Thank you, darling, for your concern. Ann was my first sweetheart, and I was her only lover. Our families had devastated us when they barred us from getting married because of our racial and religious backgrounds. Ann is your sister's mother. She took care of Ayita on her own. The CIA murdered her parents and grandparents. Ayita and I are the only people who care for her. Thank Ann for looking after your sister, who loves you. The love between Ann and me is not a sin. I believe you understand."

Two months later, Albert got a phone call.

"Hello, Albert. This is Mariam."

"Hi, Mariam. How are you doing? How is your family in Lebanon?"

"I am doing fine. The family was so happy to see all of us."

"Great. What is the news?"

"Wadie and his wife and Najla are doing good. When are you coming to see me?"

"When are you free?"

"Come for lunch this Saturday. Zita Marino will interview me in the morning. I will cook special food for you."

"Thank you. I will come."

"By the way, before his death, Edward asked me to donate his books to Columbia University. Bring a bag to pack books."

"That's very kind of you."

On Saturday morning, Albert stopped his Toyota car on West 119th Street, opened the trunk, and got a brown duffel bag. Later, he hugged Mariam and her daughter and Zita Marino. "How is everyone?"

"We are fine," Mariam responded. "Come to the dining table. I know you love our Lebanese cuisine."

When Mariam and her daughter were in the kitchen, Zita Marino sat beside Albert and inserted a small, white envelope in his jacket pocket. "Open it in the car."

After lunch, Zita thanked Mariam and her daughter and left the apartment. Mariam touched her daughter's shoulder. "Excuse me. Albert wants books. See you later." She and Albert entered Edward's white office. There were cartoon boxes on a table and on the floor.

"I will help you pack the books."

"Forget that. Take this file."

"What is this file?"

"It is about the CIA's undercover operations."

Albert noticed his name on the file. He opened it and found official documents comprising the names of CIA agents. "Many people have been looking for this file. How did you get it?"

"Someone asked Edward to give it to you."

Albert selected books and thanked Mariam for her cordial hospitality.

After sitting behind the steering wheel of his car, Albert opened Zita's envelope, picked up a card, and read, "Urgent. Residence Inn. LeCount Place, New Rochelle. Room 61. Zita. Love xxx."

Thirty minutes later, Albert knocked on the door of room 61 in Residence Inn.

Zita, wearing a deep plunge white neckline playsuit, opened the door. Albert entered the room with a smile. Zita locked the door and leaped on his chest, wrapping her bare legs around his hips and kissing his lips. "I miss you so much."

Albert carried her to the bed, loosened her playsuit, and kissed her lips, neck, chest, stomach, and thighs. "That is enough." He sat beside her.

She gazed at him. "Why did you stop?"

"I am married now."

"I know you are married. You have been my lover and best friend for twenty-two years. You have always made love to me and caressed me, even after I got married and became a mom."

"That's when I was unmarried. Sarah is pregnant. She differs from Rachel and Hannah. I do not want to cheat on her."

Zita pinched his nose and writhed her body. "Cheat on her? Your half-lesbian, holier-than-thou wife had sex with Olivia for two years. And what about your romance with Ann Stone? Wake up, old man. You and I believe in free love. We made love after you married Eva and when Rachel and Hannah were your girlfriends. Since when did we care about cheating on our gonzo partners? Sometimes I feel you are weird despite your genius mind. We made love in the Scottish Highlands, and then you married a student who looks like Olivia. There should be a news headline that says, 'Breaking news. An eminent philosopher marries his student.' What happened to you?"

"I love you, but it is different now. When Eva was alive, she allowed you to sleep with me because both of you were girlfriends. What do you want me to do?"

"First, I want you to love Sarah as much as you can. I do not want to take you away from her. Second, I need love. Our love is innocuous and a matter of life and death for us. We can see each other when we are free."

She sat on his midriff, and he put his right hand on her left cheek. She sucked and fondled his fingers. "Do you know my biggest regret in life? I regret I turned down your proposal in 1982. I was a big fool."

"But you asked me to marry Eva."

"We were a threesome. I did not want to break Eva's spirit. She loved you so much."

"Why did you ask me to love Sarah?"

"I asked you to love her, not to marry her. I wanted you to come to America, so I can see you."

His fingers smoothed her arching eyebrows. "What happened? You look heartbroken."

"I did not have sex for eight months. Do you believe that?"

"Why? What's going on?"

"I broke up with my brainless, old man. I oppose Bush's wars, and the idiot supports them. He became so conservative that he asked me not to wear short and tight clothes."

"Why didn't you tell me?"

"I was busy reporting the bloody war in Iraq, and you were sad because you lost Edward Said and your dad."

"Where do you live?"

"I bought a six-bedroom house in Mount Kisco. You should see it."

"What about your children?"

"James is at Harvard, and the girls see me two days a week."

"Do you have work tomorrow?"

"No."

"Come to our house. I should introduce you to Sarah and Olivia."

She kissed his lips. "Thank you. But, please, I do not want Sarah and Olivia to know about our affair. They won't understand our free spirit."

"Don't worry. They are not religious."

She tickled his chest with her fingernails. "Wait here. Don't go anywhere. I have something for you." She dropped her playsuit on the floor and went to the bathroom. Ten minutes later, she walked out, and Albert became astounded and terrified when he saw her wearing a motorcycle navy suit and a Che Guevara helmet, and holding a long-barrel, silenced handgun. Pulling his knees up to his chest, he recalled the mysterious motorcyclist who followed him to Asia, Europe, and Latin America, and gave him top-secret documents on the CIA and its covert activities. He recalled Hannah, who informed him about the masked assassin who killed CIA mercenaries in Latin America.

"Who are you, Zita? Are you a journalist or an assassin? Please, put the gun down."

Zita put her gun on a table. "Catch." She took off her helmet and threw it at him. She removed her Che Guevara leather mask and Che Guevara beret and put them on the gun. "That's me. Don't move a flesh." She somersaulted forward and landed on his crotch. "Ouch!" She paused and touched his face. "Honey, come on. Why are you crying?"

"I don't believe my best friend is a serial killer. Am I supposed to love female killers? Eva killed a British officer because he shot an IRA man, and Hannah killed CIA guys. How many people did you murder?"

"Wait a minute. I am not a serial killer. You also executed the guys who killed Bishop Oscar Romero."

"That's when I was a revolutionary."

"How did you kill them without using a gun?"

"A Shaolin monk taught me the iron palm to smash bricks, and I used his technique to crack ribs and necks. Are you Homatakawa?"

"No."

"I thought you were a man. Why do you wear a mask and a helmet?"

"To hide my identity. I work for Nahatatama."

"Who is he?"

"He is a specter."

"How do you work for a mysterious man?"

"Peter Stone asked me to trust him."

"Why did you kill people?"

"Don't judge me before you know the truth."

"Which truth? I talk about love and peace, and you shoot people?"

"I shot the criminals who killed my family, and I saved your ass many times. Did you forget the assassin who wanted to kill you in El Salvador? If I had not saved your life, you would not have met Sarah, and Olivia would have been an orphan. I saved your life fifteen times. Sarah and other women talk about love in words, but no one of them has risked her life to protect you. So, don't tell me I don't deserve your love."

"But why do you kill?"

"Be rational. What would you expect me to do when somebody points a gun at you to kill you? Call the cops? Sit and cry? I protected you."

"Are you the Che Guevara guy who gave me the CIA classified documents?"

"Yes, and sorry for kicking your chest in London. You

shouldn't have chased me."

"Did you kill CIA agents in Central and South America?"

"Yes. I sent them to hell."

"How did you kill them? Do you work for the Italian Mafia?"

"No."

"Tell me the truth."

"All right. I have been one of your secret bodyguards. I assassinated the CIA thugs who killed my family and wished to kill you."

"But how and why?"

"Do you remember how I saved your life and how you saved mine in New York in 1982?"

"Yes."

"After that dreadful day, I promised myself to protect you because you saved my life and because you were my first boyfriend. Besides, you married Eva, my best friend. As you know, I am a professional gymnast. I use my gymnastic skills to perform extraordinary things. I gave you documents to read them and get an idea about the CIA's perfidious work, but you published them under your name and endangered yourself, and that made my task dangerous. Do not publish classified documents and use your real name. The American government can imprison you for life in the name of national security. Do you understand?"

"How did you get classified documents from the CIA and the Pentagon?"

"The Italians know how to get things done. Refrain from asking me questions about my sources. I don't want a hoodlum to kill you."

"What about Hannah?"

"She leaked classified documents."

"Does she know you?"

"She knows me, but she does not know about my work for the Anonymous."

"Homatakawa saved Olivia's life last year."

"I know. He and Nahatatama are the most wanted persons in the world."

"Who are they? Why do they protect us?"

"No one knows."

"What about Peter Stone?"

"Peter met me in 1984 and told me the CIA had assassinated my parents. He taught me how to be a good investigative journalist and asked me in 1988 to contact the Anonymous and set up an assassination group to assassinate the evil guys in the CIA."

"But Peter was a peaceful man."

"Yes, he was a peaceful man, but the Vietnam war had changed his mind."

"How did you know the CIA's hitmen who wanted to kill me?"

"That was Hannah's risky mission. You must praise her for what she did for you. I asked you to love Sarah because I have a plan for all of you."

"How do you communicate with Hannah? I mean, how do you get classified documents from her?"

"I send her a printed card that says, 'Wish you a lovely vacation,' and she travels to Mexico and leaves the documents with a revolutionary friend at a distant place."

"What about the hacktivist group Anonymous? Do you have any connection with it?"

"Unknown guys founded an Anonymous group to

hack into the database of the intelligence agencies. They send the hacked documents to the Anonymous. Yes, they spy on us, and we spy on them."

"It is hard for one to believe a gifted, charming news anchor is the assassin who killed fifteen CIA agents. How did you learn to use a gun and kill?"

Zita opened the top drawer of a side table and picked up a portable DVD player. "Please, take off your jacket and shirt. I want to touch your body and show you something excruciating and private."

Albert took off his jacket and shirt. Zita pressed the Play button and embraced his chest.

Albert stared at the DVD player screen. A group of five armed men, led by a masked man, entered a house. "Albert, this was my dad's house in Brooklyn. This masked guy is called the Black Wolf." The Black Wolf pointed his automatic rifle at an Italian man holding a young girl in his home office. "This man, Giovanni Marino, was my dad. He was a human rights judge. That's me when I was three."

The Black Wolf frowned. "Where are the classified documents?"

"Which documents?"

"The documents about the so-called human rights abuses by the U.S. Army and the CIA in South-East Asia and Central America."

"I don't have the documents."

"Where are they?"

The Italian man's wife came into the office. "Oh, my God! What's going on?"

"This woman was my mom. Her name was Jemma."

The Black Wolf pulled a pistol and killed her.

The young girl shrieked and climbed on her mother's chest. "Mamma. Mamma." The Black Wolf tried to kill the girl, but one of his associates prevented him from shooting her. "Please, leave the girl."

Giovanni threw a book at the Black Wolf. "Bastard. Why did you kill my wife? She did nothing to you."

"Answer me. Who took the documents?"

"Who are you?"

"We are members of the Special Operations Division." The Black Wolf shot Giovanni's right thigh. Giovanni wailed. "Oh, my God! Leave me alone. What do you want from me?"

"Where are the documents, Italian fool?"

"I don't have documents. Kill yourself."

The Black Wolf fired two shots and killed Giovanni.

Zita pressed the Pause button and wiped her tears. "Do you know why I always need you?"

"That was awful and disgusting. Thank God the thug did not kill you. What happened to you?"

"The fake media claimed that the Gambino family had killed my parents. The vicious murder of my parents had forced the Italian Mafia to kill many police officers in New York."

"Who looked after you?"

"My uncle, Mariano, took care of me and taught me how to use a gun. I am now the *madrina* of the Marino family in America. We are the good Italians." She kissed Albert's right nipple. "Do you remember how we made love on a table in my uncle's restaurant?"

"Yes. We were mad."

"That was the beginning of our love story. Do you understand why the CIA wanted to kill you? Do you know why Hannah spied on you? And do you know why the Anonymous and I had to murder the jerks who wanted to kill you? I will allow nobody to harm you." She inserted her hand under the bed mattress and picked up two envelopes.

"What are these envelopes?"

"This envelope has all you need to know about Michael Rogers, Hannah, and the CIA agents who killed Michael. The other envelope has the names of the CIA agents who plotted to kill you in Central and South America."

"Hannah has been looking for these papers for many years. How did you get them?"

She smiled. "I got them from you."

"How?"

"Peter Stone was my dad's close friend. He wanted me to get the documents and did not want the CIA to suspect me. Therefore, I asked you to meet him. When you looked at his library, he inserted the documents in your briefcase. After that, you visited me. When you were in the bathroom, I opened your bag and got the documents."

"What happened when I was in New York in 1995? Security men looked for me."

"When the CIA asked federal agents to raid Ann's apartment and look for a classified document about the CIA and the FBI, Ann hid the document in your bag. The agents could not find the document, and somebody informed them that Ann had given the document to you. So, I removed the document from your bag and gave it to Edward Said. So, in 1995, FBI officers wanted to arrest you and search your bag, but the Anonymous warriors punished them. You see, no woman in the world loves you more than I do. I put myself in extreme danger because of you. Don't I deserve a kiss for what I had done for you?"

Albert kissed her lips. "But promise me not to kill more people. The world needs love and peace."

"I promise, but I have one condition."

"What's it?"

"I remain your secret lover. Do you understand? We will talk about Sarah later." She gave Albert a sealed envelope. "This is from Peter Stone to you. He gave it to me before his death."

Albert opened the envelope and read these words: "Dearest Albert, when you get this letter, I want you to give your allegiance to Zita Marino. I believe in peace, and your grandfather Bertie advocated peace, though both of us had concluded that violence is imperative in certain circumstances. For instance, we agreed that the war against Nazi Germany was inexorable. What the U.S. military and the CIA are doing is tantamount to genocide. We must stand up against their imperialism. I have created an artificial intelligence group called the Anonymous to fight for the oppressed peoples and to diminish the arrogance of power of governments. The group has the best minds in technology, military intelligence, and the media. I want you to be the intellectual and spiritual mentor of this group. Zita will guide you through articulating and identifying the right strategy.

Trust nobody but Nahatatama, Homatakawa, Ann, Hannah Rogers, and Zita. Love and support them. Do not forget to give your allegiance to Zita in a Sicilian way!

I wished to see peace in the world, but I saw endless wars and sufferings because of immoral politicians and barbarous men willing to kill and die for despicable ideologies and jingoism. I hope you will find love and peace.

Sincerely yours,

Peter Stone."

Albert paused and thought of his grandfather's redolent words and work. He gazed at Zita. "Who is Nahatatama?"

"He is the supreme leader of the Anonymous."

"And who is Homatakawa?"

"He is the military commander of the Anonymous."

"What is their background?"

"Nobody knows. Their language is cryptic, and their warriors are cyborg assassins. They are the backbone of the Anonymous. They wear masks before they go into action."

"Who is the leader of the Anonymous in America?"

"That is another big question mark."

He touched her lips. "What is the Sicilian way?"

"Stand before me and bow."

Albert stood before her and bowed. "You can kiss my hand now."

Albert kissed Zita's right hand, and Zita kissed him and took off his shoes, socks, and pants. "Come with me. I want to have a shower with you."

After the shower, Zita got a gray duct tape from her handbag.

"What is this?"

"I want to stick the envelopes to your back. I do not want people to see you walking with me and holding envelopes. Please, do not tell Sarah and Olivia about the documents. Hide them in separate and secure places. And do not you ever call me on the phone or send me emails to say secret things. The CIA, the NSA, and the FBI monitor your phone calls and communications."

Zita attached the envelopes to Albert's back and dressed him. "Let us see your lesbian family."

"I want to make a phone call." Albert called his daughter. "Hi, darling."

"Hello, dad. When are you coming home?"

"Soon. Is the guest bedroom clean and tidy?"

"I think so. Why?"

"A dear friend is coming to stay with us. Should I bring food?"

"No. I have made dinner."

"Excellent. See you shortly. I love you."

"I love you too."

Later, Albert astonished his wife and daughter by introducing them to Zita. "This wonderful woman is the remarkable news anchor, Zita Marino. Zita is my oldest friend."

"What do you mean by my oldest friend? You see, Sarah, your churlish husband thinks I am a harridan." They laughed.

"Sit at the dining table. I will join you after five minutes." In his office, Albert picked up scissors and cut the duct tape around his belly. He hid Zita's envelopes in a photo frame and selected a photograph album. After resting beside Sarah, Olivia sat next to Zita. "What have you cooked for us?"

"Parsnip and apple soup, roast chicken, grilled vegetables, and a carrot cake."

While they were devouring their dinner, Albert glanced at Sarah and Olivia. "I want to tell you my biggest secret. Zita has been my greatest friend for the past twenty-two years, and she will be my best confidante for the rest of my life. Without her, I would not have a story to tell. She saved my life in 1982."

Sarah bit a carrot. "How?"

Zita smiled. "He also saved my life."

"I was in New York City in 1982 to give speeches against the abhorrent massacres in Syria and Lebanon. A white supremacist pointed his shotgun at me. Zita–by the way, Zita is an expert gymnast–kicked his hand, and another quick kick slapped his terrified face. The guy collapsed unconscious in his chair."

"Tell them how you saved my life."

"The guy's friend pulled a bayonet out and was about to stab Zita's back after swearing at her. After jumping, I kicked his forehead and gave him a one-inch punch on his sternum. That's how Zita and I became best friends."

Sarah had a sip of wine. "Amazing."

Zita chewed a piece of chicken. "Tell them how you saved my life in Italy."

"When a Mafia car bomb killed Zita's uncle, Paolo Borsellino, in July 1992, Zita and I flew to Palermo in Sicily. Olivia was with my mother in England. One day, Zita and I were having a beer drink at a bar near the sea. I looked at an old building, and something flashed on its rooftop. A hitman pointed his sniper rifle at us. I bounced on Zita to protect her with my body just a couple of seconds before a bullet shattered her glass."

Olivia gaped. "What happened after that?"

"I kissed your papa." Zita laughed.

"We tracked the sniper for twenty minutes and knocked him down near a theater. Three police officers showed up and caught him. He was a notorious member of the Mafia family that killed Zita's uncle."

"Tell them about our adventure in France."

"I can't talk about that."

"Why not? Sarah and Olivia are mature and intelligent women."

"OK. Zita asked me in 1993 to travel with her to France to meet a female member of the German Red Army Faction, who knew about the attacks against U.S. military facilities in Germany. Her name was Sigrid. We met Sigrid in a cottage near the city of Metz. When Sigrid said the CIA was behind the death of Gudrun Ensslin and Andreas Baader, two armed men invaded our place and bawled. 'We want the German woman.' We raised our hands above our heads, and Zita winked at me. I gave a man a flying back kick to his chest, and Zita kicked the other guy's genitals and knees. When we seized their guns, Sigrid picked up a firearm from her shoulder bag and killed them. We later realized these two men were special agents for the FBI."

Sarah dropped her fork. "Oh, my God!"

Olivia straightened her back. "You and Zita should make a James Bond film."

"It was that interview with Sigrid that made Zita a leading political journalist." Albert opened the photo album, which he brought from his office. "That is me and Zita at her uncle's Brooklyn restaurant in 1982 ... Olivia, this is your mom and Zita on a beach in New York."

"Wait, dad. Did my mom have a tattoo on her back?"

"Yes. A tattoo of our names. Here is Zita with your mom when she was pregnant ... Threesome! I, your mom, and Zita are in one bed. Your mother idolized Zita. She and Zita were like twins ... Zita and you when you were one year old ... Zita and I at Peter Stone's funeral ..."

Sarah recalled Olivia's inconclusive stories about her

father's secret mistresses and felt amazed to know all these details about Zita. She became convinced that Zita was more than a friend to Albert. "Zita, were you Albert's girlfriend?"

Zita laughed with gaiety. "I have never been Albert's girlfriend. We have been special friends. Albert married Olivia's gorgeous mom, and I married an ugly pig in New York."

"The other thing I must say is that I am indebted to Zita for making me a popular intellectual celebrity. Zita interviewed me many times. How many times did you interview me?"

"Sixty-two times."

On that night, Sarah touched Albert's hand in their bedroom. "I love Zita. She is a fascinating woman."

"Yes, she is gorgeous and affectionate."

"I sense there is so much love between you and Zita. Please, I am not like those narrow-minded wives who feel jealous when their husbands go out with beautiful women. We are polyamorous. Visit Zita and spend time with her, but please, do not leave me."

"Thank you, darling. I will never leave you for another woman. Zita knows that. Nasty guys killed Zita's parents when she was three years old, and her husband divorced her last year. She needs our sympathy and love."

Zita stayed two nights with Albert and his family and invited them to spend the next weekend in her spacious house in Mount Kisco. On the weekend, Zita gave Albert a house key and accepted his offer to be his copy editor to conceal their liaison. She felt happy to rejuvenate her special friendship with Albert, her intimate lover for over two decades. Her overriding concern was not about having an affair with him. She needed a confidential friend to care for her and understand her emotional needs. To her, Albert is the ideal best friend. He consulted her, hugged her, kissed her, and held her hand even when Sarah was with them. Most important, he is the confidant who knows about her assassination mission and the leakage of classified official documents.

Albert told Sarah about his personal meetings with Zita. She loved Zita, visited her house, and felt there was no need to question her husband's exceptional intimacy with her.

Chapter 11

After her graduation in May 2004, Sarah gave birth to a baby boy. She named him Edward after her late teacher Edward W. Said. Albert seized this occasion to tell Sarah about her mother. "You need to speak to your mom. You have not seen each other for three years. Love overcomes bitterness. Anger from the past should not dictate what we do today. She wishes to hug you and her grandchild. I should pay her a visit."

"Don't go. I will call her."

Sarah called her mother and invited her to visit and see Edward. A day later, Hannah came and loved to carry her first grandchild, though she wondered why Zita Marino was in Albert's house.

"Hi, Hannah. How are you? Are you ready for an interview?"

"No interviews, please. I assume you realize now why I

visited you in 1995."

"Your grandchild is beautiful. He got your sharp eyes."

"Thank you."

Hannah snooped on Zita to delve into her unusual friendship with Albert and his wife. One day, she parked her car on Deer Knoll Street and used Porro-prism binoculars when Albert and Zita sauntered near Howlands Lake. She sensed they discussed private matters.

Two months later, Albert traveled to Toronto for academic reasons. Hannah seized this opportunity to stay in his house and look after her daughter and grandchild. One night, she entered Albert's home office when Sarah and her baby were sleeping upstairs. She searched around and noticed dust on the wall portraits. After fetching a glass cleaner spray and a kitchen tissue roll, she removed the pictures from the walls. While cleaning a frame, a dull rustle sounded at the back of the photo. She detached the back side of the mount, opened an envelope, and found CIA classified documents and a cassette recorder. She gasped when she saw Michael Rogers' list of politicians, bankers, traffickers, and CIA operatives. Resting her head on a hand, she pressed the Play button of the cassette recorder and listened to this conversation.

"Raymond, what did you do in the clinic?"

"I gave Michael a dose of strychnine."

"Who changed the brake pads?"

"Joseph Anderson. He also took out the fluid from the front hydraulic pipes."

"What about his widow?"

"Hannah is twenty-one. She's a student at Yale and has a little girl."

"Did anybody find Michael's list?"

"Larry Clark searched Peter Stone's house and found nothing. We think the list is a hoax."

"Who authorized the operation?"

"Jim Simons, Robert Buckley, and the Black Wolf."

Hannah examined Michael's list and wrote seven names. She put three question marks after the nickname the Black Wolf.

Two weeks later, Albert sat on a couch and switched on the TV to watch the Nightly News. The news anchor Billy Williams made an announcement. "Breaking news. An unnamed person has killed Robert Buckley at his Ipswich house in Essex County in Massachusetts. Robert was the director of the Defense of Clandestine Service in the early 1980s."

After a week, Albert and Sarah watched the TV when a newsreader said, "Breaking news. Joseph Anderson, a former director of the Defense Intelligence Agency, has been found slain on a footpath in Bradbury Mountain State Park in Maine."

Ten days later, Albert and his family were having dinner when a CNN news reporter stated, "We got a breaking news story for you coming in from the State of Vermont. Authorities believe they have found the body of Kevin Walker, a former CIA operative, at Kent Pond in Gifford Woods State Park in Vermont."

Albert twisted his closed mouth. "God doesn't chuck stones."

Sarah looked at him. "What do you mean?"

"It is a Syriac proverb, which means God has His own way of vengeance against the wicked people. Kevin Bill Walker and other ruffians had caused tremendous harm to many innocent people."

Five days later, an ABC News correspondent said, "Police have discovered the dead body of a CIA operative named Larry Clark at Echo Lake in Franconia Notch State Park in New Hampshire."

After watching the news, Sarah fingered her hair. "Something uncanny is going on in New England. The assassin killed Larry Clark and other CIA operatives in parks in Maine, Massachusetts, Vermont, and New Hampshire. The killer knows them and lives in a northeastern forest."

"What can I say? More people get killed in this country than in Afghanistan and Iraq."

Two days later, Albert thought Zita had orchestrated the execution of the four CIA agents because she spoke of their activities. He drove to her house in Mount Kisco and rang the doorbell.

Zita opened the door and kissed him. "I have been thinking of you. Give me a big kiss."

He closed the door and grabbed her hands. "What have you done?"

"Done what?"

"You know what I mean."

"No. I don't know what you mean."

"Who killed the four CIA agents?"

"Not me."

"You promised me not to kill people."

"I didn't kill them."

"Your documents mention their names."

"So? I did nothing. Believe me."

"Where did you get the documents?"

"I told you not to ask about my sources."

"Please, tell me the truth?"

"My Italian associates are my sources. I can't give you their names."

"One document mentions seven CIA agents."

"Four of them are dead."

"Who are the other men?"

"Raymond Harris, a retired CIA military officer, the Black Wolf, and the chairman of the Faux News Channel."

"Do you have any idea about the killer or killers?"

"No. Why are you worried?"

"Something is not right. What should we do?"

"Stay away from this dirty mess. I will do what I can."

"Be careful."

"Enough of that. Come here, sexy man, and touch me. I feel horny."

Zita and Albert kissed and caressed. His arms carried her to a bed, and he persuaded her to sit on his knees. She lowered her body and shrieked. "Oh, my God! Get up."

"What's wrong?"

"I remembered something. Robert Buckley was the CIA's boss who ordered agents to kill Michael Rogers. He retired before the CIA and the NSA put you under constant surveillance. The other assassinated agents had taken part in murdering Michael. Their execution has nothing to do with you. I have a strange feeling that Hannah has killed them."

"How? She is a university professor?"

"Don't undervalue what women can do when they are furious and vengeful. Did you show her the classified documents?"

"No."

"How did she discover who killed her husband?"

"Oh dear! She stayed in my house for a week when I was in Canada. Let us go home."

After greeting Sarah and kissing Edward, Albert and Zita entered the office. Albert removed the cardboard of a portrait. "The envelope is still here. Nothing is missing."

"Where is the other envelope?"

"I hid it behind a wall in the bedroom."

They looked around in the office for fifteen minutes. Zita opened the top drawer of Albert's desk and drew a notebook. "Albert, look here."

"It is an empty paper."

"Crazy. Give me a magnifier."

Albert opened a drawer and gave Zita a gold-rimmed magnifier. "You see? Hannah wrote the seven names."

"You should be a forensic detective."

"I asked you to keep the envelopes in safe places, not in a picture frame. Ah, crazy men! Hurry. Do something before your splenetic ex-lover kills another guy."

Albert called Hannah. "Hello, mother-in-law."

"Hi, Albert. How are you doing? How is the baby?"

"We are fine. I want to give you a copy of my new book. Can I visit now?"

"Yes, you can."

"See you soon."

Albert looked at Zita. "Please, darling, stay here with Sarah. I want to see Hannah. I will be back soon."

Later, Albert knocked on Hannah's door.

Hannah opened the door. "Hello, Albert."

"Close the door."

She closed the door. "What's up?"

"I want to kick your ass."

"This is an inappropriate language. How do you talk to

your mother-in-law like that? Where is the book? Why are you angry?"

"Why did you kill the CIA agents?"

"Do I look like a murderer?"

"Stop lying. You killed CIA operatives in Hong Kong and elsewhere. You conducted the recent killings of CIA agents. Revenge and killing evil people would not bring Michael back. Do you want to spend the rest of your life in jail? Please, do not endanger your daughter and grandchild. Do you want me to call the FBI?"

"What are you talking about?"

"You looked at classified documents in my house. I can take Sarah and Edward to a secure place in England and leave you alone. Do you understand?"

Hannah threw her arms around his neck and wept against his shoulder like a tortured girl. "Please, don't leave me. I am scared. You do not know how I felt when I saw Michael's gruesome death. He called me an hour before his death and said, 'the doctor says we can have babies.' He wanted to have sex with me and make me pregnant, but the CIA murderers killed him in cold blood. I went through hell because of his death. I am afraid. Please, protect me."

"I will. How did you kill the agents?"

"I did not do it. I asked the Anonymous assassins to do the job."

"Get clothes and come with me."

Forty minutes later, they were in Albert's house. Albert stretched her arms toward Sarah. "Surprise! Your mom will stay with us tonight. Let us have dinner."

After dinner, Albert asked Zita and Hannah to come to his office.

Hannah stared at Zita. "Can we get some privacy?"

"Zita knows everything."

"What should we do?"

"There is an idea in my head."

"What's it?"

"Leave this matter to me. Please, I don't want Sarah to know about this matter. Let us see her and have a drink."

Three days later, Albert traveled to Monterrey in Mexico and met a bearded, Marxist friend called Antonio Martinez.

"Hello, comrade Albert. Great to see you again. How is your life with Uncle Sam's imperialism?"

"Uncle Sam is in deep trouble in Afghanistan, Iraq, and elsewhere. The Muslim lunatics will blow up his ass very hard. You know how I feel about greedy capitalism, hegemony, and war. The current U.S. president is an evil psychopathic moron. He disregards human life and suffering. I snickered when he said on an aircraft carrier, 'mission accomplished.' Where?"

"On the moon. American troops killed and maimed tens of thousands of innocent families in Afghanistan and Iraq. Stupid and arrogant Americans don't admit their crimes."

"Are you free?"

"I am always free. I have never been a slave."

"Can you take me to our old shack at La Estanzuela Park?"

"I can. We will take the truck."

Albert and Antonio went to a remote cottage near a waterfall at La Estanzuela Park. Albert put his right hand on a stucco wall. "Do you remember this place in the revolutionary days?"

"Yes. Here we trained our comrades and printed pamphlets for the insurgencies in America."

"I am thinking of making a new revolution."

"With Nahatatama and Homatakawa?"

Albert stared at Antonio with concerned eyes. "Have you met them?"

"I did not meet Nahatatama, but I saw Homatakawa from a long distance, fighting with incredible bravery like a Shaolin monk. He lived with an indigenous tribe in the mountains of Oaxaca and learned native dialects. He moved to America in 1995."

"In 1995? I came across him when he punished the federal officers who pursued me in 1995."

"He is the fastest and fiercest man on earth. He uses hatchets, swords, arrows, spikes, bayonets, and other tools to butcher our adversaries. Only a missile or an atom bomb can stop him. A young assassin called Tilatowate is his assistant. Their mission is to defend our group and execute our enemies."

"How do the members of the Anonymous interact with Nahatatama, Homatakawa, and Tilatowate?"

"Only one person can contact them. We call him the Messenger or Hatakachita."

"Who is he?"

"He is the hidden mastermind of the Anonymous intelligence unit. He lives in the U.S. and conveys Nahatatama's orders."

"Have you seen Homatakawa's face?"

"No. Homatakawa wears a mask and a helmet. People say he wears a mask because something burned his face. How is your work with Zita Marino? Do you still see her?"

"Zita? Do you know her?"

"Yes. Zita is one of our trustworthy comrades. I gave her guns to kill CIA operatives in Latin America."

Albert paused with staring eyes and cogitated for a moment. He thought no one else knew about Zita's deadly mission. "One of your trustworthy comrades?"

"Yes. Zita's mission was to execute the CIA officers who formed the death squads in Latin America. As a skilled shooter, she shot down CIA airplanes in 1984 and 1986 and a chopper in 1987. She stopped her military activities in 1990 to look after her family."

"Wow! Who gave her guns in South America?"

"José Mujica's comrades."

"Who funds your group?"

"Our comrades and a rich American businesswoman named Hannah Rogers fund the group."

"Oh, my God!"

"God? Which God? The poor guy who was crucified in Palestine?"

"I am shocked. Hannah is my mother-in-law."

"She is a dedicated lady. She leaked CIA documents to me, and Zita came here to get them. For personal reasons, Hannah vowed to wipe out the CIA agents outside America. She poisoned and exterminated imperialist mercenaries on four continents. She spies and works for our Anonymous group."

"Your Anonymous group? I thought Peter Stone had founded the group."

"That's true. Peter Stone and his son Jamie had founded the group and set up a sophisticated international network of radical activists. There is an Anonymous boss in every country. You see, we do the dirty job, and you fight books and theories. I am the boss in Mexico, and

Hannah is the Anonymous leader in America.”

“Oh dear. No one would believe Hannah is the most dangerous woman in America.”

“That’s why we call ourselves the Anonymous. There are over one thousand Anonymous warriors in the U.S. They use digital and laser technology. Homatakawa is their commander.”

“How did they enter the country?”

“From Mexico to Arizona, Texas, and California. The Anonymous warriors are digital illusionists and masters of disappearance. They hypnotize the border patrol agents and live in private houses in the major cities.”

“What if people betray the Anonymous? What would happen to them?”

“Our assassins would execute them without delay.”

“Do you cooperate with the Internet hacktivist group Anonymous?”

“Some of our guys are Anonymous hacktivists. Our scientists and information technology engineers insert electronic chips in electrical and mobile gadgets. The old method of espionage is over. We get information from intelligence and military institutions without making a stink.”

“I learn new things every day. However, something is bothering me.”

“What is it?”

“Why does the Anonymous protect me?”

Antonio put his arm on Albert’s shoulders. “Because you are the mind and heart of the Anonymous.”

“Can you explain?”

“You advised us in the early 1980s to create robot assassins, a network of magicians, and an international organization to confront imperialism and the traitors of justice. You said the problem with political activists is that they do not work like intelligence agents. Peter Stone and his son Jamie took your valuable advice and formed the Anonymous. By Nahatatama's orders, the members of the Anonymous must pledge to guard you."

Albert rested his face on his hand in disbelief. "Why? Am I Jesus Christ's son? How don't I know that? This is the weirdest thing I have ever heard. I do nothing for the Anonymous."

"Your intellectual work is our overall strategy."

"Why does the Anonymous spend so much time, money, and effort to safeguard me?"

"Only Jamie Stone and Nahatatama would answer your question. They said we must protect and save you to preserve our artificial intelligence robot technology."

"Which robot technology? I am the last guy who would figure out this type of technology."

"Jamie Stone founded an underground laboratory for robot and cyborg technology."

"Where?"

"Somewhere in East Asia."

"What is the connection between this lab and me?"

"I do not know why our technology experts want to keep you intact. Anyway, against whom do you want to rebel?"

"Against the warmongering prigs in Washington, D.C." Albert unzipped his bag, opened his laptop, and typed.

"What is this language?"

"It is Arabic."

"Is it about Iraq?"

"Yes. Wait to hear the news. Trust me. Iraq will turn into an inferno for the U.S. troops."

Antonio smiled and patted Albert's shoulders. "*Viva la revolución.*"

Albert typed five-hundred Arabic words. "Antonio, take me to an Internet shop. But before that, I need a Mexican hat."

They returned to Barrio Antiguo in Monterrey. After eating spicy food at a restaurant, Albert bought two Mexican hats. "This is for you, my dear comrade. You are a great friend." Later, he entered an Internet shop and sent an attached message to an Islamist website.

"Done. Thank you, comrade Antonio."

Four days afterward, Albert and Sarah were in their home. Albert turned on the TV. "Let us watch Zita."

Zita started her nightly news. "Good evening. We have a breaking news story for you. Abu Musab al-Zarqawi's al-Qaeda terrorist group in Iraq has claimed responsibility for the brutal assassination of the former CIA agents Robert Buckley, Joseph Anderson, Kevin Walker, and Larry Clark ... We will show you now the video that the terrorists have released."

A masked militant appeared. "In the name of Allah, the Most Gracious, the Most Merciful ... We have executed the CIA filthy infidels Robert Buckley, Joseph Anderson, Kevin Walker, and Larry Clark in the heart of America, the land of the oppressive unbelievers who have caused the death of thousands of our brothers and sisters in Iraq ... Allah is the Greatest, and death to the enemies of Islam."

After the news, Albert called Hannah. "Good evening, my favorite mother-in-law."

"Yes, my favorite son-in-law."

"Can you come for dinner tomorrow? Edward wants to kiss his gorgeous grandma."

"Tell him his gorgeous grandma will come to kiss him."

The next day, Albert kissed Hannah's face and hissed. "Have you seen the news?"

"Yes. You are incredible."

"Go to my office. A special guest is waiting for you."

Hannah entered the office and saw Zita sitting at Albert's desk.

"Come in, darling. Close the door."

Hannah sat on the opposite side of the desk. "Hi, Zita. What are you doing here?"

"I am not here to interrogate you. I want to discuss how we can collaborate."

"What do you want?"

Zita opened an envelope and showed Hannah a photo. "What is this?"

With a shy face, Hannah stared at Zita. "How did you get this photo?"

"What were you doing with these binoculars at the Kisco River? Were you spying on Albert and me?"

"Sorry for that. I wanted to know about your special friendship with Albert. Do you have an affair with him?"

"I am his copy editor. Be careful. Italian men don't like the stalkers who spy on their women."

"What else?"

"Peter Stone asked us to follow Nahatatama's orders and protect Albert. We need to do good things for Albert and Sarah."

"Peter Stone. Nahatatama. Sarah. Why are you here?"

"How is the Anonymous company?"

Hannah scowled at Zita with challenging eyes. "What

is the Anonymous company?"

Zita gave Hannah an envelope containing four photos. "These photos are evidence of your covert work for Latino guerrillas."

"How did you get the photos?"

"I am the best investigative journalist in the town."

"What is your point?"

"You funded my guerilla operations in the 1980s. I shot down the CIA planes. You gave Antonio Martinez CIA documents, and I got them from him. I know you finance the Anonymous organization and its lab. Should I mention the agents whom you killed?"

"You didn't answer my question."

"I have two plans for your daughter and against the CIA?"

"What do you want from my daughter?"

"I want to make her the most powerful woman in New York."

"Is this a joke? How?"

"First, I want her to be the next mayor."

"The next mayor? Are you kidding?"

"No. I need your cooperation."

"What about the CIA?"

"We wish to do something about the CIA's mayhem."

"What do you want to do?"

"I want you to get me maps of underground tunnels that link the CIA headquarters to nearby areas such as George Mason University."

"Why?"

"I want to organize a carnival."

"What if I say no?"

"You can't say no. I will send your military photos to

the CIA and the FBI."

Hannah lost her patience. "Are you threatening me? Are you a journalist or what?"

"Calm down, honey. I am your boss."

"No one is my boss. You are a lunatic sociopath. I am leaving."

Zita opened a box and placed a Che Guevara helmet on the desk. "Wait. Do you like to buy my helmet?"

"I don't drive motorcycles."

"What about this mask?" Zita put a Che Guevara leather mask on the desk. "Do you remember San Pedro La Laguna in Guatemala? Who saved you?"

In the haunting recesses of her memory, Hannah recalled the harrowing encounter with the masked woman, a mysterious figure shrouded in the iconic visage of Che Guevara. The troubling backdrop was the dense and foreboding forest near San Pedro, a labyrinth of uncertainty during the tumultuous Guatemalan civil war. "Oh, my God! Are you the Che Guevara girl who saved my life in Guatemala?"

"Yes, and sorry for the rough ride on the old motorcycle."

Hannah placed her right fingers on her mouth and feared Zita. "Do you work for the Anonymous?"

"Maybe. Are you the leader of the Anonymous?"

"You said you are my boss."

"OK. I am the head of the Anonymous in America. Are you going to collaborate?"

"Yes." Hannah hugged her. "Thank you so much for saving my life in 1988. I am alive because of you."

"You are welcome. Does Albert know Nahatatama, Homatakawa, and Tilatowate?"

"No, I don't think so."

"Are you ready?" Zita extended her right hand, and Hannah kissed it. "Thank you. You have remained loyal to the Anonymous."

"Does Sarah know what we do?"

"No, and she will never know. Be vigilant. The CIA and the NSA want to find out more things about Albert's contacts with our comrades. Leave no evidence in your house."

"I am careful."

"Do you know the real name of the Black Wolf?"

"No. You and I had executed his filthy operatives. I think the chairman of Faux News, Jim Simons, knows him."

Zita looked at her polished fingernails. "How is your relationship with Jim?"

"He is a close friend."

"I will ask activists to hack his emails and phone calls. Can you ask your guys to install cameras in his offices?"

"I think so. Can you tell me something about our leaders, Nahatatama and Homatakawa? Where do they live?"

"The Anonymous does not allow us to ask these questions."

"What should we do for Albert?"

"He is a man of love and peace."

"Is Ann Stone his secret lover?"

"She is the mother of his eldest daughter. She lived a hard life after the murder of her parents and grandparents." Zita kissed Hannah's lips. "Let us go out and kick some asses."

Chapter 12

Mary became Olivia's inextricable lover and partner in the pacifist struggle against injustice. In August 2005, they returned to Columbia University to do a master's degree in broadcast journalism. After their graduation in 2006, they worked as beat reporters and photographers for news agencies and renewed their human rights, feminist, and peace activism. They crusaded for lesbian legal rights, and Olivia became a celebrated TV host of a controversial show called *Lesbian Talk.*

As a tireless activist in New York, Olivia felt her need for her father's erudite knowledge to give her activism a boost. One evening, she invited him to deliver an informal lecture at her Lesbian, Gay, Bisexual and Transgender Community Center in Manhattan.

The festooned hall of the LGBT Center was full of feminist and latitudinarian women. Albert was the only heterosexual man there, and before his lecture, Olivia stood and held a microphone.

"Dear gorgeous friends, a warm welcome to you all. You might have already speculated on why Dr. Albert Russell is here. He is here to talk about our freedom to love, our freedom to choose, our freedom to be who we are. I assure you he is more feminine than many women. At least he is more womanlike than George W. Bush's warmongering Secretary of State Condoleezza Rice."

"Oh yeah," the crowd roared.

"How do I know that irrefutable fact? Well, he is my adorable father."

"Wow! Wow!" the audience screamed.

"Our wonderful sweetheart and patron Sarah Rogers will make an important announcement after the lecture. Let me now invite Dr. Russell to speak."

After opening her ochre purse, Sarah picked up a tissue paper and wiped two tears. Zita touched her left hand and grinned. Albert stood behind a rostrum, glanced at his wife, Olivia, Mary, and Zita, who were in the front row, and the audience.

"Good evening. How are you today?"

"We are all right. We are good. Thank you," the crowd yelled.

"The title of my lecture tonight is 'Freedom and Love.' People, in general, say they respect the law of the land and advocate freedom. They may mean freedom of speech and political emancipation. But when it comes to our natural instincts, many people prate about false gods, outdated laws, and obscurant taboos to control our freedom. They tell us whom we should love, and whom we must not love. They do not realize that our emotions, desires, passions, and imaginations are who we are. Who can regulate our emotional desires and dictate to us how we should love? They say God created Adam and Eve, not Adam and Steve ... If the world is a man's heart, the heart is a woman's world ... Woman was not created for love, but love was made for her. Love is a woman's whole being, a woman's history ... A woman filled with love cannot be defeated. Let me end this lecture by saying that when you stand on your feet, you occupy a small place in the world. When you stand for love and good principles, the world becomes a small place for you. I love you."

The women in the hall cheered and clapped. Olivia hugged and thanked her father after he finished his thought-provoking lecture. Old and young women shook his hand and expressed their heartfelt appreciation of his advocacy for lesbian rights.

Sarah stood. "The two-party political system in our country is cruel and ineffectual. The mayors of the great New York City have been sexist and partisan men. It is the time for a liberated woman to be the next mayor. I announce my intent to run for mayor. Thank you."

Olivia's extraordinary love for her supportive father had intensified after he became her consultant on LGBT issues. Meanwhile, her affection for Mary had grown profound and irrepressible. This was the opportune time to prove her quintessential commitment to their love. One day, she and her father visited Greenwich Jewelers in downtown New York City and examined expensive rings before they picked up a gold one and diamond earrings.

Olivia planned to celebrate Mary's twenty-seventh birthday in the Holiday Inn restaurant on 39th Street. They went there on Mary's birthday, sat at a square table, and ordered food and wine. Olivia touched Mary's hand. "Sweetheart, you are my love and soulmate. Do you have any idea how much I love you? I want to be with you forever."

Mary beamed. "I want to be with you until the end of the next century."

Olivia inserted her hand into her sparkling pink purse and opened a ring box.

"Honey, will you marry me?"

"Let me think." Mary winked and paused for a second. "Oh, my God! I will never say no to that. Yes, love, I will marry you. This ring is very chic. Honey, I love you so much."

They kissed, touched hands, and wept with joy. After dinner, they moved up to their hotel room and made love.

In the morning, Olivia kissed Mary, who was still in bed. "I need fresh air and want to call my dad."

Olivia, wearing high-waisted shorts and a T-shirt, left the room barefoot, walked to the end of the carpeted corridor, and relaxed on wide stairs. She used her cell phone. "Dad, love, I have good news for you."

"What is it, darling?"

"Mary and I have agreed to get married."

"Congratulations! Darling, I am happy for both of you."

"My love for Mary will never overcome my love for you and Sarah. Please, dad, I need you more than ever. I need your love. Marriage will be a massive thing in my life. I want you to be with me at this crucial time. The conservative imbeciles will do their worst to annul the marriage. They say same-sex marriage is illegal."

"Sweetie, I will be with you and stand up for your rights. I will fight for your right to marry Mary. Come here and give your daddy and Sarah big hugs."

Two months later, Olivia called her father. "Dad, my big day will be on the 23rd of this month. Please, take note of this day."

"We will be with you, but I have one condition."

Olivia gaped at her cell phone. "What is it, dad?"

"I, Sarah, and Mary's parents must have breakfast with you at ten o'clock in the morning after the wedding day. This is an English tradition."

"That is all, cheeky monkey? I thought there was a serious problem, you horrifying devil. OK. We will have a super breakfast together. Do you have another life-threatening condition, sexy dandy?"

"Yes, I want tons of hugs and kisses."

"You will get tons of hugs and kisses. The wedding party will be in the Plaza Hotel."

A week before the wedding day, Olivia, Sarah, and Albert walked on Madison Avenue in the Upper East Side to get clothing. "Look over there. To the right. Intrusive camera operators are following us and taking photos."

"Dad, we are popular celebrities in New York. This is normal."

As they entered a fashion store, Albert saw a camera operator taking unauthorized photos of them. "Wait here. I want to reproach that impudent cameraman."

Sarah smiled. "Leave him. We are in a public place. This is America, not England."

"He has left the store."

"These snoopy people want photos for celebrity magazines."

Olivia selected glamorous underwear and party garments and asked her dad and Sarah to come into the dressing room. She tried on clothes and wanted to know their view. She felt it was natural for her father to glance at her body and see her change clothes. There was no chichi posturing, and there was no sense of fake shame. Olivia wanted women to love their fathers as she loves hers. Wouldn't life be more enjoyable and pleasant?

On that day, Olivia wore a sleeveless, red party dress in her house and asked her father, Sarah, and Mary to comment on her choice of clothing. "Gorgeous," they said. After that, Olivia took off her dress and satin shelf bra and let everyone see her naked body.

Mary turned her face up and looked sullen. "Olivia, what is this? Change your clothes in another room. Don't you see? Your dad is here."

"Yes, this man is my dad. I know that."

"I don't stand naked in front of my dad. This is inappropriate and rude. You are a big woman now."

"What? I changed my clothes when your sister was with us. What is the difference between your sister and my dad?"

"He is a man."

"What does that mean? Do you mean my dad is a depraved man? Or you think my dad will rape me if he sees me naked? No one, and I mean no one, will separate my dad from me. Yes, there are demonic dads who abuse their daughters. Don't you know my dad? You and I are lesbians and attracted to women. You will not mind if a woman friend looks at our naked body. Why can't my dad see my body? Please, darling, I dislike our religious and social cant."

Albert placed his left arm around Mary's shoulders. "Let us discuss the wedding party."

On the wedding day, Albert, Sarah, Ann, Ayita, and Olivia went in a black Chrysler car to the United Church of Christ on Broadway. As predicted, there were media reporters and Christian protesters carrying anti-gay banners, such as "Not Blessed Just Cursed," "God Hates You," "You Are Going to Hell," "Homosexuality is an Abomination to God Almighty," "God is Your Enemy," "Repent or Perish," "Homosexuality is a Threat to National Security," "Homo Sex is Sin," "Homosexuals are Possessed by Demons."

"Here are the conservative jerks and the evangelical dullards." Olivia glowered and left the car. A reporter asked her. "Ms. Olivia Russell, how do you feel today?"

"This is a wonderful day for women's freedom and choice."

Zita Marino was there that morning. "Hello, Albert."

"Hi, Zita."

She held a microphone. "What do you think of gay marriage?"

"I advocate free love and the liberty to choose. We cannot tell people whom they must love."

"Do you have any concern that your public presence at your daughter's lesbian marriage might undermine your reputation?"

"My beloved daughter is more important than my academic stature. Please, have a seat in the church and take photos."

"Yes, sir." Zita entered the church, sat on a front seat, and reflected on her love relationship with Albert.

Albert held Olivia's arm and moved into the church. When they walked down the church aisle, he sang in a faint voice. "Here comes the bride. She is six feet wide."

Olivia glanced at him and beamed.

When the wedding service finished, Olivia kissed Mary, Sarah, Ann, Ayita, Hannah, Zita, and Barbara. She cuddled her father. "I will give you a big kiss later, my lovely man. I love you." She hugged him again and wept.

Albert stared at the church door and thought he saw Homatakawa. "Just a moment, darling." He sprinted to the door and looked around, but Homatakawa vanished into the air.

"Dad, what happened? Why did you run?"

"Something in my head has prompted me to look for someone I know."

They left for the Plaza Hotel on Fifth Avenue, and there were over 250 feminists and lesbians. In a stunning, sleeveless, white frock, Olivia danced with Mary and lesbian friends. After a while, she saw her father dancing with Sarah.

"Dad, can I dance with you?"

"Yes, sweetie. I would love to dance with you. Excuse me, Sarah."

Olivia put her left hand on her father's right shoulder and gazed at his beaming face. "Oh, dad, I have always dreamed of dancing with you on my wedding day. I have always thought of my unbreakable love for you. My love for you is true and everlasting. I wish to hug and kiss you all the time. You are my spirit, soul, and joy. Do we need to live away from each other? You have taught me love and what love means. You are the only man I love. Thank you for everything you have done for me. Thank you for all the love you have given me. I love you so much. I wish my mom ..." She broke down and swooned to the floor. She could not get up on her feet.

"Olivia, darling," Albert screeched.

Mary, Sarah, Ann, Ayita, and Zita jumped off their chairs, and other people halted their dance and encircled Olivia. "Olivia, are you OK?"

Tears ran down her cheeks. "Yes, I am fine. I am just exhausted. It has been a long day."

Albert lifted her up. "Stay with Mary."

After the party, Olivia, Mary, and their families moved to their hotel rooms. The next day, Mary and Olivia wore bright dresses and descended to the hotel restaurant. Mary's parents and sister, Albert, and Sarah sat at a round table. Albert was in his midnight blue suit. Sarah was resplendent in a light pink bodycon dress, and a pearl necklace gleamed on her bare neck and shoulders.

Olivia sat beside her father and Mary. She looked, with a cheerful smile, at her father. "Good morning, dad." She gave him a soft kiss beside his lips.

After they chatted and finished breakfast, Albert whispered into Sarah's right ear. Sarah beamed, and Albert stood. "Sweethearts Olivia and Mary, we wish you a fantastic life full of happiness and love. Excuse us. Sarah and I ought to go now. We want to talk about Mr. Obama."

"Obama?" Olivia reacted.

Albert held Sarah's left arm, and both walked away from the table. A moment later, Sarah turned her face back. "What's wrong with politics in the morning?" She glanced at Albert's face and rested her head on his right shoulder.

Chapter 13

The 24th of August seemed like an ordinary, sunlit day in the indefatigable New York City. After wearing a white shirt, a carmine jacket, and a short black skirt, Olivia kissed her wife and got a taxi to Bloomberg Tower in Midtown Manhattan, where she hosted her galvanizing show. When the cab stopped on Lexington Avenue, Olivia noticed, through the taxi window, the unusual collective presence of news reporters holding microphones and TV cameras.

She left the cab and encountered the scrambling reporters who encircled her from all sides, and the camera people who took flash photos and baffled her.

"Good morning, Ms. Olivia Russell. What do you say about the present allegations against you?" a corpulent reporter inquired.

Olivia clutched her maroon leather purse. "What are

these allegations?”

“There are serious accusations regarding your incest relationship with your father,” a reporter answered.

“This is fictional.”

“Do you mean you don’t have sex with your dad?” a pyknic journalist asked.

Olivia struggled to quell her rising rage. “This is preposterous. How do you ask me such a foolhardy question? I don’t have sex with my dad. I am a married lesbian, as everybody knows.”

“Excuse me. What about the erogenous photos which the newspapers have published today?” a female reporter asked.

Agitated and disturbed, Olivia could say nothing further. She scurried into the colossal building and ascended to her exclusive office. She turned on the TV and, with a sense of foreboding, watched the dismaying news about her, and about her father and Sarah. One rotund Republican commentator pilloried. “They say Ms. Sarah Rogers is the illegitimate child and wife of a Columbia philosopher of religion. He is a philosopher of disgusting filth.” A supremacist expositor on another TV channel had scorned. “How could our universities hire a British thinker involved in a sexual liaison with his unchaste daughter? This is egregious and repulsive.”

Meanwhile, Albert walked to the kitchen in his house to eat breakfast and watch the TV. He opened the fridge to get milk and twisted his face toward the TV after he heard a news anchor mentioning his name.

“Unbelievable! Total garbage! Welcome to America, the fertile land of scandals.”

He dashed to his bedroom and removed his clothes.

Sarah and Edward were in bed. "Albert, where are you going?"

"I need to see Olivia."

"Why?"

He picked up a remote control and switched on the TV. "That is why."

A news reporter held a microphone. "We are still waiting for a response from Professor Albert Russell. The evidence we have suggests he is married to his daughter and has an affair with his lesbian daughter."

"The jackasses have published private pictures of us. They have been spying on me."

Sarah raised her head. "Who are they?"

"They are the big brothers of the deep state and the bellicose dolts who hate peace and who think they can subdue me. This vitriolic fuss is about you, not about Olivia and me."

"What do you mean?"

"The grouchy conservatives do not want you to be the mayor of this city."

The phone buzzed. "I will be there shortly."

"Who was that?"

"The Dean of my department wants to see me. Do not worry, darling. I always have an alternative plan for such cases."

"Which plan?"

"Whether they like it or not, you will become the city's mayor. I promise."

"How?" Sarah glared at the TV. "Oh, my God! Do you have an affair with Olivia?"

"Don't be daft. I will force your mom or another guy to disclose a big mystery about you."

Albert left the house. There was a group of reporters and camera people waiting for him. Albert saw Zita Marino and preferred to talk to her.

"Good morning, Professor Russell."

"Good morning, Zita."

"I want to ask you two straightforward questions. Is your wife your daughter? Do you have a secret liaison with your lesbian daughter?"

"I do not deny that my daughter and I love each other. Having incest with her is ridiculous. Both of us are public figures. I renounce the lie that my wife is my biological daughter. Excuse me, please. I must go to my university. Thank you."

The defamatory news and remarks had perforated into Olivia's mind like a poisonous dagger. A brunette secretary came in with a memo. "Chairman Mark Johnson wants to see you right away in his office."

With an aching, trembling heart, Olivia passed up her flabbergasted colleagues and trod to the Chairman's office.

"Good morning, Olivia. Please, sit here," Chairman Johnson spoke with an emotionless tone. "You have confounded us. What is going on in your life?"

"What have I done to deserve this hatred?"

Johnson rubbed his jutting chin, shrugging off her simple answer. "Didn't you read the papers and view the news this morning?"

She gazed at his flinty stare. "I saw the news. What should I do?"

He sneezed. "What do you say about these damaging reports?" He threw five tabloids on a square table beside her. Some headlines were, "LESBIAN OLIVIA RUSSELL AND HER LOVE AFFAIR WITH HER FATHER," "A

COLUMBIA SCHOLAR IS MARRIED TO HIS DAUGHTER," "THE SECRET LIFE OF A LESBIAN," "A PERVERTED PHILOSOPHER AND HIS LIAISON WITH HIS DAUGHTER," "SARAH ROGERS: LOVE CHILD OF A COLUMBIA SCHOLAR," "OLIVIA RUSSELL: LESBIAN OR NOT?"

Inflamed and dumbfounded, she could not provide a cogent argument. "This is nonsense. This is untrue."

"Is it untrue? What do you say about these shameful photos?" Johnson pointed at romantic shots of her and her father in the tabloids.

With a worrisome soulfulness, she glimpsed at the photos on the front pages. "There is no sex here. These are hugs and kisses."

Johnson tittered. "What do you call these hugs and kisses? Do good daughters sit on their dads' knees and kiss their mouths in Central Park?"

"I am a free and conscientious woman, and I love my dad. The hateful conservative Republicans and the Tea Party dweebs are targeting me because of my lesbian show and candid criticism of their ideology and politics."

Chairman Johnson knew that Olivia's show had attracted millions of viewers nationwide and generated millions of dollars in revenue. "I have trusted you and appreciated your innovative talents and creativity. Big shots had scolded me when I hired you because you are an outspoken lesbian. I need clear answers before I decide about your job here."

"Please, give me some time to resolve the matter."

"Your show today will be the last one. Do not panic. You have eight weeks to give me a reliable response."

"Thank you."

"You can leave now."

Olivia left Johnson's office and noted her colleagues were staring with pejorative suspicion. The incest accusations were grievous and malicious, and she thought she must defend herself and her father.

Back in her office, she stretched her legs on a counter, thinking of what she should do. She mulled over her fascinating life with her wife, father, Sarah, and homosexual friends. She felt the disturbing news had provoked them. How would a young woman like her challenge the powerful media? When she twisted her bobbed hair and pondered her hapless predicament, her phone rang.

"Honey, I am bugged. It seems this is our new battle. You have my full support," Sarah said.

"I have no clue about the vindictive accusations. The news has surprised me, and the diabolical conservatives are playing a dirty game against you and me."

"Honey, you are a public figure and need to be careful. Did your dad speak to you?"

"No. I guess he is meeting the board of the university. Love, I will talk to you later. I want to sort out this crappy mess."

"OK, sweetheart. Take care. I am thinking of you. I love you."

"I love you too."

In the Department of Philosophy on 1150 Amsterdam Avenue, Albert met the Dean, the Provost, the Secretary of the University, executive vice presidents, and senior scholars. With a serious face, the Dean began the meeting. "Dear Professor Russell, we acknowledge your immense contribution and sincere dedication to the university. It is the policy of the university not to interfere in people's private lives, and to advocate equality and freedom. The university received calls from influential groups and organizations asking us to terminate your work. May I request you to tell us the truth?"

Albert smiled with amiable lips. "Thanks for calling me. I did not and do not have a sexual relationship with my daughter. Almost everyone in this city knows she is a radical, lesbian activist who behaves like a free libertarian feminist. My wife, Sarah Rogers, belongs to a well-known American family. Her mother is a famous Yale scholar and a great-granddaughter of William Barton Rogers, who founded the Massachusetts Institute of Technology in 1861. Thus, the canard that the powerful Rogers family had allowed Sarah Rogers to marry her biological father is unthinkable. Thus, the current defamation is preposterous and nonsensical. The unfounded allegations relate to my critique of the White House, the Congress, the CIA, the Pentagon, the Department of State, the evangelical churches, and other hawkish institutions that promote regressive fundamentalism and aggressive foreign policy. The homophobic, misogynist accusers avoid the avaricious producers of violent pornography, which fills our homes and streets with degrading vulgarism, and point their lethal guns at a young lesbian feminist because she hugs and kisses her father in public places."

"What are you going to do?" The Secretary asked.

"I will litigate a case against Faux News Corporation and hope you will postpone your decision on my work until a court makes a verdict."

The Provost rested his hand on the table. "You can continue to teach or apply for a vacation until the university discovers the full truth. Please, avoid having public interviews at the university."

After the meeting, Albert called his daughter. "Hello, sweetie. How are you, darling? How did you receive the abject slanders?"

"They have made me miserable. Did you listen to the news?"

"Do not worry at all. I will explain a few things when I see you. I will always be there for you. Yes, I listened to the unfortunate news. Welcome to America!"

"Dad, what do you think we should do?"

"We should sue Faux News Corporation. I do not have a qualified lawyer. Do you recommend a brilliant one?"

"I work with a good and dauntless lawyer. Her name is Lauren Jefferson. She campaigns for the gay rights in the State of New York. I will give her a visit soon."

"Darling, I am proud of you. Do not let the corporate news ruin your life and marriage. Your dad will forever be with you."

"I appreciate that. Talk to you soon. Bye for now. I love you."

Olivia checked her cell phone and made a call. "Hi, Lauren. This is Olivia Russell."

"Good morning, Olivia. Oh dear, what is the story this time?"

"The conservative barbarians say I have a sexual relationship with my dad."

"I watched the distasteful news. This is weird. You are a married lesbian activist. But, dear, the photos with your dad are out of the norm. How did they get them?"

"They have been spying on my dad and me."

"Yes, we know their cruddy work. What are you going

to do about the defamatory allegations?”

“We want to sue Faux News Corporation. Can you take up this case?”

“I will pursue the case for the sake of your sexy eyes. Can you come here before we do anything?”

“Can I visit you right now?”

“Yes, you can.”

Olivia got a taxicab and visited Lauren Jefferson in her office. She gave Lauren a swift kiss on her face and rested on a brown leather seat.

Lauren, with an oblong face and brunette hair, sat opposite to her, crossing a leg over the other and smiling. “Tell me, Olivia, and be honest with me. Do you have an affair with your father?”

“I refuse to call it an affair. My dad loves me, and I love him. I always make it clear to my friends that my dad is the only man I love. This love does not mean I have a sexual relationship with him.”

“What about Sarah?”

“Sarah is not my dad’s daughter. The asshats want to destroy her because she wants to be the new mayor. I hug and kiss her when I meet her. I don’t have an affair with her.”

“What about the photos?”

“I kiss my dad when we see each other. My wife kisses him too. I also kiss my lesbian friends. We do not suck lips and tongues and make love to each other. The conservative schmucks think my swift peck on my dad’s lips is incest. We do not. The Mediterranean peoples kiss their relatives and friends.”

“Yes, but your soothing arms around your dad’s neck and seductive kisses show you are in love with him.”

"He is my dad, for God's sake. I am in love with him without a shred of doubt. What is wrong with that? Please, I am a committed wife, and my dad has a beautiful wife. I do not make love to my married dad. Kissing or holding hands in public places is not sex."

"That's fine. First, I will speak to Faux News and try to negotiate an acceptable deal. I will ask them to offer an official apology and financial compensation for the emotional and psychological damages that were incurred because of the false allegations. We will then initiate a formal lawsuit in the court if they refuse. What do you think?"

"Do your best."

"Remember that going to a court means prosecutors and lawyers will force you to expose confidential details about your private life. This includes your father's academic reputation and his relationship with Sarah."

"My dad and I are not afraid of talking about our private life."

"That's good."

Amid the shadows of despair, Olivia found herself once again at the imposing edifice of Bloomberg Tower. Clinging to the frayed strands of hope, she forged ahead, determined to embark on her program with a resilience that belied the turmoil within.

In a quiet moment of introspection, she sought refuge in a bathroom. As the cool water cascaded her face, she wrestled with the burden of her circumstances. Yet, undeterred, she adorned herself with a veneer of strength, painting her lips with an audacious stroke of glossy red lipstick.

A female guide, marked by over-the-ear headphones,

led her into a surreal pink-hued studio. The atmosphere crackled with an unspoken tension as Olivia took her place on a gamboge seat.

With shorn locks and a gaze, she crossed her legs, and her hands rested on her bare knee. As the studio lights cast a glow, Olivia fixed her gaze upon the eye of a TV camera.

When a director showed her a go-ahead signal, Olivia began her show. "Good evening, ladies and gentlemen. I am Olivia Russell. Welcome to *Lesbian Talk*. Well, there are exciting surprises today. I will tone down the topic of lesbian marriage for personal reasons.

I guess you have read the papers and watched the news. What I wish to say is that I am innocent and did no wrong. As I have defended lesbianism and my right to marry my girlfriend, I will fight for my affection for the only man I love. Yes, I say to everybody watching me now that he is the only man I love from the deep bottom of my heart.

It is unfair for the media and individuals to form judgments about me without first reading my story, which is a narrative centered on pure love. In its essence, love is not a crime, nor is it a sin. Love is not sex. Love is not anti-Americanism. We should make love our drink, food, and air. Love is the most significant sign of justice. It exists to let us forget the pain of death. Are we scared of love? Why do people associate love with sexual intercourse? We love our families, our country, our homes, our clothes, our cars, our games. Is love more treacherous than the heartless men engaged in gruesome wars? What prevents us from choosing whom we love?

The religious fundamentalists in this great country advocate animosity rather than love. They endorse war over justice and peace. Despite declaring ourselves the wealthiest and most powerful nation, a sizable portion of our population struggles with poverty, homelessness, and illness. Instead of moral sanctimony, our fellow citizens need care and compassion. It is paradoxical that, while proclaiming our trust in God, we inflict harm on others in the name of this very deity. Yes, don't look down on others because their sins differ from your sins.

Who can regulate our natural feelings and instincts? The devilish conservatives impel us to stamp out our genuine emotions and passions. They want us to be phonies. They talk about Jesus Christ, who was born in a mucky manger and died on a cross, and all they care about is money, power, and war. Jesus said, 'love your neighbor,' and they say, 'hate your neighbor.' Jesus said, 'blessed are the peacemakers,' and they say, 'blessed are the warmakers.' Jesus said, 'know the truth, and the truth shall make you free,' and they say, 'stay away from the truth because we don't want you to be free.' Where is our freedom to love whom we choose? We must live in love, with love, and for love.

I wish to inform you that I will talk in public about my true story with my father. It is an inspiring story about a daughter's unblemished love for her adored father. I am not afraid of saying I love my father. This love is not about sex. Rather, it is about unending affection, care, compassion, and warmth.

What causes us to suppress our innate emotions and sentiments? Why do we refrain from expressing our true thoughts and feelings within us? Could it be a desire to keep a favorable image in the eyes of society? Are we apprehensive about challenging ingrained and oppressive societal norms? Many individuals in this wonderful nation cannot confront the oppressive, bureaucratic system that governs them, relying on influential institutions and their support networks. You know the identities of those pursuing power and wealth at the cost of our freedom. I invite you to delve into my story before passing judgment. I love you."

After the show, Chairman Johnson met Olivia, who was in tears. "Your show was excellent, terrific. Let us see what you want to say in court. By the way, you are not fired; you are just suspended for a while." Johnson grinned and tapped on her shoulder.

In the morning, Lauren Jefferson called Olivia. "Faux News has refused to apologize publicly. I suggest we file a lawsuit for defamation and libel."

"Go ahead."

"You need to be plucky. Prepare yourself for the worst-case scenario in New York. Your demonic opponents are opulent and powerful. They finance and support many conservative organizations."

"I have no other choice left but to fend off these allegations and stand by my dad."

Hannah tremored when she saw the disturbing news. She called her daughter and Albert and pledged to pay the expenses of hiring lawyers. A day later, she called the white-bearded, portly chairman of Faux News, Jim Simons.

"Hi, Jim. This is Hannah Rogers."

"Hello, Hannah. I am pleased to hear your voice."

"What is going on? I thought we were friends."

"We are friends. What is the problem?"

"Your news company is denigrating my daughter and accusing her of indecency."

"Oh dear. Come to my new house in Sands Point to discuss the matter."

"When?"

"Come tomorrow at 6:00 pm."

"Thank you."

On the next day, Hannah visited Jim and rested in his home office. He drew out a case and lit a cigar. "What is the story?"

"Your news company has distressed me, and your baleful journalists say my girl is married to her dad. Do you think the Rogers family and I had allowed my daughter to marry her dad?"

"What do you want me to do?"

"Can you keep your guys quiet?"

"Over two hundred journalists and reporters work for my corporation. How do you want me to keep them quiet? You and I believe in the freedom of speech."

"But this is not freedom of speech. This is about my daughter and me and the Rogers family."

"Why did your daughter marry this English guy who hates America?"

"He doesn't hate America. His daughters and wife are American citizens. He just disapproves of America's wars."

"But he keeps criticizing the conservative people."

"He is a freethinker. Anyway, I am not here to analyze him. There is no need for your company to besmirch my daughter and me."

"Don't worry, dear. I will talk to the managers." Jim picked up a checkbook and signed a check. "Take this."

"What is this?"

"A check."

"Five million dollars? That's a lot of money. For what?"

"For you and your daughter. Our friendship is worth much more than the news."

"I don't need money."

"Just keep it. You might need it for the court."

"Which court? I don't need a court."

"Dear Hannah, I am not an autocratic dictator like the Saudi king. I cannot order my journalists to shut up. Some of them have been in the journalism business for forty years. I assure you things will be fine. Just ask your son-in-law and his girl not to sue my company. They cannot win a case in the court."

Olivia's attorney, Lauren, rejected Hannah's plea not to take legal action and filed a formal lawsuit in the New York State Supreme Court in Manhattan. In return, Faux News escalated its accusations against Albert and Olivia and commissioned the notorious conservative Attorney Daniel Brown, a dogmatic believer in the absolute inerrancy of the Bible, and who proclaims that lesbians are dissolute sociopaths and destined to Hell.

Drowning in the turbulent waters of scornful accusations, Olivia felt the weight of nervousness pressing upon her. Yet, amid the abrupt storm, the unwavering support from her family and the LGBTQ community stood as a resilient bulwark, infusing her with new strength. Bolstered by this support, she mustered the courage to instruct Lauren to beseech the Supreme Court for permission to broadcast its proceedings. The libel case looming over her and her academic father was not only a personal ordeal, but it had grown into a matter of profound public interest, demanding the stark spotlight of media scrutiny. The managers of Faux News thought she was inane and jejune. This was their ultimate opportunity to nail her down forever and gain financial profits. The Supreme Court approved Lauren's request since Faux News had offered no objections.

Meanwhile, Ann Stone and her skilled journalists of *The New York Times* published classified documents on the underhand connections between the CIA and Faux News. Provided by Hannah and Zita's Mafia, the reports accused the CIA and Faux News of promoting anti-liberalism and warmongering and of illegal involvements in covering up torture and inhuman abuses in Iraq and Afghanistan. This indomitable reporting had incensed the intelligence community.

One evening, Ann entered her building. A gunman followed her and was about to shoot. She turned her face back when she heard a bump and saw a man lying on the floor and carrying a pistol. Albert appeared and seized the gunman's card wallet. "Ann, darling, I am here."

Ann froze. "Did you kill the guy?"

"He is not dead. I gave him a rabbit punch."

"What are you doing in my neighborhood?"

"Getting fresh air."

"Can we be serious for a moment?"

"I am serious. A recondite voice in my head has asked me to come here and protect you. We need to know this oaf and his supervisors who want to kill you." Albert opened the gunman's card wallet. "His name is Thomas Stevens Weber. Date of birth is January 8, 1970. His address is 367 Ocean Parkway, Brooklyn. Let us go up to your apartment."

Ten minutes later, Albert and Ann heard sirens of police cars and ambulances. They opened a curtain and saw Thomas Stevens Weber hanging on a street light.

Albert rested his hand on Ann's shoulder. "Who would do such a thing?"

"Only the Anonymous warriors would do that."

"Why?"

"The Anonymous warriors follow you wherever you go."

Two days later, Hannah informed Albert that Thomas Stevens Weber had planned to assassinate Ann and him after he had a secret session with Jim Simons. Albert spoke to Zita, who had always concealed her anger with Faux News. It was Faux News which averred that the Gambino Mafia gangsters had murdered her parents. This time, Faux News had targeted her best friend and secret lover. She protected him in the old days and assassinated the CIA mercenaries who tried to kill him. One day, she made a quick phone call. "*Diamo inizio alla festa.*"

"*Sì, la signora Bertina.*"

Two dark-haired Italian Americans, wearing black suits, left a red-bricked apartment on Pleasant Avenue in East Harlem and sat in the back seat of a black Ford Ranger. One of them made a call. "*Tempo di festa.*" A minute later, a masked sniper, on the top of a building on West Forty-Eighth Street, fired six shots at the windows of the Faux News building on Sixth Avenue. No one was injured, but six windows shattered. The driver of the Ford Ranger drove to Jim Simons' mansion in Sands Point. At the gate of the estate, the Italians executed two bodyguards with silenced guns. An Italian talked to Jim and said he is Bill Wilson, an FBI agent investigating the last shooting at the Faux News building. A minute later, the two men, in the back seat, left the car and knocked on the door of the mansion.

"The FBI, please."

An elderly woman opened the door. "Yes."

The two men opened their wallets and showed the lady their FBI badges. "The FBI."

"What's wrong?"

"Nothing is wrong, ma'am. We just need a word with Mr. Jim Simons."

When Jim came to the door, the two men shook his hand. "Good evening, sir. Sorry to disturb you. Can you come with us for a minute? We want to discuss security matters and show you photos related to the shooting tonight."

"OK."

Jim Simons walked with the two men to their car. One of them asked him to sit in the back seat. When they sat beside him, they put their guns to his chest and asked the driver to drive the car away from Sands Point. One abductor taped Jim's mouth and covered his head with a wool mask.

In Harlem, the trio of kidnappers escorted him to a deserted ballroom, where they peeled off the tape and removed the mask, only to secure him to a steel chair.

"What happened to my bodyguards?"

"We sent them to heaven."

"What do you want from me? Don't you know who I am?"

They laughed. "We know who you are."

"Who are you, guys? What do you want? Money? Ten million bucks? Twenty million dollars?"

"Shut up."

A minute later, Zita, wearing her distinctive gear and Che Guevara helmet, entered the hall, with her chest and head up, and attached a gray silencer to her long-barrel pistol. Jim stared at her and became paralyzed. After turning left, Zita marched toward Jim and placed her gun on his forehead. She put a small piece of paper in front of his eyes. The paper said, "Who is the Black Wolf?"

Jim said nothing, and Zita walked away from him.

"Damn you, filthy killer. You killed my brother and friends in Nicaragua."

Halting her stride, Zita paused, nodding for five seconds. With a quick pivoting movement, she directed a forceful back kick toward his chest. The impact sent him into the air, and he landed on his back with a resounding thud on the damaged floor. She put her gun on his penis and showed him the paper that said, "Who is the Black Wolf?"

One abductor bowed. "Tell us about the Black Wolf, and we will let you live. We promise."

"He is Chris George Lewis. He lives in Dover, Norfolk County, Massachusetts."

An abductor smiled. "Good boy."

The three abductors hoisted him with his chair and left the ballroom. "Where are you leaving me?"

"We will be back soon."

Zita remained in the ballroom and remembered how Jim Simons wanted to kill Albert during the Nicaraguan general election in 1990. She glared at him. "Why did you want to kill Albert Russell?"

"So, you are a woman? Who are you?"

"I am Albert's angel. Why did you want to kill him?"

"He is a renegade harboring disdain for America. While professing to be a philosopher, he is, in reality, a traitorous spy working for leftist terrorists. His rhetoric dismisses

Western civilization as nothing more than a myth created by racist white men to hegemonize the world. Read the news. He had sex with his daughter. His wife is his daughter. He is a vicious pig."

"Really?"

"Why do you care about him? Are you his mistress?"

Loaded with fury, Zita removed her helmet. Jim's face became blanched with horror. "Zita Marino! The Mafia's whorish floozy. Oh, my God! What are you doing, bitch?"

"Bitch?" She turned her face toward him. "This is for Albert Russell." She pointed her gun at his forehead and shot him dead.

When she left the hall, she saw her cousins lying on the ground and groaning. "What happened?"

"A masked guy beat us."

"You are three strong men. How could he beat you?"

"We think he is Homatakawa. He is fast and a martial arts master."

"I touched his arm. It is solid as a steel pipe."

"OK. Let us get out of here before the cops come."

The next day, Chris George Lewis, a six-foot-tall, slim man, walked with a German shepherd near Charles River in Dover. Zita jumped in front of him. "Hello, the Black Wolf."

Chris quivered because a few CIA hitmen knew his sobriquet, the Black Wolf. "Who are you?"

"I am Albert Russell's angel?"

"I see. Buzz off, stupid woman."

Zita unzipped her leather jacket and pulled her gun. "Do you remember the little girl in Brooklyn when you murdered my dad, Giovanni Marino, and my mom in front of me? Kneel."

Chris kneeled before her. "Please, don't shoot. I will give you what you want."

She fired a bullet into his chest. "This is for my mom." She fired another bullet into his right thigh. "This is for my dad." The third shot knocked his skull. "This is for Albert." He died on the spot, and his dog escaped. Zita booted and rolled the lifeless body into the river.

The next day, Albert and Sarah watched the TV when Zita announced that the police had found the dead body of Jim Simons in an abandoned ballroom in Harlem.

Sarah grabbed his arm. "Oh, no! Faux News will accuse us of killing him."

An hour later, Zita declared that Chris George Lewis was found shot dead at the Charles River in Dover.

"Blimey! What's going on in this crazy country?"

The next morning, Albert met the reporters who flocked in front of his house. "I want to confirm that we condemn the barbaric killing of Jim Simons. We know what Jim Simons' news company has said about me and my wife and daughter. But be assured that we hold no grudge or ill will in our hearts. We extend our heartfelt condolences to his family. I always say the world needs love guided by positive knowledge. We need to unite against the recent wave of religious terrorism. I request our politicians to let the Arabs and Muslims solve their own problems by themselves. We are not their wardens and guardians. I dare say there will be more terrorist attacks. I hope the President and his government understand what I am trying to say. Thank you."

An hour later, two FBI agents visited Albert. "Can we talk to you in private?"

"I hide nothing from my wife."

"Where were you when Jim Simons died?"

"I was in the house or in the university. As you see, journalists and reporters escort me everywhere."

"Do you have a gun in the house?"

"No. You can search the house. With due respect to the Constitution, I oppose the idea that the people have the right to keep and bear arms. Guns killed over sixteen thousand people last year."

"Do you have any idea who the killer might be?"

"No. But think of it. Jim Simons' news channel has spawned many adversaries because of its scathing attacks on liberals, leftists, and Islamist groups."

"Anyway, thanks, Dr. Russell. We appreciate your kind cooperation. We are sorry for any inconvenience."

"No problem at all. You are welcome."

Later that day, Hannah visited her daughter and hugged her several times. "Mom, what do you withhold from me?"

"Nothing. I am worried about you. I don't want the Simons family to think we planned Jim's death."

"Mom, you know Albert. He can't kill a spider."

Three days afterward, Albert read an article in *The New York Times* on the Black Wolf and his covert operations. He recalled Zita, who told him that the Black Wolf was the culprit who murdered her parents and uncles. He folded the newspaper and stuck it underneath his left arm. An hour later, he used a key and opened the door of Zita's house. "Zita, are you here? Zita, are you there?"

"I am here in the bathroom."

Albert opened the bathroom door and saw Zita puffing a white cigarette and mourning in the foamy bathtub. After taking off his jacket and rolling up the sleeves of his blue shirt, he kneeled beside the tub and put his right hand on her neck. "Give me your cigarette." He dropped the cigarette into the toilet and caressed her back. "What is wrong, darling?"

"Please, stay with me."

"Why are you sad? Your eyes are red."

She kissed his hands. "Chris Lewis was the ratbag who murdered my dad and mom. He wanted to kill me when I was three and tried over seven times to kill you. I dispatched him to hell. This is the first time I execute a CIA officer in America."

"Oh, dear!" Albert hugged her and pecked her neck.

"Who am I? Why am I here? Am I doomed to be a serial killer? The stupid media says I am the most beautiful and intelligent journalist in America, but I am a lousy bitch. I wish to live a normal life."

Albert thought of Jim Simons' death. "Who killed Jim Simons?"

"I killed him. The scumbag tried to kill you during the general elections in Nicaragua in 1990."

"The police found his body in Harlem. How did you get him there?"

"My cousins helped me."

"Don't you watch *Forensic Files*? Aren't you afraid of the FBI?"

"My cousins wear latex masks and gloves. The FBI won't dare touch me because my people keep classified official documents and raunchy photos of politicians, businessmen, attorneys, and military personnel that nobody wants to see." She rubbed her face on his hand. "Ah, Albert, I am the most powerful and dangerous woman in the world today. My relatives made me the godmother of the most powerful Mafia in America. I tried hard to control myself when I reported the death of Jim and Chris. I could not sleep, and my mind thought of you. Am I a rotten bitch? I executed all these miscreants because they slaughtered my family and plotted to kill you. When will I stop killing people because of my family and you? I loathe myself. I need love. My life is shit and horrible ..."

She jumped out of the bathtub and vomited in the washbasin. Albert covered her body with a towel and rinsed her face. "Wear the bathrobe and sit beside the chimney. I will make soup for you." After cleaning the washbasin and his hands, he picked up his cell phone. "Sarah, darling, Zita is very sick, and I need to be with her tonight. I will phone Olivia and ask her to be with you."

"Tell her I am sending my love and best wishes. Take care, love. See you tomorrow."

After calling his daughter and asking her to be with Sarah that night, Albert entered the kitchen, opened a minestrone can, and put a pot on the stove. Five minutes later, he poured the cooked soup into a bowl and rested beside Zita. "How do you feel now?"

"I feel better because you are with me. Thanks for the soup." Later, she switched on the TV. A news anchor said an Islamist terrorist group had released a video claiming that "a soldier of Allah" had assassinated Jim Simons because his news channel "spreads false propaganda against the true religion of Allah and Muslims." Zita cachinnated and turned off the TV.

"Why are laughing?"

"These deranged psychopaths are hilarious. If a hurricane kills Americans, they will say they have ordered the hurricane of Allah to extirpate the American infidels."

"They think God is their military commander."

She hugged and kissed him. "I love the way you speak. How does Sarah feel about us?"

"She knows you are my best friend?"

"What does she think of me?"

"She loves you and feels you are one of our family."

"I hope she would someday forgive me."

"Why do you say that?"

"We have been secret lovers for twenty-seven years. I killed bad guys because of my love for you. It is so hard for me to stay away from you. My love for you is natural, and I have no sense of guilt at all. I hope Sarah realizes I love her so much because she allows you to spend time with me. I will do my best for her."

"We are just concerned about the court thing."

"Nothing will happen to you. I have something for you and Olivia."

"I don't want more killing."

"There will be no killing but Italian fun. Give me your cell phone. I want to call Sarah."

"Hi, Sarah. This is Zita. How are doing, honey?"

"I am good. How is your health?"

"I am getting better. Thanks to Albert. Would you, please, pack clothes for you and for Edward and Albert? Get heavy raincoats. I want to take you all to a special place."

"For how many days?"

"For a week."

"Thank you."

"Sarah, I hope you know you and Albert are my best friends. Do not worry about anything. I will do my best for you. I really love you."

"I love you too."

"Good night. See you tomorrow morning."

"Good night."

Albert touched her hair. "Where do you want to take us?"

"I have a luxury yacht at North Cove Marina. We will go to a place called Bald Head Island in North Carolina. I have a house there."

"That would be wonderful."

She winked. "Let us go to bed and do something special."

After entering the bedroom, Zita requested him to face away and shut his eyes. As he complied, she, holding a baseball bat, contemplated delivering a blow to his head. Yet, her overpowering love for him had stayed her hand. Setting the bat aside, she opted for a kick to his rear and leaped on his back. "Why did you lie to me? Why?" She drubbed his neck.

"What's wrong, love? I have never lied to you."

"Don't you ever, ever beat my boys. I will kill you if you touch them again. Do you understand?"

"Who are your boys?"

"My Italian cousins."

"I haven't seen them for ages."

"Why do you lie to me?"

"I do not lie. What are you talking about?"

"You are the only kung fu master I know. My cousins said a kung fu guy beat them. Are you Homatakawa?"

"No. That's not me. I swear."

She opened a wardrobe drawer and got photos of murdered CIA officers. "Look at these photos. Martial arts weapons killed these CIA agents. You are the only guy who knows how to use these Chinese weapons. Are you Homatakawa?"

"No. No. I talk about love and peace. How do you think I am Homatakawa who executes people? I am not a robot assassin. I am honest. What happened to you?"

"Did you kill these CIA operatives?"

"No."

"Are you Tilatowate?"

"No. I don't drive motorbikes, and I don't murder people." He paused. "Oh, my God! Do you think Hannah is the masked motorcyclist? We know she killed CIA officers."

"I don't think so. Hannah does not know kung fu. She told me Homatakawa had saved her life."

"Why does Homatakawa protect us?"

"I don't know. I tried to know his identity, but to no avail."

"Do you want to apologize for hitting me?"

"I am so sorry. I thought you were Homatakawa, who assaulted my cousins. What about a kiss?"

On the next day, Zita put a suitcase and a box of food in Albert's car. Albert drove the car to his house, where he and Zita kissed Sarah and Edward.

"Are you ready?"

"Yes. Albert, take the two bags to the car."

"I will take Edward."

Two hours later, they were on a fifty-foot-long white motor yacht. Zita switched on the engine and cruised south. Albert and Sarah stood beside her.

"Albert, that's Governors Island. Look to the right. That's Liberty Island ... That's Hoffman Island ... That's

Swinburne Island ..." Zita continued to tell Albert and Sarah about places on the east coast till she stopped the yacht in the ocean, not far away from Atlantic City.

Late that night, Albert and Sarah were in a bubbly, four-seater, rectangular jacuzzi. Zita, holding a glass of white wine and wearing a green high-neck bikini, sat opposite them. Sarah knew personal facts about Zita in the last five years, yet she yearned to learn more about her love for Albert.

"Sit beside Albert."

Zita sat next to Albert. "Thanks."

Sarah ran her right fingers over Zita's left arm and induced her to place her hand on Albert's knee. Zita smiled.

"Zita, have you ever made love to a woman?"

"Just to Olivia's mom. We were a polyamorous tribe of hearts and Albert's lovers."

"How?"

"Eva was irreligious. You can say she was an anarchist and radical feminist. Because of her Irish background, she supported the Sinn Féin party in Ireland and the socialist revolutions around the world. I was her best friend when she married Albert. One day, we had a bath together, and on another occasion, she came to my bed, and we made love. Anyway, I am a heterosexual."

"Did the three of you have sex together?"

"No. I couldn't make love to Albert when Eva was with us."

"Why?"

"Because I was selfish. Albert was my only true love."

"How many times do you make love to Albert in a month or a year?"

Zita grinned. "Ha! What are you looking for? I don't

have sex with Albert."

"I don't believe it. You charm everybody."

"My love for Albert is not about sex. I think you know that. Albert is the only friend who knows who I am. We love to hug and kiss."

"I love you. I have no problem if you need to spend more quiet time with Albert. You can see him every fortnight."

"Wives get angry if their spouses see other women. Why aren't you angry with me? Aren't you jealous?"

"Not at all. Because of my lesbian feelings, I see a woman friend. To me, the love shared among two or more consenting adults is far from a crime against humanity, especially when we compare it to the backdrop of our troops causing so much harm to innocent lives. Disillusioned by our societal moralities that seem hypocritical in the face of widespread bloodshed, I question and reject the virtues upheld by the society we inhabit. Freedom and happiness should be our priority. Albert and I enjoy each other because we are free. We understand each other's desires. He will never leave me, and I know you will never take him away from me. We are a trio now." Sarah placed her right hand on Zita's face and kissed her lips. Zita blinked and felt overjoyed to hear Sarah's reassuring words.

Albert splashed water on their faces. "Don't I have a say in all this debate?"

"Be quiet," Sarah replied. "When women talk, men listen."

In the morning, Hannah wore a black pantsuit, a cashmere coat, and black leather gloves. Her hair was loose with a side parting. She got her car and attended the grand funeral of Jim Simons, anticipating his influential family would stop the media vilification of her daughter. Meanwhile, Zita and Sarah gripped each other's hand and jumped into the blue ocean. Albert exulted in seeing his wife with his best friend swimming and fondling with stimulating vitality. Later, they cooked, ate, and drank with glee. Edward, in his own way, was a major source of their delight.

The next day, the new chairman of Faux News, Paul Simons, rejected Hannah's demand that his company should make a public apology to her daughter, arguing it was not his role to hamper the performance of his competent reporters and journalists.

In the meantime, Zita and her dearest friends were joyful when they arrived at Bald Head Island. Albert and Sarah felt astonished at Zita's five-bedroom house in this remote place.

"Here is where I stay away from civilization."

The next day, Sarah sat on a balcony overlooking a grassy field and the North Atlantic Ocean. Zita put her hands on her shoulders. "What are you thinking?"

"I am worried about the court."

"Honey, take it easy and trust yourself. Don't trouble yourself about anything."

"The guys of the Faux News are powerful and rich."

Zita smiled. "They are not more powerful than me. I will not allow them to demean and malign you. They will pay you money, and you will know the truth."

"How?"

"I am Italian. Trust me. Come with me."

Zita opened a room door. "Get a bicycle. I will show you the Island."

Zita and Sarah rode their bicycles and made their way to Federal Road and North Bald Head Wynd until they halted at Bald Head Lighthouse (Old Baldy). When they stopped under a lonely tree, Zita put her hands on Sarah's face and kissed her lips. Sarah loved the kiss.

"Do you want to be the next mayor in New York?"

"Yes, I do."

"Kiss my right hand if you wish to be the next mayor."

"Why your hand? I ... I can ... I can kiss, kiss you."

"No. I want you to kiss my hand."

For an eerie moment, Sarah recalled *The Godfather* film series, and fearing the unknown, she bowed and kissed Zita's right hand.

"Good. You are now a member of the family."

"Which family?"

"My family. Your family. Our family. Be who you are, and I will make you the next mayor."

"You? You are a journalist. I do not understand what you say. You asked me to kiss your hand. What does this have to do with the mayorship?"

"I told you I am Italian. I am the big sister of the good Italians. Honey, listen. The more you love Albert, the more I will love you. I have a cute son and two gorgeous daughters. They, Albert, and you are all I have now. I did many things for Albert and want to do more things for him and you. Love him as much as you can, but remember, I love him too. You need his love, and I need his love too. Do we have a deal?"

Sarah stuttered for a while. "I love you and will never stop Albert from seeing you. I told you he can see you, and you can see him when you want. You can come to our home whenever you like. I know how both of you feel about each other."

"But I don't want the media to say we have an affair. What should we do?"

"I should be with Albert when he visits you. You can take him upstairs if you need private time with him. But what about Edward? I don't want him to think his mom and dad have many lovers."

"Your mom and my daughters can look after him if we need a special space for ourselves."

Sarah's lesbian sexuality had pestered her emotions. She felt a romantic affair between Zita and Albert would do injustice to her. "What about me?"

"What about you?"

"You can see Albert, but what about me? Don't I merit your love? I have intense feelings for you. I wish to make love to you."

Zita laughed. "I am not a lesbian, but you will get what you want. You can see me in private. But, honey, you need to discipline yourself and stop being obsessed with your vagina if you want to be a politician in New York. Do we have a deal now?"

"Yes, we have a deal. What about the court?"

"Forget the court. I am the toughest investigative journalist in New York. I am more formidable than the guys of Faux News."

"How?"

"Sorry. This is not a part of our love deal."

Four days later, they were back in New York. Zita became busy preparing something for Albert and his household. She made four phone calls, saying. "*Voglio ballare.*" To her Italian collaborators, this means, "Let us do a sleazy work." One evening, she picked up a vocal microphone from her car and entered Albert's house. "Albert, come to the office."

In the office, she took off her jacket and shirt, revealing her scarlet balconette bra and seductive cleavage. "Get me scissors."

Albert picked up scissors and stood behind her. Sarah opened the door and ogled Zita's tempting shoulders and arms. "What's going on?"

"Come in. I want Albert to cut the paper gum tape."

Albert touched two envelopes attached to Zita's back. "What are these envelopes?"

"Open this one."

Albert opened an envelope and saw erotic images of a topless woman. "Who is this woman? What does this have to do with the court?"

"The topless girl is Attorney Brown's daughter. This blockhead is the big guy of Faux News. This is what I call Italian fun."

"What would we do with these photos?"

"I will send them to newspapers and magazines. Give the other envelope to Ann Stone. An eye for an eye, and a tooth for a tooth."

Albert called Ann. "Good evening, Ann."

"Hi, love. How are you doing?"

"I am doing great. Can I see you tomorrow? I want to give you a copy of my new book."

"You are always welcome. Can you see me at four?"

"OK. I will see at four."

The next day, Albert visited Ann. When she closed the door, he kissed her. "I miss these beautiful lips."

"Naughty man."

"Where is your laptop?"

"On the desk over there."

"Come, darling. I want to show you something." He fetched the laptop and sat beside her on a couch.

"What is this CD?"

Albert hugged her. "This is about the death of our parents and grandparents."

Ann inserted the disc into the laptop and stared at the screen. Three armed men entered Peter Stone's home. An obscure man put his rifle on Peter's head. "Where is Michael Rogers' list?"

Peter took off his glasses. "Which list?"

"I said Michael Rogers' list. He gave you a list of CIA names."

"I don't have it."

"Where is it?"

"I said I don't have it."

"Don't let me blow up your freaking ass."

"If you kill me, the Anonymous will assassinate your men one by one until the end of time."

The veiled man snickered. "The Anonymous? Who is the Anonymous?"

"The Anonymous is the most powerful assassination organization in the world. The Anonymous warriors do not forgive, and they do not forget. They have your names. Expect them everywhere and anytime. They wear masks and hoods, and their bodies are made of steel. Yes, it will be a war without end, a war that will make the CIA a piece of garbage."

"Screw you, thickhead. Who is the double agent who leaks classified documents? How did Albert Russell get secret documents from the CIA?"

"Ask him."

"But he was in your house."

"Dr. Russell is a world-renowned philosopher, and his grandfather was my best friend."

"Did you give him the documents?"

"Go to hell."

"You asked for it, you piece of garbage." Gunshots echoed through the room as the masked man discharged three rounds. The lifeless body of Peter crumbled to the ground. Undeterred by this murder, the masked assailant moved into a nearby bedroom. Peter's disabled spouse, unsuspecting and defenseless, became the next victim of a malevolent act. "Let us get the English pig."

Ann held Albert's hand. "Oh, my God! How did you get this CD?"

"Our grandfather installed hidden cameras in his house. He knew the CIA and drug warlords would kill him. A masked motorcyclist threw the CD in my car in the morning."

"How does he look like?"

"He wears a Che Guevara helmet and a Che Guevara mask." Albert had declined to mention Zita Marino.

"Oh, my gosh! That is the mysterious assassin who fought the CIA in the 1980s. How did he get the CD?"

"I Guess he took it from our grandfather's house."

"How?"

"I don't know. Watch this one. It is about our dad and your mom."

Four armed men entered Jamie Stone's house. One of them poked him in the face. "Who are the Anonymous?"

"What is the Anonymous? I am a scientist."

"Your obnoxious father said the Anonymous would kill us. Who are they?"

"Ask my dad."

"Your dad is dead, moron. Who is Nahatatama, and who is Homatakawa? Who made the robot assassins?"

Jamie chortled. "Robot assassins? Are there robots and assassins? You are funny."

"We know you invented the cyborg garbage. Where is the lab?"

"I don't believe in science fiction."

"I will count to ten."

"The Anonymous is nameless. Its fighters are killing machines. They are coming to kill you all."

"Nine. Ten. Go to hell." Two gunmen fired shots and killed him. The other two went upstairs and murdered his ill wife in her bedroom.

Ann and Albert watched the odious crimes and cried.

"Do you know who killed them?" Ann embraced Albert.

"No. Their leader is called the Angry Jaguar."

"I realize now why the CIA wants to kill you. Our dad loved you so much."

"I want a favor from you."

"What?"

"Can you upload the video clips on *The New York Times* website and ask your journalists to publish articles on the horrible death of our father and grandfather before the court date?"

"Yes, I can."

"Thank you. I love you." Albert placed his hand on her bosom and kissed her. His kiss and touch had aroused her. "Come with me."

"Where?"

"To your room."

They entered the room. With her right hand between his thighs, she pushed him to the door and kissed him. She prompted him to put his hand on her breast. "Touch me. Here ... Slowly ... Bite me ... Bite me ... Harder ... Harder ... Yes, yes ... Wow! Holy Ghost! ... What am I doing? ... Honey, I am sorry."

"No problem, love. I know it is painful to see the horrible murder of our family and be single."

"What can I do? I wish to kill your mom."

"Oh dear! Why?"

"Why did she say you are my brother? I wished to be your wife. I can't forget our sex. Do you remember that midnight when you put noodles on my chest and licked my breasts?"

"These were the merry days ... How do Hannah and Zita communicate with the Anonymous?"

"I do not know. Our granddad recruited them and requested them to obey the Anonymous. He was wise. The Anonymous is his creation."

"I wish to know Nahatatama and Homatakawa."

"Me too."

"Take off your bra. I want to massage your back."

Ann took off her bralette and lay on her front. Albert massaged her neck and sang. "Oh my lovely rose of Clare, you're the sweetest girl I know. You're the queen of all the roses like the pretty flowers that grow. You're the sunshine of my life ..."

"It is a beautiful song. How do you know it?"

"It was Eva's favorite song. She sang it for me every day."

"Do you miss her?"

"Yes, very much."

"What about Sarah and Zita?"

"Sarah asked Zita to be her lesbian lover."

"She is delirious."

"I know. I love you, Ann. Thanks for the tremendous work you do for me."

"I love you too. Please, be careful. The imperialist world wants you dead."

"I am not afraid of anybody. Anyway, we need to adopt a bloodless method and employ violence only in self-defense. Do you know the Internet hacktivist group Anonymous?"

"Your wife founded it."

"Sarah?"

"Yes."

"Why?"

"When the conservative critics abused you in 2002 because you condemned George W. Bush's plan to invade Iraq, Sarah created Anonymous to expose them."

"How do you know that?"

"She cooperates with me."

"Sarah, the witch."

"She idolizes you. How many lovers do you have?"

"Sarah is the wife, Zita is the mistress, and you are the queen."

She kissed his hand and shed a tear. "I love you. This is a happy moment in my life. You are my joy. Call Sarah and tell her you want to stay with me tonight."

"My pleasure. You are the sunshine of my life so beautiful and fair. And I will always love you, my lovely rose of Clare ..."

Chapter 14

After a plodding routine of technical procedures, Olivia found herself in the witness box as the first testifier. Her family, media correspondents, camera operators, and other concerned people had filled the packed courtroom.

Olivia's lawyer, Lauren Jefferson, stood before her. "What is your name?"

"My name is Olivia Albert Russell."

"What do you do?"

"I am a lesbian activist and a television show host."

"Who is Albert Russell?"

"Albert Russell is my biological and legal father."

"Do you love your father?"

"Yes, I love him."

"Can you explain?"

"My mom died in an airplane crash in Japan when I was one year old. Albert has been my dad, mom, and mentor all my life. I revere him for his exceptional care, affection, and responsibility."   *

"Have you ever been alone with him?"

"Yes, countless times because, as I have said, I grew up without a mother or a sibling. What's wrong with being alone with my dad?"

"Are you engaged in a sexual affair with him?"

"No. This is inconceivable because I am a married lesbian."

"Who is Sarah Rogers?"

"She is my dad's wife."

"Are you involved in an intimate liaison with her?"

"No. I don't have a sexual affair with Sarah."

"Are the pictures of you and your father genuine?"

"Yes, they are authentic. Spiteful villains had taken them without our permission."

"What do you say about them?"

"They show me kissing my dad in public places, not in striptease nightclubs. Kissing my dad for a second is not incest, as the anti-gay conservatives say."

"So, you do not have sex with your father?"

"No. I do not call my love for him sex."

"There are rumors about your father's wife. What do you make of them?"

"Sarah is not my father's biological daughter or my sister. I hold a high opinion of her as a wonderful, caring stepmother. We are like twins."

"You often say you are a lesbian feminist activist. What does this mean?"

"It means I advocate and campaign for the human, legal, and social rights of lesbians."

"Can you tell us about your TV show?"

"I call my five-day-a-week show *Lesbian Talk*. It debates lesbian issues with professional experts and criticizes the homophobic, misogynist attitudes toward the lesbians."

"Did your media corporation suspend your work because of the current allegations?"

"Yes."

Lauren glanced at Judge Allen Redford for a moment and shifted her sight toward the seated people. "Your Honor, ladies and gentlemen, Olivia Russell's honest and public work has attracted harsh criticism from the xenophobic, homophobic, transphobic, and misogynist conservatives, who say Ms. Russell's lesbian feminism threatens their traditional values and interests. Before these latest allegations, Faux News and its affiliated newspapers and magazines called Ms. Russell's show 'A Whore's Show.' On July 13, the *Conservative Voice* newspaper said, 'Olivia Russell preaches debauchery and hedonism in our American society.' On July 19, the *Tea Party* newspaper called Ms. Olivia Russell 'The Dildo Harlot.' So, the fabricated accusations against my client are driven by conservatism and fanaticism, which say our multicultural and multiethnic country is a Christian nation that the Bible and white Protestant Christians must govern. The unauthorized photos show Ms. Olivia Russell kissing her father. Yes, some of you may say mature women should not kiss their fathers in public spaces. But there is no evidence that Ms. Olivia Russell is involved in a sexual affair with her father. Thank you."

Attorney Daniel Brown stood, staring Olivia in the eye, and giving her a derisive smirk. "Your Honor, ladies and gentlemen, as a family man, I do not like to interfere in people's private lives. I will say thank you and goodbye if

Ms. Olivia Russell and her father drop the insubstantial lawsuit against my client. I say we have hard evidence that proves Olivia's liaison with her father, as well as with her half-sister and stepmother Ms. Sarah Rogers. What do you say about this matter, Ms. Olivia Russell?"

"Hard evidence or hard ...? You are ridiculous. It is too late. Stop blithering."

"You ask for it."

Attorney Brown brought in a shopping cart carrying 25 inches x 40 inches framed, colored photos. He showed Olivia and the crowd a picture of her and her father when they kissed each other in a New York park.

"Who is in this photo?"

"This is me sitting on my dad's knees."

"And?"

"Kissing him."

"Do you sit on your dad's knees and kiss him in a public park?"

"What's wrong with that?"

The Attorney pointed his left fingers at the photo and tittered. "Yeah, what's wrong with that? Interesting. How many women kiss their fathers like that?"

"You tell me. You are the oracle."

"None. The photo shows your pink painted lips on your dad's mouth. Your short dress shows off your bare thighs. What do you call that?"

"I call it love."

"Love? Our daughters love us, but they do not wear short dresses, and sit on our knees, and put their lips on ours. Only lovers do that. You are a glitzy lesbian and should admit that."

"I do not call that sex."

"If you do that with your father in downtown places, what do you do with him when he is in your home?"

Lauren stood with a livid face and blazing eyes. "Objection, Your Honor. It is not our line of work to meddle in people's lives behind the closed doors."

"Objection sustained. Proceed, please."

"Yes, it is not our business to bring to light what people do behind closed doors and walls. But Ms. Olivia Russell accuses my client and the whole media of fabricating the indubitable fact about her love affair with her father." Attorney Brown pulled another photo. "This photo shows Ms. Olivia Russell leaning on a maple tree in a New York park and kissing her father's lips. As you see, Olivia's hands are on her father's backside. Only lovers do that. Did you have sex with your dad, Ms. Russell?"

"I answered this dippy question. I did not and do not have sex with my dad."

"Are you sure?"

"Yes, I am positive."

Attorney Brown carried the third enlarged photo. "Tell us about this photo."

"It is a photo."

"Yes, we know it is a photo. But who is on your bare thighs?"

"She is my stepmother."

"Do American women sit on the unclad thighs of their stepdaughters and kiss their mouths?"

"Ask them. What do you mean by American women? Many American women are offenders in prisons. My stepmother and I are American citizens. So, please, stop generalizing about the American women. I love my stepmom, and she cares for me. I do not make love to her."

"Do you love her?"

"Sarah is a special woman because she cherishes my dad. I do not care what other women do. Our kisses are natural."

The Attorney glared. "Natural? Do women kiss or suck the lips of their stepmothers and say this is natural? Is it natural or erotic, Ms. Russell?"

"The main point is I love her. She is my best friend."

Attorney Daniel Brown picked up the fourth photo. "Ladies and gentlemen, as you see, Albert Russell is wearing blue swimming trunks and lying on a beach. His wife, wearing a fringe bikini, is sitting on his chest, and his daughter, wearing a strapless bikini, is resting on his stomach, and hugging her stepmother. Olivia's hands are on Sarah's chest. Do you know any decent woman who hugs her stepmother like that? There are two options here. Either they are sisters, or they are lovers."

"Keep guessing till the Judgment Day."

Attorney Brown requested the court to play a DVD. "Your Honor, ladies and gentlemen, this clip shows Ms. Olivia Russell holding party dresses and gossamer underwear in a New York fashion store. She enters a changing room and removes her clothes in front of her father."

He turned his stern face toward Olivia. "What do you call that, Ms. Russell? Tell us the truth. You have taken an oath to tell the truth. Did you take your clothes off in front of your father?"

"Yes. So, what is the problem?"

The Attorney twisted his receding chin. "Yeah, what is the problem?"

Olivia gaped at him and stretched her arms up over her

head. "Yes, what is your problem?" She wrapped her arms around her waist. "Didn't you see your daughters naked when they were girls? Normal parents see their naked kids and bathe them. Many parents walk naked in their homes. In a free country like France, topless daughters swim with their dads and brothers. My dad is my parent. He can see my body when I am an adult. We did not make love in the fashion store. Sarah was there. You can ask her about that."

"Why didn't you take your wife to the fashion store? Why do you take your father to women's stores?"

"What is the difference between my wife and dad? My dad is a special person."

"Do you mean your wife is not a special person?"

"I adore my wife."

"That's fine. You love to take your father to fashion stores. But why do you like to take your clothes off in front of him? Why do you show him your underwear?"

"Where do you live, old man? Don't you go to the beach? Don't you see women wearing all types of bikinis? Albert is my true father, for Heaven's sake."

The Attorney took a photo. "This photo shows you and your father in a women's underwear store. Can you tell us what your father was doing in a women's underwear store in Manhattan?"

"I wanted his thoughts on the clothes I got."

"Clothes?" Attorney Brown placed his right fingers on the photo. "Huh! Do you call your translucent underwear clothes? Yes, we go out with our daughters to clothes stores, but do dignified fathers go with their married daughters to women's underwear stores?"

"My dad is different."

The Attorney stretched out his hands and jeered. "Yes, he is different. He is a professor of religion! Yet, he skulks around with his lesbian daughter in a women's lingerie store. Is this a British thing? In America, decent fathers do not run out with their grown-up girls to department stores to buy women's underwear."

"They are benighted and conventional fathers. My dad is different."

With a dour face, Attorney Brown placed two photos on wooden drawing stands. "Yes, your father is different! This steamy photo shows you holding bandeau bras and tangas. The second photo shows your so-called different father going with you to a changing room for women. Did you change your dresses in front of him?"

"Yes, I removed my dresses when he was with me. Why the furor? He was not there to rape me. I wanted his opinion on the clothes I selected."

"Bizarre. Did you want your father's opinion? Did you need his opinion on your bras and briefs?"

"Yes."

Attorney Brown asked the court to play the second DVD. "Your Honor, ladies and gentlemen, this vulgar clip shows Ms. Olivia Russell holding bras, briefs, and, of course, her father's hand. She and her father enter a changing room. Ms. Olivia Russell did not realize that the door of the dressing room is about one foot above the floor. She did not notice there was a long mirror in front of the door. As we have seen, Ms. Russell had taken off her jeans and shirt when her dad was alone with her. Ms. Russell moved closer to her father. As you have observed, she raised a bare leg and hugged him for ninety-five seconds. So, Ms. Russell, did you touch your father when you were naked?"

"I was not naked."

"Excuse me! We saw your pants and shirt on the floor."

"But you didn't see my underwear."

"Underwear? Were you wearing a skimpy G-string? Did it cover more than an inch of your crotch?"

Lauren stood in anger. "Pardon me, Your Honor. We can't allow the use of indecent language in the court."

"Sustained."

"I apologize. Ms. Russell, I repeat my question. Did you touch your father?"

"Yes, everybody knows I touched him. Could I hug him without touching him?"

"I mean, did you sensually touch him?"

"What do you mean?"

"Do you understand my American English? Did you touch your father sexually?"

"I have never had sex with my dad."

"We saw your bare legs. Did you kiss your dad in the changing room?"

"Yes. Where is the problem?"

"Were you topless?"

"No. I said I was wearing underwear."

"When you hugged him, did you think of having sex with him?"

"What do you want to know? My dad was wearing his suit, as we had seen. He didn't take his pants off."

"You embraced him for ninety-five seconds. Did you make love to him in the changing room?"

"No. I said my dad was wearing his suit. We will never make love to each other."

"If your father cares about his academic reputation,

why did you hug him in a lingerie store for a minute and a half?"

"I love my dad."

"If sexologists, including your lesbian psychologists, see the latest DVD, they would adduce you intended to make love to your father."

"They can say what they want."

"Did you intend to make love to him in the changing room?"

"No. I kissed and hugged him."

"I believe you wanted more than a kiss and a hug."

Olivia gazed at her father. "No."

"You did not answer my question. Did you wish to make love to your father?"

"I am a married lesbian, and I will never make love to a man. I will never make love to my adorable dad."

"Unbelievable. You take off your clothes in front of your father, and then you say you would never make love to a man? We are not fools, Ms. Russell. Answer my question. Why did you hug your father?"

"Because I love him."

"Why did you hug him for a minute and a half? Did you want to make love to him?"

She sobbed. "I love him so much."

"I repeat. Did you wish to make love to him?"

"I wish to be with him all the time."

"Doing what? Ms. Russell, answer my question. Did you want to make love to him?"

"I will never make love to my wonderful dad."

"Are you afraid of telling us the truth because your wife is in the courtroom?"

"No."

"What do you call your compulsive lust for your father, Ms. Lesbian?"

"I call it true love."

"Is your incest a true love?"

"You call it incest, and I call it true love because my love for him is immutable." She wept and placed her fingers on her watery eyes. "I will never have a sexual relationship with my remarkable dad."

Sarah put her face on her husband's shoulder and cried. Mary cried too.

"Ms. Olivia Russell, do we require more explicit evidence to substantiate your dissolute misconduct with your father?"

With a wrathful look, Mary stood and wanted to swear at the Attorney. "Listen, you son of a ..." Albert placed his hand on her mouth and asked her to calm down.

Olivia realized fiendish agents had kept her father under constant surveillance for political reasons. She gazed at Sarah and Mary.

"I will tell you the truth. I will tell you why I hugged my dad in the changing room for ninety seconds. When my dad was in the changing room, he looked at me and wept. He said, 'You always remind me of your beautiful mom. I have never loved and will never love a woman more than your mom. I wish she is alive to see you now. My heart is aching. I miss her very much.' That is why I hugged my beloved dad in the changing room. The conservative dunces like you don't understand this sacred love and bond." Olivia bit her lower lip and became tearful.

Olivia's warm tears and emotional testimony had distracted and puzzled the Attorney. "Your Honor, no further questions to Ms. Olivia Russell, who tongues the lips of her father and stepmother. May I request the second witness to come forward?"

After stepping forward, Albert hugged his daughter and rested in the witness box. Lauren stood beside him. "Professor Russell. Can you tell us something about yourself and work?"

"Yes. My name is Albert John Russell. I am a British citizen and Earl, and a professor of philosophy and comparative religion at Columbia University."

"What is your relationship with Ms. Sarah Rogers?"

"Sarah is my wife."

"What is your comment on the published photos? Did Olivia kiss you in open places?"

"Yes. Olivia kisses me when she meets me, whether in the house or in a country park. She adores me, and I adore her."

"You are a distinguished philosopher and a public figure. Why do you permit that in public places? Why don't you kiss her in the house?"

"If I see my daughter, say, at Times Square, do you want me to say, 'Darling, I cannot kiss you here. Let us go to the house?' This is risible. Olivia and I do not think kissing each other for a jiff is a vile sin or flagitious treason against the U.S. Constitution and homeland security."

"We are not talking about sins, Dr. Russell."

"This is how Olivia and I express our affection."

"What do you mean?"

"I mean, we consider the kiss a manifestation of goodwill, equality, love, and respect. French, Italian, Russian, and Arab men kiss their male siblings and friends. This does not indicate they are bisexuals or homosexuals. Kissing is not a divine criterion for ethics because it is a socio-cultural practice."

"Let us talk about your wife. Is Sarah Rogers your daughter?"

"Impossible."

"Published photos show you and Sarah's mother holding hands and kissing each other when you were an undergraduate in Hong Kong. Did you have sex with Sarah's mother?"

"Sarah's mother, Hannah, was a member of my sports club for two or three weeks."

"You didn't answer my question."

"I did."

"Did Hannah tell you Sarah is your daughter?"

"Why would she say that?"

"How do you confirm Sarah is not your biological daughter?"

"I met Hannah in March 1981. Sarah was born on February 23, 1982. Do the calculations. Sarah cannot be my daughter unless you prove I had sex with her mother and pregnancy can last eleven months. Medical labs had examined our DNA."

Lauren smiled. "Faux News says you had sex with your daughter. Is this correct?"

"This is rubbish."

"You are a prolific author. How many books have you written on religious fundamentalism in America?"

"Five books."

"Stupendous. Do you think religious fundamentalism is good?"

"Like all ideologies such as Communism, Nazism, and Fascism, religious fundamentalism is false and harmful."

"How many books have you published on the wars in Afghanistan and Iraq?"

"Three books."

"What do you think about the wars?"

"They are illegal, unethical, and nefarious crimes against humanity. They will never bring about peace in the world. Islamist terrorism will spread in many countries. Five days ago, a brainwashed Muslim terrorist killed thirteen people at the Soldier Readiness Center at Fort Hood in Texas."

Lauren walked across the crowded courtroom. "Your Honor, ladies and gentlemen, the allegations against Dr. Russell have been motivated for political and religious reasons. On July 6, Faux News said, 'Dr. Russell believes that our troops in Afghanistan and Iraq are mass murderers.' On July 8, the *Wall Street Journal* said, 'Dr. Albert Russell thinks Western Christianity is a false and dangerous religion.' On July 16, *Chicago Tribune* said, 'Albert Russell, a Columbia University philosopher, calls John McCain, Sarah Palin, Bill O'Reilly, Sean Hannity, and Glenn Beck the hypocritical devils of self-righteous conservatism.' These quotes are proof of intentional propaganda against Professor Russell." Lauren held a copy of *The New York Times* newspaper. "Have you read the papers today? This headline says, 'The CIA Killed Peter Stone.' Peter Stone was the greatest journalist in New York. The other headline says, 'The CIA and Albert Russell: Mission Impossible.' So, we know who murdered the great investigative journalist Peter Stone. The criminals in the CIA had wished to kill Albert Russell. Again, the printed photos do not show sexual acts between Dr. Russell and his daughter. There is only a conjectural assumption. Serious and legal accusations must depend on irrefutable evidence, not on fictional suppositions. If people implicate themselves in love liaisons, they will work hard to conceal their affairs. Dr. Russell and his wife and daughter kiss each other in public places. They are eminent public figures in New York. If Dr. Russell has a sexual affair with his famed daughter, he will try to cover up his relationship with her. Thank you."

Attorney Daniel Brown got up, gawking at Albert's face, and walking a few steps to the right side of the courtroom. "Dr. Russell, your university and the media have told us you are a professor of religion. Fascinating. Which religion do you teach?"

"Religion here means all religions."

"You teach students about all religions?"

"Yes. That's correct."

"Didn't it occur to your intelligent mind that a professor of religion should not do things that religion forbids?"

"I delve into the study of religion because of its significant impact on society and human thought and relations, not because I subscribe to religious beliefs."

"Do you suggest you do not believe in religion?"

"There is no one true religion in a philosophical sense. A few religious concepts are admirable and beneficial, and some religious dogmas and practices are superstitious and detrimental."

"Are you an atheist?"

"No."

"Agnostic?"

"No. I am a spiritual humanist trying to be a sane human in our turbulent world."

"Let us go back to my point. Don't you think your personal life shocks your students who expect you to behave like a professor of religion?"

"No one, except my wife, may intervene in my private life. However, I am a dedicated scholar. Many scholars disagree with my philosophical opinions and personal behavior, but no one has lamented my sincere devotion to knowledge."

"In your book *Free to Love* you say, let me quote you here, that 'we cannot tell people whom they should love and whom they should not love. People must be free to love anyone they want.' What does this mean?"

"It means people have the right to love whom they want. We cannot rule their hearts and feelings."

"You say people must be free to love anyone they want. Does this mean brothers can love their sisters, and fathers can love their daughters?"

"Your problem is that you associate love with sex. I love my books. Does this mean I have a sexual affair with them?"

Sarah, Mary, Olivia, and other people chuckled. The judge banged his gavel against the table. "Quiet, please."

"But you understand I am not talking here about nostalgic or spiritual love; I am alluding to sexual love. Any impartial person who looks at these erotic photos would say you have a sexual relationship with your lesbian daughter."

"This is if you think kissing lips is a sexual act."

"Professor Russell, you teach philosophy and logic. Be sincere with us. If you see your daughter sitting on a man's knees and kissing his lips in a public place, what would you say about her?"

"I would say she is in love with him. But this does not mean she has a sexual relationship with him."

"How do you know that?"

"And how do you know that they have a sexual relationship? You need to see the sexual deed to affirm they have a sexual relationship. You can say I *think* they have a sexual relationship, but you cannot say I am *sure* they have a sexual relationship. There is a significant dissimilarity between probability and certainty."

"Do you think your daughter's obsessive love for you is anomalous and compulsive?"

"I do not think so. I had petitioned for her right to be a free lesbian and marry her girlfriend. Her hugs and kisses are symbolic expressions of gratitude. I do not see a complication in a daughter's kisses in a country where perpetrators brutalize and rape tens of thousands of women every year. Fathers are parents. Why is it deemed acceptable for a daughter to change her clothes in the presence of other women, while it is considered unacceptable for her to do so next to her father? Who makes the rules?"

Attorney Brown scratched his goatee and shrugged, sensing his inability to argue with a shrewd, logical philosopher. "Your Honor, no further questions to Dr. Albert Russell."

The third testifier was Olivia's intrepid wife, Mary Hanks. When a court man asked her to place her left hand on the Bible to take the oath, she refused. "I don't believe in the Bible."

Mary sat with imposing confidence in the witness box, and Lauren approached her. "Can you tell us your name and who you are?"

"I am Mary Jeffrey Hanks. I am Olivia's official and lawful wife."

"In short, does your wife have a sexual relationship with her father?"

"No way. Our relatives and friends know Olivia loves to hug and kiss her dad when she sees him. There are no hidden secrets about this fact. I have no problem with that if they don't sleep together in my cozy bed." She laughed.

"Thanks. Your Honor, I have no further questions to ask."

Attorney Brown had declined to question Mary because he thought she would use swear words when she insults the conservatives and Faux News.

The fourth witness to sit in the witness box was Sarah Rogers. Lauren got close to her and beamed. "Hello. Can you tell us who you are and what you do?"

"I am Sarah Rogers and Professor Albert Russell's wife. I am the Chairperson of the New York Center for Women's Human Rights."

"Have you ever felt anything indecent between your husband and his daughter?"

"No. I have seen nothing aberrant between them. Olivia is our special soulmate. Albert and I love her for many reasons. I know my husband very well. He is one of the kindest men in this world."

"Everybody here wants to know the truth about your relationship with your stepdaughter. Do you have an affair with her?"

"No. There is no affair between Olivia and me. Olivia and I are married. I will never hurt the feelings of my husband or Mary, my doughty partner in the struggle against the enemies of women. Yeah, I kiss Olivia because she is my darling and the daughter of the man I love. My kiss is a big thank you."

"Thank you."

Attorney Brown frowned as his wide eyes glared at Sarah for a moment. "You are Albert Russell's wife. Why isn't your name Sarah Russell?"

"Women are not men's possessions."

"Is Albert Russell your father?"

"A stupid question deserves no answer."

"If Albert is not your father, who is your father?"

"Ask your omniscient God."

"Do you mean you are an illegitimate child?"

"Total nonsense. I am a real human being and a legitimate U.S. citizen."

"Ms. Rogers, you are a vocal activist in New York. Your homosexual and trans buddies parade topless on our streets."

"Is this a puzzle?"

"Do you make girlie parties in your home for Olivia's lesbian friends?"

"Yes, I do."

"Recent studies on American lesbianism link it to female crimes, hermaphroditism, and sex work. They say young lesbians are engaged in orgiastic parties and sleep freely with each other. I mean, do you make parties for lesbians to conceal your affair with Olivia?"

"Wow! Amazing! You are the best authority on lesbian sexuality!" Sarah scoffed. "What do you know about lesbian feminism? Do lesbians sleep freely with each other? Do you watch porn movies?"

"I don't watch pornographic films. I am referring to biological and psychological studies that say lesbians join lesbian clubs and experience sexual intimacy."

"You and your ilk are ignorant of lesbian feminism. Olivia, Mary, and I are devoted feminists. We fight for women's human rights. Though we believe in sexual freedom and have no problem with eroticism and social nudism, we confront violent heterosexual pornography because it shows physical aggression and portrays women as submissive slaves for those rotten men who masturbate like baboons and dream of raping women when they see sadistic filth. The voracious media portray lesbians as escorts, perpetuating a distorted image that encourages sleazy men to view them as promiscuous sex workers."

"Again, do you have an affair with Olivia?"

"I do not. The end of the story."

The fifth witness was Hannah. She was unhappy with this public spectacle. Lauren stood with a tender smile. "Your Honor, ladies and gentlemen, Albert and Sarah have done two DNA tests. I tell you, there is a sinister side to our case." She turned her face toward Hannah. "Hello. Please introduce yourself?"

"I am Hannah Thomas Rogers. I am a Yale professor and the CEO of Rogers Corporation. Sarah Rogers is my daughter."

"When did you first meet Albert Russell?"

"In 1981."

"Where?"

"In Hong Kong?"

"Were you married when you met Albert?"

"Yes. I was married then."

"Did you have sex with Albert in Hong Kong?"

"I joined his martial arts club for three weeks."

"Do you imply you had an affair with Albert?"

"I imply nothing more than acquaintance."

"Did you think Albert was your daughter's father?"

"I said Sarah and Albert have the same eye and hair color."

"Why did you say that?"

"Look at them."

"I want to thank Albert, who gave me his 1981 diary. Let me read what he said. '4 March: I met a young American woman in a restaurant today. Her name is Hannah Rogers. I will take her tomorrow to my kung fu club. She is beautiful.' '23 March: Hannah did not come today to the club. Maybe she is ill.' '24 March: I looked for Hannah in many places. I do not know what happened to her.' '26 March: No trace of Hannah anywhere.' According to Albert's diary account, you disappeared on Monday, March 23. Let us suppose you had sex with Albert on Sunday, March 22. Let us also assume Albert did not use condoms and his Chinese herbs did not erase his crazy sperms. The official birth documents say your daughter was born in New Haven on Tuesday, February 23, 1982. How would Albert be your daughter's parent?"

"Ask the fake news."

"One of your daughter's excellent traits is that she kept your passports in a wooden crate." Lauren picked up a passport from a folder. "This stamp proves you left Hong Kong on March 22. What do you say about that?"

"That was a long time ago."

"Let me remind you of another fact." Lauren held a copy of a newspaper. "This newspaper, dated Friday, April 10, 1981, says your husband Michael Rogers had died on April 9. Let us assume Michael had sex with you on April

9. This proves Michael Rogers is not Sarah's father. So, who is Sarah's father, Professor Rogers?"

Sarah wept, and Albert hugged her.

"You tell me."

"I will let you know Sarah's father, but tell us how you do not recognize your daughter's father? Stop playing games."

"I don't play games. I was young, and my husband's terrible death had traumatized me."

"Really?"

Hannah seethed. "You are confusing everybody. What is your point?"

Lauren opened a briefcase and picked out a file. "This medical report says your husband was sterile. It means he could not make you pregnant. Your Honor, I have no further questions."

Attorney Brown left his seat, gazing into Hannah's eyes and sniggering. "Professor Hannah Rogers, we appreciate your kind coming to the court today. You authored a critical book called *The Culture of Pornography* and many articles on sexual behavior. What do you say about Olivia's photos?"

"You could say they are suggestive and provoking. But this is reasonable in Olivia's case. She lived with her father for many years. They formed a strong affection. She also loves him because he championed her legal right to marry her girlfriend. Sometimes, a daughter sits on her father's thighs to gratify her subconscious needs."

"What do you mean by subconscious needs?"

"People get attracted to each other to satisfy latent feelings that logical thought can't explain."

"Are these normal kisses?"

"They are not normal in a conservative society like ours."

"Do these photos point to Albert's affair with his daughter?"

"Cultural and social discourses construct morality. In some societies, such as in the Amazon and Papua New Guinea, male and female nudity, for example, is not a moral obliquity."

"Were you Albert's girlfriend?"

"No. We were friends."

"Why didn't you have a relationship with him?"

"We have different views on life."

"Can you explain?"

"Albert is a humanist philosopher and freethinker, and I am a Catholic. That's all I can say."

"I guess he is like his grandfather Bertrand Russell, who believed in free love and had a few love affairs."

"Albert does not believe in religious morality."

"Who is Barbara Rogers?"

"She is my sister-in-law."

"Is she single?"

"Yes."

"Why does Albert travel with her?"

"They are prolific authors. I think we are here to talk about my daughter."

"Thanks, Professor Rogers. No more questions, your Honor."

Lauren stood again and stared at Hannah. "Why does Sarah adore her husband?"

"He is famous, and it is typical for a young woman to seek fame."

"Seek fame? Let us discuss your own fame. Here is a

transcript of Michael's will. It says if he dies before you become pregnant, his family will get you a two-bedroom house, and you would receive $100,000. But if he dies after you become pregnant, you would inherit his estate and thirty percent of his company's shares. You had two choices. Either you stay without a child and get a small house and $100,000, or you become a mother and inherit Michael's home and shares worth millions of dollars. So, you planned to become pregnant by any means. You had sex with a man. This man is Sarah's biological father."

"Your argument is a piece of typical fluff. I was unaware of Michael's will."

"Your Honor, the allegations against my clients are false. The other party has shown us photos that prove nothing but hugs and kisses and bespeak the grotesque intrusion of people's privacy. This, Your Honor, concludes the argument I wish to submit on behalf of my clients. I hope the court will take the right actions to the full extent of the law."

The judge announced the next hearing session would be at 2:30 pm and left the courtroom.

After a break for lunch, Albert and his family went back to the courtroom at 2:15 pm.

Lauren stood. "May I request Ellen Jones to come to the courtroom?"

A forty-eight-year-old blond, blue-eyed woman rested in the witness box.

"Hello. Can you introduce yourself?"

"I am Ellen James Jones."

"Where do you live?"

"In Greenwich Village."

"What do you do?"

"I am a journalist. I work for Faux News."

"Do you know Hannah Rogers?"

"Yes."

"How did you come to know her?"

"Hannah was my cousin's best friend."

"Who is your cousin?"

"Linda Jones."

"Where is she?"

"She died in Papua New Guinea in 2000."

"How did she die there?"

"The Anonymous terrorist group killed her."

"Why?"

"The terrorists hate America."

"What did Hannah tell you after she met Albert and Sarah in May 2001?"

"She visited me in the house and said she was upset because Albert married her daughter without her consent."

"What else did she tell you?"

"I can't remember now."

"With no warning, you published trenchant essays against Albert Russell since the year 2001. Why?"

"We live in a free country. Journalists and writers are entitled to criticize anybody."

"Entitled? Were you entitled to abuse Albert and call him 'a shameless, reprobate philosopher,' 'a brash English aristocrat,' 'a presumptuous advocate of sexual decadence,' 'an unscrupulous proponent of Oedipal sexuality,' 'an unabashed hater of Western civilization,' and 'an immoral exponent of libidinous promiscuity'? Do decent journalists use this type of acrimonious vocabulary?"

"I am free to debunk spurious scholarship."

"Spurious scholarship? Let me caution you that your

colleague Diane Walters has professed in the morning that it was you who reported the alleged blood relationship between Albert and Sarah. Why did you say Sarah is married to her father?"

"I have my own sources."

"Stop lying. The only person who fabricated the alleged relationship between Albert and Sarah was you."

"That's your assumption. Hannah told me she had an affair with Albert before the death of her husband. So, who is the father? Use your logic."

"This is not an assumption, and you know it. You became antagonistic because Hannah refused to be your girlfriend. You have never been with a guy because you are a lesbian. How did Faux News get pictures of Hannah and Albert when they were in Hong Kong in 1981? How much did Faux News pay you?"

"Nonsense. I was not in Hong Kong when Hannah met Albert."

"Nonsense? You found Hannah's pictures in Linda's home. How did Linda get the photos?"

"I do not know. Linda is dead."

"Linda was a CIA agent. The CIA asked her to spy on Hannah and her husband. Why did the CIA and Faux News ask you to traduce Albert and his family?"

"I do not believe in your conspiracy theories."

"Do not compel me to send your intimate photos to the media."

"Objection, Your Honor. This is blackmailing."

"Sustained."

"You became incensed when Hannah told you Linda was a member of the CIA group that tried to assassinate Albert outside the U.S. You wanted to exculpate your cousin and disguise the secret relationship between the CIA and Faux News. This explains why you discredited Albert and Hannah and disputed their academic credentials."

Ellen rubbed her hands on her thighs and felt afraid of public defamation and legal prosecution. "Yes, I told Faux News about Albert's incest. I must defend our democracy. Albert and his leftist Marxist terrorists are an existential threat to our security and values."

"Your Honor, ladies and gentlemen, we know who told the Faux News reporter Diane Walters about the alleged blood relationship between Albert and Sarah. Don't these reckless fools realize that our medical and forensic experts can test people's DNA?"

Lauren sat in her seat, and Attorney Brown found it problematic to question Ellen Jones after she disclosed the source of the sexual allegations.

Lauren rubbed her hands and got up again. "May I request Henry Simons to come to the courtroom?"

A fifty-three-year-old handsome man came to the courtroom and sat in the witness box. Hannah nodded and covered her face.

"Thank you for coming. Can you tell us your story?"

"I am Henry Simons, a Republican businessman and Congressman, and a candidate for the New York City mayor's office. My father, Jim Simons, was the Chairman and CEO of Faux Entertainment Group. Before his death, Michael Rogers was my best friend and business partner. I attended his sad funeral in April 1981 and gave a speech on our friendship. A week later, Hannah told me about her depression. By the end of February 1982, she called me and said she had given birth to a girl. I went to her house to see her daughter. Three months later, she contacted me, saying she could not understand her husband's complex business, and asked me to buy some of her company's shares. I bought shares for twenty million dollars. In 2001, Hannah told me she lost her mind because her daughter, who was a nineteen-year-old student at Columbia University, had married a British philosopher. She did not know what to do about that. Three years later, Sarah became a mother and reconnected with her mom.

After that, Hannah put an end to her friendship with Ellen Jones. So, Ellen became cranky and discredited Hannah and her folks. In the meantime, secret agents contacted Faux News to see how they could calumniate and revile Albert Russell. After getting money, Ellen conducted the shameful task of vilification. She told Faux News about the alleged blood relationship between Albert and Sarah, and about Albert's assumed incest with his daughter.

Meanwhile, Sarah announced her intent to be the next mayor of New York. I realized my dad and his Faux News had smeared her, not because they cared about her sex life, but because Albert Russell's wide influence is a significant challenge to the systematic corruption of the financial and political institutions in our country. Our government, intelligence agencies, and politicians say Albert poses a severe threat to our national security to preserve their interests and corrupt politics."

"Thank you for this impressive introduction. You said you met Hannah a week after Michael's funeral."

"Yes. That's true."

"What did you do with Hannah?"

"We dined and talked about our families."

"Did you sleep in Hannah's house that night?"

"Yes. We slept together."

"Did you have sex with Hannah?"

"Yes. It was consensual."

"Why did you have sex with her?"

"Hannah was my best female friend."

"Why did you buy Hannah's shares?"

"I said I was Michael's business partner."

"Did you have an affair with Hannah?"

"No. I got married."

"Why did Hannah continue to visit you?"

"We are close friends, and there is a strong relationship between the Rogers family and me."

"Are you married?"

"No. My wife died of cancer two years ago."

"When Sarah ran for mayor, Faux News began a virulent campaign against her."

"I agree. But I have never said a bad word against Sarah, who is my best friend's daughter. For the record, I am not responsible for the Faux News Channel and its reporting, though my dad was the owner of the company. I would never speak ill of Hannah's daughter."

"In a recent interview, you said the malignant reports, which say Sarah is Albert's daughter, have disgusted you. Why didn't you meet and talk to Sarah?" Lauren picked up a bank statement from a file. "This bank statement verifies that Faux News had given Ellen Jones $250,000 just a week before the allegations had surfaced in the news. Is this coincident?"

"As I have said, I am not responsible for Faux News. I will talk to my brother about the matter."

"Your Honor, I have no further questions."

When Attorney Brown stood, Henry Simons raised his left hand. "I have no time for you." After leaving the witness box, he waved to Hannah and Sarah and rested on a seat.

Lauren stood. "I would like to invite Dr. John Alfred Palmer."

Dr. Palmer sat in the witness box. Silence ensued in the courtroom, and the seated people drew their attention to the renowned forensic investigator.

"Thank you for coming to the court. Please, tell us about your work."

"I am an FBI director and a forensic expert."

"With great admiration, we watch your inspiring interviews and marvel at your phenomenal expertise and incredible findings. You solved many complicated crimes."

"Thank you."

"I want to ask you two precise questions. Is Sarah Rogers Albert's daughter?"

"No. My team and I have examined Albert's and Sarah's DNA."

"Is Henry Simons Sarah's biological father?"

"Yes, he is the biological father of Sarah Rogers."

Albert and his family and Henry Simons stood in shock and peered at each other. Mary yelled. "What the f...!" There was an outburst of quibbling uproar and chaos in the courtroom. In a nearby bar, a shaggy man banged on his table and spoke to his companion. "Holy crap! Did you hear that? Henry Simons is Sarah's dad."

The judge declared that the court would hold a final hearing at ten o'clock in the morning and ordered everybody to leave the courtroom, except Lauren,

Attorney Brown, and Dr. Palmer.

After getting up, Sarah hurtled toward Henry Simons and filliped him on the chin. "Listen. You have never been my dad, and you will never be my dad. Do you understand?"

Albert embraced her. "Sarah, please, do not speak to your father like that."

"He is not ..."

Albert closed her mouth. "Henry, I am sorry. Can we talk?"

He rubbed his chin. "Yes, of course."

Albert, Sarah, and Henry sat in a closed room.

Henry gazed at Sarah. "I swear by God, I have no idea at all. Your mom had never said I am your dad."

Albert gave Henry a C4 envelope. "This envelope has classified documents and a CD that holds the names of CIA officers and politicians involved in the death of Michael Rogers. These individuals used fake bank accounts to launder illegal money derived from arms and drug trafficking originating in Central and South America. The official documents include the names of the firearms manufacturers who, with the aid of banks and CIA agents, sold weapons to Asian and Latin American terrorists to topple socialist governments. I regret to say that the lists include your father's name."

"Oh, my God!"

"I think your daughter deserves a hug."

After standing, Sarah and Henry wept and hugged each other for a minute. Hannah came in and kissed Henry Simons. Sarah glared at her. "God damn you, mom. Why didn't you tell me about my dad? Why?"

"It is a long story. I didn't know."

"I will tell you," Henry interposed. "Michael didn't want your mom to take over his wealth, but I forced him to state that she must get $100,000 if he died before impregnating her. I made love to your mom when we had a lot of drinks because I wanted her to have a child and get a third of Michael's wealth. But when your mom became pregnant, she told me the pregnancy happened because she had an affair with an English guy in Hong Kong. That is why I did not marry your mom. Anyway, I have been seeing your mom for a year. We love each other and want to be together."

Hannah rested her hand on Henry's shoulder. "But now we must finish the job. So, call your brother, Paul, and tell him we want to see him at six o'clock."

"OK. I will call him. Please, can you all come to my home? I want Sarah to meet her brother and sister."

Albert, Hannah, and Sarah went to Henry's home in Midtown Manhattan and greeted his daughter, Ashley, and son, Liam. At five-thirty, Hannah and Henry moved to Paul's house in the Upper East Side. Paul asked them to come to his office.

"Wow. Congratulations. I have a new niece. What can I do for you?"

Hannah put her purse on her lap. "I want two things. First, I want our daughter Sarah to be the next mayor. Second, Sarah needs a token reparation and an apology from Faux News. Only if these conditions are met, you will see your niece. And then all of us will live happily ever after, as they say. Albert and Olivia need nothing."

"The family and I have no objection if Henry wants Sarah to be the next mayor. Money is not a problem. But I do not think I can issue an apology to Sarah or to her husband and his daughter."

"Why?"

"I told you I can't force our reporters and journalists to stop criticizing Albert and his lesbian daughter."

"I think you can."

"Please, this matter is beyond my managerial capacity and the objective of my job. Politicians and powerful institutions want to do something about Albert's irritating and needless interference in our American politics."

"I am not talking about Albert. All I am asking for is that your company apologizes to my daughter about the sexual accusations."

"I cannot do that."

"Sarah is your niece, and I will be your sister-in-law."

"We are a lovely family, but I can't make a public apology. Sorry."

"Try to understand that the Anonymous warriors will kill more Americans if your news channel harms Albert and his family."

"This is America. We are the greatest nation on earth. We are not afraid of a British philosopher and his stupid robots."

Feeling embittered and betrayed by Faux News, she opened her handbag with a furious face. In a dramatic and shocking gesture, she withdrew a silver handgun and pressed it against Paul's forehead. "I swear to God."

"Hannah, what are doing?" Henry yawped.

"Sit, Henry." She swung the gun at Paul. "Listen to me, you piece of garbage. I swear to God I will blow up your head if you do not apologize in public. The court has humiliated me today because of your evil company. And, yes, your evil dad was the one who killed my husband."

Hannah gazed at Henry. "Yes, Henry, your dad murdered your best friend to cover up his criminal dealings with the CIA. Your dad tried to kill Albert. I could have killed him, but I kept him alive for the sake of our friendship." She shifted her face to Paul. "If you call the cops, I will let the entire world know your father was a contemptible criminal and a big crook. Do you understand?"

"OK. Calm down, please."

"Something else. I do not want to see the piece of trash Attorney Brown in the courtroom tomorrow. Is this clear?"

"Yes. I will do what you want."

In the morning, Albert and his family and Henry Simons and other interested people came back to the courtroom. Henry stood. "Your Honor, I now speak on behalf of Faux News."

Lauren stood. "Please, may I ask Dr. Palmer to come here?"

Dr. Palmer sat in the witness box.

Lauren glanced at him. "Is there the possibility of an error in the DNA testing?"

"No. We used the best laboratories in the country."

"Do you like to add anything?"

"Yes. Ms. Olivia Russell does not have a love affair with her father. If she had an affair with him, the NYPD and the FBI would have known that."

"Are you certain?"

"Yes. The FBI, the NSA, and the CIA put Dr. Russell under constant surveillance, before Mr. Obama became the president, because of his public speeches against the wars in the Middle East."

"Thank you, Dr. Palmer." Lauren turned her face to

the left. "Your Honor, ladies and gentlemen, Sarah Rogers is not Albert Russell's biological daughter. The Republican Congressman Henry Simons is Sarah's biological father. Here is the official letter of the DNA tests. My client, Ms. Olivia Russell, is innocent. The photos and the clips we have seen prove nothing but guiltless, loving, and emotional behavior. Remember, the baseless, defamatory allegations are about an incest relationship between Ms. Olivia Russell and her father. As I have said before, if two distinguished public figures want to have a love affair, they would not hug and kiss each other in populated parks and public places. They would not kiss each other near their workplaces. Secret lovers go to distant motels, private resorts, hotels, and secluded places, not to Central Park and fashion stores. On a further and important note, how do we allow intruding photographers to invade our privacy? How do we allow the intrusive paparazzi to take photos of us when we are in the changing rooms? Would we license photographers to install hidden cameras under our desks and seats, and in our bathrooms and bedrooms? The sham accusations are based on ideological and political considerations, and on an infringement of my client's privacy.

But the real question is why the conservative media has defamed Dr. Albert Russell? For your information, CIA agents had tried over fifty times to assassinate him in Asia and Latin America. Why? Do you know why? I will tell you why. Because Dr. Russell has this authentic video that incriminates the CIA for executing the celebrated investigative journalist Peter Stone and his wife and their son Jamie, who was an esteemed genius scientist. Please, play the video."

The callous murder of Peter Stone and his wife and their son by CIA operatives had appalled the people in the courtroom. Lauren pointed at the screen. "The second clip will show you a private meeting between a CIA director called the Black Wolf and Jim Simons, the founder of Faux News Corporation."

The amazed crowd in the courtroom watched and listened to this conspiratorial dialog. "What should we do to Albert Russell? We lost many men because of him. And now he wants his wife to be the next mayor in New York," the Black Wolf spoke to Jim Simons.

"I will handle this matter. I know his wife's mom. We will say his wife is his daughter, and he has sex with his other daughter."

"I wish to kill this British asshole, but the leftist terrorists and the Anonymous would blow up our cities and massacre millions of Americans."

"We don't need trouble with the Anonymous and the British government. We should hire a drugged hitman to kill him."

Lauren switched off the video. "Sad to say, Muslim terrorists killed the Black Wolf and Jim Simons a few weeks ago. And before I leave you, have you seen the papers today?" She opened a carton box and pulled out newspapers. "Here is a seminude lap dancer on the thighs of Faux News Chairman Paul Simons. And this topless girl is Attorney Brown's daughter in a Playboy club. I have no problem with that, but the hypocrites see the specks in other people's eyes and do not see the logs in their eyes."

The judge said the court would deliver a verdict at 2:30.

Albert and his family left the court building and

declined to talk to the reporters who encircled them for a while. They had lunch in a quiet restaurant. Later, they were in the courtroom, waiting for the final verdict. Sarah carried her son Edward, and Olivia sat between Mary and her father.

Judge Allen Redford said Olivia had won the lawsuit and ordered the other party to pay her $650,000 in compensation for the damages caused by the malicious accusations.

Olivia sprang up and hugged Mary, Albert, Sarah, and Barbara. When they exited the court building, reporters were waiting for them.

A female reporter held a black blimp microphone and stopped Olivia, who was in tears. "What do you say now?"

"I hope this is the happy conclusion of a long and painful story."

Another reporter approached Sarah, who held her son and Albert's hand. "Ms. Sarah Rogers, what do you think about the verdict?"

"I am happy. We won the lawsuit, and it is a beautiful day for the celebration. We will not allow the conservative Bible bashers to rule America. They hate freedom and the gay people. This is a free country and will always be free. We filed the lawsuit against the unfounded accusations because of our eternal love for Albert."

Sarah and Olivia kissed Albert's lips. "You can take photos now. We love him and will always love him."

Albert whispered to Olivia and Sarah. "Have you seen Zita?"

"No. She was not here," Olivia replied.

"You must see her. She is a great woman. She has done so many good things for us. I will be in the house to keep the bed warm for you," Sarah said.

Albert drove his car to Zita's house. Zita was standing near a front window, carrying a cup of tea, and waiting for Albert. She grinned and wept when she saw him leaving his car. After placing her teacup on a table, she opened the door and kissed Albert's lips as if she had not seen him for a long time.

"I knew you would come."

"Oh, Zita, how can we thank you?"

"I did what I did because of my love for you. Go back to your home and have a wild party with your gorgeous daughter and wife. I can be patient for another day. Our love story is not over yet."

Chapter 15

In his home, Albert seemed frazzled and distracted. "My body needs repose and the bed."

"You look haggard."

"You know, exacting things have exhausted my brain in the last three months. The slander. The court. And now you have a father, a brother, and a sister. Life is life. Wonderful."

"I wonder if I would love my dad, though he is sympathetic and generous."

"Fill your heart with gratitude. I need to sleep. Good night."

At six o'clock in the morning, Albert's phone rang. "Albert, I need to see you right now," Ann said.

"OK. I will see you shortly."

Ann kissed Albert in the family room and held his hand. "My sources inform me that local anti-American terrorists are going to blow up the CIA headquarters in Virginia. The terrorists say today is the judgment day. This will put our lives in danger. Do you know anything about this matter?"

"No. My leftist and Muslim sources said nothing. I heard there were roadworks in Langley."

"My sources confirm the obliteration is today and inevitable. What should we do?"

"I should contact my informants. Let me first meet Hannah. She might reveal something."

"I will come with you." She picked up her cell phone and pressed a button.

Hannah welcomed them. "Good morning. This is an early visit. What's going on?"

"Unknown terrorists want to raze the CIA headquarters to the ground."

"Why?"

"Maybe to avenge an offense. Do you have any idea who would conduct an assault on the CIA?"

Hannah contemplated for a while. "Oh, my God. I gave Zita a construction map of the tunnels under the CIA headquarters. She said there would be an Italian festa."

"Oh dear. Zita and her Mafia clique want to vindicate the massacre of their clan. I will talk to her."

Albert and Ann visited Zita.

"Good morning. How are you today?" Zita tried to kiss Albert, but he moved his head away from her.

"Tell me the truth. What will take place today?"

"Nothing. I am not going anywhere."

"What are you going to do?"

Zita smiled. "I want to have sex with you. Ann, with

due respect, why are you here? What can I do for you?"

"Who will attack the CIA today?"

"Why do you ask me this crazy question?"

"What is the judgment day?"

"You are a professor of religion and should know that."

"Stop playing childish games with me. Do not oblige me to bring an end to our friendship."

"Wow! Are you drunk? Did you have a riotous party with your wife and daughter? We kissed yesterday. What's wrong with you? Why do you talk like that?"

"Are you going to commit a massacre?"

"I am not a witch."

"OK. This is the end of our friendship."

Zita grabbed his hand. "Crazy man, I am your best friend. I thought you came here to spend a day with me. You can't finish our friendship like that."

"Why not?"

"Don't you know why? I love you. We have been best friends for twenty-eight years."

"Tell me the truth if you love me."

"Which truth?"

"You have a minute to tell me your plan against the CIA."

"Which plan?"

"OK. I am leaving you forever."

"Dammit! You are going nowhere." She opened a drawer and got a pistol. "Sit, both of you. Please, Albert, don't let me lose my love for you."

"Why are you holding a gun? Do you want to kill me?"

"How do you say that?" She rubbed her mouth and goggled at him with her seductive eyes. "OK. I want to blow up the CIA headquarters. It is the time I avenge the death of my parents and uncles."

"Are you nuts? Do you want to slaughter thousands of innocent people?"

"Innocent people? Did you forget? They massacred and mutilated millions of people in Japan, Korea, Southeast Asia, Latin America, Somalia, Afghanistan, and Iraq. The CIA psychopaths killed my mom and dad. You should understand how I lived without my parents."

"The people who murdered your parents and uncles are dead. You will gain nothing. George W. Bush exploited the terrorist attacks to justify his wars on Afghanistan and Iraq. The U.S. may drop an atomic bomb on a poor country if you destroy the CIA headquarters."

"I don't care anymore. It is too late now. The bombs will explode in two hours."

He looked at his Bulova watch. "Do you have the detonators?"

"No. Nobody can go there except the Anonymous warriors. My guys attached the bombs to explosive liquids in sewers."

"I can't stay here. We are leaving. I ought to notify the security agencies."

"What happened to you? Sit. Don't make me mad."

Albert and Ann sat on a sofa, and two sturdy Italian Americans came out of a room and stood behind them.

"Do you want to die? Nahatatama, Homatakawa, and their Anonymous assassins killed the guys who threatened me."

"Shut up and be quiet. The Anonymous will never attack me because I am one of them."

A moment later, a ninja throwing spike smashed a front window and injured Zita's right hand. She squealed, and her pistol fell to the floor. The two Italians left the house. A masked person thrashed them with a three-section staff and fractured their heads, legs, and arms. The masked person stormed through the door and entered the house. When Zita tried to pick up her gun, the masked person jumped and kicked her face and chest. Zita fell into a coma, and Ann got her gun. "Albert, we need to go now."

Ann and Albert left Zita's house. Albert stared at the masked motorcyclist who fled away. "Who was that guy?"

"That's Tilatowate."

Albert made a phone call.

"The White House."

"I am Professor Albert Russell. Please, I want to talk to the President as soon as possible."

"You need an invitation."

"Please, the terrorists will launch an immediate attack on the country. The President is my friend. Ask him to talk to me as quickly as possible."

"OK, sir."

Fifteen minutes later, Albert's phone vibrated.

"Good morning, Dr. Albert Russell. This is the President. What's up, man?"

"Please, sir, ask the CIA personnel and everybody in Langley, Virginia, to leave the area promptly."

"Gosh! Why?"

"The terrorists will blow up the CIA headquarters after ninety minutes."

"Who told you that?"

"Some of my students spy on the terrorist groups."

"Are you sure? We have the best intelligence agencies in the world. How don't they know this matter?"

"I can't answer your question on the phone. Please, Mr. President, order the CIA employees to move out."

"OK, buddy. I have always trusted you. If this is false information, I will kick your ass and deport you."

Ann touched Albert's face. "What did the President say?"

"He said he would deport me if nothing took place."

She patted his hand. "Be confident. I will be with you."

Albert and Ann went to the house in Larchmont and saw two suited men leaning on a car hood. "Yes, how can I help you?" Albert asked.

"We are Sarah's bodyguards."

Albert and Ann entered the house and greeted Sarah. "My dad has asked us to have lunch with him."

"Who are the two guys outside the house?"

"They are my bodyguards. My dad hired them. Are you coming?"

"I can't go. You go, darling."

"You look stressed. What's wrong, love?"

"Something bad will happen."

"Where?"

"The barbaric terrorists want to ravage the country. Please, darling, go to your dad and tell him I am busy. Give me a kiss."

Sarah and Edward left the house. Albert hugged his sister. "So, darling, when will the wise people put an end to this murderous bedlam?"

"Blame the CIA that started all this bloody mayhem. It wants the U.S. to control the world and be the only superpower. This will never happen."

They looked at the TV screen. A CNN news anchor frowned. "This is a breaking news alert. We are getting reports that the government has asked the employees at the CIA headquarters in Virginia to leave the area for security reasons."

Ann rested her head on Albert's right shoulder. "Oh, my God. Zita is imprudent, and nobody would stop her Mafia group. She is like a zombie ghost."

Albert looked at his wristwatch. "I hope they will hurry and escape away. Ten minutes remain before the scourge."

"Ten minutes?"

"Yeah. Zita said the blasts will start at one o'clock."

The tension in the room escalated as Ann and Albert glued their staring eyes to the live news coverage. The screen flickered with chaotic scenes of terrified people sprinting through the nearby forests, their desperate escape taking them in all directions.

Moments later, the tranquility of the place shattered. Multiple explosions rocked the county, their deafening blasts annihilating car parks and unleashing fiery infernos. The landscape transformed into a nightmarish tableau of destruction, as massive mushroom clouds billowed into the sky.

Albert held Ann's hand. "Here is a repulsive example of human insanity. What will we benefit from this barbaric carnage and slaughter?"

Ann caressed his arm. "Love, I am worried about you. The CIA and the FBI will ask you many questions about the explosions."

"I know that. I will not say a word about Zita and hope to talk to the President."

In the morning, Albert's phone rang. "Good morning, my dear friend."

"Good morning, Mr. President."

"We lost the car parks, but the central buildings are intact. The explosions caused no human casualties. On behalf of the United States of America and the American people, I want to extend our deep gratitude to your tireless efforts to keep this country safe and secure. I need you to be my advisor on global terrorism. This, of course, is an unofficial offer because you are a British citizen."

"Mr. President, I am very honored and thankful. The most important thing is human life."

"Thank you, Dr. Russell. I will see you soon. God bless you and the family."

Three days later, Albert got another call from the President. "Dr. Russell, can I meet you on Friday at the White House?"

"Yes, sir. When?"

"What about 10:30 in the morning?"

"Great."

Albert and Ann flew to Washington, D.C. on Friday morning. Albert got a taxi and headed to the White House. While he was on his way to the Oval Office, he met the director of the CIA, Lorenzo Pedrotti, and shook his hand. "Good morning, Dr. Russell."

"Good morning, Mr. Pedrotti. Please, don't leave the White House. I have something important about the security of this country. Let me first see the President."

Albert entered the Oval Office. The President stood and gave him a hug. "How is my pal? How are you doing? Please, sit here."

"I am fine, sir."

"How is the family? I heard your wife is running for the mayor's office in New York."

"Yes, that's true."

"She has my full support."

"Thank you, sir."

"You have been in this country for a long time. Why didn't you apply for the U.S. citizenship?"

"Who doesn't want the Queen?" They laughed.

"You should become a U.S. citizen. This country needs people like you."

"Thank you, sir."

"Please, stop calling me sir. You were my mentor."

"OK."

"So, Dr. Russell, who was behind the evil attack on the CIA headquarters?"

"The al-Qaeda terrorists."

"How?"

"They have three or four sleeper cells in New York, Chicago, and California. I have met Lorenzo Pedrotti. Please, ask him to come here. I have something significant to say."

"What is it?"

"It concerns Osama bin Laden."

The President made a call and asked for Lorenzo Pedrotti. He smiled and sat beside Albert. "What do you know about bin Laden?"

"I know where he lives."

"Wow. That is incredible. Where does he live?"

"In Islamabad." Lorenzo Pedrotti came into the Office.

"Hi, Lorenzo. Please, have a seat. Yes, Albert, what do you want to say?"

"Before I say anything regarding bin Laden, I want to request the CIA to stop its war against me."

The President gaped. "Which war?"

"The CIA had conspired to kill me since I published

official documents in 1990. The Anonymous killed the CIA operatives who tried to assassinate me."

"Oh, my God. What are you talking about?"

"Yes, Mr. President, the Anonymous executed over thirty CIA agents in the last ten years because they sought to kill me."

"Unbelievable. What is the Anonymous?"

"It is a secret organization of qualified robot and cyborg assassins who are my undesignated, unsanctioned bodyguards. They obey the leftist revolutionaries, who consider me their intellectual hero. They look after me wherever I go. I am a man of knowledge, love, and peace. I am the only person who can stop the Anonymous. Therefore, I implore the CIA to cease trying to harm me." Albert looked at Lorenzo. "I request you, I beg you, I ... I order you to stay away from my family and me. The Anonymous will wage a new world war and murder millions of Americans if the CIA kills me. No army in the world can defeat the Anonymous warriors because they are invisible and equipped with the most advanced artificial intelligence technology. They can appear anywhere, and no walls or borders can stop them."

"Incredible. Lorenzo, what do you say?"

"I don't know about the CIA's plans to assassinate Albert. I will investigate the matter."

"The CIA killed this country's greatest journalist Peter Stone and his wife and their son, who was a remarkable scientist. These people were radical and influential thinkers. The Anonymous avenged their death by killing many CIA operatives. Three or four CIA agents abducted my daughter a few years ago. The Anonymous killed them and saved my daughter."

"Albert, I thought you are here to discuss the attack on the CIA headquarters."

"First, I want a deal and a pledge. I will tell you where Osama bin Laden lives if you promise me to stop the CIA's violent intervention in my personal life."

"What do you want me to do?"

"Please, ask the CIA and other intelligence agencies to stay away from me. My family and I want to live in peace and dignity."

"OK. I will direct the CIA to stay away from you."

"Thank you, Mr. President." Albert opened a leather briefcase and drew a Google map. "Osama bin Laden lives in this house in Islamabad."

"Are you sure?"

"Yes. Three members of the Pakistani ISI know about this matter."

Albert left the White House and met Ann at the airport. They flew back to LaGuardia Airport. After their arrival, Ann drove her silver Hyundai Santa Fe. "Have you seen Caumsett State Historic Park Preserve in Lloyd Harbor?"

"No."

"I will take you there." Ann parked the car on Watch Way, near a place called Northwest Bluff. "Albert, get the binoculars. You can see your house from here."

When Albert bowed his head to get the binoculars, Ann groaned. "Oh, Gosh! They are here." She picked up her cell phone and sent a text.

Three Chevrolet Tahoe cars blocked Ann's car. Albert squeezed Ann's hand. "Stay calm. We will fight them when we are in danger."

Eight armed men left their cars. One of them glared at

Ann. "I am Allan Marshall. We are federal agents. Please, get out of the car."

Albert and Ann walked out of the car. Albert gazed at Allan. "What is going on, sir?"

Allan asked them to stand beside a tree. "How did you know about the attack on the CIA headquarters?"

"Sir, please, Ann has nothing to do with this matter."

An agent searched Ann's car. "She is American. This is her passport."

Allan opened Ann's passport. "What do you do, Ann? Why are you here?"

"Don't you recognize me? The country knows my newspapers and magazines."

"Why are you here?"

"I want to ask Albert about his important meeting with the President in the morning."

"Here?" Allan looked at an agent. "Take her there."

Allan stared at Albert. "How did you learn about the assault on the CIA?"

"Sir, I met the President in the morning and told him the truth."

"You didn't answer my question. Who told you about the attack?"

"Two Muslims had informed me about the attack."

"Who are they?"

"They live in Pakistan."

"What are their names?"

"Qadir Khan and Ahmad Qadiri."

"Who is Nahatatama?"

"What is this strange name?"

"Don't you know him? Who is Homatakawa?"

"Why do you ask me?"

"The Anonymous murdered four dozen CIA officers because of you."

"I did not kill them."

"I said the Anonymous killed them. How don't you know the people who protect you?"

"The Anonymous assassins are not people. They are machines appearing like people. They speak a strange language that I do not know, wear masks and hoods, and call themselves the Anonymous. So, how would I know them?"

"Don't you know the guys who care for you? We do not wish to hurt you. Again, who is Nahatatama? Who is Homatakawa? Who are the Anonymous?"

"Do I need to repeat myself? I told you I ..." Three masked, hooded motorcyclists, carrying crossbows, shot a volley of steel arrows and killed three officers. When the other officers pulled their guns, the motorcyclists threw spikes and stars and injured their arms and legs. One of them jumped and kicked Allan Marshall's frightened face. "Tilatowate, leave him," Ann said and retched when the motorcyclists executed the others by using broadswords and fled the site.

Albert grabbed Allan's neck and hustled him back, pressing him against a thick tree. "Who asked you to follow me?"

"You are playing with fire and making a huge mistake."

Albert kicked his left knee. "Answer me, or I will kill you."

"He is Aaron Buchman."

"Who is he?"

"He is the White House Chief of Staff," Ann said.

Albert thwacked Allan's neck and killed him. Ann

hugged him. "Oh, my God." Albert looked at the dead officers. "These filthy animals do not understand. I thought it was over. Who are the motorcyclists?" Albert moved an FBI car and cleared the way.

"Get in the car. Let us go home."

"How do they know me?"

"Who?"

"The motorcyclists. Why do they protect me? Do they collaborate with Zita and her vicious Mafia? They are professional assassins. Let me call Zita."

Albert got his cell phone and made a call. "Hi, Zita. How do you feel?"

"I am well. I am sorry. Please, forgive me."

"Don't worry. I will contact you soon. Take care."

Albert glanced at Ann. "The motorcyclists are not Zita's hitmen." He made another call. "How is my favorite mother-in-law?"

"I am OK, my favorite son-in-law. What are you like? Did you meet the President?"

"Yes, I met him. Can I meet you tomorrow?"

"You can."

Albert looked again at Ann. "Hannah is in her home. She is not one of the motorcyclists. Strange. My American friends do not have motorbikes."

In the morning, Albert got a copy of *The New York Times* newspaper and read the bold headline, "**The Anonymous Are Back: Carnage in Long Island.**" In the evening, he visited Ann Stone, who touched his face. "You look tense."

"I have been thinking of the obtuse federal officers who died on Long Island. After I met the President, the White House Chief of Staff, Aaron Buchman, had asked the federal agents to follow me. I saw him glaring at me and using his cell phone on my way out."

"Aaron was a Deputy Director of the CIA. He supports the CIA's targeted killings."

"Why did your newspaper say the Anonymous killed the federal officers in Long Island?"

"We have good connections with the NYPD."

"But the Anonymous didn't make any statement. So, how did the NYPD know?"

"The motorcyclists used martial arts weapons that have the Anonymous symbols. Anyway, how's Sarah doing?"

"She is fine and happy. She spends most of her time with her father."

"Do you like to stay with me tonight?"

"I wish, darling. Thank God the agents did not kill us. I want to go home and relax."

Ann put a hand on Albert's face and kissed him. "I love you. What would I do without you? Come on the weekend. I need a massage and hugs and kisses."

Two days later, Albert was with Sarah when he switched on the TV. A news report said an unidentified killer had slain the White House Chief of Staff, Aaron Buchman, in his car, and the police found an Anonymous card in his mouth.

Sarah yawned. "The Anonymous guys are like ghosts. They are here and there and everywhere."

The next evening, Ayita, carrying a leather knapsack, entered Ann's apartment. A mysterious man wearing a ski mask placed his hand on her shoulder. She punched his wrist and gave him a roundhouse kick. He grabbed her foot and pushed it down. After twenty seconds of swift punches and kicks, Ayita jumped and gave him a tail kick to his face. He tumbled down behind a couch. Ayita pulled a nightstick from a console table. "Who are you, blockhead?"

"Ayita."

"Dad. Dad. Jesus Christ. What are you doing here?"

He removed his wool mask and wept. Ayita sat beside him on the floor and hugged him. "Dad, I am sorry. I thought you were a burglar. Why were you wearing a mask? I could have killed you. Please, dad, stop crying."

"I am crying because of you."

She sat on his thighs. "Because of me?"

"I know who you are."

"Of course, you know who I am. I am your girl."

Ann came into the apartment and saw Ayita's arms around Albert's neck. "Is it a daddy-daughter time?" She looked at their tears. "What happened?"

"My dad was wearing this mask. I kicked his face. I thought he was a robber."

"What is going on, Albert?" Ann sat beside him on the floor. "Why did you wear a mask?"

"I know Ayita."

"Dad, don't be silly. You know I love you very much."

"I and Shaolin monks taught you the best techniques of kung fu. Tilatowate uses the same kung fu styles which we taught you. I saw your kung fu skills in action. Thank you, sweetheart, for looking after me."

"Dad, what are you saying?"

Albert's hand touched Ayita's face. "Darling, don't you trust your dad, who adores you? Who was the masked motorcyclist who kicked Zita in her home? Who kicked Allan Marshall's face and executed the special agents at Caumsett State Park? Please, tell me the truth."

Ayita hugged him and lifted the back of her red hair. Albert stared at a minuscule tattoo of an eagle. "That was me. I am Tilatowate or the Flying Eagle."

"Who murdered the two agents in the May Fair Hotel in London? I saw a Band-Aid on your hand after their death."

"I killed them. They wanted to blow up your room and kill you and your wife."

"Who executed the CIA officers in Latin America and Hong Kong?"

"That was not me."

"Who executed them?"

"Homatakawa."

"Do you work for the Anonymous?"

Ann looked at Albert's face and kissed him. "Yes, we work for the Anonymous. I love you." She cried. "The CIA gangsters killed my parents and grandparents. They tried over fifty times to assassinate you. Ayita and I will never allow the barbaric guys to harm you. I have known you since you were born. I kissed you when you were ten, made love to you when you were fourteen, and became the mother of our beautiful daughter. You have been my sweetheart for forty years. I could have married a rich man and lived a luxury life, but I resolved to avenge the murder of my parents and grandparents and guard you."

"Only I and you knew about Aaron Buchman. Who killed him?"

"We do you want to know?"

"I guess I have the right to know what you do behind my back. Ayita, did you kill him?"

"No."

"Who slew him? Don't you trust me?"

"We trust you." Ann paused. "I asked Homatakawa to kill him."

"How do you know Homatakawa?"

"I am Hatakachita or the Messenger. I am the only person who can contact Homatakawa."

"Who is he?"

"We don't know his identity."

"How do you trust him?"

"My dad made him a bionic assassin to protect us."

"Where does he live?"

"I can't tell you."

"Why?"

"He would kill me."

"Homatakawa?"

"Yes."

"Who is the leader of the Anonymous?"

"What do you want to know about him?"

"I need to figure out why he and the Anonymous care about me."

Ann wiped her tears and kissed him again. "Go to your room. I want to show you something." She entered the kitchen and fetched a black crowbar. After pushing Albert's bed against a wall, Ann removed a rug and three floorboards. There was a cellar under the wooden floor. Ann glided down and got an electronic gadget and a set of cards.

Albert wiped the gadget. "What is this machine?"

"This is the voice changer device that my dad made before his death. Listen." Ann pushed a button. An orotund male voice said, "We know who you are and what you do. We will get you out of your holes, and then we will kill you. We are a regiment. We do not acquit. We do not neglect. We do not rest. We are the Anonymous." Ann smiled and showed Albert the Anonymous cards.

"Are you the leader of the Anonymous?"

"No." She put her hand on his face. "You are the leader of the Anonymous. You are Nahatatama, or the Blue Chief, because you wear blue suits."

The revelation hit him like a thunderbolt. A shiver raced across his skin, with disbelief gripping him as he grappled with the realization that he was at the helm of the world's most dangerous assassination organization. He punched the floor. "How?"

"The Anonymous protects you because you are our leader and because you carry the secret code and design of my dad's robot technology."

"I don't understand."

Ann brought a scanner attached to a laptop. "Put your hands on the scanner." The scanner photocopied Albert's palms. Albert stared at the laptop screen and saw digital diagrams and electronic images of bionic technology and humanoid robots. "I still do not understand."

"Our artificial intelligence technology requires a secret password to access the database that is stored in you. Your palms are the password, and your brain thinks and manages the overall operations and stratagems of the Anonymous. The Anonymous assassins read your mind and follow your subconscious orders. My dad scanned your hands and inserted a silicon chip into your body in 1988. So, the Anonymous tracks and guards you to preserve the database."

"Where is the robot laboratory?"

"It is beneath a vast mountain in Yunnan province in China. In the beginning, Vietnamese fighters lost their limbs because of the American bombardment. My dad turned these Vietnamese into robot warriors. Our global scientists developed and programed the Anonymous warriors to fight like the Shaolin monks. That is why they are kung fu experts."

"How does the Chinese government allow the Anonymous scientists to create cyborg warriors in China?"

"We are helping the Chinese army create artificial intelligence warriors and the best weapons in the world."

"What is the language of the Anonymous fighters?"

"My dad compiled a dictionary of ancient and extinct Native American words. The Anonymous fighters use this dictionary."

"If the Anonymous fighters use Native American words, how do they understand my English language? I think, write, and dream in English. How do they get my instructions?"

"Turn your head." Albert turned his head, and Ann pressed the bottom of his neck and throat. "Talk."

"*Hau. Na* Albert. *Itan can kin he mi ye* [Hello. I am Albert. I am the boss]."

Ann pressed his neck again. "The Anonymous fighters have an artificial-intelligent translator. They translate your thought and commands into their language."

"How do they appear everywhere and disappear?"

"They use transformative digital technology and can make themselves invisible. That is why the security agencies cannot capture or destroy them."

"How many people know I am Nahatatama?"

"Only we and Homatakawa."

Albert hugged Ann and Ayita. "Thank you for caring for me for many years. I am very proud of you. Please, tell me where Homatakawa lives. I must see him in person and thank him for his great work. You and Homatakawa are the true leaders of the Anonymous."

"He lives in a big detached house at Beach Road in Huntington in Suffolk County."

The next day, Albert parked his car on Bay Ave and walked to Beach Road. He squatted behind a dense thicket and found Homatakawa's house at the beach. Ten minutes later, an aged East Asian man stopped his van at Homatakawa's home, carried a dark briefcase, and buzzed the doorbell. A bowed, hooded person in a wheelchair opened the door. Albert thought he was at the wrong address. He looked at his cell phone to check the address. He was in the right place. Twenty minutes later, the East Asian man put the wheelchair masked person in his vehicle and zoomed away. Albert moved to the back of the house and saw an open window on the second floor. He clambered up to the side of the house and went into a room. After switching on his torch, he opened a drawer and saw women's underwear. After a while, he found photos of him and his family. There was a noise at the main door. He hurried downstairs and stopped behind the door. The wheelchair hooded person entered the house and closed the door. Albert touched the person's shoulder. "Who ...?" The seated person grabbed his arm and threw him on a coffee table as if he was a basketball. Albert broke the table and groaned. "I am angry. Say your last prayers," a robotic voice said.

Albert raised his head from the floor and rubbed his neck. "Don't kill me. I am Nahatatama. I am Albert Russell. Who are you? Why do you protect me?"

After pushing the wheelchair away, Homatakawa stood

and removed the hood and wailed. "Albert. Albert." A woman cried and switched on a light. She put her right hand on her chest. "Eva. Eva."

Albert wriggled and sobbed. "Eva. Eva. Oh, my God. Eva. You are alive."

Eva sat on his abdomen and kissed his face and lips for a minute. "I love you. I love you."

Albert touched her face and wept. "Oh, sweetheart, what happened to you?"

She pulled her hair up. "I miss you so much." She paused and cried. "The CIA scumbags abducted me when I was in Haneda Airport ... They molested me ... They interrogated me to know about my connection with Fusako Shigenobu and your grandfather Peter. I refused to talk ... They put me in a military helicopter ... When they heard about the crash of the Japan Airlines Flight 123, they tried to drop me on the crash site. I resisted for a while and jumped off the helicopter using a raincoat as a parachute. My legs and arms broke, and tree branches ripped off the skin of my face and damaged my throat ... A Japanese monk found me unconscious and sheltered me in a forest house ... When your grandfather came to Japan to investigate the crash, a Japanese friend brought him to me ... The sight of my fractured limbs and face devoid of skin had left him in shock ... I told him the story ... I told him about the pigs who wanted me dead. He broke down in tears and vowed to take revenge ... He asked the monk, Japanese friends, and your dad to treat me in secret ... Your grandfather and dad traveled to Japan to look after me ... Medical and technical specialists inserted fibers and prosthetic material into my body and made a silicon mask to cover my face. I have bionic limbs."

"Oh, darling, we thought the explosion of the plane had reduced you to ashes. I saw you today with an East Asian man. Who is he?"

"He is the leading Japanese specialist who looks after me. He removed the mask today. How do I look?"

Albert kissed her. "You are gorgeous, my sweetheart. Are you Homatakawa?"

"Yes. I am the most wanted person in the world."

"What about the assassination business?"

"The Japanese monk and his disciples taught me ninjutsu and how to use weapons ... Your dad visited me in 1989 and told me he created an army of robot warriors to avenge the murder of his parents. He enhanced the power of my arms and legs and asked your sister, Ann, to keep me updated on your life and travels. I moved to Mexico and turned into a killing machine. Ayita and I had protected you for many years. Yes, my love, do not believe the liars. Your daughter, the Anonymous warriors, and I are your true bodyguards. Ayita and I are the military commanders of the Anonymous. Ann is the mastermind of our operations."

She kissed Albert. "You know, I cried because you said to Olivia, 'You always remind me of your beautiful mom. I have never loved and will never love a woman more than your mom. I wish she is alive to see you now. I miss her very much.' I love you, Albert. Isn't our daughter brave and gorgeous?"

"Yes. I am proud of her."

"Love, I am still your wife. No woman, and I say no woman in the world, will take you away from me. I want to be with you till the end of my life. No more sleeping around. Do you understand what I say?"

"I understand."

She smiled. "Guess what? I am a Japanese citizen, and my name is Kanako Sakamoto. Come up to my bed."

They went to bed and made love. Eva left the bed and got an envelope from a locked drawer. "This is for you. It is from your granddad."

Albert opened the envelope and found a handwritten letter. "My beloved grandson, Albert. Your wife Eva is alive, but she cannot see you now because she is paralyzed, and her face has no skin. She declined to tell me about the people who betrayed her and told the CIA about her trip to Japan. Look after yourself and Olivia. P. Stone."

"When did you get this letter?"

"Before his death." She placed her head on his chest. "I know who murdered your dad and granddad."

"Who killed them?"

"Lorenzo Pedrotti."

"The CIA director?"

"Yes. He is evil."

"How do you know that?"

"I forced Aaron Buchman to tell me the truth."

"Did you kill Aaron?"

"Yes. Aaron was a filthy villain. Lorenzo Pedrotti will be in New Jersey tomorrow. I must kill him. Come with me to see your wife in action."

"What do you want me to do?"

"Wait for me at Sacred Heart Cathedral tomorrow at five p.m. The Cathedral is near Branch Brook Park in Essex County, New Jersey. Go home and rest. Wait." She gave him a CD and a cell phone. "Use this cell phone when you contact me. Press this button for an emergency. Our warriors will protect you all the time."

"What is this CD?"

"It is Paddy Reilly's song 'My Lovely Rose of Clare.' Do you remember? I sang it for you every day."

The next day, Eva met Albert near the Sacred Heart Cathedral and asked him to get in her car. She drove to Stonebridge Road in Montclair. "That's the house."

"It is a mansion. I see three security cars."

"Don't worry. Let us eat and rest. We'll start the action at eleven o'clock."

At a quarter to eleven, Eva moved to her car and fetched a tanto, a sword, and ninja spikes and stars. She hid the swords in her sleeves and glanced at Albert with a grin. "These are my toys. Wear these gloves and shoes. Go to the main door after I kill the guys in the security cars." She pressed a button on her cell phone. "Strike. Strike."

Eva stomped to a black GMC car and knocked on a window. "Hello, guys. Do you want a kiss?"

"Are you drunk, lady?" a security guard said.

"Yeah, I am drunk. Give me a big kiss." She jabbed the driver's face. When the other two guards in the car wanted to pull their guns, she threw a spike and a star, piercing their necks. Two Anonymous warriors used hatchets and killed them. Eva threw a tanto at a security guard sitting behind a steering wheel and slew him. After thirty seconds, she and her warriors murdered four agents in their cars and gave Albert a signal.

Albert proceeded to the main door. Two armed men stopped him. "I am Professor Albert Russell. I need to meet Mr. Pedrotti."

"At this time?" one asked.

"Yes. Please, make a call."

When one of them snatched his cell phone, Albert

delivered powerful punches to their necks and vicious kicks to their chests, leading to their demise. He heard a clunk behind him and saw a dead agent holding a pistol. "Hi, dad. Be careful. Watch your back."

Albert saw his daughter carrying a silenced gun. "Ayita, what are you doing here?"

"I cut the communication and surveillance lines."

Eva came. "How can we get in?" Albert asked.

She smiled. "Through the door."

"How?"

"Follow me." Eva and Ayita kicked the door with all the force they could mobilize, and one part of the door fell to the floor. With fast speed, they jumped into the house. Eva killed two suited men with throwing spikes, and Ayita assassinated two men with butterfly swords and shot another man in the head. Albert kicked Lorenzo Pedrotti's back when he tried to use a cell phone. With a dismayed face, Lorenzo stuttered. "Albert Russell, what are you doing? Don't you know me? You are committing a despicable crime."

"Indeed. I am here to tell you two facts. The first fact is that you murdered Peter Stone and his son and their wives. The second fact is that I am Nahatatama, the leader of the Anonymous." Albert wished to punch Lorenzo's abdomen, but Eva caught his fist. "Albert, wait." Eva glared at Lorenzo. "Your swine raped me, and you threw me off the plane in Japan."

His eyes bulged in fear. "Impossible. Eva Kelly is dead."

"I am alive, gobshite. This is for Jamie Stone and his wife, and this is for Peter Stone and his wife. And this is for me, fecker." Eva stabbed his face and slaughtered him with a samurai sword. She got a red marker and wrote on a mirror, "The Anonymous were here." She picked up her cell phone. "Fire. Blaze." Three Anonymous warriors appeared and burned the mansion.

In the morning, the Governor of New Jersey declared a state of emergency. The TV news channels broadcast breaking-news stories about the death of the CIA director and his colleagues. The President condemned "the horrible terrorist attack" in New Jersey and vowed to "bring the barbaric killers to justice." A law enforcement spokesperson said the Anonymous had committed "war crimes against America and her citizens and institutions."

The next day, Albert and Eva went to see Zita. When Zita opened the door of her house, she was surprised to see Albert with an attractive Japanese-looking woman in a wheelchair. After closing the door, Eva clenched her fist and thumped Zita's jaw.

"Eva," Albert shouted.

Horrified and stunned, Zita rubbed her chin and stared. "I don't believe this. This is impossible. You are Japanese. You do not look like Eva. Eva died."

Eva kicked Zita's belly. Zita's back hit a bookcase. Albert grabbed Eva's shoulder. "Eva, what are you doing? This is Zita, our best friend."

"This crone told the CIA about my secret meetings in Lebanon and Japan."

"How was that?"

"Tell Albert the truth or I will kill you."

"Please, Eva, switched off your Irish crap. The CIA abducted me and forced me to talk about your connection with the Japanese Red Army. Yes, I was jealous because you took Albert away from me, but I had never, ever thought of harming you. You were my love and best friend, though I felt sad because you married Albert and took him away from me. We were supposed to be threesome lovers, but you asked me to stay away from Albert after you gave birth to Olivia."

"Was that a reason to betray your best friend? I was your girlfriend. The CIA psychopaths raped me and threw me out of a plane. I let you have an affair with Albert for a long time. I could have slaughtered you, but Albert loves you. It is over now. You will never see Albert again." She spat in Zita's face.

"Please, Eva, let me talk."

"Shut up. You lied to Albert and Hannah and said you work for the Anonymous. You claimed you were Albert's bodyguard. You lied to Hannah when you said you are the Anonymous boss in America. How dare you ask Sarah to kiss your hand and join your Mafia dung? You are a fat liar. I protected Albert and Hannah and my daughter. You forged Peter Stone's letter and said he wanted Albert to be loyal to you in a Sicilian way. Peter had never signed his full first name. He had never typed a letter to Albert. You have betrayed us." Eva placed her hand on Zita's face.

Zita got scared when she touched Eva's strong arm. "Who are you?"

"I am Homatakawa." Zita fainted.

Albert embraced Eva. "Please, forgive her. That was the past."

"I can't keep her alive."

Zita opened her frightened, dozy eyes. "Eva, for God's sake, let me talk. I was with Peter when he asked me to type a letter to Albert. That was before he founded the Anonymous. When he said Albert should give his allegiance to me, I said, 'Do you mean in a Sicilian way?' He said, 'Yes, in a Sicilian way.' Peter wanted Albert to join my Italian group. Yes, I lied because I wished to know the leaders Nahatatama and Homatakawa and wanted to know why the Anonymous killed the people who worked to kill Albert. I thought Albert was Homatakawa. Please, I am now a different woman. I love Albert and Olivia and their families. God knows what I have done for Albert and for your daughter. Please, honey, I am so happy to see you, though you look different. I love you so much. I have a son and two daughters. Please, let me live. I beg you. I will do anything you want." Zita cried and covered her face with her hands.

"Too late." Eva fastened her fingers around Zita's neck.

Albert grabbed Eva's shoulder. "I beg you to leave her. Zita has been a great friend."

"OK. I want you to dismantle your Mafia crap, or I will kill all your Italian family. If you say a word about me, I will decimate your son and daughters and let the world see this picture." Eva unzipped her leather jacket and threw a photo on Zita. The image was of Zita when she killed Jim Simons.

"I love you, Eva. Did you forget our sex and intimacy? I blew up the CIA's headquarters and killed Jim Simons because of my love for Albert and Olivia. Why did you punish my cousins? Why? What did they do to you? Albert, tell Eva what I did for you and for your family."

Eva's eyes became tearful as she recalled her friendship and sex with Zita. She put her hand on Zita's face and brushed her lips for ten seconds. "I am sorry for hitting you. I love you. You are welcome to join the Anonymous and be one of us. Be prepared and ready. Lie beside Albert and put your head on his thigh."

Zita rested her head on Albert's thigh and wondered what Eva wanted to do. Eva ripped off Zita's shirt and licked her face and chest. Zita removed Eva's jacket and blouse and kissed her.

Albert lowered his face. "Perverted women."

"Close your eyes and be quiet."

In the evening, Albert visited Ann. She looked up at his pale face. "What's happening now?"

"Eva is alive."

She gazed and hurrahed. "Oh, my God. How?"

"Eva is Homatakawa. Our dad and grandfather knew she was alive in Japan."

"Why didn't she contact you?"

"She had broken limbs, and her face was skinless."

"How is she now?"

"She is attractive and fearless and has a Japanese face. She asked me to be with her. What should I say to Sarah?"

"Sarah adores you. Tell her the truth. Tell her Olivia's mother is alive."

"Eva wanted to kill Zita today."

"Why?"

"Because Zita told the CIA about Eva's contacts in the Middle East and Japan. Eva was not in the doomed Japanese airplane. CIA agents abducted her and threw her out of their plane. She killed the CIA director because he asked his thugs to rape her in Japan. However, after some skirmishes, Eva and Zita fondled each other beside me."

"Ha! The threesome is back. They will never change."

"How did Eva know what Zita had told me in 2004? How did she know about our grandfather's letter to me?"

"I don't know. Only you, Olivia, and I know that.

Does Olivia know her mom is alive?"

"I don't think so."

"I think Olivia had spoken to Eva about you and Zita. Don't underestimate her intelligence."

"Olivia said nothing to me about her mom."

In the morning, Albert's phone rang. "Hello, Albert. Can I see you today?" Eva said.

"Yes. Where?"

"The Peninsula Hotel on Fifth Avenue. Room 74."

"OK. I will be there after an hour."

Sarah hugged him. "Who was that?"

"An old friend wants to see me."

"Where?"

"In Midtown Manhattan."

Albert did not know what to say to his wife. How would he tell her his first wife is still alive? An hour later, he was with Eva in the hotel room. They kissed for a minute and cried. "God knows how I lived in Japan and Mexico. It had been a long time. I wished to kiss you and talk to you, but a solid mask covered my face. I love you so much." She wept.

"I cried every year. I thought you were dead. You are gorgeous. I remember our first date and kiss. How are you, love?"

"I am good. I have strong limbs, fresh skin, and a Japanese face."

"I realized that after you touched me. How did you survive?"

"Peter and Jamie gave me four million dollars. I work for *The Japan Times*."

"How did you know about Zita's private chat with me?"

"Olivia has been my informer. Before the court, she

thought Zita was manipulating you and ruining your marriage. OK. Let us stop talking. Give me your hand." She grabbed his right arm and flipped him over on the bed. "Take off your clothes."

She made love to him and rested her head on his chest. "Call Olivia. I miss her so much."

Albert called his daughter. "Darling, can you come to The Peninsula Hotel? I am in room 74."

"Why are you there?"

"I want to spend some time with you. I need a hug."

"OK, dad. I am at the Museum of Modern Art. I will come soon."

"Please, darling, do not tell anyone about this matter."

Thirty minutes later, Albert welcomed Olivia with a loving hug and a warm kiss. She felt surprised to see a charming woman sitting in a wheelchair.

"Dad, what is going on?"

"This lovely lady wants to see you."

"Hi." Olivia shook Eva's hand. Eva stood and hugged her. Albert cried and put his hand on Olivia's shoulder. "Darling, this is your mom, Eva."

Olivia jerked backward. "My mom died a long time ago, and this woman looks Japanese."

"Honey, I am your mom."

Olivia remembered the tattoo on her mother's back. "Please, turn around." She uncovered Eva's lower back. Her body convulsed, and she screamed when she saw the tattooed names of her parents. "Mom, mom." They hugged and wept. Eva kissed her for two minutes and opened a sideboard. "Do you recognize this mask and this hood?"

"Oh, my God. Mom, are you Homatakawa?"

"Yes, love. I was your guardian." She glanced at Olivia's

neck. "I gave you this necklace in Thailand."

"Why didn't you talk to me?"

"My face and lips were without skin. I couldn't talk. The Anonymous scientists programed me to speak like a robot."

"What happened to you? Oh, my God. What about Sarah? Does she know you are alive?"

"I am your mom, not Sarah. We will talk about Sarah later. Sit on the bed to hear your mom's story."

Eva sat between Olivia and Albert. "Before I tell my story, call your partners and say you want to spend the night together." Five minutes later, Eva held Olivia's hand. "Are you ready?"

"Yes, mom."

"I went to Japan in August 1985 to meet relatives of the members of the Japanese Red Army after I met Fusako Shigenobu in the Middle East ..." Eva spent an hour explaining her horrific ordeal in Japan and resolve to protect her family and punish the CIA agents who tortured her. Albert and Olivia cuddled her and appreciated her incredible perseverance and intrepidity. Later, a man knocked on the room door. "Room service."

Eva jumped off the bed and sat in her wheelchair. After opening the door, a young waiter pushed a food trolley into the room and wheeled it next to a table.

After dinner, they slept together in one bed.

In the morning, Albert suggested they should go to his home to see Sarah and Edward. When Albert opened the door of his house, his son ran toward him. "Daddy, daddy." Albert held and kissed him. Sarah came out of the kitchen and stared at Eva, who was in a wheelchair. "Sarah, darling, this wonderful lady is Olivia's mom. Her reappearance has shocked and surprised us."

With a graceful smile, Sarah hugged Eva and Olivia. "Before you say anything further, I want to ask you a question. What about Zita?"

"Zita is our best friend. She was so happy to see Eva. All of us need her."

"OK. I have a dad, and Olivia has a mom. Fantastic. Who says miracles do not happen? Let us be like the Mormons. Albert, I do not mind you have two wives. Keep this matter a secret until I become the mayor. I am so delighted to see you together. I am overjoyed to see you, Eva."

Eva kissed her hand. "Thank you, honey. Albert adores you. I will never take him away from you. As you see, I am paralyzed and cannot do much."

"You can stay here."

"No. Thanks. You need to feel free in your home. I have a house on Long Island."

"Okay, let us have a drink and a party. Olivia, call Mary and ask her to come, and I will call my mom." She fetched a wine bottle and four glasses. Mary and Hannah came, and Eva enjoyed meeting them. They drank alcohol and ate delicious food and were merry. But in the evening, they heard a hail of bullets outside the house. "Go upstairs. Move," Eva shouted.

Olivia looked at her. "Mom, we cannot leave you."

"Go upstairs and stay with your dad. All of you go upstairs."

They moved upstairs, and Sarah held her son and Albert's hand. "Do something for Eva. You cannot leave her alone."

"I will. Go to the bedroom and lock the door."

Eva made a call. "Kill. Kill." After abandoning her wheelchair, she held her bag and left the house. Sitting behind a tree, she saw Sarah's bodyguards dead beside their car. Five armed men fired at two Anonymous fighters using laser machine guns, and two hitmen, carrying submachine guns, approached the house. Eva threw a steel star on a hitman's face and jumped on the other hitman and slashed his hand with a Japanese tanto. "Who are you, dickhead?"

"Screw you."

Eva inserted a spike into his shoulder. "Who sent you here? I will let you live if you tell me the truth."

"OK, do not kill me. Paul Simons and Jason White asked us to kill Albert and his family. Paul is furious because the court thing has demeaned him, and Jason White wants to avenge the death of the CIA director and his colleagues."

"Who is Jason White?"

"The acting CIA director. He is now with Paul Simons in Manhattan."

"What is your name?"

"Dylan."

Filled with rage, Eva smothered him to death and took his cell phone. A masked motorcyclist came to the scene and killed the last hitman. "Eva, take the motorcycle, the mask, and the hood. I will stay here to protect the family."

"Thanks, Ayita."

When Eva rode Ayita's motorcycle, she looked at a helmeted motorcyclist beside her. "Who are you?"

Zita removed her helmet and swung her hair. "An old friend."

"I love you, saucy vamp. Let us kick some asses." Ten

Anonymous motorcyclists followed Eva and Zita and moved fast toward Midtown Manhattan. While driving on 6th Ave, Eva held Dylan's cell phone when it blipped.

"Dylan, did you finish the job?" Paul Simons asked.

"Ha. Ha, dog." Eva cackled.

"Who is this?"

"I am Homatakawa, the slayer of men."

Appalled and frightened, Paul dropped his cell phone on a table in his office, and Jason White stared at him. "What's wrong?"

"Homatakawa and the Anonymous are coming."

"Don't worry. I will call the NYPD and the FBI."

Eva, Zita, and the Anonymous warriors parked their dark motorcycles near a bar on West 48th Street. An Anonymous female warrior gave Eva a Samurai sword. Eva put her hand on Zita's shoulder. "I do not want you to fight. Prepare your camera." She looked at her Anonymous warriors. "War, war. Let us screw them."

"Fire, fire, Master," the warriors responded.

They marched toward 6th Avenue. Eva picked up her cell phone and called Albert. "The war has begun. Keep Olivia with you. I love you. We are a regiment. We do not acquit. We do not forget. We do not rest. We are the Anonymous."